KERRICK GRIFFIN

The Mavericks, Books 1–2

Dale Mayer

THE MAVERICKS, BOOKS 1–2
Beverly Dale Mayer
Valley Publishing Ltd.

Copyright © 2019, 2020

All rights reserved. Except for use in any review, the reproduction or utilization of this work in whole or in part by any electronic, mechanical or other means, now known or hereafter invented, including xerography, photocopying and recording, or in any information storage or retrieval system, is forbidden without the written permission of the publisher.

This is a work of fiction. Names, characters, places, brands, media, and incidents are either the product of the author's imagination or are used fictitiously. Any resemblance to actual events, locales, or persons, living or dead, is entirely coincidental.

ISBN-13: 978-1-773364-45-2
Print Edition

Books in This Series:

Kerrick, Book 1
Griffin, Book 2
Jax, Book 3
Beau, Book 4
Asher, Book 5
Ryker, Book 6
Miles, Book 7
Nico, Book 8
Keane, Book 9
Lennox, Book 10
Gavin, Book 11
Shane, Book 12
Diesel, Book 13
Jerricho, Book 14
Killian, Book 15
Hatch, Book 16
Corbin, Book 17
Aiden, Book 18
The Mavericks, Books 1–2
The Mavericks, Books 3–4
The Mavericks, Books 5–6
The Mavericks, Books 7–8
The Mavericks, Books 9–10
The Mavericks, Books 11–12

About This Bundle

What happens when the very men—trained to make the hard decisions—come up against the rules and regulations that hold them back from doing what needs to be done? They either stay and work within the constraints given to them or they walk away. Only now, for a select few, they have another option:

The Mavericks. A covert black ops team that steps up and break all the rules … but gets the job done.

Welcome to a new military romance series by *USA Today* best-selling author Dale Mayer. A series where you meet new friends in this raw and compelling look at the men who keep us safe every day from the darkness where they operate—and live—in the shadows … until someone special helps them step into the light.

Kerrick

On the precipice of change … Just not the way he'd expected …

Kerrick is tagged to join a new elite group, where he'd have more say and less rules on missions. Working mostly alone, he's to track down a kidnapped victim suspected of being in England, and likely she's not the only one. This is his kind of job; finding out a longtime friend is his backup makes this mission a go.

Amanda is snatched at the end of her workday while walking to her vehicle. Days later she wakes to find she's imprisoned, alone in a small cement cell. One rotting meal a day is provided, and that is it. Once she realizes someone else is here–a young boy—she's even more determined to escape. And to take him with her. Running into Kerrick wasn't the plan …

Escaping is only one part of the puzzle as the truth drags them to Europe and beyond as they sort out how the two kidnappings are related, who's behind it all and why … Before they are run aground and imprisoned all over again …

Griffin

Helping Kerrick was one thing, getting tagged for a mission of his own quite another …

His heart ached to hear a young girl had been kidnapped while at a hotel in Thailand, waiting for her father to arrive. But nothing is ever as it seems, and this case isn't even close to simple.

Lorelai spent the last seven years enjoying her young charge, Amelia Rose. Tutoring the daughter of a wealthy business owner added perks to the job, like holidays around the world. In all these years Lorelai had never once seen the downside to having big money–until the holiday in Thailand where Amelia Rose is targeted, and they were both kidnapped.

Griffin managed to rescue the kidnapped victims, but tracing the kidnappers was a whole different story and brought the group a little too close to home …

Sign up to be notified of all Dale's releases here!
https://geni.us/DaleNews

KERRICK

The Mavericks, Book 1

Dale Mayer

CHAPTER 1

KERRICK CASSIDY LOOKED at the text message and frowned.

Meet at 1830.

He knew who the sender was, but he hadn't heard from this guy in a long time. He had always been a bit on the raw side, a law unto himself, a maverick among humans. Kerrick had heard he'd gone into the military but had lost track of him. Was it the same friend? Kerrick's phone ID'd the man's name and number. Or rather, a version of his nickname.

Kerrick sent a quick message back. **Where and why?**

Waterside Pub. That pub—or dive—was just inside the San Diego city limits but still close to where Kerrick now stood in his apartment in Coronado. Waterside was more of a locals' hangout, and one Kerrick knew well. As he thought about it, he realized it's where he'd met this friend a long time ago. But there was no explanation as to the *why* part of the message. At that, he frowned, checking his watch. It was 5:35 p.m. now. He had no plans. He had enough time to make the meeting, even with Friday night traffic.

So, was that a coincidence, or was something else going on here? He sent his old friend an affirmative reply while standing and staring out the window of his small apartment. He was living on the Coronado base in standard base housing, but that was short-term. As in, very short-term.

Like, … his entire military career was soon over. He was done with the navy. At least in the capacity he'd served.

He was at a crossroads in his life, one that he looked forward to but, at the same time, he'd given a lot of his best years to the navy. He'd been part of their elite group, but sometimes the people around you changed, and the people above you changed, and Kerrick had been chafing at the rules and the regulations for a long time. He was one of the more senior guys and knew that he should be moving on. Others had gone on to have life partners and families, rounding out their lives. Kerrick didn't have either of those things to keep him grounded.

He used to, but that was a long time ago. He and his wife had been childhood sweethearts. He'd only been in the navy a couple years and hadn't even made it to his elite group yet when she and their six-month-old daughter had been killed in a car accident. Some men hit the bottle; others managed to recover from life-changing events like that. In his case, Kerrick locked all the hurt inside and had faced the world, angrier, harder, and more determined to bury himself and all his pain in his work.

Kerrick stared at his phone, frowning, wondering if he should show up for this meet. He didn't have any reason not to. The thing was, the longer he'd been in the service, the more Kerrick understood other men's struggles with the regimented lifestyle. While Kerrick had taken solace in the rules and regulations, others had chafed at the restrictions. Kerrick had more of a get-along-with and do-the-job type of attitude. He'd been all about the team.

As the teams had expanded, and as the number of members in this elite group had totaled several thousand, the atmosphere had changed. It was great if you could stay in the group that you loved and with the men who you knew and trusted. But, when they left or were transferred, it became an ever-changing sea of faces. The status was changing too, and he wasn't sure he wanted to have unknown guys, untested guys, guys ten years younger than him watching his back.

And he knew that they looked at him and worried that maybe Kerrick was past his prime. Just the thought of that angered him. No way he was washed-up. Not at thirty-four. But something was definitely different in his outlook now. And it went beyond the everlasting agony of losing his wife and child. It was another kind of ache in his soul. He wanted to do more; he wanted to go into foreign countries and take out the insurgents like they needed to be taken out.

But he was forever being held back by the politically correct actions as dictated by the brass above. And sometimes it really chafed to have men a long ways away make decisions about matters they couldn't possibly comprehend, not without boots on the ground. Hell, even friendly fire was an issue on the bases. If the brass couldn't handle the fights in their own bases, how were they deemed worthy to supervise any op in a foreign country?

He shook his head, grabbed his keys, and walked out. He locked the door behind him, feeling a sense of finality in the movement. Although he slept here, he didn't really live here. He kept his civilian clothes to a minimum. He was always ready to leave at a moment's notice, and he cared about nothing in that place. The memories of his wife and daughter were the only things that still mattered, and he kept those inside. Sure, he'd had relationships since losing them, but those quick hookups had been more for him to reconnect to the world and maybe to let off some steam and just to have a bit of fun every once in a while. His heart, however, was well-guarded.

Nobody walked away from an experience like his without some scars to show for it. And he had yet to find a way to manage those scars. And the physical scars on his body? Well, he didn't give a crap about those. They were beyond fixing and were so much a part of him that even he'd forgotten how he'd gotten a lot of them. And none of them bothered him, yet he knew it would bother other women. Not the females he tended to spend time with now. They couldn't care less. They just wanted a good hard ride, and he was up for that any day.

But the softer side of a real relationship—with love, true love, like that special relationship he'd had with Aurora—that part he kept hidden. He was afraid his ability to give true love had died permanently with her but held out hope that one day he'd find himself responding emotionally to another woman.

When he walked into the pub five minutes early, he didn't recognize anybody in the smoke-filled room. He ordered a draft off the bar and took it outside. He always preferred to be outside anyway. He found his friend sitting there, in the far corner on the patio, waiting for him and watching him approach. Kerrick studied him as he sat down. "The years haven't been kind," Kerrick said bluntly.

His friend smiled, shook his head, and said, "No, they haven't been. Doesn't look like they've been too kind to you either."

Kerrick shrugged, still bristling at the idea that he might be past his prime, and said, "I'm doing fine."

His friend nodded, and Kerrick stared at him.

"What name are you going by these days?" Kerrick asked.

His friend just smiled and said, "Call me Beta."

Kerrick's eyebrows rose. "As in, second in command, with a leader called *Alpha* above you?"

Beta chuckled and said, "There is a ladder. But I didn't tell you that."

"Sounds like you're still a bit of a maverick." Kerrick crossed his arms, not willing to give an inch to the man trying to read him intently. "Why am I here?"

"Maverick?" Beta rolled the word around on the tip of his tongue and smiled. "I like that. We can use that. Now as to why you are here – answer that question yourself. Why *are* you here?"

Kerrick frowned. Because, of course, that was exactly what he needed to know too. "Curiosity," he said. "Trying to figure out the voice from the past."

"Heard you were having some trouble."

"Not really," Kerrick said, reaching for his beer. He lifted it and sipped but never took his gaze off the man across him. "Just an interesting stage of life. Nothing I can't handle though."

"Do you care to handle it any longer?" Beta asked, leaning forward to study his buddy's eyes.

"Not sure what that means," Kerrick said in a calm tone. "Have you got a job for me? Because I'm no mercenary."

A grin flashed, Beta's white teeth lighting up the evening settling around them. It should have been a hot and sunny day in California, but, with overcast clouds, it wasn't. A storm threatened on the horizon, adding an electric crackle to the air around them. Just the kind of weather that matched Kerrick's mood.

"It would be government-sanctioned," Beta said. "Black ops. Small teams on the ground. Mostly two working alone."

Kerrick felt the shock waves rock through him. "You do know what I have been doing for the last decade, right?"

Beta nodded. "One of the topmost decorated Navy SEAL officers. I'm really proud of you."

"Why?" Kerrick asked. "I never did quite understand the thing about getting medals for doing your damn job."

Beta cracked a smile again. "Still the same old Kerrick. You have a set of honorable rules to live by that few men can match," he said, leaning back casually as he picked up his own beer and drank.

Kerrick nodded. "Definitely have my own set of standards and my own honor system, and I'm loyal. Which is why I can't ever do anything of a mercenary nature."

"It's got nothing to do with that," Beta said calmly. "But I need to know if your heart's still with the Navy SEALs or if you're ready to take a step into something ... different."

"How different?"

Beta chuckled. "Maybe not very different at all. We're talking two-man undercover missions, possibly larger teams as we recruit a few more men."

"Who's leading?"

"I am, from a distance," Beta said. "But essentially you're on your own."

In spite of himself, Kerrick could feel the interest surging through him. He leaned forward, his hands gripping the tall beer glass. "How alone? For how long?"

"Only what you feel you need. You're the boss of *your* mission."

Kerrick's eyebrows shot up. "Money?"

"Are you asking about money for your bank account or money available to do what's needed to be done?"

"Both."

"Got you covered. And more."

At that sock to his gut, Kerrick stared at his friend. "How black ops?"

"It doesn't get any darker than this."

"Is this a brand-new US government department? Do we have a code name?"

"Definitely." He grinned. "I just named it The Mavericks."

Kerrick snorted at that. "So, no systems in place. You don't know how it'll work yet?"

"You'd be one of the first to implement it."

"Even if I go in alone," he said, "I still need some people to call on. I need intel. I need maybe a specialist here and there."

Beta nodded. "And you will have backup, of course."

Kerrick frowned at him. "Depends on who the backups are reporting to."

A startled laugh erupted from Beta's lips. "Yeah, the same old Kerrick. Always wanting to know who'll report to whom and who's over your head."

"I want to make sure that nobody is reporting behind my back," Kerrick said. "I want my people loyal to me, to the program, and to whoever is cutting our paychecks. But most of all, loyal to me while on a mission."

"Understood."

But Beta didn't say anything else, so Kerrick wasn't exactly sure just how much leeway he would have. He probed gently. "Budget?"

"Yes."

"How big?"

"More than you can spend in this lifetime," Beta said. And this time, there was no smile. He had settled in, just waiting to see what questions Kerrick would ask.

"I can have anything I need? Do you have the resources?"

"Interesting question."

"Up until now I just walked into the armory and signed out what I needed."

Beta's smile still did not show up. He continued to stare at Kerrick steadily.

"Meaning, I can use my own suppliers?" Kerrick asked to clarify Beta's silence.

Beta gave a shrug. "Nobody—and I mean *nobody*—in the military gets to know about this."

"So, not the usual sources," Kerrick said as he stared out into the landscape. "What about using civilians?"

"No details ever to be given."

"Some of the civilians I know," he said, "don't need to ask questions to understand what's going on."

"Exactly. And, considering it's your cover, and your ass, you might want to watch who you talk to."

Kerrick had a few more questions, but it was kind of hard to sort out details when he didn't know enough about his new employer or about what was expected from him to begin with. Typical government attitude. The navy trained them to obey and to not question. No matter how idiotic the order. And Kerrick had had more than a few of those. Luckily he had lived to complain about them. He understood that some of those follow-orders-without-thinking reflexes may be necessary when fighting a war, but, even then, Kerrick had to think there were other—and better—ways to do things. "Time frame?"

"Are you packed?"

"Always." Kerrick gave a decisive nod, sucked in his

breath, and settled back against his chair. He rapped his fingers on the table, waiting for Beta to say more. To say anything.

Beta smiled and said, "Then get some sleep. It's only chatter now. We're following a person of interest and need more people lined up anyway. We'll call you sometime in the next couple days."

Behind him, a glass shattered on the concrete patio floor. Kerrick shifted to take a look. And, when he turned back, his friend had vaulted over the small porch railing, letting Kerrick catch a glimpse of Beta just as he disappeared around the corner of the building.

Kerrick sat here for a long moment, wondering what the hell he had just got himself into.

CHAPTER 2

JUST SHY OF forty hours later, at 10:25 a.m. on Sunday, Kerrick got a phone call. Out of the blue, a strange robotic voice on the other end said, "It's time," and promptly hung up.

Ten minutes later Kerrick took a deep breath and stepped outside. No personal belongings were left here. He was no longer part of the Navy SEALs and was moving out of his austere base housing, even though the rent was paid through to the end of the month. But he doubted he would ever be back here to the base again. So, he'd taken care of business first. He didn't say goodbye to anybody because he didn't know if he would see them again and because he could see them one week later. For all he knew, this was a one-time job and nothing else. At the pub, he parked, walked inside, ordered a coffee, and headed out to the same table as before, where he found Beta waiting for him again.

Beta held a brown 9x13 envelope, gave it to him, and said, "You have just about enough time to drink that."

Kerrick nodded, checked his watch—10:58 a.m.—took a long healthy swallow of his black coffee, and then asked, "Where am I going?"

"First job's easy. You're off to England."

Kerrick smiled. "That's almost like staying at home."

"Not necessarily in this case," Beta said. "Take care of

the job, and we'll talk afterward."

And, just like that, he got up, walked back into the pub, and disappeared. Sitting outside alone, Kerrick swiftly emptied the folder and studied its contents. There was a photo of a beautiful young woman's face, her name noted as Dr. Amanda Berg. He frowned at that, her name rattling somewhere around in the back of his brain.

He quickly read her dossier, which stated she was a biochemist and had been kidnapped outside a specialized center in France. Their intel said she was somewhere in England, having been seen at the Dover ferry crossing. He frowned again. If she'd been sighted, somebody must have already been following her, and they shouldn't have lost her once she had reached the English shores. He couldn't wait to hear that explanation.

He found plane tickets between the papers. Checking his flight info, leaving at 11:24 a.m., didn't give him any time to finish his coffee. But, after a twelve-and-a-half-hour flight, involving one stop, he should be in London. He stuffed the rest of the file back in the envelope and headed to his vehicle. As he got to the parking lot, a cab waited for him, and his vehicle was nowhere to be found.

The cab driver looked at him and said, "Are you the guy going to the airport on an express run?"

Kerrick asked, "Do you have my bags?"

The cabbie nodded and pointed at a black carry-on duffel bag and a small backpack visible on the floorboard of the car.

"Good enough," Kerrick said, already in the back seat. As the cabbie pulled out of the parking lot and headed toward the airport, in the back of his mind, Kerrick wondered what had happened to his car—which wasn't worth a hell of a lot but was still his. In the taxi, he had just enough time to flip through the rest of the paperwork but not enough time to ingest it all. Just when he thought he'd gone through all the information though, he noticed a tiny microdot in the bottom of the envelope. He pulled it out slowly, staring at it.

Just then the cabbie called out, "Forgot to give you this," and tossed him a box.

In the back of the cab, almost at the airport, he quickly dismantled all the packaging. He took out a pair of sunglasses. A quick inspection didn't reveal anything special about them. Also he found a Bluetooth headpiece that went to the accompanying burner phone. One number had been programmed in.

As soon as he exited the cab at the airport, he walked to the counter and checked in, wondering why he was flying commercial to begin with. Once he was at his gate, he headed into an isolated corner. There, he dialed the one number programmed in his disposable cell. Instead of hearing a voice, a series of tumblers clicked into place. *A secure line. Interesting.*

"State your name."

"Kerrick."

"Full name."

He rolled his eyes and gave it.

"We have you at the airport right now," the voice said. "You will arrive on target according to our schedule."

"Yes, according to the current airport schedule."

"The microdot has information you need," the voice said, "use the sunglasses."

Hmm. The sunglasses can send info to me? On the lenses themselves, I presume. Interesting.

"We'll contact you when you land."

He shut off the phone, tucked it in his pocket, and wondered about the cell phone. Depending on how dangerous this op turned out to be, this disposable cell would be one of the first things he dumped. But he couldn't do it yet. He looked at the microdot and sunglasses, finding a small hole to drop in the dot. Then he put on the glasses and stared out the window. Immediately information flowed on the glass lenses, displaying further details on the case. He didn't know what anybody's involvement in this kidnapping was yet. Including his own. If he hadn't known Beta, Kerrick wouldn't have taken this step at all. Beta already knew about Kerrick's history and knew where he was at in this stage of his life. But then, of course, Kerrick had been targeted just for that reason.

DR. AMANDA BERG shifted uncomfortably on the hard bed. It wasn't concrete but it was more like an old metal cot with a mattress on top. Or what had been a mattress at one point in time. It was so thin and so flat that no cushion was left to it. In addition, she only had a thin blanket for warmth. Her initial panic over being kidnapped and drugged had subsided somewhat, and her brain was now finally working again.

She'd been taken off the street right outside the building where she worked, in broad daylight, a hood pulled over her head before being tossed into the back of a lorry, and then locked up in this windowless hellhole. The only glimmer of light that she saw came from outside her solid wood door. All had been a nightmare of silence and fear, but her anger simmered deep beneath the surface.

Was this because of her research work? She came from a wealthy family, but did these kidnappers know that? That didn't matter to her as much as her research. She was working on specific cancer genes and cures too, but did her kidnappers care about that? Not likely. The only person she knew, who hated her, was her ex-husband. Their nasty divorce was still fresh on her mind, even five years later. Probably more on his mind than hers though. She'd figured that she was safe when the ink was finally drying on the legal document, but was she? Was he behind this? In which case, he might just leave her here to rot.

She had married in the thralls of her first real love affair and had found out very quickly that her husband was nothing more than a user, after her family connections and money. He'd never intended in any way to be monogamous. The shattering of her dreams had sent her spiraling into depression, her anger not far behind. Six months into that marriage, she had discovered one of his affairs. They had fought over it, only to have him confess to multiple affairs; then he had brutally taken his fist to her jaw. She vowed that no man would ever hit her again.

She had managed to escape from him once and had yet to come face-to-face with him again. She wouldn't be surprised if he was behind this. They had signed prenups at her father's suggestion which she then insisted on. With her divorce, that meant her ex-husband got nothing. He had fought hard on that issue, but, with only six months of marriage and the physical proof of her injuries, the divorce had been swift and easy on her side.

The judge had ruled in her favor, and her ex got nothing. Which was, as he had put it, a waste of an eighteen-month investment, and he should have at least gotten the house. But her house was worth almost one million dollars, so how he figured a year of dating and half a year of marriage should have garnered him that, she didn't know. Or her father's side, he'd been worried and upset but had been pretty caustic in his tone when saying, "I told you that he was nothing but a user."

Being told *I told you so* at that time of her life was not exactly a highlight either. Regardless, that had been almost five years ago. Surely her ex would have gotten over it by now. She hadn't seen him since, but her name and her work had recently been in the news. Had that set him off again? She was still in the same house, and she'd worried about that at the time of the divorce, but her father had set up a high-end security system.

But the trouble with her home security system was that it only worked if she were inside her home. The minute she went outside, she was fair game, and that's where she had been taken. She groaned as she shuffled on the lumpy excuse of a mattress. She closed her eyes, feeling sleepy. After all, without her watch, she was listening to her internal clock, which told her that she had woken up in the middle of the night several times, needing a bathroom.

A chamber pot was in the far corner of her cell, and she had been forced to use it several times. Even now, once again, her bladder was bursting. And yet, she'd had very little water. They had thrown a bottle in with her originally, but she'd had no food, and she didn't have a ton of body fat to begin with.

She had to escape before she was too weak to fight. If they didn't give her any food soon, that point would be facing her within hours. She got up, forced herself to the pot, where she relieved herself yet again, and then laid down on the cot once more.

Surely this nightmare would be over soon.

CHAPTER 3

AMANDA SLEPT FOR a while, woke to use the chamber pot yet again, fell asleep only to wake up chilled on the uncomfortable cot, contemplating what day it was. She counted this as Day Two of her captivity, but she had no way to confirm that. Something odd sounded outside her door. She bolted to her feet, swaying a bit with the effort, and tiptoed to stand behind the door, her ear flat against it. She heard sobbing. Horror swept through her. She wasn't alone? It's one thing if she was the only prisoner, but to think that there might be others? It was definitely a female crying too.

A hard rap came on her door, and then a voice called out, "Step away from the door."

She frowned but immediately obeyed and stood about four feet back from where the door would open. When it did, a man dressed all in black, his rifle over his shoulder, held a tray in his hand, while a second gunman stood guard. The first thrust the tray forward, and she grabbed it immediately. Without another word, the door slammed in her face. She stared in shock at her first contact with anyone since she'd been here. Not a word, not an explanation, nothing.

Just silence. Even her neighbor no longer cried.

Horrible thoughts assaulted her mind. She shook her head, not able to handle all this … evilness.

She slowly walked back to her cot and sat down with the tray. There was a sandwich and a bowl of what appeared to be a thin soup. The food was lukewarm, but it was food. She ate slowly, knowing that she would need all the sustenance she could get, and, if she was only getting fed once a day or every other day, this wasn't enough. Still, she would survive.

They gave her another bottle of water and something in a cup too. She looked at it and frowned, wondering if it was safe to drink. Then again, was any of this food safe to eat or drink? Not that she had much choice. She picked up the sandwich, studied it carefully—old stale bread with mayo and what looked like tuna and lettuce. She took a tentative bite and then couldn't help herself from taking several bigger bites. Her hunger clawed at her, digging deep into her stomach.

She could only hope that somebody had seen her as she was snatched off the street or that someone had at least put out a call of alarm when she hadn't shown up for work the next day. Somebody should have contacted her father. And, if that had happened, he would have contacted somebody. He was high up in the government in Norway, but her birth in the States gave her dual citizenship in America. Her mother was a politician in Maine, but her parents had divorced long ago. Amanda had remained much closer to her father than her mother. Surely, between her parents, somebody would have put out a call for help.

After her initial bites, she slowed down and ate the rest of the food slowly, nibbling away at it, trying to make it last. When she'd eaten half the sandwich, she lifted a spoon and tried the soup. Canned tomato but, again, it was food. And she couldn't afford to be picky. She sipped it as slowly as she could. She needed the liquids too. She put the tray down with half the sandwich still on it but with all the soup gone. Then she picked up the cup of what? Coffee? And sniffed it. For whatever reason, she was more afraid of drugs being in the coffee than in the soup. The soup was pretty acidic, being tomato. And she hadn't tasted anything off in it. She took a tentative sip of the coffee, lukewarm but soothing.

Something else sat in the last dish on the tray and jiggled at her every move. Jell-O? That didn't make any sense, unless she was in an institution, like a hospital, where they give you the whole meal all at once. Was that a possibility? She studied her concrete cell, built of cinder blocks but missing windows. The floor was concrete as well. If she was in an institution, maybe it was a prison, and she was in solitary confinement because that's what it looked like. Or a storage room?

Then another thought came to her, and she was afraid that, if they came and took away the tray, they'd take away any remaining food too. She couldn't take that chance, so she ate the second half of her sandwich and then her dessert, polishing off the last of her coffee at the same time. She automatically checked her wrist. Old habit. But they had taken her watch, so she couldn't confirm the time or the date. But approximately an hour later she heard voices yet again. She stood with the tray in her hand as the door opened. The guard looked at it and gave a clipped nod. He took it and disappeared.

Amanda called out, "I need another chamber pot." It made him hesitate, but he still slammed the door shut. She groaned. "Surely, if this were a prison, there'd be a toilet."

As she sat on the cot again, nobody returned to talk to her. She pulled the thin blanket over her shoulders, her stomach finally full for the first time in recent memory. But now she was worried. Her mind tried hard to work on solutions to getting out of here, but, unless she was capable of fighting two armed gunmen, both apparently trained and healthy, she didn't have a hope.

Mentally she reached out and said, *If anybody out there is looking for me, please don't take too long…*

KERRICK HAD SLEPT on the plane enough that, as soon as it landed, at roughly 8:00 a.m. Monday, London time, he was energized, despite the eight-hour time difference between here and San Diego. And, with a transatlantic flight, he had also had time to review the materials given to him so that he could move forward with this op. With his carry-on bags in hand, his mind buzzed with all the intel, yet with no leads, as he tried to figure out where Dr. Berg was being held. In his head, he called out to her and said, *Amanda, I'm coming. Hold tight.*

The trouble was, he didn't really know what resources he had available to find her. The wad of cash in that envelope had been in the local currency. That helped. Also the microdot had revealed a series of bank accounts and related statements—hers, her father's, her mother's, even the corporation Amanda worked for, but Kerrick's quick review of the screenshots revealed only one year's worth of statements from each source. Yet nothing stuck out as a questionable transaction.

Kerrick had hoped his new employer would have provided him with more. Having been thrown into the deep end with little explanation or underlying supporting information, Kerrick was walking in the dark.

Still, he'd spent years walking in the shadows. He was plenty used to it.

Outside, he stopped and looked around, but nobody waited for him. He headed over to a rental car office. His envelope had also contained fake IDs. Using one of them, he quickly rented a car and headed to London. For all he knew, Amanda could have been flown to a different country by now. But this kidnapping had only recently been reported, not even fourteen hours ago, although her kidnapping had originated earlier, around 2:00 p.m. on Sunday, Paris time. Why had she been under such close scrutiny in France by Kerrick's new employer, who even now remained nameless? Why did the kidnappers take her to England at all? Scotland and Ireland were options as well as all of Europe.

Once he booked into a small cheesy motel, keeping his budget money in mind, he tossed everything onto the breakfast table to figure out his next step.

He pulled out his personal laptop, hooked up to the internet, and downloaded the research he'd gathered while in the air. He had done a background check on her history and had collected any connections Berg might have to England that he could get, courtesy of science conventions, medical conferences. Technically he didn't find much. But Amanda was a reclusive researcher, not a party girl tweeting incessantly or taking selfies and updating her dating status on Facebook.

So, while he was online, he checked his email. Almost immediately a small window opened on his laptop with a message at the bottom and a link. His first thought was that he had been hacked. Then he shook his head. Yeah, he had been hacked all right—by his new employer. He studied the message and the link. Then he clicked it.

The message gave him an account login, while the link took him to a strange site that he'd never seen before. Hesitantly but willingly, he typed in the required login information. He was logged into a server instantly. Immediately a chat window popped up.

Welcome to England.

Well, I'm here, but I'm not exactly sure what I'm supposed to do.

If you don't know by now, then you're the wrong man for the job. And, with that, the chat window disappeared.

He glared at it. "Well, that's fine," he said to the empty room. "It's not that I don't know what I'm doing. *Study the victim first. Then study the crime scene to get a feel for your enemy.* I'm just not exactly sure how I'm doing it yet, with my newfound parameters."

Irritated, he ignored the chat box and resumed his research, checking for any connections and further history on Amanda Berg. The web had scant information on her marriage and divorce, but, just when he had settled into studying her childhood and early school years, the chat window popped up again. He wanted to ignore it but knew that was foolish too. Words formed on the chat window.

Time is running out.

Do we know what the end game is? He typed his question, hoping his terse and direct communication with Grumpy—as he deemed his helper—if this *was* still Grumpy, would get Kerrick what he really needed: intel, not lip.

No.

Father, ex-husband, company?

Possibly all of the above or none.

Studying her history online right now.

At that, a couple more links appeared. He clicked one to see a full dossier on Amanda, much more complete than what had been given to him before on the microdot with its single sheet of data regarding Dr. Berg, some three hundred words tops. More than what he could dig up on the internet. He now read her detailed history. It was all about her schooling, her university, the awards she'd won, and the company she worked for.

The fact that she was doing cancer research could mean her kidnapper wanted Dr. Berg to treat them as a private patient, who had then kidnapped the good doctor because it was the only way they thought they could get her attention. Or possibly her kidnapper was somebody who didn't want Dr. Berg to find a cancer cure, when she seemed at a breaking point of something big per the recent newspaper articles.

Kerrick studied the various links which Grumpy had provided, realizing he was in a database. A government database that somehow Kerrick had been cleared to use. He didn't have a clue as to what his clearance would be normally. But this? Pretty awesome. He read on. ... Both her parents were politicians. Immediately he asked in the chat box, **Blackmail? Kidnapping note? Ransom?**

None yet. All things are possible.

Do parents know she's missing?

Yes, father contacted us to find daughter.

How did he find out?

Unknown to us but he refused our additional security services to protect him as he had his own private security.

Mother?

She knows but doesn't have any further info to be of assistance in this matter. Father has deployed security

measures of his own to watch over mother, even though they are divorced.

More family?
Only child.
Aunts, uncles, cousins?
None.

At that, Kerrick's eyebrows raised because it was very unusual not to have *any* extended family. But who knew? It was what it was. While he read more of her expanded dossier, the chat sent a couple more links, which Kerrick immediately pulled up and read. **I need information**, he typed.

About what?

Her coworkers. Is she close to anybody in particular at work? The state of her actual research. Is she truly close to making a breakthrough, or is that just media hype in the newspapers? Is she working for any special funding group?

Back in five. And then whoever was on the other end of their chat left.

Frowning, Kerrick quickly returned to reading everything else he had been given on Amanda and realized that she'd been seen in a blue four-door vehicle, not the lorry that had taken her away initially, yet both had been on the ferry. Or at least he thought the original lorry used in the kidnapping had been with the blue car on the ferry. Somebody had tried to track her using the car's license plate, but the vehicle was lost on the other side of the ferry crossing at Dover.

He reviewed the other photos in the brown envelope but saw none from the ferry crossing. Supposedly, she'd been laid down in the back seat and covered up, as if asleep, to give her an almost normal appearance, so as not to alert the ferry authorities. And that made Kerrick wonder just how correct their intel was.

In the chat box, he quickly asked that question and then sent a second question about tracking the vehicle itself. When the responses came back, an image was attached, showing a birthmark high on her cheek, near her right eye. It correlated to the same facial mark found in his file.

Both vehicles lost almost immediately in Dover, the lorry and the blue car. License plates no longer visible, so we assumed they were switched. Either switched vehicles or switched license plates.

Kerrick nodded. All too often, that was an easy option.

Not close to any coworkers. Works solo on her own research. Reliable sources state she is on the verge of finding a cancer cure. While she has been awarded several grants over the years, her current funding group is her employer, Scion Labs.

Well, that was not much.

As he learned more about the kidnapping victim, who this woman was, he found nothing in the files or in his research to dislike. She was known as a champion of lost causes—being a member of both the dance club and the genius club in her school years as a teenager—which led to her being very popular, as she helped everybody to meet and to organize various social parties, trying to get the wallflowers off the wall and onto the dance floor.

He smiled at that. Of course she'd been a social butterfly type coming from her political family of origin, but obviously, as an adult, she could be an introvert too and have hidden depths if she was also a chemist, working on cancer research. And that sent him down another rabbit hole. He went to the chat box again. **What prompted cancer research?**

Best friend died in college.
Name?

Alice Durnham.
Should have been in the dossier.
Ask and you shall receive.

He snorted, wondering if this was still Grumpy but reformed, or if Kerrick was getting bounced between five different people, like some call center located wherever on this planet. Regardless he resumed his own research into Alice Durnham. And, indeed, she had struggled with breast cancer as a young woman, not knowing she had the disease until it was too late to treat.

It had affected Amanda deeply. She had lost a lot of her bubbliness since then, and she had changed the direction of her research to find a cure for cancer. Something interesting in that same vein had been how she had also lost another friend. It was briefly touched upon, but this other mutual friend had introduced her to her future husband. Kerrick searched for the name of the friend and couldn't find it. He typed in the chat box once more, and the reply came one minute later.

Bridgette Hampton. Died in a car accident. Ruled an accident. No reason to consider otherwise.
How soon after introducing the husband?
One month.
Would help the bonding.
Yes.
Any connection from ex-husband to any extremist groups?
Under investigation but nothing points in that direction at this time.

Aah, so the chat box people didn't have all the answers. He frowned because he really didn't want to find limits to what he needed to know. He quickly typed in another question. **Any connection to anything suspicious?**

Lots.

Such as?

He received a list of associations that the ex-husband had dabbled in. Everything from vegan groups to gun groups to divorce groups. He frowned as he thought about that. **That's a lot of nothing.**

Yes.

Cover?

Possibly.

Location of ex-husband and whereabouts for the last thirty to seventy-two hours?

Was at work Friday. Went missing over the weekend. Has a new lady friend. Possibly they went on a trip.

It's Monday.

Hasn't shown up for work.

Suspicious.

Yes.

Father?

Looking into potential blackmailers.

Should have had a ransom note by now.

Not necessarily.

Let me know if you find the ex or if the father gets a blackmail demand.

Okay.

And it went on and on as Kerrick kept delving in, trying to get more and more information. **We need a location in England. She was being followed by someone, who reported it to her father, I presume. Do we have that info? Can we contact the security detail?**

No. Not available. We have nothing else.

He sighed and groaned. **She could be anywhere.**

Yes.

That's not helpful.

No.

Tracking device on her?
No.
Tracking device on the blue four-door?
No.
Health issues that might necessitate her needing medication?
No.

He groaned. **Satellite?**

Absolutely.

I want to see the image from the day she was taken, and I also want the camera feeds from the bridge as she came off the ferry. I want to follow those two vehicles.

Just a moment.

Also need weapons and tactical gear.

When the response came he stared. **Already loaded in car.**

Really? He didn't want to check now. He'd have to continue to trust. He continued to go through the paperwork that he'd been given and realized that he should have picked up food before he came here. He got up, walked over to the window, and stared around at his nearby surroundings. A small diner was at the end of the block. That would do. **Grabbing food,** he typed in the chat box. **Back in ten.**

Then he quickly locked up the motel room and headed across the street and into the small diner. There, he ordered a meal to-go, coffee, and picked up several muffins and some doughnuts. Sugar was always good for a hit of energy as long as in moderation. Back in his room, he still had no answer from the chat window. He sat down with the laptop in front of him and ate. Then he cleaned up his garbage and sat back, doing more research.

Time was wasting, but, if they didn't have any intel, even England was way too damn big for Kerrick to start knocking on doors. When his laptop beeped, he clicked his computer to see the satellite feed. Then he clicked on the chat window. **I need remote access to an imaging program.**

There was silence for a long moment while he continued to study the feed, and then he was given a set of logins and a link. He quickly hit the link and logged in. Opening up that video, he zoomed the images to a much higher pixel count to see exactly what he needed to look at. Sure enough, the woman "asleep" on the back seat of the car under surveillance had a scar on her right cheek. The mark was on one of the earlier photos of Amanda that he had, but he had missed it on the first go-around because he had only looked at the background in her picture, taking in the scenery behind her head. But on further examination, there was a definite triangular or kind of heart-shaped scar on her right cheekbone, high and close to her ear. It happened to be that side of her facing up in the photo too. She appeared to be drugged. He did a quick perusal, studying the vehicle, writing down the type and the make and that a rear light was broken.

Check for an accident report, he typed into the chat box. Then he kept on searching the satellite feed, going through every angle on that ferry, trying to get something on the driver. But all Kerrick got was dark hair on a hairy arm by the open window. He was the only other person in the vehicle.

No accident on file regarding ferry passengers for that date and time using data available and as reported.
Single driver with "sleeping" passenger confirmed by birthmark as Amanda Berg, he typed into the chat box.

But then he stopped and wondered about the lorry

parked right behind the car on the ferry. He zoomed out, taking a look at the distance between them. A transport truck would make a lot more sense for a kidnapping, where she wouldn't be visible. So, was this the lorry that had first taken her? Then, before reaching the ferry, they had moved her to the blue car, like she was sleeping, instead of remaining in the back of a lorry, where an unconscious woman would look particularly suspicious, should the ferry authorities demand a search?

And then the kidnappers transferred her back into a lorry—or *the* lorry—after the ferry landed? Or was this lorry just a decoy? Either way, these kidnappers had done this before. Kerrick pressed Play on the video feed, moving it forward, and the car went ahead, exiting the ferry, with the lorry following. They both took the first exit, and then another vehicle jumped in between the car and the lorry, making Kerrick even more suspicious. Or it could be a total random event.

As he kept watching, the video feed cut off.

He immediately asked via the chat box for access to the transit cameras at that intersection. Their chat continued with more links followed by more links. He kept looking, following the car, but, for at least one mile, blank spaces and blind spots filled the camera feed. The transit cameras could only do so much.

He kept following the video until he found yet another blind spot, and, when he came up on the other side of that suspicious part of the feed, the car was gone. So was the lorry and the middle car. He backtracked and looked at the online map he had pulled up into a new tab to see where else the car could have headed. He kept on searching down the optional roads on various feeds and then asked for another feed. He quickly clicked on the new feed and reviewed it.

He needed to grab all these logins to put into a master file to memorize for other cases. He didn't want to keep asking for access. Almost at this train of thought, the chat window's new message read **Watch your back** and then disappeared.

Chat was gone. To the empty room he whispered, "Thanks for that." Luckily he had some feeds still open on his laptop.

He studied the blind spot and noted another road heading off to the side. He picked up the next transit camera intersection four blocks away, but he saw no sign of the blue car anywhere in the next hour's worth of feed. That bothered him, but he couldn't get a view of that corner. It was about forty minutes away from where he sat. He quickly packed up his laptop and the rest of the equipment that he had, as well as his ready bag, just in case, and then headed out to his rental vehicle.

He drove to the point where the blue car had been lost in the traffic feeds. He still had the camera feeds up on his laptop, so he could double-check the area around him. He drove forward and around several blocks. Then, with his instincts prodding him, he pulled off onto the shoulder and got out. It was now three o'clock in the afternoon, Monday. *Damn it! Where had the time gone?*

He noted traffic was everywhere, and it was a hell of an intersection to try to disappear into. But, at the time of the supposed kidnapper's Dover crossing, it would have been about 7:00 that Sunday evening. So, if this were truly the kidnapper's car driving outside of London, about 9:00 p.m. that Sunday, as evidenced by the time stamp on the satellite feeds and on the street cameras, then that vehicle pulled safely off the shoulder here. Kerrick walked up and down the first hundred yards from where the camera went blind, checking on both sides of the road. He stood for a moment with his hands on his head, swearing.

What had happened to the car? It hadn't gone forward, and it hadn't been seen on the other side. But then he remembered the lorry. How big was that damn lorry?

He got into his rental and searched his feeds and confirmed his initial assessment—it was a large lorry, like a moving truck. And then he knew what had happened. He quickly zoomed in on the feeds, picked the ID number off the lorry and its license plate number, and ran a search. Because, of all the things, if the blue car wasn't here, and he couldn't find any sign of it, that meant it wasn't here. There was no ravine to have gone down; there was no cliff to have gone over; there were no houses with garages. Nothing but straight traffic thoroughfares.

There were subdivisions all around, but no exits here accessed them. Which meant the lorry had pulled ahead, and the car had driven up on a ramp into the back and could even now be inside that damn lorry. He needed help. He picked up his disposable phone and quickly dialed its only saved number. When the other voice asked for his identification, he gave it and said, "I need the chat."

Instantly the chat window opened up, and he gave them the license plate and the lorry ID number. **Find that sucker.** Then he typed alongside that **The car's inside it.**

The chat box disappeared for a long moment while he drove around and parked on higher ground, where he could get a better view of the overlaying area. The lorry could have driven for another eighteen hours across country, but he suspected—now that the car had been hidden inside the lorry—that the kidnappers were close to their true destination.

So they had driven to another place near London, where they were probably safe to park and able to work there. But where did one park a huge lorry like that? It had a company's logo on one side, but, as he saw from the various video camera feeds, it had a different logo on the other side. So it had been repurposed from its original intent, which made a lot of sense but would also throw people off.

Different witnesses would give differing reports to the authorities, sullying their veracity. *Smart move, from the criminal's mind-set.* He hadn't seen anybody try that before, but it made sense. It also gave credence to his working theory that the lorry had swallowed up the car. Using the live camera feeds, he backed up the feeds and then quickly searched through them for the appropriate time stamp; he needed to see where that sucker went.

There. And it did drive down near here. It headed through that intersection, then picked up again on the main route, and headed forward. It was slow and painstaking to get through these rudimentary street-camera feeds. The software used for a video game for home use had more viability than these city street cameras. Kerrick shook his head at that.

Just then the chat window offered a new link. He quickly tapped on it to see the lorry turning off into a large parking lot, and its corresponding street address popped up below. A trucking company. Another good idea. Hide one lorry among many other lookalikes. He immediately entered the company's address into his GPS and drove. He didn't know where the hell that vehicle was now, but he needed to find it. The kidnappers might not have unloaded the car yet, but they sure as hell would have unloaded the passenger—unless she was already dead.

CHAPTER 4

AMANDA WOKE UP bitterly cold, her body shivering, trying to warm up in her cool cell by rubbing her hands along her arms. She followed the innate wisdom of her internal clock and deemed this the next morning. But how could she tell for sure? It could be just the continuation of what she had earlier deemed as her second day here. Or … hell. Still her first day here. Actually that made more sense. Time would drag by here, she suspected.

She shook her head. The drugs and lack of light messed with her senses.

She had to once again get up to relieve her bladder. And found that the pot had been emptied. Did they do that at night, when she slept? That gave credence to this being a new day, Day 2? Or Day 3 of captivity for her?

She frowned; somehow she'd slept through the night and hadn't even heard her visitor. That wasn't good. But her next thought was not any better. The only way for that to have happened was either the room was gassed or her food had been drugged.

Surprise, surprise.

She didn't know how much longer they were planning on keeping her here. There hadn't been another sound or another voice crying since she'd heard the first one. That was disturbing.

Then she turned bitterly cold, both inside and out. She laid here for a long moment, distracting herself by listening intently, but there was nothing to hear. She got up and systematically walked from wall to wall, trying to listen to the other side, tapping to see if she could find a hollow space in the walls—or to hear tapping in return from another captive like her. But she found no weakness in the walls and no neighbors.

Then, back at the door, she held her ear against the wood and could hear something banging outside. She tested the doorknob, but it was locked. There was no opening or window in it, so she had no way to see out. She studied the door hinges, wondering if she could take it apart. But she didn't have any tools. Nothing here could even possibly undo those screws. And they were pretty intense-looking screws. A drill would be required, and, if the screws were really old, like the rest of this place seemed to be, then they were probably rusted, and she couldn't do anything with them anyway. The pins were also long and deep and rusty looking so no budging those.

Just then a hard pounding came at the door. She jumped back in shock, and a voice called out, "Stand away from the door."

Shivering in the cold, with her arms wrapped around her, she stepped back a few feet and waited until the door opened. It was the same man who had delivered the tray of food to her once, but he carried no food, only held a gun this time, which he pointed at her, while another man in a white lab coat stepped inside.

She stared at her boss in shock. "Dr. Hinkleman?"

He gave her a fat smile and nodded. "Glad you're awake enough to know my name."

She stared at him in bewilderment. "Why am I here?"

"Because you won't do what you're told," he said in exasperation.

She shook her head. "I've been working under you for years. Of course I'm doing what I'm told. What is this all about?" She threw her arms wide open. "Do you have any idea how cold it is in here?" At that, her teeth started to chatter too.

Immediately the doctor frowned, turned, and barked an order in another language to the man behind her. Who barked an order to somebody else, somebody out of her sight and probably standing in the hallway. Of course nobody would leave her alone long enough to retrieve a blanket for her, but her mind spun off in a million directions, trying to figure out what had been said. Why was her boss here? Where was she?

"What is this about?" she asked.

"A couple things," Hinkleman said smoothly. "Your work, for one. Somebody who doesn't want you, for another, and somebody who is happy to get back at your father, for a third. I'm basically collecting on two points and getting what I want at the same time. Bonus."

She took a deep, slow breath, trying hard to calm her pounding heart as she realized just how many people could be involved in this. "Are you saying you coordinated with two groups of people to have me brought here?"

"I coordinated with a lot more than that," he said. "But it doesn't really matter because you're here. I've been paid times two and get your research for my own."

"If you wanted my research, you know it was yours anyway, based upon the employee agreement I signed when I hired on with Scion Labs. They get ownership of any patents or trademarks, etcetera, of my creation while under Scion Labs employ," she said, struggling to focus on one of these issues. "This doesn't make any sense. The one who wants to get rid of me would be my ex-husband, but he should have done that before I signed the divorce papers. The one trying to get back at my father ..." She turned to the doctor and snapped, "Could be anybody in the world."

"Keep your temper. But you certainly nailed the people, yes. As for your research, you haven't been letting me know about all of it, have you?"

She frowned blankly at him but knew he wasn't fooled. "You know that I'm not supposed to give you anything until we have surety," she said slowly. "And obviously I haven't hit that point, or I would have told you."

"It doesn't matter," he said, "because somebody else who works with you told me all about it. And I'm very disappointed you didn't tell me first. Now you'll be sorry too."

KERRICK PULLED INTO a large parking lot, past the one he was interested in. He had slowed as he had driven by the first one, but he confirmed it as his destination as he saw a lot of lorries parked outside. He pulled up, parked on the side of the building housing Hope Rims Company, and pretended to walk toward its office.

Instead, he dodged past, as if heading to the loading zone. There, he hopped over the fence into the neighboring property and snuck up against the building for the trucking company. He tried to listen in on any conversations in the parking lot, mostly drivers razzing and joking about how their weekend plans had worked out. That wasn't exactly what Kerrick cared about.

He studied the vehicles parked in the large lot, waited until the men outside loaded up and pulled out, and then walked among the lorries, looking for one in particular. It was the fourth one from the back along the fence, but it was pulled forward so the back could be accessed. He took several photos, sent them to his contact, and checked that it had the expected license plate number and the right lorry ID number. Then he swung open the large rear door to the storage area and hopped inside.

It was completely empty. Of course it was. Knowing the car was long gone, he checked to see if there was any sign that it had been here. He found a few drops of oil. He stopped, took a picture of it, took a sample of it using a Q-tip in a Ziploc bag, and popped it into his pocket, just in case it might be of need later. Then found more oil at the opposite end of the lorry. *Strange.* He took samples of it too.

He slipped out, shut the door softly, and walked up to the front of the cab. It was unlocked, so he hopped inside now, quite content that nobody could see him unless they came to move this particular lorry. He checked the logs in the glove box. The insurance was in the name of the company on whose property he sat, which made sense.

Kerrick thought about the traffic feeds and realized he hadn't checked the side panels of the lorry. It's quite possible somebody had changed the logo. He took several photographs of the insurance papers and the logbooks, but nothing here noted that this lorry had taken the ferry over from the mainland. *Interesting.*

Yet an employee of this company was more likely involved in the kidnapping itself, not so much the company. The employee just needed his employer's lorry. Kerrick made his way back outside and checked the logos on each side of the lorry. And, sure enough, one side had the permanent company logo painted thereon. On the other side? The same logo replication. Whatever had been there before was no longer present. It must have been a large plastic or magnetic sign that the employee could easily put on and take down again. *Again, interesting.*

Kerrick quickly walked around the parking lot, took several license plates photos from other vehicles, and then stepped up toward the main office. A young woman sat behind the counter, typing. He waited until she was free, then smiled, and told her that he was looking for the driver of lorry 714.

She looked up at him in surprise. "Why?" she asked suspiciously.

He gave her a winning smile and said, "He's a friend of mine." It was almost comical how much relief crossed her face when she heard that.

"That's Jimmy's lorry," she said. "He knows everybody." She waved her hand. "You just missed him."

"Surely that wasn't him who just drove out?" he asked with an exaggerated frown.

She nodded. "He's got a delivery down the road. He should be back in a couple hours."

He looked outside, checked his watch, and looked outside again. "How late are you open?"

"If you can't wait, just come back," she said. "The office closes at six. But Jimmy will return the lorry whenever he's done, if it's later than that."

"Or I could check him out at the job. I was hoping to make plans for the coming weekend."

"He's gone to the commercial growers up the road with

a big load of fertilizer and chemicals to drop off."

Kerrick waved his thanks, stepped out of the office, heading for his rental. He drove up the road, looking for the growers, found the location, and plugged it into his GPS. He pulled off to the side in time to witness the men unloading the delivery.

He didn't know which one was Jimmy or who the other guy was. From his vehicle, he took several photos of their faces and quickly sent them off to his one and only contact on his burner phone, with a note saying he was looking for Jimmy, the regular driver of lorry 714 which had come across the ferry. Just an update for Beta.

Kerrick figured that *his people* would get to him as soon as they had anything further or something new. At least he hoped so. He wasn't used to having zero contact with anyone in person and just waiting until things were deep-sixed in the internet, the equivalent of filing things in the circular file. On the other hand, there was a certain amount of freedom without having to check in.

He waited in his vehicle until the delivery men were more or less done. Then one of the men walked into the storefront. Kerrick walked in after him and listened as he talked to the women up front. They called the dark-haired man Tom, which meant Jimmy was the one outside and still at the lorry. Kerrick walked toward Jimmy, standing beside the lorry, lighting up a cigarette.

Kerrick gave Jimmy a smile, pointing at his lorry, and said, "Hey, didn't I just see you on the ferry coming from the mainland yesterday?"

Jimmy ground out the cigarette and gave him a blank stare. "Not me. Not my rig."

Kerrick backed up, looked at the number on the rig, and

said, "Same tag, same type lorry, wrong number though. It was seven-one-four that I saw on the ferry."

Jimmy shook his graying head. "Well, that's my rig, but I wasn't driving it over there, that's for sure. And not on no Sunday."

"Well, it was definitely on the ferry. Pretty sure you were the driver." Kerrick frowned as if he was really confused, reaching up to scratch his temple. "But maybe not. It was definitely your lorry though." Then he walked to the other side and said, "Part of the reason I noticed was it had two different logos. One on each side of the lorry."

Jimmy gave him another blank look.

"You don't know anything about it?" Kerrick asked in surprise.

Jimmy shook his head. "No, not me. You must be talking about somebody else."

"Maybe not you. But it was your lorry. Maybe I'll head back to the trucking office and see who that was then."

"Why do you care?" Jimmy asked.

"Oh, I care," Kerrick said. "Had a little bit of a confab with that vehicle."

"What kind of confab?" Jimmy asked, getting upset. "My lorry's not banged up at all."

"Didn't say it was a lorry confab, did I?" Kerrick said.

"Well, if you had a dust-up with a driver, you'd have known it wasn't me."

"Good point," he said. "I think I'll go find that lorry. Your company's yard is just a couple miles from here, isn't it?" Then he pulled up his phone, nodded, and said, "Yep, I'll find out who that driver was."

"When was that again?"

Jimmy didn't appear to understand what was going on,

which kind of put him into the *might be innocent* category. But, at the same time, Kerrick had seen a lot of men who could lie so well that you'd never know. He gave Jimmy the time and date of the ferry crossing per the pictures he had on his phone.

Jimmy shook his head over and over again. "I was home with my wife. My rig was in the yard."

Just to prove the point, Kerrick brought up the picture of the lorry and the ferry number on his phone, then held it up to Jimmy.

Jimmy was flabbergasted. He just stared, his jaw dropping. "Well," he roared, "that son of a bitch."

"You want to clarify?"

"Hell no, I don't," Jimmy said. "That suffices to say that somebody I know took that lorry when he shouldn't have."

"Well, that might be," Kerrick said, "but it's your assigned lorry. Do you want to get in trouble or should your buddy?"

Jimmy glared at him. "Why? Who are you, and why do you care?"

With a hard smile, Kerrick pulled out one of his many IDs and held it up. "Somebody who cares," he said. His voice went low and hard. "Whoever you lent that lorry to was up to no good. Illegal activities with that lorry have been photographed."

Jimmy's face blanched. "I didn't have nothing to do with that," he snapped.

"Bullshit," Kerrick said. "If that's not you driving that lorry, you obviously know who is." He pulled his phone down and checked through his photos and then, finding one of the cars ahead, he held it up and said, "And do you recognize that car?"

Jimmy sucked in a breath. It seemed he knew a hell of a lot more than he had said so far. Slowly he nodded his head. "I do," he said, "but I don't know what the hell's going on."

"And why is that?"

"Because the guy who owns that car doesn't work for the company anymore."

"But let me guess, he's friends with the driver who borrowed your lorry?"

Jimmy winced.

"And they paid you to look the other way. Is that it?"

"Yeah," he said, shamefaced. "But I thought it was just to pick up a few extra moving jobs on the weekend or after hours during the week."

"*Moving*, indeed," Kerrick said starkly. "I wonder if you have any idea what they were moving this time."

Jimmy shook his head. "No, I don't think I want to."

"No, you don't," Kerrick said. "But I'll tell you anyway. We've got a missing woman, and she'd been ID'd in the back of this car in front of your lorry, which then picked up the car and hauled it in the back of the lorry, moving this kidnapped woman somewhere else."

Jimmy stepped back, his face turning beet red, his hand at his chest. For a moment, Kerrick thought Jimmy would have a heart attack, watching him carefully, but eventually Jimmy caught his breath and then in a panic said, "I didn't have nothing to do with that."

"And we're back to the same point where we were earlier," Kerrick said coolly. "Who was driving the lorry?"

Jimmy worked a hand through the wispy white hairs at the top of his head, obviously not sure what to do.

"That's fine," Kerrick said. "I can haul you in and will question you and your family as to what connections you have to this kidnapped woman."

Immediately Jimmy backed up several paces. "I didn't have nothing to do with it." He held up his hands in front of his chest, waving Kerrick back. "Nothing, you hear me?"

"I want a name," Kerrick said. He pulled up his phone and quickly took a snap of Jimmy's face. "Just so we can find you whenever we want you," he said.

At that, Jimmy started to talk. "Stanley. Stanley Warrick," he said. "The guy used to work at the trucking company."

"So he's the one who owns the blue car?"

Jimmy nodded.

"And he's the one driving the lorry onto the ferry last night?"

Again Jimmy nodded.

"But he's no longer employed by your company, right?"

"Yeah, he was fired about six months ago."

"Why?"

Jimmy took several deep long breaths and finally blurted out the truth. "He was taking the rigs, disabling the GPS, and driving them after-hours."

"Interesting," Kerrick said. "And, since he got fired, your friend is now getting you to cover for him while he does the same thing. Right?"

"Yeah, but honestly, I didn't think it was anything like this."

"Did your employer ever find out what this Stanley guy was doing with the rigs?"

Jimmy shook his head. "Not back then. But it was nothing like this. Stanley didn't go very far. We figured he was just bringing over and distributing shipments of imported illegal goods."

"Such as?"

"Maybe some wines that didn't have the proper papers, maybe some easily sold items ..." Jimmy looked at Kerrick, still half panicked, and said, "I didn't have anything to do with that shit. ... I promise."

"Promises don't mean anything when a woman's life is in danger," Kerrick said. "Who else would be involved from the trucking company?"

At that, Jimmy stopped, looked at Kerrick, looked again at the storefront where his coworker still was, and said, "I don't think there's anybody else."

The way Jimmy was eyeing the storefront meant this had to be about Tom too. "Well, there's at least two vehicles directly involved," Kerrick said. "Stanley's car had to be driven by somebody because you just said Stanley was driving the stolen lorry. So, if two people are driving around, chances are more people are involved."

Jimmy shook his head, his wispy hair flying around as he said, "I don't think so."

"Well, somebody's got to be looking the other way. What about the extra mileage on the rigs?"

Jimmy's face turned bloodred, and he looked to see if his partner had come out of the store yet. He then faced Kerrick. "Sometimes I change the mileage back a bit."

"Really? And nobody's thought to check them? And nobody's thought to check with your rigs during the weekend or at night?"

Jimmy flushed and looked downward.

Kerrick nodded and said, "You disabled the LoJack, didn't you?"

"Only a couple times early on. When I was afraid they'd check. But they never did so ..."

"And they don't track the GPS on the lorries and check it against mileage records?"

"Not yet," he said glumly. "But they probably will now that you're here."

"And how long have you been doing this?" Kerrick snapped. "Do you always steal from your employer?"

"I've been here forty years," Jimmy snapped back. "I got another year, and then I'm out. Do you think they'll give me anything but a handshake and a pat on the back that says thanks?"

"And why do you deserve more?" Kerrick asked. "Did they not give you a paycheck all these years? And I presume a decent one because you stayed."

Jimmy blinked several times at that. And he shrugged. "But I don't have enough to live on if I can't work."

"So were you involved in Stanley's smuggling operations too?"

Behind him came a voice, saying, "What are you talking about? Smuggling?"

The voice was young and light. Tom was half whistling as he walked toward them. "Anybody who knows Jimmy would know that in no way would he do anything wrong." Then the young guy grinned at Kerrick, held out his hand—a hairy hand full of black hair—and said, "Now, me, Tom Paine, well, you know what? I might have been known to nick a few things in my time."

And Tom must have driven Stanley's blue car onto the ferry with Amanda unconscious in the back seat. So that third vehicle could very well have been driven by my man Jimmy here.

Jimmy opened the cab door and said, "Come on, Tom. We got to go."

"Now we're not in that big a hurry," Tom said. "What's

the rush?"

Jimmy shot a dark look toward Kerrick. "Nothing. We're late, and I want to go home." He hopped in, slammed the door, and turned on the engine.

Tom lifted a hand and said, "Hey, my ride's leaving. Anytime you want to talk to me, give me a shout."

"At what number?" Kerrick asked drily. But, to his surprise, the kid peeled off a number. Kerrick quickly added it to his cell phone and nodded. "Maybe I'll do that. How long have you worked for them?"

"About six months," he said with a big grin. "It's a really good paycheck. I like the hours, and I like the work. They're really very good to deal with."

"So, you wouldn't be involved in anything shady then, would you?" Kerrick's voice was low and curious.

Tom opened up the passenger side, just as Jimmy attempted to move forward. Tom hopped up before it took off on him, and he said, "Nah, no way. The owners, they're really good to deal with."

"Yeah, you must be related to them."

Tom chuckled. "I am. They're my grandparents."

No wonder Jimmy didn't want to speak up. He was nearing retirement age, didn't want to screw that up. But he was already in enough hot water letting Stanley, who was fired, still use the company's lorry, while Jimmy covered for Stanley by tweaking the mileage records. Now Jimmy surely didn't want to name the bosses' own grandkid as their accomplice to a kidnapping, not to mention bringing up the smuggling issue as well.

And, with that, the two lying employees tore off down the road.

CHAPTER 5

AMANDA WOKE UP again, trusting her internal clock to remain accurate, shivering once again. The windowless cold gray walls stared back at her. Her stomach churned violently. Nothing was more unsettling than knowing you were getting sick unless it was knowing that you were locked up as a prisoner in a dark cold room with only a full pee pot to throw up in. Just the thought of getting up to hang her head over the top of that thing made her balk. The smell alone would make her erupt violently.

Trying to focus on anything else, she laid in bed, gasping, willing her gut to calm down. Finally she was forced to sit up, hanging her legs over the edge, dropping her head between her knees, hoping to still the stream. Was it the little bit of drugged food they'd given her, or was it just the lack of food? She had tried so hard not to eat, but it was impossible when the hunger got to her. And, of course, these assholes knew that. Hinkleman also hadn't returned. He had just laughed at her circumstances and had walked out even when she had cried after him, "What do you want?"

He had lifted a hand goodbye and left.

The fact that he was getting paid several times over to keep her captive was mind-blowing. She hadn't made a name for herself. Not yet. Her father had, as a politician. As had her mother. And sure, Amanda wanted to feel the rewards for her research work on cancer. Several of her patients had gone into remission after taking her drug, but, of course, her patients were of the four-legged variety, not the humans who she needed to try her cure on.

But getting human trials approved was something else. And she didn't understand why Hinkleman would be upset that she was to the point of applying for those. Couldn't he appreciate what she had done? His name went on all the papers anyway. Although hers would go on the papers too. She was his underling.

Was that it? Was he not willing to share the glory? Pretty upsetting if that's the case because he already had several awards in his name, but they were from decades ago. Yet he clung to them and reminded everybody of them almost weekly. But this level of curing-cancer research, of course, was where everybody wanted to be. A cure for cancer was the Holy Grail. Why wouldn't Dr. Hinkleman appreciate that, no matter who found the cure?

Even before all her formal upper-level schooling, she'd been very young when joining the Mensa group. There she'd met many people who were doing awesome things in life, inspiring her to do even more. After Alice's death, Amanda had chosen to work on improving the human condition by finding a cure for breast cancer.

As she sat in the darkness, she could feel the tears well up, and she called out to her dead friend. "Alice, I sure hope you're doing well in a better place. There's a good chance I could be joining you soon."

Of course Amanda heard no answer. There was never any answer. She'd been talking to Alice since her death. She knew, every once in a while, her coworkers caught her mumbling to herself. And that was fine. The problem was, she was mumbling to a specific person, knowing full well that she wouldn't get an answer back but needing to converse with her anyway. After all, Alice was why Amanda did this. To save others like Alice. She'd been so young when she had been diagnosed with breast cancer, of all things.

In Amanda's mind, she'd always thought that breast cancer belonged to middle-aged or older women who'd already had their two-point-five kids and the breasts themselves had been worn out and used up. But instead, her friend was only twenty-six and yet to be pregnant, and she had died so soon afterward. How was that fair? And, of course, it wasn't, but Amanda's situation wasn't fair either. Life was a bitch sometimes.

Just then she heard a gentle tap, but she didn't understand from where. She hopped out of bed, instantly woozy and unsure on her feet, stopping to steady herself, and still not knowing what time it was exactly in the darkness. She was losing track of most of her senses now.

She walked over to one wall and tapped gently. Nothing. She walked to the next, tapped again and again, and at the door she tapped as well. And just as she went to do that on the next wall, another tap sounded, but it came from the ceiling above her. She slowly stepped onto her cot, steadying herself again, not surprised by her weakness, and tapped back. There was almost a startled sensation, and then two more taps came. She tapped twice back.

At least this way, they knew that she had heard and that they were communicating. Didn't mean that they knew *what* they were communicating, but she'd take any sign of human existence that she could.

When the taps came back three times, she got a little pissed, but she tapped three times back as well. Her worst nightmare was of a child playing up there, letting people know that the floor was talking to them. And then she noted the ensuing series of taps and breaks. And it repeated over and over again. She caught her breath, dragged her mind back to the Morse code that she had learned when interested in navy life. She realized that somebody was signaling to her. She listened to it tapped out over and over again: H-E-L.

Her heart sank and her eyes closed when the *P* came.

She didn't know what to say. She tapped her reply slowly. *Yes, please help me.*

Another startled moment could be heard from above and then another set of taps. *Can't* came back. And then *Help me?*

Tears dripped down Amanda's cheeks as she realized that, indeed, somebody else was being held here too, another prisoner, not just the crying woman heard earlier on Amanda's same floor but also above her. She tapped back slowly. *Can't. Locked in.*

The answer came as *Me too.*

Needing to know that somebody was out there, somebody who maybe could tell her father, she tapped out her name and added *Chemist kidnapped.*

What came back was a name. *Brandon Coleman. Kidnapped.*

And then the next part broke her heart. *Ten years old.*

She screamed a cry of rage, a cry of pain and anger. A little boy was up there, a child held captive. Like her. She sent another message back. *Why?*

Father bad.

Not.

They say so.

Doesn't matter. Stay strong.

You?

Ex-husband mad at me. Also some enemy of my father involved. Not sure what to say next, she sank onto her cot. When she heard footsteps outside, she quickly stood and tapped *Quiet. Someone's coming.* The last thing she wanted was for anybody to know that they were communicating.

Someone pounded on her door.

When the order came for her to stand back from the doorway, she climbed off her cot, automatically took several steps backward, and stood at attention.

The door opened, and Hinkleman walked in. He glared at her. "We need you."

She opened her eyes wide. "Of course," she said. "What do you need me for?"

"Your notes," he snapped. "They don't make any sense."

She frowned. "If they don't make any sense, it's because you're not following them. Or ... someone has altered them."

"You?"

She shook her head rapidly. "You know I would never corrupt the data. That's everything to me."

He stared at her for a long moment and then, without warning, smacked her hard across the face. The blow sent her reeling, and she collapsed on the cot. He turned and walked out again.

She lay here, her anger returning. Memories of her ex hitting her added to her ire. Yet through it all she knew she hadn't heard the hard *snick* on the lock as the door was slammed behind her.

Slowly, with her ear against the door, she pushed down the handle and tugged the door toward her. She only opened it a little bit to see if anybody would slam the door in her face. But nobody appeared to be outside her door, at least not in the three feet before her door. The hallway was disjointed, if it were a hallway at all. By the time she took three steps and reached the next corner, she peeked around, and she could now see that her short hallway joined a long and dank hallway, but faint running lights ran above her on the ceiling. Multiple doors were on both sides. This hallway was also completely empty.

She had waited for one opportunity, and she took it.

THE TRUCKING COMPANY had closed for the day at 6:00 p.m., and it was almost 7:00 now. Kerrick sat in his vehicle in an empty lot several blocks away and quickly researched the employee names he had been given from the very helpful front-desk lady. All it took was the mention of Stanley Warwick, and she wanted to do everything possible to make sure nobody was doing that again. Kerrick had already sent those names to his contact. When he received a text message to **Call**, he picked up his phone and waited for the tumblers to connect him to a secure line.

Then he asked, "What's up?"

"One of the trucking company employees used to work for a biochemical research company," said the quiet voice on the other end of the call.

The voice this time wasn't Beta's, his old buddy. Yet another new voice without a name in this new government division.

"He was a delivery driver for them until he got fired six months ago."

Tom Paine. "The owner's grandkid. And?"

"It's the same company she worked for."

Instantly he went "Yes!" This is exactly what they needed. It was a break, and it was something to blow open this case. "Perfect," he said. "I need to know everything about the biochemical research company. I want to know all the details, no matter how small."

"It won't help much. It's in Paris."

"Everything helps. She was kidnapped after work in front of that building. Every little tidbit helps," Kerrick said firmly. And then he swore. "I don't want to take the time to hop over there, but I might have to."

"Tell us what you want."

He ran off a list of all the questions he wanted answered about the company. Then, when he finally ran out of steam, he said, "And get it to me later tonight."

The voice laughed. "You don't ask for much, do you?"

"You want the girl saved, don't you?"

There was silence for an instant. "You'll get your answers," the voice said, and then it rang off.

Kerrick wished he could send a message to Amanda herself, letting her know that somebody was coming for her. Letting her know that somebody cared. Because, in spite of himself, he was starting to care about this victim. He'd been on several teams that had rescued kidnapped victims before, but there was just something about that clear and direct gaze of Amanda's ... That purpose in her eyes, that sense of self, as if to say *I know exactly what I'll do. I know how I'll do it, and, Cancer, you better damn watch out because I'm coming for you.*

He recognized that look because his gaze held the same kind of look. Only, in his case, it was all about him coming for her. The emotions he felt hit him sideways. Odd to think about caring for this woman when he hadn't cared for anyone after all these years.

As he looked out the window of his vehicle, he could see the day waning away, but he'd gotten a lot done so far. He'd get back to his motel and stay at it. He didn't have a clue when his people would contact him again. At least he had a good start on solving this case. Now, if only he could force the cops to drag in Stanley, who owned the car on the ferry, for questioning. Would Stanley say anything though? Not likely. He probably has been well paid for his part in this.

And Tom Paine? The cops needed to talk to him too, but Tom wasn't any mastermind. That much was for sure. Yet he had the connection to Scion Labs, Amanda's employer. So was Tom getting paid too, directly from his previous employer to screw over his current employer, meaning, his own grandmother and grandfather? *Family*, ain't they just grand at times?

Well, at least Kerrick knew where to find Tom tomorrow. At work.

Kerrick drove back to the motel, stopping to pick up food. He ordered another burger and fries, hating that he was eating a lot of fast food but needing the sustenance, and parked outside the motel.

Back in his room, he quickly set up his laptop again and researched Stanley. What if, on his own, Kerrick could contact Stanley directly? Maybe scare the crap out of him to get him to talk? Kerrick searched online for a physical address or anything that would give him a location, but he found nothing. And, if Stanley no longer worked at the trucking company, what's the chance he would talk anyway? It's not like he could lose a job he didn't have anymore.

By now Jimmy, the nervous weasel, would have forewarned both Tom and Stanley. Sighing, Kerrick bet that Tom Paine would *not* be returning to work tomorrow.

It was well past business hours now and getting darker out and now thirty-one hours of captivity for Amanda. And that's why Kerrick needed to track down a few more of these people. He hated to lose all of the night to sleep, although he did have to catch some shut-eye to be able to do this job right, to divert any jet lag. So much information still had to be found, and Kerrick had absolutely no inkling where Amanda was being held.

What if Jimmy or Stanley or Tom didn't disengage the GPS on that lorry? Surely one of the three of them would have covered their asses. Still, after meeting two of them, Kerrick decided to see what information that GPS could give him.

He contemplated breaking into the trucking parking lot overnight and then wondered if he could hack into the computer system instead. He quickly opened his special chat window and ordered the GPS tracking info on the lorry. The answer was a single question mark.

He typed **Do it.**

He sat here and ate his burger and fries, wishing he'd picked up at least one coffee. When he was done, he tossed his garbage, grabbed himself a large glass of water, and drank that down. By the time he returned to his laptop, the chat window had a message waiting for him and a link. He quickly went into the link, and, sure enough, it provided the LoJack mileage data on lorry 714 to date. He went back to the day in question, and there it was—the path that the lorry had taken on Sunday.

Even with three guys involved in using a stolen lorry, not one had considered disengaging the LoJack on it. Wow, talk about cocky. Or just plain stupid. But while the LoJack gave Kerrick the total mileage traveled on that Sunday by the stolen lorry, it didn't tell him anything about the locations reached along that journey. And the mileage racked up that day indicated one hell of a trip. Like to Paris and back?

He went back to the chat window. **Get the map for Sunday's route from the LoJack company.**

Almost immediately, as if having already anticipated what he needed, another link popped up. And there he was, into the security system and checking the exact route the lorry had traveled. With that, he brought out his paper map, courtesy of the local airport—and always good to have on hand as a backup. He spread out the map on the bed with his laptop beside him. He quickly used a highlighter to mark off the lorry's route on his physical map.

As expected, it was a circuitous route. The lorry had traveled to France to kidnap Amanda from Scion Labs in Paris and had returned to England, obviously meeting up with the blue car on the French side of the ferry. And the two vehicles had crossed together, as confirmed on the ferry images. Why two vehicles? The only thing Kerrick could think of was the kidnappers feared the lorry would be searched before being allowed on the ferry.

For sure, a "sleeping" woman in the back of a lorry would raise eyebrows. Whereas a "sleeping" woman in the back seat of a car, obvious for all to see, didn't seem so suspicious.

Regardless, Tom and his hairy arm drove Stanley's car onto the ferry and then onto land in England, while the lorry driven by Stanley soon took the lead and headed into the Liverpool area. There, it had stopped at a couple spots—one Kerrick suspected was where the car had been loaded into the lorry. The lorry had driven another seventeen miles before it stopped again, dropping off Amanda, then had returned to the trucking company yard.

This last stop had likely been where the car had been removed, simply because of the way the lorry was parked away from the fence, like to secretly unload a car. But all that conjecture did not tell him where the car had gone afterward. He again typed into the chat box and asked if there was any sign of the blue car yet.

No.
We need to find it.
On it.

Of course they were on it. The car could be key to finding Stanley. But at least now he knew where the lorry had stopped, where the lorry might have dropped off Amanda. It was a run-down commercial area of town; Kerrick could get back into the traffic cams to find the car hopefully. Moving his laptop from the bed back to the table, he sat down, logged again into the traffic center, and searched through the feeds. He didn't have access to the main city of Liverpool, though he quickly asked the chat window for the login. It took a moment, and then he had another link. He was loving this. He seemed to have access to anything. Granted, he didn't have free *direct* access, but, if it was a reasonable request, so far he had been given whatever he needed.

Back in the traffic cams, at this one location where the lorry had stopped—at least as far as he could tell from this particular angle—was a large loading bay. And that would make sense. There would not likely be any cameras picking up the lorry, but, ... if Kerrick was lucky ... He sat here for the next several hours, fighting exhaustion and jet lag, skimming through the traffic feeds and looking for the car or the big lorry. Then his laptop dinged as the chat window provided another link. He clicked it to see a video camera feed of a big lorry backing up to a loading bay off to the side of some huge industrial building, its rear doors open. As he kept watching, the blue car reversed out of the lorry and drove away. He crowed in delight. **That's it.**

Instantly a thumbs-up emoticon appeared in the chat window.

He laughed. **So you do have a sense of humor. We need to track that car now.**

But, of course, they already were. It took another two minutes, and then his screen flashed. Frowning, he checked out what was coming—a feed recorded earlier, showing the route that the blue car had traveled. Unfortunately he never saw the driver. It could have been Stanley, since it was his car. Or it could have been Tom, since he was mainly driving the car that Sunday. Hell, both men could have been in the vehicle for all Kerrick could tell. That left Jimmy to return his lorry back to the overnight parking lot at the trucking company. So he was driving that third vehicle after all. Kerrick never tracked it very far, only seeing it a couple, three times. And then it disappeared—into the back of the lorry. Pretty brilliant for three stupid crooks.

"Interesting," he murmured as he quickly took notes. The car headed past a hospital, turned around into the back, but then, almost as if thinking it was in the wrong place, pulled back out again and headed away. He frowned at that. "What's the matter? This guy not know where he's going?"

He kept watching as the vehicle pulled ahead into another large medical complex with a huge but run down sign out front. There, it went into an underground loading area, where Kerrick couldn't see it anymore. Kerrick waited and watched but in Fast Forward mode. The vehicle came back out close to forty minutes later per the time stamp on the video. The thing is, this time, from what he could see of the driver, just his shirt-covered chest, it looked to be a different driver, a bigger guy. Kerrick zoomed in as the car took an incline and could see it was a larger man with a beard now.

"Damn it." He sent a screen shot to his people via the chat window. **Got a partial facial photo but try to match it.**

Won't be easy. Only got his beard to go by, and the beard covers major facial markers needed to ID him.

Do your best.

Kerrick frowned, wondering what had happened to the original driver—Tom? Stanley? Jimmy? Someone else?—and that's where the feed ended. He immediately dropped back into the chat box, asking for the rest of the feed. **We need to find that vehicle**, he added on his message.

He was given immediate access once more. He quickly searched and watched as the car was picked up by various traffic cameras on its route, and then finally he could see it off in the distance, heading toward a country pasture. Another vehicle was close behind it, with only a driver inside—and this car was *not* the third one used earlier as a diversion at Dover. These two vehicles got up to a bridge, and Kerrick lost the blue four-door there. He kept searching and waiting, but nothing else showed up again. Kerrick sighed. It was a blind spot in the cameras. But he did catch the other vehicle, a gray two-door, driving away, and this time two people were in the front seat. The picture was grainy, the car too far down the road. *Interesting ...*

That canal needs to be checked up at the bridge. Stanley's blue four-door car will be down there. Still, we could find the dead bodies of Stanley, Tom, and/or

Jimmy anywhere anytime now too. Let me know what you find.

There was an acknowledgment on the chat window, and Kerrick was happy to have the help on that because Kerrick didn't have time. He checked his watch and realized it was almost midnight. He needed at least four hours of sleep a night, but that would have to come later. He closed the chat window, dropped the lid on his laptop, made his preparations quickly, gathering all he would need for his upcoming night maneuver, and had a hot shower.

CHAPTER 6

THE DARKNESS PLAYED with her senses. Amanda lived in an unceasing cycle of dim light. She tried all the doors in the hallway for her floor, deemed the basement as far as she knew. Every door was locked. A knock and her whispered, "I'm here to get you out," didn't get any responses. Only her door was unlocked. She quickly dashed to the far side of this building, but she was in a corridor of more locked doors. She opened one to find it was a closet. She stepped inside, looking for anything to help her. She found a pair of coveralls that she hastily pulled on over her dirty clothes and an old hat. She stopped, looked around for a weapon, finding instead a mop and also a bucket—not much of for weapons. But both would give her a bit of cover.

She grabbed them and carried them out into the hall and checked every one of the doors on each side of this hallway and again found nothing unlocked and nobody responded to her whisper at each door either. She headed back down the third hallway, doing the same checks for each hallway for each side of this building. There had to be a way to get out of this damn place. She passed a double door and stopped. She opened the door, relieved to find that it wasn't locked. It led her to stairs heading up *and* stairs heading down. Her heart pounded, worried that a ton of the bad guys were in this building and that she wasn't the only kidnap victim here.

Up or down?

She hesitated, but the little boy who spoke to her in Morse code was up one floor. So she bolted up the stairs, still carrying her mop and bucket as she headed to the next flight. She could see a small window showing the outside world, so this floor where the boy was held was at ground level. Which meant she had been incarcerated belowground, and yet, another floor was below hers too, given the up and down staircases she had just seen.

Where the hell was she? What was this place? It was dark outside, but her days and nights were all twisted up and turned around, so that she didn't know if this was dusk or dawn. She should have warned Brandon that she was coming, but there'd been no time. Neither could he likely tell her where he was located in this mausoleum. Still, she had a good idea where she had been, and he was directly above her.

She went into the first hallway on this floor and again found it empty, nobody responding from behind the locked doors. She didn't have a clue what all these rooms held. Around the corner was the next hallway on this floor and had almost no doors. She kept tracking the direction to where her room would be underneath. Why had she seen no workers here? Orderlies? Guards? For all she knew, this building was empty and deserted, except for its captives, with a crew coming once a day or every couple days to throw food and water at them.

She raced as fast as she could, using long strides to get down to what she thought would have been the equivalent of her room below. She stopped at the corner, considered how many doorways were to the left, then walked over by three and grabbed the knob and turned it. It opened. But the room itself was empty.

Shit. She stopped. She reorganized her thoughts, trying to figure out how many doors to the left down *her* hallway were there, but this was the corresponding room she was searching for on this level. She was sure of it. However, just in case the floors weren't quite exactly duplicates, she went one door to the left and opened it. It was also empty. Cursing, she went one door to the right, and it was locked. She tapped on the door, and there was a delay before she heard a responding tap. She then tapped a question in Morse code. *Is it you?*

The answer came back *Yes.*

She tried the door again, but it was locked. She could hear him pounding on the door. She waited until he stopped and then tapped *Stop. Be quiet. I have to find out how to open the door. I'll be back.*

And then she left. A matching closet should be down the little boy's hallway as well, if this floor was anything like her floor. There, she raced inside, looking for anything. Again she found nothing to use as a weapon. But there were more coveralls. She quickly checked inside the pockets of each pair, looking for keys that would unlock that door, but found nothing. Then she found the mother lode. A large key ring. Hanging on a hook on the wall.

She stared at it in joy but then realized it could take her an hour to figure out which one belongs to which door. And surely it was just keys to places that didn't matter, right? Because they wouldn't leave prisoners behind locked doors and also leave behind the keys displayed openly on a wall, would they?

Pulling out one of them, she smiled because it was a

master key. She headed back to the same room, and, just as she was about to put the key in the door, she heard voices. She immediately disappeared around the corner and returned to the closet. She rehung the keys on the wall but not before she took the master key. She tucked it into her pocket and disappeared, hiding behind the rack of coveralls.

The only way to make this work was if she tried to be as flat as she could with the coveralls hanging before her. She heard the voices come down the hallway, but they didn't open the door to the closet. She waited, knowing that, if they went one direction, they had to come back again.

But how long would they take? As she waited, she heard the footsteps again. This time they stopped at the door. Somebody opened the closet and said, "This is just the broom closet, in case we need something for spills or to clean up the blood. If it's a big job, we call in the cleaning crew."

She frowned at his tone and his wording, almost as if giving a tour to somebody on his first day at a new job. But the sound of cleaning up blood didn't make her feel any better. And, if it was bad, bringing in a cleaning crew? Yeah, she could imagine.

The voices continued, and she heard, "During the night, we clean out the chamber pots. It's gross. Every one of these rooms should have their own bathroom. If they were in the upstairs rooms, they do, but these downstairs rooms don't." Then the closet door was closed again, and she heard their footsteps getting farther and farther away.

She snorted silently. "Great," she muttered. "I get to be in one of the worst rooms. Doesn't that just suck?"

When she thought it was long enough, she slowly opened the closet door and stuck her head out. Saw no sign of anyone. She stepped into the hallway and raced back to

Brandon's door, hoping that the men hadn't taken the kid away. Using the master key, she quickly unlocked his door. A terrified pale-faced boy stood on the other side. "Brandon?" She opened her arms, and he raced into them. She quickly shut his door again and whispered, "We have to go now."

He wore just shorts and socks and a T-shirt. He held his shoes in his hands, almost as if he thought he could sneak out quieter without wearing them. She motioned for him to get those on fast. She looked around, thinking of anything else in that closet which would be of help to him. *That old jean jacket.* She held up a finger, raced back, quickly snagged it, and brought it to him, putting it around his shoulders. And then she led him back to the stairs. What she didn't know was how to get out of this building.

"Do you know where we're going?" Brandon asked in a loud whisper.

She shook her head. "No. I found stairs but no exit yet."

He nodded. "We need to find that first."

"Suggestions?" she asked, hating the idea of going down the hallway any farther. "That's where the men came from," she said, pointing. "I just about got caught by two of them."

His only response was to stare at her, and she could see the whites of his eyes and how his mouth was pinched tightly together.

She nodded, as if making a decision, then said, "The stairs have to go somewhere."

He stayed close to her as they headed to the stairwell.

There, she motioned up top and said, "Let's go up one more flight. I can see light there, and I know we're above-ground here, but we should check the next level anyway. Then decide on our next move."

They quickly made their way upstairs to what appeared

to be the main floor, and, sure enough, they found a door, with an alarm at the top. She hesitated, pointed at that bright red light, and said, "When the door opens, an alarm could go off."

"But we still need to open it," the boy said as he peered through the nearest window into the darkness. "Do you think there's any chance of getting away from here?"

"This *is* our chance," she said firmly. "If we don't get away on this attempt, we're in deep trouble. They'll lock us up, throw away the key, and then we won't even be given that little bit of food that we've had so far."

"What food?" he mumbled. "I could eat this jacket by now."

"Well, let's hope it doesn't come to that."

Just when she was about to take a deep breath and open the door, they heard voices again, and the door at the top of the stairs opened. They stared at each other in horror. She quickly grabbed him and pulled him back so they were out of view—as long as nobody came down the stairs—hoping that the new arrivals were going up instead.

The voices at the top of the stairs called out, "So do we need to show you the downstairs again too?"

That sent Amanda and Brandon silently scampering down to his floor. Again. Where they waited to see what the newcomers did next.

KERRICK HAD PARKED one-quarter mile away and hiked the rest of the distance to the GPS location where the lorry had unloaded the car, and hopefully Amanda too. Google Maps had ID'd the location as a huge sanitorium that had closed down and been left derelict. And yet, if it was derelict, this building shouldn't have been powered, and there was definitely power. He could see lights on inside. A few vehicles were parked around the building too. So obviously not derelict, no matter what Google told him.

He headed toward the side fence and jumped over it, just in case working cameras checked out people at the main entrance. If other people were held in here, then it was quite possible that the kidnappers had a very extensive security system. Kerrick hoped not but knew he would do what he could to not trigger any alarms. "Hang on, Amanda," he whispered. "I'm coming."

Once he got to the building, he quickly geared up, shaking his head at the surprising haul hidden in his car. Bolstered to have everything he needed, he walked around, looking at the six stories rising above, potentially a seventh or a penthouse that he couldn't quite see. He had no idea how many stories deep it went. But, depending on how many rooms filled each floor, there could be hundreds of patients held here. There was no business sign, no welcoming entrance, and not even a set of double doors that evidenced any kind of regular interaction with people. And yet, this place appeared operational. He crept alongside the building, noting the exits. Two were at the back, with a fire exit on the other side.

Kerrick also found a shipping bay for deliveries on the right-hand side. The driveway dipped into a floor-to-ceiling gated area and went down where a series of raised docks were for unloading at the same level as the lorries. All in all, pretty standard stuff for a commercial building. But the double doors on the bays looked old, as if they probably wouldn't even open. At least, not easily. And that was something else to consider.

If that's where the lorry had driven, which to the best of Kerrick's knowledge it was, why here? Why not just park in the front, unload the woman, and take her in that way? Unless it was just easier down there. It's also possible no cameras were down there to ID the woman. Although the street cams had caught sight of the lorry as it backed up here.

With that thought in mind, he crept his way down the back of the building in the darkness, dressed fully in black, his face blacked out too, and checked for an unsecured entryway, finding an unlocked side door. He opened that and stepped inside. He wore night-vision goggles, which made it easier to see anything. He moved slowly, getting his bearings on the inside of the building.

While the bay door area was for trucks to drive into the lower levels of the building, Kerrick noticed the downward slope of this more pedestrian area, diving deeper into the same area, he presumed.

One of the things about large and supposedly empty buildings like this was that it was often easy to lose track of your navigation sense. And that's something he couldn't afford to do. He kept on moving quietly through the floor. Boxes were off to one side, which he noted without investigating them further, but then farther along he found large pallets. He checked to see it was foodstuffs, and that meant people lived here, so they had to feed them. And they were feeding lots of people because there were multiple pallets.

He kept on moving, but he took photos as he went. He still saw no signs of anyone. It was a small operation based solely on how few cars were here, but he had already taken images of each of the vehicles parked out front—two lorries, a car, and an SUV. He did a complete search of this floor and counted how long that took. Twelve minutes. Realizing how long it would take to check every floor—even without opening every door to every patient room—he had to pick up his speed. But it was just him out here and no backup. He didn't like that part at all. His phone vibrated at his hip, and he pulled back into a far corner and checked it.

Are you in?

He tapped the phone twice for a *yes.*

Backup is on its way.

He smiled at that. **Who?**

Friend.

He stared at that word, but no further messages came. He pocketed his phone and went up one level to get a bird's-eye view. He located a newly installed elevator at one corner and three sets of stairs at the remaining three corners. He was still in the basement area of the building. After taking one more set of stairs, he could look out the nearby window and see the ground below.

Just as he went to the front of the building, passing more windows, he caught sight of somebody dressed in black, skirting around to the far side. He immediately tracked the newcomer to the back wall and then waited for the door to open. Just as it did, it seemed somebody instinctively knew Kerrick waited here. So, he tapped out his name in Morse code. He froze, and then, on the other side of the door, someone tapped out an affirmative *Yes.*

And then he asked, *Who the hell are you?*

Griffin.

Kerrick opened the door and flashed his light in the man's face. Eyes bright and deep emerald green stared back at him. They were twinkling. Kerrick reached out a hand, and Griffin caught it and squeezed hard. Kerrick didn't have time for explanations or questions, but he pulled his buddy in and shut the door tight. In a low whisper, Kerrick asked, "Are you up to speed?"

Griffin nodded. "Have checked out the grounds. All clear. But doubt it will stay that way."

Kerrick nodded and stepped through to the stairwell and said, "Down here first."

But Griffin pulled him back and pointed down.

Kerrick couldn't see anything.

By his ear, Griffin whispered, "Somebody's on the landing below us."

"Got it."

He stepped off to the side to peer down the stairwell, seeing two bodies pressed tight against the stairwell below. So, they heard him coming? That was just too damn bad. If they got in his way, he would take them out. But ... one was small, in baggy coveralls. The other smaller. He held up a warning hand to Griffin, who joined him at his side, and they studied the two in shock. They looked at each other, and then, in a sudden move, Kerrick, using the railings, jumped up to the landing below in two moves, his weapon up tight against the taller of the two people frozen in front of him. And damn if that same clear and directed gaze from one of his photos didn't shine back at him.

"Who are you?" she snarled. Even with his gun poking her in the ribs, she raised her fists as if to clock him.

He quickly grabbed her hand, twisted it around her back, and pulled her tight against him, so she couldn't hit him. The child beside her immediately punched and kicked at Kerrick, but Griffin grabbed him and wrapped him up tight.

Kerrick whispered in the woman's ear, "Amanda?"

She froze, then slowly nodded.

"Good," he said. "You're the one we came for."

"But Brandon comes too," she was quick to demand.

With her in his arms, Kerrick raced back to the door where Griffin had entered. With both captives safely in their custody, they stepped outside into the cool night air. Kerrick whispered, "Don't make a sound. Don't make a move. Not until we tell you."

"How do I know whose side you're on?" she asked in an angry whisper.

He could see the fear in her gaze and also her determination to not let that stop her. But, as she stared into his eyes, she seemed to relax a bit. He smiled and said, "Well, I have a code word for you. Would that make you feel better?"

She frowned and said, "I don't know any code word."

"And why is it that you do cancer research?"

She stared at him, shook her head, and he whispered, "Because of your friend Alice."

She sagged against him, and he picked her up and carried her off into the night.

CHAPTER 7

AMANDA DIDN'T KNOW if she should trust this stranger or not, but the fact was, she was outside her prison and breathing fresh air again. That was the best feeling ever. She held Brandon close in her arms. The poor kid was terrified. He had his arms wrapped tight around her waist, as they both stared up at the men with darkened faces. The men motioned them to move with them quietly.

Just as they headed down the path toward the front of the building, several vehicles pulled in, lights blazing. The two men grabbed her and Brandon and pulled them back behind the building.

She could hear one man swear under his breath. She looked around the property, but the fences were high and would be hard to cross. "Maybe we should go back inside," she whispered.

"Or maybe not," the other man said, his voice low. "If they're coming inside, we want to make sure that we're not caught in there. As soon as they go in the building, we need to get away from here."

"I don't know if there's any way out the back," Amanda stated. "Do you guys know?"

The second man looked over at the first and said, "Kerrick?

So that was his name. It's not like they had had time for

introductions.

Kerrick shook his head. "I didn't see anything. It's this fence all the way around."

The first man nodded. "Makes perfect sense. They shepherd people in, so they only have one direction to go."

"Like cattle," she supplied calmly. She waited to see if the footsteps sounded closer to them. But—other than being flat and tight against the building with the two men both ready and armed—there was just complete silence. Then shortly thereafter she heard car doors closing and lots of laughter from the people walking into the building that angered her more than anything.

They thought this was funny? They thought this was a good thing that she and this poor child and how many others had been imprisoned, freezing, day in and day out, surviving on moldy food and using piss pots instead of toilets? Just the audacity of these people made her so angry. She could feel the tremors running up and down her thin frame. And maybe Kerrick noticed too because he gripped her shoulder firmly and whispered, "Stand steady."

She just glared at him. He flashed a smile in her direction, but she didn't move. The second man leaned forward, ever-so-slightly, and held out three fingers and then dropped one. She waited, wondering what would happen when he dropped the other one. He dropped the second one, and Kerrick whispered, "As soon as he signals it, we'll run. Be ready."

"Great," she muttered, "but where?"

"We'll stay to the right and go through that open gate."

"A getaway vehicle would be better," Brandon muttered against her waist.

She felt more than saw a chuckle come from Kerrick. He

patted Brandon on the shoulder and then reached out a hand, grabbing both of theirs when the second man dropped his final finger. They bolted as fast and as silently as they could, racing along the fence on the right-hand side to the double gates that stood open. Then they were through. She wanted to scream in victory when she hit the other side, but the men weren't giving her a chance to catch her breath, and she knew that they were a hell of a long way from being out of danger.

Just when she thought that maybe they'd cleared the danger zone, they heard voices shouting behind them. With her breath coming in gasps and her chest burning, they raced faster. She thought they were heading for a road, but instead they pulled them into another building, and then they stopped, pressing up tight against another wall. She closed her eyes and tried to calm down her breathing. But each breath rasped out, sounding like a huge cacophony of noise that people miles away would hear.

Brandon looked over at Kerrick and said, "Please tell me that you have a car or a truck to take us away."

Kerrick smiled at him and said, "Yes, but we don't want to be seen getting into it because then they'll follow us too easily."

Brandon smiled for the first time. "Good. If they try to take me a second time, I'll make them pay."

Amanda gave him a quick hug, then said, "The bad guys aren't taking us anywhere again. You and I have both had enough of that crowd."

She could feel the shiver of fear run over him, and she realized just how terrifying an event this must have been for the young boy. It had been bad enough for her. She couldn't imagine how he felt. He was only ten. The machinations of these evil and greedy people were not something any child should be exposed to. Not like this.

They waited again in complete silence. The trouble was her heart just kept pounding against her rib cage. The adrenaline still coursing through her bloodstream kept her revved up, unable to calm down. She could feel her blood pounding at her temples. Her breathing rasped hard in her dry throat from the mad dash. It was all she could do to get her breath under control, just in case she had to run again. It wasn't something she wanted to think about, but she would run until she dropped if it meant avoiding that nightmare.

JUST THEN THE second man stepped forward and farther away from them.

Kerrick called out in a low, urgent voice, "Careful, Griffin."

Griffin? Neither were names that she recognized, yet both were strong, warrior-type names. She appreciated that they were here with her and Brandon. She couldn't imagine escaping on her own, although she'd done well enough before these men had found her and Brandon. She'd gotten them out of their locked cells. These men had helped get them out of the building, but she couldn't put her trust in them too far. For all she knew, they wanted something else from them. How devastating would that be? She studied Kerrick's face, looking for any signs of deceit or betrayal, but it wasn't that easy. It was dark outside, and, short of staring into his eyes again, there was no way to know.

Griffin made a hand motion, and they crept forward. She heard people running, probably searching the grounds all around them for their escapees. So far, nobody had come onto this property.

"How did you know this building was empty?" she asked.

"I scoped it out earlier on a satellite feed," Kerrick said. "Griffin came out earlier this evening too. I knew we could get in this door because I'm the one who unlocked it."

She smiled. "Glad to hear that. It would help if you locked it now though, and then they couldn't get back in again."

"It's already done," he said.

And, realizing that the men seemed to have this well in hand, Amanda sagged against the wall and groaned lightly.

Immediately Brandon turned to look up at her. "Are you okay?" he asked anxiously. Then he spun to look at the other man. "She hasn't had much food or water for the last couple days, by my count of her captivity. She can't do much more of this."

She had some questions for this special little boy, but they would have to wait. Meanwhile she reached out a gentle hand and patted his shoulder. "I'll be fine. Remember how you haven't had any food or water either. Which may have been the better option, as mine were drugged."

"Just stay close," Kerrick said. "And stay silent. We'll get you where you need to go."

"That better be to a shower, a buffet table, and a hot bed," she said and then added, "And communication with the outside world."

"We'll be your outside communication for a while," Kerrick said.

"Are you turning us over to the police?"

He shook his head. "We're not sure the police even

know you're missing."

She stared at him in shock. "What?"

He nodded.

"But surely my father would have contacted them."

"He contacted our group instead," Kerrick said quietly. "And thank God that he did."

"He would do that," she murmured. "He's got connections I can't even begin to guess at."

Just then Griffin made a sound. Immediately Kerrick placed a finger on her lips. She stared at him wordlessly. Her mind was still trying to comprehend the situation. So, no law enforcement, which meant her father didn't trust the police. So, those connections he had, who she didn't know about, he had thought that this was the time to call on them? She shook her head.

All she wanted to do with her life was to cure cancer and to help save women like her best friend. And yet, men like these were out there who did this with their lives instead. It was almost too much to imagine what a life of darkness they led. A life of danger. A life of walking and living in the shadows. Did they ever come out for light? Did they have a normal life? Did they have wives and kids? Did they mow the lawn on Sunday and sit in the backyard and have a beer with a barbecue?

They didn't seem the type, but then what did she know? This was their work persona. It's what they did on their off time that had her curious. Just then they were moved gently to another location within the same building. And that didn't seem like a good idea to her.

She looked over and opened her mouth, but Kerrick gave a sharp shake of his head. Immediately she shut up again. At the back of the building, they stepped outside and moved across the property and around another building. She didn't know what was going on, and she had lost track of where they were as they wove between buildings, back and forth and around. And then, all of a sudden, Griffin was gone. She gripped Kerrick's hand and whispered in a low but urgent voice, "We have to wait for him."

Kerrick looked at her, squeezed her fingers, and said gently, "He's gone to get the car."

She stared up at him blankly, then looked around. "Oh."

"It'll be fine. Just give us a minute to get you into the wheels, and we can get away from here."

She looked over at Brandon to see his huge eyes shining in the darkness. He was tired and exhausted and famished, but also an element of excitement was evident in his expression. This was a story to tell whatever friends he had back home. These superheroes had dashed in the middle of the night to save them. She knew her own role in Brandon's tale was probably as the lost dumb blonde. That filled her with amusement rather than disappointment.

She was okay with whatever version he had to tell to get himself to move forward on this one. She didn't even know what she would say herself except she wanted to block it all out. But how was she supposed to do that when Hinkleman was her boss? Who was *she* supposed to tell this tale to?

Hinkleman was one of the shareholders who were part of the board of directors for her employer, Scion Labs. Hinkleman was highly regarded in his field. Or had been decades ago. And only by people who didn't deal with him day to day. Among those at Scion, Hinkleman was more feared than revered. She had seen him totally lose it, and it wasn't fun to watch. He was more of a bully and a blowhard in her opinion—probably who he truly was. He had been even more volatile lately. But he was unpredictable at best. She had just kept her head down at work, happy to have this huge lab facility at her disposal, to be paid to do what she loved and would have pursued regardless, what she felt was her purpose.

But Hinkleman had been here at this facility, knowing she was locked up like a prisoner. And he had hit her because her data was corrupt, when in reality he just couldn't read it. She shook her head at that. Frowning, she wondered how deep or how high this corruption went within the ranks of Scion. She, as a part owner too, as a major shareholder, felt partly responsible for cleaning up this mess. Why wasn't there any internal oversight as to Hinkleman within Scion? Surely there had been signs … and not just as to the verbal abuse of his researchers.

She desperately wanted to get back to her office and to see what had happened to her research, but she was a long way from doing that. Not to mention the fact that, if the company hadn't called about her absence from work, maybe they were in on this whole scheme too. Maybe it wasn't as great a company to work for as she had always thought. Maybe Hinkleman was just one of many on the board who was involved. Those were more thoughts to send shivers down her body. With her whole world collapsing around her, she could hear sounds of a vehicle coming closer. She stiffened and stared up in a panic at Kerrick.

He smiled and said, "It's Griffin."

She took a deep breath and let it out very slowly, then nodded.

KERRICK WAITED AS the vehicle pulled up within ten feet of them. It didn't have its headlights on, but the back door opened, and he quickly ushered them toward the car. They were placed in the back seat, and Kerrick took the front passenger seat, and, just as silently, the vehicle pulled forward and headed away from where she and Brandon had been prisoners.

"Not exactly a textbook escape," Kerrick said to Griffin as he sent a message to have the rental picked up. He might need more of the goodies that were still there too.

"Wasn't far off though," he said with a big smile. "Now to make sure we get a couple hundred miles away from these guys."

"We have to go back though," Brandon said.

Kerrick turned to look at him in surprise.

"It wasn't just us there," Brandon explained. "There are other prisoners."

"Did you see other people?"

He nodded. "When I first came in, I saw two others, a man and an older woman, but they were sleeping."

At the *sleeping* comment, Kerrick and Griffin exchanged hard glances.

"Were they on beds?" Griffin asked.

Brandon nodded. "Yes, like those hospital and ambulance gurneys. They were bringing them into the center."

"Did you recognize who they were?"

He shook his head. "No. The guards said something about Cynthia and Peter."

"And you think they were from the same family maybe?" Kerrick asked.

"The guards didn't mention that," Brandon said. "Adults always talk around kids. They think we don't hear anything."

Kerrick chuckled. "Well, they were wrong in your case. Anything else you can tell me?"

"The ambulance number was 41058," he said immediately.

Griffin stared at him in surprise. "Did you recognize the drivers or the men who were pushing the gurneys or anybody who was involved in kidnapping you?"

Kerrick wondered at what the kid could have seen, but, when Brandon started to talk, Kerrick quickly pulled out his phone and hit Record because it seemed Brandon had an incredible sense of recall. Whether it was his imagination or not was too early to tell, but he gave everything about the two guards, from the color of each guy's hair to the type of shoes each wore. Kerrick and Griffin exchanged hard glances as they listened to Brandon. When he finally ran down, Kerrick said, "Well, that's an awful lot of detail. I hadn't expected that much."

"Photographic memory," Brandon said quietly. "Most people laugh at me for it."

"We're not laughing," Griffin said. "We're ecstatic. Because you've given us lots of information, and hopefully we can use that information to help solve this."

Kerrick heard Amanda asking Brandon, "Do you have any memories of when you were locked up? Who came to see you? Who brought you food? What was in your room? Maybe it was different than what I went through."

Brandon shrugged and said, "It was four walls, a floor, and a ceiling. All appeared to be concrete."

And then he went into the same detail that he had spoken of before, describing the type of rotten food—which he refused to eat for the most part suspecting drugs but was smart enough to mash up and add to his chamber pot—who had brought in the food, how they were dressed, whether they had keys, and what kind of weapons they had.

Kerrick was stunned. "Is there any reason to suspect that your photographic memory is something that they know about?"

"I don't know how they would," he said.

"Does your father brag about it?" Amanda asked.

"My father thinks I'm a freak," Brandon said, his voice calm, like he was used to saying that a lot.

"You were smart enough to know Morse code and to use it, so I highly doubt that," Amanda rushed to reassure him.

But Kerrick had seen a lot of fathers who were assholes, so he wasn't so sure.

Brandon immediately said, "I don't mind. My father's kind of weird too."

"In what way?"

"He sells body parts," he said.

"As in organ-donor body parts?" Amanda asked.

There was silence first, and then Brandon, his voice very small, said, "Something like that."

Kerrick's heart hardened. If Brandon's father dealt in the black market for body parts, that put these kidnappers into a whole different level of criminal activity here. "Do you think that's why you were kidnapped?"

"Part of it, I'm sure," he said. "But it could be any number of things."

"Well, I'm interested in hearing your theories," Kerrick said, struggling to believe he was talking to a ten-year-old.

"Well, there's my dad's business," he said. "Plus, I'm one of those students who everybody loves to hate."

"With a memory like that, I'm sure you get straight As

all the time, don't you?" Griffin asked, looking at Brandon in the rearview mirror but smiling at him in a friendly and best-buddy way.

Brandon nodded. "Yes. I get very little wrong. And that makes everybody upset, including the teachers."

"They should be happy you're a star pupil."

He just shrugged and stared out the window. "Still makes me a freak. In the world, nobody likes freaks."

Amanda gripped his fingers and said, "I understand. But it gets better as you get older. I know. So, freak or not, I like you anyway."

Brandon chuckled at that. He turned to look at her and said, "Not many women know Morse code."

He was blissfully unaware of how sexist his comment came across. Whether it was his own upbringing or his limited experience, Amanda didn't know, but he'd completely slapped Amanda into a category of potentially being a dumb blonde. She just laughed, her voice soft and mellow as it floated through the vehicle, showing no signs of the strain of the last couple days. Low, melodic, and almost mesmerizing.

Kerrick struggled to keep all the details of her separated in his mind as the information flowed through the car. He was grateful he had his phone on Record because so much was discussed right now. It was hard for him to keep track of it all.

"I'm not a dumb blonde," she said gaily. "I'm not quite in the genius category as you are, Brandon, but ..."

"*Amanda?*" Brandon said, his voice raising, as if something suddenly clicked into place. "*Amanda Berg?*"

"Yes," she said. In the review mirror, Kerrick could see her staring at Brandon in surprise. "What did you remember about me?"

"You're a Mensa, aren't you?"

She studied him carefully. And then she nodded, a grin spreading across her face. "I am, and so are you, *Brandon Coleman*. Aren't you?"

He gave her a big flash and a white smile. "Absolutely." He reached out of hand and said, "Pleased to meet you. You're more my kind than I thought."

While the two in the back seat carried on a quite animated conversation, Kerrick brought up a completely new point. He glanced over at Griffin and muttered, "What's another reason why the kidnappers would be collecting brains?"

"None I want to think about," Griffin said. "Particularly after somebody who provides body parts seems to be involved in this."

An edginess shifted down Kerrick's spine as he contemplated Griffin's answer. This was ugly. But it could get a whole lot uglier yet.

Kerrick directed Griffin to drive toward Kerrick's motel but had him bypass it and went on to another one he had seen not too far away, set off in the back corner of its property. It was little more than a dive, but it was a motel and had a second floor with direct outdoor access.

When he pulled their vehicle in front of the motel office, Griffin hopped out, leaving the car running, and headed inside. He came back less than two minutes later with keys, chuckling as he sat in the car again. "I didn't think the clerk would take my cash at first. Seems my burglar outfit scared him." Chuckling still, Griffin turned to face the two in the back seat. "Don't you like my pleasant and honest smiling face?"

Amanda groaned. "I'm sure you'd scare children and most adults with all those black marks on your face. But the clerk won't tell anyone that we're here, right?"

Griffin shook his head. "I made sure of that. He'll keep our secret to his grave."

Amanda's eyebrows rose as she looked at Brandon. "Good thing he's on our side, right?"

Now Brandon giggled too.

Griffin drove them around back, parking their vehicle between two huge SUVs, basically hiding it in plain sight. The two men quickly escorted their guests up to the second floor and into the double rooms that shared an interconnecting door. Griffin locked one front door, crossed over to the other room to the join the rest of them, and said, "I'll be back in a little bit."

"Don't you want to take the paint off your face first?" Brandon asked.

Griffin gave him a white-toothed smile and said, "Nope, not for this job." And he disappeared into the darkness of the early morning hours.

Kerrick motioned at the double beds in this room and said, "If you guys need to sleep …"

"We need to eat, to drink, and I need a shower," Amanda announced.

Kerrick smiled and said, "Your bathroom's right there. Food's coming."

When Amanda took off for the bathroom, he pulled out his laptop and sat down.

Immediately Brandon hopped up at the kitchenette table across from him and said, "I really need to use your laptop."

"Why is that?" Kerrick asked, still struggling with the wise man inside the boy's body.

"To tell my dad that I'm safe."

Kerrick was busy on the chat page, letting his cyberteam know their latest location and that they had rescued Amanda and a kid but also warning his contact person that a lot more people were potentially being held in the same building. "Let me have my people do that, so nobody can trace our call. Is that okay with you?"

Brandon nodded.

"But I need to give them a quick update first, okay?"

Brandon nodded his head again, patiently waiting on Kerrick.

Kerrick wrote a short rundown and then uploaded the video and the audio tape that he had taken on his phone, mostly the ton of details that Brandon had handed over. It would be great if Kerrick's *people* could pull that together and maybe dredge up some matches to Brandon's descriptions via facial recognition software.

"You'll get to speak to your dad directly after we catch some of these bad guys, okay?" He nodded at Brandon, who seemed to understand, and asked, "Do you remember any names?"

Brandon blinked and, almost like a film reel rolling, started spouting names.

"I meant names from being kidnapped."

Brandon just gave him a droll look before spouting those in a fast string.

When he ran out of names, Kerrick made him repeat them, while checking his handwritten list and realizing he'd caught all but two of them. He sent that list off to his contact also, surprised to see Amanda joining them so soon. Her hair was dry, so she hadn't had her shower yet. "And you're both in the Mensa club, right?" He looked over at

Amanda and then back at Brandon. They both nodded. "Is there a special ranking system in the club?"

"Just our IQ level," Brandon said. "People like me love to be ranked. But, if you're not at the top, nobody wants to be ranked."

Kerrick chuckled at that. "Well, when you're the best of the best, nobody wants to know that they're the worst of the best."

Brandon laughed with the lightheartedness that a ten-year-old could.

Kerrick glanced at Amanda to see a wry look on her face. "Is it rude of me to ask, but is there a major difference between your IQs?"

She shrugged. "I don't know."

Brandon immediately popped up and said, "I'm 175."

She laughed. "Well, his IQ is higher than mine by one point."

"Is that enough to make a difference?"

She shrugged. "Not for me, no."

"Not enough, no," Brandon said.

"Did any of the people," Kerrick said, talking slowly, "and think about this now, were any of the people who you saw involved in this kidnapping mess, are their names associated with the Mensa group?"

Brandon's eyebrows shot up, and he sat back. "Interesting theory."

"But one we need to consider," Amanda said. "In my case, it was Dr. Hinkleman. In my opinion, he only joined Mensa for the public attention, for more accolades. But he was not actively engaged with the other members as far as I could see."

Kerrick turned to look at her in shock. "You know who

kidnapped you?"

"I don't know the men who took me off the street. I was grabbed by two men, and a hood was thrown over my head. Then I was tossed into the back of a lorry, alone. They remained on the street. The lorry drove off almost faster than my kidnappers could close the rear door. Then I heard the driver and his passenger talking at some point. So I counted four different men involved in my kidnapping.

"So the driver and a passenger were already inside the lorry. I didn't recognize their voices. So no idea who those men were either. I don't remember anything else until I woke up in this dark room, like a jail cell, and then yesterday, the day before, whenever"—she waved her hand as if she'd lost track of time—"when the guards came in, Dr. Hinkleman came in too."

"Interesting. So Hinkleman had no problem letting you see his face, correct?"

"He was my boss, supervised my work. My cancer research," she said slowly. "And when he came back a second time to see me in my cell, he was angry. He said something was wrong with my data."

"Was there?" Kerrick asked.

Brandon snorted. "Only that the others probably couldn't read it, right?"

Amanda gave a small shrug. "Potentially, yes."

CHAPTER 8

AMANDA DIDN'T KNOW how to explain it but tried. "When I do my work, I must always consider theft issues, and people like to question your results and to test you, even when you haven't had a chance to finish your own experiments. So I've gotten into the habit of writing in a short form when doing theorems, doing that right from college. It's faster for me, and other people can't read it."

"So, when your boss said your data didn't work, was it because he couldn't read your shorthand?"

"It's possible," she said slowly. "But he did say that one of my coworkers had been working with my research. And, if it was somebody who I work with closely, they would have known ahead of time about my shorthand."

"Meaning, they should have been able to read it."

She shrugged and sat down on the third chair at the table. "Potentially. I don't know how hard it is for others to read. How long until we get food?" she asked, holding out her hand, palm up. She stared at her fingers, a little worried because they shook so bad.

"It's coming," he said, noting her concerned expression and her visibly shaking hand. "You should be eating within twenty minutes."

She nodded and said, "That'll be fine."

Brandon quickly reached out, grabbed one of her hands,

and held it in his. "Do you have blood sugar problems?"

"Only when I've been starved," she said, joking.

"Right. I thought my stomach would eat itself," he complained. "Don't they know how much food a ten-year-old needs?"

"Apparently not," she said, "or they didn't care."

"They didn't care," he said. He stared out the window, even though it was completely closed off with the blinds, his face glum. "I think that's the story of my life."

"What? That nobody cares?" Amanda asked.

"I think my father only kept me around because of what I could do for him."

Kerrick leaned forward suddenly. "Maybe you should tell me what you do for him?"

"Run probabilities, analyze the company data, and figure out where he'll make more money," he said. "It's pretty simple. He doesn't run a very complicated business, so it's not like I need a whole lot of financial education for his purposes."

Amanda smiled. "But so many people don't know how much we do understand and how much we don't, once we're labeled as a Mensa. It's expected that we know the velocity for traveling to the moon and what speed we need to lower to and how many feet off the surface."

He looked at her in surprise and nodded. "You *do* understand."

"Absolutely," she said as she leaned forward with a smile at the corner of her lips. "When I first started working at the lab, and they found out that I was a Mensa, people would ask me all kinds of questions, almost all to test my knowledge. But they were stupid questions, like, *Do you know how many skin cells are on an armadillo?*"

Brandon snorted at that. "You know what? I can't imagine the animal would sit still long enough for us to count, but we'd be talking minuscule amounts. Skin cells are sloughed off every twenty-four-hour period, so you'd be forever dealing with the fact that some of the skin cells would be falling off, and some would be ready to peel off. So, are they talking about the skin cells underneath *and* the skin cells that are in progress of being dumped?"

She nodded. "Exactly." She glanced up to see Kerrick frowning at her. She smiled and said, "Don't worry about it."

But his gaze darkened, and he shook his head. "It's amazing for those of us who don't have your brains to see just how much ability and smarts you guys have."

"Which is why I wanted to direct mine into cancer research," she said. "Particularly breast cancer. But then you already know that."

"I do," Kerrick said, "and I'm sorry for the loss of your friend."

She acknowledged his statement with a gentle nod of her head. "It was a very difficult time." She glanced over at Brandon suddenly and asked, "Where's your mother?"

His shoulders sagged, and he shook his head. Kerrick picked up the conversation. "Do you remember her at all?"

He shook his head again.

"Sorry, dude."

Brandon just shrugged. Amanda reached over and gripped his fingers. "It's tough, but it's something we end up living through."

"Exactly."

Just then a car door slammed outside.

She gasped, and her fingers started to shake. Brandon

gripped her hand tightly as they stared at each other in fear. Kerrick stood and peered through the blinds. "Dinner's here. Or whatever you want to call a meal at four in the morning." He got up, walked through the adjoining room, then stopped, and looked at them. "Do not *for any reason* open any door, do you hear me?"

They both nodded. She watched as he disappeared into the adjoining room, leaving the adjoining door slightly ajar, and then opened its outside door. She could hear him conversing with somebody, and she thought it was Griffin. She slowly relaxed. "It's okay," she said to Brandon.

When Kerrick returned with a large bag in each hand, she was surprised to find him alone. "Did you order delivery or something?"

"Or something," he said, deliberately not letting her know anything.

There had been a lot of secrecy between her and him. She really wanted to get some answers, but it was hardly the time or place. And she didn't know how much was necessary for Brandon to know. That massive brain of his was already churning through the details and trying to figure out this mess. It might be a good thing for him to face this head-on or for him to solve this all by himself even, but, at the same time, she wasn't sure he needed to know much more about evil human nature at this point.

Then the smell coming from the bags hit her, and she groaned. "Is that Chinese food?" she asked.

"We have Chinese food, fried chicken, and burgers," he said. "I didn't know what you wanted, so I ordered up a bunch of all of it."

Brandon gave a yelp of joy and raced toward the second bag. "Burgers? With fries?"

"Yes, but if you wanted anything special," he warned, "you won't be happy because I ordered straight off the basic menu."

"It's not the time to be worrying about specials right now," Brandon said. "That can wait until tomorrow."

"And what kind of special things do you prefer?"

"I hate pickles," he said. "Only drink one kind of pop. Chips have to be rippled and plain."

"Well," Kerrick said, "we don't have any chips nor do we have any pop. You can take the pickle off your burger." He quickly filled the table with food and handed a burger to each of them.

Amanda looked at hers and passed it over to Brandon and said, "You can have them both."

He turned toward her, frowned, and said, "You have to eat too."

She nodded. "I do, but I'll have my vegetables first."

He wrinkled up his nose at her as if to say, *Why on earth would anybody want vegetables?*

She laughed and said, "You'll understand this a little better as you get older."

He shook his head. "Hard to understand that theory. Vegetables are nasty at any age." His face wrinkling, he watched as she pulled out multiple boxes and containers of Chinese food and chopsticks.

She opened the containers, checked inside, grabbed the chopsticks, looked around, and asked, "Are there any dishes here?"

Kerrick got up to check the little kitchenette and shook his head. "Can you eat out of the container?"

When he turned around, she smiled, her mouth already full, and mumbled, "Absolutely."

She settled back and had a portion of each of the different dishes, everything from almond chicken to diced chicken to beef and broccoli as well as several noodle dishes too. Her stomach registered as full in no time, and she was scared to overload it after so many days of contaminated food and water. When she looked at Brandon, both his burgers were gone and so were the fries.

He eyed her Chinese food, slowly reaching out.

When she pointed out the box of fried chicken, his face lit up, and he reached in and grabbed a leg.

She smiled and had one for herself too. She looked over at Kerrick and asked, "Is this supposed to be food for you and Griffin too?"

"Griffin will bring more back," he said. "I'm waiting for coffee."

She moaned at that thought. "I would absolutely love a coffee. But now that the food is in me, I'm scared to put too much more in my stomach." Then she turned to Brandon. "Don't eat too much. It might come right back up again."

He nodded and said, "But I doubt it." And then he reached for another piece of chicken.

She got up, walked around, had a drink of water from one of the bottles that Kerrick had brought, and said, "Now I'll have that shower." She looked down at her clothes. "Unfortunately I have no clean clothes to change into."

"Not yet," Kerrick said. But he didn't give her any reassurances that clean clothes would be coming anytime soon or that she'd be heading back to her own apartment in the near future either.

But still, a shower would make a huge difference. She smiled, nodded, and said, "Don't get into any trouble while I'm gone, you guys."

Kerrick faced Brandon and said, "Now that your stomach's almost full, is there anything you can tell me about Amanda that would help us find out what was going on in her world?"

"She's doing cancer research. Her next step is to get approved for human trials," Brandon said as he reached for yet another piece of chicken.

Human trials. Bingo. He'd float some theories on that by Griffin. But right now he didn't want to focus any more on human body parts with Brandon. Kerrick was amazed at how much food that kid could put down. He might be ten years old, but he was eating for three grown men.

"So you didn't eat any of the food that they gave you?"

"Only enough to keep alive. Even if it was poisoned, in the amounts I ate, it was not enough to put me under." Brandon shook his head. "None of us have gotten much food at that place."

"Did they have trolleys outside? Did you see if the other patients were getting food trays at the same time?"

"No," Brandon said, "but the thing about being a kid is that they talk in front of me all the time because they don't think I have any smarts to understand."

"Gotcha," Kerrick said. "So, what did you overhear?"

"They were talking about Amanda. How one of the bosses was pissed right off. They didn't know if they could stop him from killing her."

"But they wanted to stop him from killing her?"

"He wanted her to go into the lab and to start working again. He wanted to keep her as a prisoner for a long time until she was done with her work."

"That's not nice," Kerrick said, frowning. In fact that was beyond ugly.

"There wasn't anything nice about those men," Brandon said.

Kerrick nodded. She could have been kept for years in that kind of a state. They would have been forced to give her food and water in order to have her brain function properly, but, if she couldn't recover her original notes or prove her theorems, they might have just thrown her out with the garbage the next time.

Brandon frowned and said, "I think they were talking about something else too. I wasn't sure though."

"Can you tell me what they said?"

"Something about multiple buyers and multiple deals for the same person."

"And did you have any idea what that meant?"

"Not really. Something about getting paid to do favors for more than one person at the time, but they were talking about Amanda."

"You heard her name mentioned?"

He nodded. "They talked about her a lot."

"How did you feel when you realized Amanda was in the room below you?"

"I wanted to tell her to run," he said. "To get away."

When Kerrick heard another sound outside, he peered once again into the darkness of the night.

But it was Brandon who said, "It's Griffin."

Kerrick glanced at him and asked, "How do you know?"

"I recognize his footsteps," he said candidly.

"You're really into this stuff, aren't you?"

Brandon nodded. "It's how I knew Morse code." Then he frowned and looked toward the bathroom. "How did she know about Morse code?"

"Because I think, like you, she has eclectic tastes and interests," Kerrick said. "Remember? She's a Mensa too."

Brandon nodded thoughtfully. "Most of the Mensas aren't even like me. I think there's something wrong with my brain. I think that's why I'm a Mensa. Not because I'm really smart but because there's something weird about my brain."

"I don't think so," Kerrick said, shaking his head. "You are a Mensa and, even if you didn't have that label, you're smart. That's the bottom line. Don't ever try to hide it. Just don't make a point of shoving it in everybody's faces."

Brandon chuckled. "I've been told that before too."

Kerrick could imagine. When a series of knocks came at the door to their adjoining room, he nodded and said, "I'll let Griffin in. You stay where you are, please."

Brandon nodded, and, as soon as Kerrick turned away and then glanced back, Brandon had already reached into the bucket of chicken for another piece. At this rate, they would need to buy the same food all over again. The kid was a bottomless pit.

Kerrick went through the connecting door, barely shutting it, and opened the front door of the other room for Griffin, who stepped in and handed him two more bags.

"I hope more of this is food," Kerrick said. "That kid's eating us out of house and home."

Griffin looked over at the adjoining door to see that nobody was there, and, in a lowered voice, he said, "There's been no call about the kid being missing. We tracked his father down. We know who he is, but he hasn't put out the word to anybody as far as we can tell."

"What's the chance that this is a punishment of sorts for the kid? Or maybe his father was just happy to get rid of him?"

"There are a lot easier ways to get rid of someone that are more permanent and more cost-effective," Griffin whispered. "His dad will never be Father of the Year material in my eyes. So, playing devil's advocate, he could just take him out back and deep-six him. Better than that, his dad might as well sell his body parts and get some money."

"Sad to say, just knowing that his dad didn't report Brandon as missing, I can see his dad doing the worst possible thing—that second theory you mentioned." Kerrick grimaced and shook his head. "Something weird is going on there."

"I know. It did occur to me that, letting me again play devil's advocate, what if the kid's a spy?"

At that, Kerrick's eyebrows shot up as he contemplated it. "Interesting theory."

"Maybe, but doesn't mean I'm wrong. We have to keep an eye on him."

"Agreed. It would be an interesting twist to the tale. What else did you find out?" He made his voice louder as they walked through the connecting door to the other room. Kerrick put down the bags on the table and then took the coffee cup holder from Griffin and put it on the table too.

Brandon looked with interest at the cups, but Kerrick shook his head and said, "You don't need any caffeine."

"No," he said. "I need sleep. And preferably a warm bed. And I suppose she'll make me take a shower too."

"When was the last time you had one?" Griffin asked.

Brandon just shrugged and said, "No clue."

"Well, there's your answer," Kerrick said.

Just then the bathroom door opened and a smiling pink-faced Amanda walked out in the same clothes but with a towel wrapped around her hair. Immediately she looked at Brandon and said, "Your turn."

He frowned at her, not moving.

She shook her head and pointed.

He groaned, but he got up obediently. Then, before really surrendering, he said, "Don't finish the chicken when I'm in there."

"I promise I'll save you *one* piece," Griffin said as he reached into the bucket and pulled out three for himself.

At that, Brandon raced into the bathroom. "I'll be superfast."

"Make sure you wash behind your ears," Amanda scolded. "And, if you come back out and that hair is not clean, I'll take you back in there myself." The door was slammed harder than necessary on her words.

She chuckled and said, "Boys will be boys." She walked over, looked at the food with interest, and then nodded and reached for a piece of chicken herself. "I think I'm full, and then, after a few minutes, I realize that I really want more food."

"That's fairly typical too," Kerrick said.

She waited a few minutes, with her head cocked, and he realized that, once the water could be heard running in the shower, she turned and said, "Okay. Now, what did you find out?"

Kerrick sighed, motioned at the nearest empty chair for her, and said, "There's no word at all about Brandon. Nobody's looking for him. His father hasn't called anybody, as far as we can tell."

She sat down while staring at him in horror, and then, with a lowered voice, she said, "Do you think he paid to keep him there?"

"But why?" Griffin asked her on a mouthful of fried chicken. "Why would he?"

She sat back and thought about it. "I guess there are cheaper ways to get rid of a child these days, particularly given Brandon's father's line of business."

Kerrick immediately nodded. He had his laptop up and was working away, his fingers clicking on the keyboard.

"So, what are we doing from here?"

"We'll hang low for the moment," Kerrick said, without looking up. "So get as much sleep as you possibly can. We'll stand watch in shifts, and then, hopefully by dawn, we'll have new plans."

"I don't know if I can go back to my apartment or my job," she said abruptly.

"Obviously we don't know everything about this," Griffin said, "but your boss is definitely involved. That puts the spotlight on the company, Scion Labs, and its people will know where you live. It's not even a possibility to consider going back to your office or to your home."

She sagged in place. "I need my laptop," she said quietly. "You have to understand. It's got my life's work on it."

"Your place has probably been cleaned out of anything useful. Just think about it. Your boss was after your work already. And, when they found what they had was corrupt, don't you think they would have immediately gone to your home office and took your electronics?"

"I had a laptop with me, when they kidnapped me," she said. "They probably thought it had my research work on it."

"And does it?"

She shook her head. "No, I ran a home server. It's hidden."

"Back to that *scared of somebody stealing your research*?"

She shrugged. "Maybe."

"Can you log in to your server remotely and download the information?"

She looked at his laptop, frowned, and said, "Maybe."

"Can you give me your router ID?"

Surprised, she nodded and said, "Well, I could, but what good would that do?"

"I could log in to your router and, therefore, into your network, if you've got the passwords memorized. And potentially we can access everything and download it to this laptop."

She frowned as she thought about it. "I have a lot of it on cloud storage but that last bit, I need to get from the server."

Brandon bounced out of the bathroom, already reaching for more chicken.

Amanda smiled. "Your hair is wet. Did you wash behind your ears?"

Brandon grimaced, immediately looking guilty.

"And did you wash all over, including your hair, with soap or shampoo?"

"Yes." At Amanda's questioning look, Brandon groaned. "May I eat more chicken before Griffin eats it all?"

At her nod, he ate like a starving kid.

Kerrick twisted around his laptop so she could see the screen and pointed her to the little chat window. "Type the router number in there." She did that, and he said, "Then, once you see your network pop up, type in your network password." She did, and, just like that, there were her files. She shuffled the laptop a little farther away from him and started moving material.

Kerrick didn't want to butt in when she was so obviously

trying to protect her stuff, but he said, "Unless you have a key, this laptop's not totally secure either."

She nodded. "I'm moving it to cloud storage, but I don't want my footsteps tracked."

He shrugged. "I can't guarantee that's possible right now."

She looked at him for a long hard moment and then quickly moved the laptop closer to her and glanced at Brandon.

Brandon moved his chair so it touched hers. He continued to eat, but he gave her a nod or a headshake as needed with each of her looks or a finger pointing to the screen.

Kerrick didn't know what she was doing as a workaround, but he suspected that the two great minds in this room would figure it out somehow.

When she and Brandon were done, she sat back with a pleasant smile and said, "At least now I have my material."

"And you still need your laptop?"

"Preferably. I'd like to get my laptop and my server from my place. But it is all hidden. So, short of the bad guys finding it—and I don't think they did, or they wouldn't have needed one of my assistants to read my research notes—so I don't think anybody looking casually will find it."

"What about guys like us?" Griffin said.

She gave him a fast frown and said, "I don't know. Depends on how well you look."

Kerrick was interested to see what she would consider to be a hard-to-find hiding spot like that. "If it's not a priority, I don't want to make the trip to France just yet," he said. "That'll just put both of you in more danger. But I can have your electronics picked up and kept somewhere safe."

"And I can get it back when I need it?"

He nodded. "Absolutely."

"Okay then. Let me know if your guys have trouble finding it."

Kerrick smirked but said, "I will, if needed."

She glanced at Brandon and then at Kerrick. "Do you have a safe house where Brandon and I can stay for a while?"

"We have a place," he said, wondering about that himself, now typing in the chat box to find Amanda's hidden electronics at her house and then to line up a safe house. "What about your father? What's your relationship with him?"

Her face softened, and the corners of her lips tilted. "We're very close," she said.

"So we'll get a message to him that you're safe," he said. "But I don't think you should have any direct contact with him until we know more."

She groaned. "Seriously?"

He nodded. "Because we don't know yet who else is involved."

"Well, as long as you pick up my ex-husband," she said, "you've got one-third of the equation."

"What's he got to do with this?"

"No clue," she said, "but Hinkleman told me three parties were interested in getting me out of the way."

"Who?"

"My father's enemy, my ex-husband, and then … Hinkleman himself?" She shrugged.

"That's what I assumed too."

CHAPTER 9

IT HURT TO say that her ex-husband was involved. Amanda just didn't understand how or why. "He does make a good scapegoat," Amanda said. "Yet I'm not exactly sure I believe Hinkleman when he said my ex was involved."

"Why either way?"

"We signed the divorce papers five years ago, and he got nothing." She shrugged. "So him caring now doesn't make any sense."

"So he wouldn't be involved because you've already signed the divorce papers, but he would be involved because he got nothing?"

She nodded at him. "That's a good way to put it. It was a very bitter divorce, and we weren't married very long either."

"Why the divorce?"

"Because he didn't have any intention of being faithful, and I had absolutely no intention of being unfaithful while I was married. When I realized that we had such different philosophies as to what a true relationship was, I wasn't sticking around."

"So you initiated the divorce?"

She nodded. "Yes, and after only six months." She watched as he winced. She nodded. "Right. Six months and that's it."

"And he got nothing because the marriage was so short?" He nodded as if that made sense.

"He got nothing because of the prenuptial agreement I insisted he sign." There was a moment of silence as both men stared at her. "And why would I not?" she said. "It was important to me that he have no access or no benefit from control of my research, and, in some countries, material that you work on and discuss with your partner and/or research during a marriage can be something that he can claim as a part owner. I wouldn't allow that."

"Smart," he said. "There could be a tremendous amount of money involved in finding a cure for cancer."

"I already have a lot of money. It's a fallout of being a Mensa."

At that, Griffin snorted. "Are you saying all Mensas are wealthy?"

"Of course not. But, as a Mensa, it helped me to get funding, other research grants, so that I could do my research, and that took money."

"But you are working for Scion, correct? Getting paid? A company which you do not own?"

"Yes, absolutely," she said. "I'm working out of Paris for Scion Labs."

"Are you a shareholder?"

She glanced at Griffin and then slowly nodded. "Yes, I am."

"Did you have any issues with the board? Over your research?" Kerrick asked.

Before she had even answered Kerrick's question, Griffin asked, "Is that how you got to do the research that you were looking to do?"

"Well, I would hope the board had no issues with my

research, but it wouldn't surprise me if they had an issue *with me*," she said. "But I invested enough money in the company's shares that they couldn't argue about my research area, and I had a say in my own work."

"And do you think that may have pushed Hinkleman into doing what he did?"

She frowned. "I never considered what my shareholder entrance into the company might have done to him. But it's possible." She shrugged. "I own a fair bit of the company."

"A controlling interest?" Kerrick asked.

"Not half of the company, no," she said with a shake of her head.

"And what if Hinkleman suddenly found out that you were one of the major shareholders? Would that make him hate you?"

"He hates me anyway," she said. "He was all fire and brimstone when he was young, but none of his research panned out, so he's jealous of anybody who's on target and getting validated results."

"Which you think you are?"

"Which I definitely am," she said with a nod.

"Interesting," he said. "But it all comes back to that company, Scion Labs, and to Hinkleman."

"And potentially my ex. And potentially an enemy of my father too. Hinkleman said something about being paid from multiple sources. But I have no clue who that enemy of my father could be. Still, someone needs to warn him that he might have a viper close to home that he doesn't know about."

"Aah," Kerrick said, settling back. "That then makes sense of something that Brandon overheard. Makes a lot of sense now."

"What sense? Hinkleman just picks a victim, finds out how many people hate her and want her locked up, then he charges the people for kidnapping her?" she asked in outrage. "And how's that something to do with your life? Or …" She sat back. "Did someone approach Hinkleman?"

"The questions are then, who chose you, why did they choose you, and how is it that Hinkleman got involved?"

"He was the boss at the prison," she said, "so he's got to be involved with other patients as well."

"Is he a medical doctor?"

She looked at him in surprise. "I think he is. He was an MD first, and then I think he went into research because he didn't have the right kind of bedside manner for patient care relationships."

The two men stared at her, then slipped a covert glance to each other.

She wondered what that look was about but shrugged. "I just heard something about it."

"Between you and Brandon, you guys hear a lot, don't you?"

Brandon nodded, obviously listening but too busy eating still.

Amanda nodded toward him. "As Brandon said, he is a child. Nobody thinks he's important," she said. "In my case, I just put it down to being blonde and female. A lot of times men talk over us as if the conversation is just way too complicated for our fluffy empty brains."

"Well, you can bet we won't make that mistake," Kerrick said drily.

She looked at him with a smile and said, "You've already saved our lives. I don't even know how to begin to thank you."

"No thanks are necessary," he said. "But, if more people are being held there, like Brandon mentioned Cynthia and Peter, we wanted to make sure that we get everybody out. And …"

"Now that they know you two have escaped, the bad guys are already moving the rest of the prisoners," Griffin said. "I videoed as much as I could. While I was there, I saw three ambulances leave with six people total, two in each emergency vehicle."

Brandon perked up. "So that's why you left your face blacked out?"

Griffin laughed and nodded.

"Patients leaving in the same condition as they arrived?" Kerrick asked. "Meaning, likely all drugged into unconsciousness?"

"Yes," Griffin said. "You know that's the easiest way."

"They drugged us at night anyway," Amanda said in a low tone.

"But they've got to have a second location already set up and ready for the patients," Kerrick said, "particularly if they aren't ambulatory."

"Our guys are working on it," Griffin told Amanda. Then he picked up his cup of coffee and took a long sip.

As far as Amanda was concerned, Kerrick and Griffin were no ordinary team. Why did she think these rescue teams would entail at least eight guys? Or at least four to handle contingencies? But she admitted that Kerrick and Griffin were not any ordinary men either. They each counted as two men at least. Even so, but for the two of them, she hadn't seen anyone else helping out yet.

But that chat window was very interesting. She wasn't the super IT person that she wanted to be, but she knew enough about computers to hide her tracks when she moved around her research material. And that chat window of Kerrick's opened up into something very deep. She wouldn't be at all surprised if it wasn't some kind of black-ops or deep government covert operation link, superprivate, supershielded. She wanted to immediately get back into it and ask to get the information that she needed. Likely she'd get bumped out immediately.

"Well, surely somebody needs to pick up Hinkleman, while you search for others involved in kidnapping and that jail," she said, "because that's the one guy I can guarantee you was involved since I saw him in person at the jail."

"There's an alert out for him right now," Griffin said. "And on several other people involved, based on Brandon's descriptions and facial matches. We're on it. We just have to keep low until we know that everybody involved has been picked up."

"How long do we 'have to keep low'?" Her gaze went from one to the other. And back again.

They both shrugged and said, "A day? Maybe two."

She frowned and then realized she'd already spent a couple days as a prisoner, so how was a couple days being free, but with them, any different? She nodded. "Just make sure you get *all* these guys. I don't want to keep looking over my shoulder after this. And I surely don't want them after Brandon."

Brandon smiled a toothy grin her way, still chewing up the chicken in his mouth.

She patted his shoulder, then stood, looked at the beds, and asked, "How are we doing the sleeping arrangements?"

"The two beds here are for you and Brandon. One of us will sleep in the other room, while the other will be on watch here."

She nodded, walked to the bed closest to the window, and said, "In that case, I'm heading for some shut-eye."

Brandon decided he had enough food for now and said, "Me too," as he crawled into the bed across from her.

She smiled sleepily at him, forgetting to make him take a real shower before going to bed.

Then the two of them crashed and immediately fell asleep.

KERRICK RAISED HIS head from the pillow to find it was six o'clock in the morning, and he was about to switch shifts with Griffin. He heard a sound from the adjoining motel room. As Griffin's distinctive footsteps came his way, Kerrick hopped out of bed and walked into the bathroom. Quickly he used the facilities and scrubbed his face. Then he stepped out to see Griffin crawling into the other bed.

"All clear," Griffin whispered.

Kerrick nodded and headed to the desk. He took his laptop and his phone with him to the adjoining room. As he moved into Amanda and Brandon's room, Kerrick stopped to study the two sleeping people. He wasn't sure how this op had grown from saving one to two people from the get-go, but no way would he have dumped a child in the street on his own.

Although this one might be perfectly capable of handling himself, it was also obvious that he had a ton of information that was beneficial to their op; plus they needed to keep him close for his own safety. Brandon could potentially help find his dad as well as saving the other people held against their will by Hinkleman and his crew.

But what surprised Kerrick was to find both Amanda and Brandon curled up in the same bed, her arms wrapped around the child. Kerrick frowned, wondering what had happened.

Just then she opened her eyes, looked at him, smiled, and whispered, "Nightmares. No matter what kind of superbrain he has, he's still a child."

Kerrick nodded in understanding and walked over to their table, then set up his equipment. After that, he went back to the little kitchenette, where he plugged in the kettle and made himself an instant coffee. He would be up now until the day was over and needed something to keep him going.

When he passed by them, he saw Amanda slip out of bed and move into the bathroom. He expected her to go back to sleep after that, so he sat down at the table with a notepad, collating the notes they had. He was still waiting on more information and even updates. So far, nothing had come in. At least not via his phone. He hoped, when he hooked up to the internet, more information would be downloaded to his email and that the chat window sat there, waiting to help him. Preferably with answers.

He opened up his email program and waited. He heard beeps, notifying him as various emails dropped into his program. He quickly surveyed them, picked the couple that were the most important, and read some history on the background of Hinkleman, with a note that he was still at large. And then on Amanda's ex-husband. Thinking over things, he frowned, opened up the chat box, and typed, **Have you picked up the ex-husband?**
No.

Why?
No sign of him.
Crap.
Yes. We found the blue car in the bottom of the canal. And an older pickup.

He grinned. **Good. Anyone in it?**

You were right. Stanley and Tom were found dead inside, one in each. Jimmy has been picked up for questioning. We expect him to be arrested.

Good to know. Sounds like someone is cleaning up. Is her father safe? Did you inform him of her status and what she was told?

So far he's safe. And, yes, he was brought up-to-date.

After that update, he added some reminders. **I don't have full research into the company that Hinkleman and Amanda were working for.**

It's in your email.

He returned to his email and looked. And there it was, hidden among all the rest. He brought it up and hunkered down to study the information. When Amanda came out of the bathroom, she walked over to the kitchenette and had a glass of water. She studied him, leaning against the counter.

He didn't even bother looking up. "It's still early. Just go back to bed."

"What about you?"

"I'm on shift watch now," he said. He flicked through the online pages, quickly scanning them. "I'm studying the company that you work for."

"If you find anything juicy, let me know," she said. She stifled a yawn, a movement that was both graceful and not, all at the same time. Kerrick found Amanda and Brandon to be fascinating with their massive brains, and yet, in some ways, both of them were so normal and even childlike in their innocence. She stumbled on her way back to bed, and he half stood, afraid she needed assistance, but she waved him off and said, "I'm just tired."

She made it to Brandon's bed, pulled back the covers gently so as to not disturb Brandon, slipped under them, softly laying her arm across Brandon's chest, and crashed.

There was just something so disarming about seeing her like this. So far, she'd escaped her cell, then went on to save Brandon, almost escaping the building itself when he and Griffin had found them. It took a lot of guts for her to do what she did. It took a lot of courage to go back after Brandon too. He wondered often about the maternal instincts in women and whether they were all blessed with equal amounts or whether some were just so much more caring.

No doubt she had formed an attachment to the young boy and he with her, and maybe that was a good thing. They were two of a kind. Nothing quite like bonding in captivity. They were good for each other. They both appeared to be loners, each with a father potentially distant, and maybe they needed each other. Amanda had been married but had no children, at least according to her file. He looked over to ask her but realized she was out cold. So he went back to reading his research.

About an hour later Kerrick heard a whimper. He looked over to see Brandon tossing fitfully in bed, crying out words. They were unintelligible, but he was still disturbed. Kerrick frowned, not sure how to help a child like this. He could tell him that it was okay, that he was caught up a nightmare, but Kerrick didn't want to wake him and scare him because that would be one of the worst things he could do. But, at the same time, how did you soothe a child like this?

As he watched, Amanda woke up, kicked off the covers, rolled over, slipping over to the far side, and cuddled up against Brandon. Kerrick could hear her voice as she rubbed the boy's shoulder and arm, whispering, "*Ssh*, it's okay, Brandon. We're safe now."

Almost immediately the child went quiet and went back to sleep.

Kerrick thought she was asleep too, but, as he continued to work on his laptop, she murmured, "What are you doing?"

"Making sure we get all the information we need," he said.

"Why don't you come lie down on my bed," she said. "I can't sleep while you're working."

He stopped and said, "I'm on duty."

"You need sleep too," she said.

"I'm fine."

"Well, I'm not," she said. "I can't sleep while you're doing that."

He frowned.

She rolled over, slipped out of Brandon's bed, crawled back onto her bed, and glared at him. "I'm not kidding."

"What the hell?" he muttered under his breath. Then he looked at her. "Surely you don't expect me to lie down and cuddle you, like you were doing with the child."

She sat up, looked at him, and said, "Expect? No, but would it help me get back to sleep, yes." And, with that, she flopped back down, pulled the covers over her shoulders, and stared at the wall.

He didn't know what to say. So, completely nonplussed,

he got up, slowly walked over, and laid down on top of the covers, wrapped an arm around her and tucked her back up against his warm body. It took about thirty seconds, and then she let go of a really heavy and deep sigh from inside her chest. He could almost feel it rattling up her spine as she slowly let it out, and he realized all that she had been through and how hard it must be to close her eyes with strangers hanging around. "I'm sorry," he murmured. "I didn't realize."

She gave a tiny shrug of her shoulders, the movement almost imperceptible. But tucked up so close as they were, he could feel it.

He whispered against her head and hair, "Just sleep. It'll all be better now." He watched her eyes flutter closed and her breathing drop into a heavy and steady rhythm. The little heart-shaped scar on her cheek caught his eye. He found himself leaning over to kiss the spot ever-so-gently. Surprised, he sagged back and held her close. That had come out of nowhere. Or maybe not, ... not since he'd first seen that image of her.

Overwhelmed, he lay close to her, letting the emotions flow through him, marveling at the strength of them. He'd been so afraid such feelings were lost to him with the death of his wife. But Amanda was a special woman, and he'd instinctively recognized how special she was to him ...

He waited several more moments, wondering how this woman could appear so strong and so caring, and yet, at the same time, so vulnerable. He found himself not wanting to leave her, not wanting her to face the boogeyman alone, who would surely come and catch her while she was asleep.

Nightmares were like that. They were insidious dream-stealing gremlins that came into your world when you couldn't protect yourself from them. They snuck into your subconscious and twisted everything into this nasty fog and then woke you up in a panic, fear sweating through your pores.

He gently stroked her arm, reaching around to lace her fingers with his. She shuffled slightly, moving back closer against him, spoon style, and he lay here knowing he needed to get up. But it was so comforting, even to him, to just lie here and hold her. And that was dangerous.

Knowing that he was crossing a line that he didn't dare cross, he slowly disengaged himself and pulled back a little bit to let the cool air slide up between them, so she could adjust to his leaving faster, before finally sitting up. At the edge of the bed, he stopped, looked down at her, and smiled because she hadn't moved. She was now in a deep sleep, and she needed it. Her body had to recover, and that would take longer than one night's sleep.

He sat down at the table to see a chat box had brought up more information. He quickly jumped back into his research, but he couldn't stop thinking about the warm and incredible woman he'd been holding for the last twenty minutes and how much he wanted to go back and hold her all over again.

CHAPTER 10

WHEN AMANDA WOKE up later that same morning, she lay in bed, her mind still hazy and fuzzy. She had memories of warm arms wrapped around her, and it took her a moment to take stock and to realize she was alone in her bed. So, had that been a dream? She cast her mind back to earlier this morning, remembering the number of times she'd gone over to Brandon to soothe and ease the child back into sleep.

And her related conversation with Kerrick popped into her mind. She flushed, remembering how much she'd wanted him to come and lie beside her, wanting, like Brandon, to feel safe and secure, if only for a moment. And the fact that Kerrick had? … It had helped as she'd dropped into a deep sleep and even now felt one hundred times better. Her body and her mind would still take some time to recover, but she'd come a long way and all because of a good sleep. She slowly sat up and yawned. And looked over to see Griffin. She stretched and yawned again.

He smiled and said, "Good morning."

"Good morning," she said in a low voice, realizing from the light in the room that it was morning. "What time is it?"

"It's after nine," he said. "You slept well."

She stared at him in surprise and softly exclaimed, "I never sleep in."

"Well, there were extenuating circumstances this time," he said with a smile.

She nodded. "I'm glad to see Brandon is still sleeping."

"Absolutely. Kerrick's gone to shower and change," he said. "At ten o'clock we'll eat, whether Brandon's awake or not."

She chuckled at that. "It's guaranteed to wake him up if you bring food in here." She laid back down on the bed, content to just lie under the covers, feeling the softness under her back, knowing that her time in that nightmarish prison was over with. "Did you guys get any more answers?"

"Some but not too many. There's no sign of your ex or Hinkleman, but our people are watching for them. We've got the research on your company happening, and, according to the administrators, Hinkleman has taken a three-month leave of absence."

She snorted at that. "A sabbatical?"

"I don't know if you can call it that when it's from a company, at least one like this," he said. "But it's a leave of absence. That's all they would say."

"Well, *I* might be able to get them to say more, as a shareholder, but you probably have as much access as I do," she said, losing half the words in yet another yawn. She repeated her statement and then said, "But I need to be a little more awake for that."

"Well, I can offer you instant coffee or instant coffee," he said cheerfully.

She struggled with the concept and carefully said, "Caffeine is caffeine, and I can't afford to be choosy right now."

"True enough." He got up and put on the teakettle. "When I said it was nine, I really meant it was nine-twenty. So, it's almost nine-thirty now. Caffeine will help to get you awake and alert."

Amanda nodded, went into the bathroom, and washed her face. Her hair was a mess, having slept on it while wet. She hadn't even braided her shoulder-length locks. It was almost too short for a braid now, though, having cut it a few weeks before she had been taken prisoner. She ran her fingers through it, to loosen it up, and then took the brush to it. She smiled as she held the brush. The guys had a bag of toiletries for her, but none for Brandon. After all, they were only expecting to rescue her. By the time she brushed out the tangles in her hair, she felt a little bit better and a little more cognizant.

As she stepped out of her bathroom, Kerrick walked out of the bathroom in his adjoining motel room. Once all four of them were together in their rooms, the adjoining door had never been closed between them. He only had a towel wrapped around him as he sorted through clothes on the bed. She immediately averted her gaze but not before she saw the lean muscle, the sculpted abs, and that careful, and yet, very contained can-do determination on his face. She didn't want her first meeting with him to be awkward, but now it felt even more awkward.

She walked back to her bed, quickly made it up under Griffin's curious eyes, and then sat down at the table across from him. He nudged a cup of black liquid toward her. She stared at it and tried hard not to curl her lip.

"I know how you feel," he said, laughing. "But remember that *coffee is coffee* right now. When we get some food in you, we can get some of the real stuff too, but …"

She nodded and tugged the cup a little bit closer. When it was cool enough, she lifted it and took a small sip. Like he said, coffee was coffee, and she really had no right to complain after the sludge she'd been fed the last couple days in her prison cell. As she sank back into her chair, Kerrick joined them on this side and cast her a curious glance. He didn't appear worried by the previous event in the wee morning hours and didn't look bothered by the daytime recognition of having slept together, in the strictest sense, where she felt both, only for different reasons.

"You look better," he said.

She nodded. "I finally managed to get a deep sleep. Thanks." She tried to keep her tone neutral and noncommittal. If he could talk to her like they were friendly strangers, that worked for her too. It's not like they were any more than that. The fact that he was a stunning male and had held her so gently so she could go to sleep wasn't something she wanted to bring up with Griffin here. But she appreciated it nonetheless. She motioned toward Brandon. "He's still sound asleep."

"The innocence of a child," Kerrick said. "Oh, now we're back to instant coffee too?" He looked at Griffin, raising a brow.

"You can go," Griffin said. "The fresh air will help you out. I want to finish tidying up these notes first."

"What are we going for?" she asked.

"Coffee and breakfast," Griffin said without lifting his head.

"Do I get to choose what I want for breakfast?"

"As long as it comes from one of the two fast-food chains around the corner, yes," Kerrick said cheerfully.

She winced. "I need a lot of food though. I'm really hungry."

"I doubt it's anything compared to what Brandon will need," Kerrick said. "I'd ask if you wanted to come with me, but I don't want you outside. We need to keep you hidden. We can't take the chance that somebody is tracking you."

"Could they find me if I was just walking around the corner?"

"It's an intersection," Griffin interrupted. "And that could quite easily mean cameras. And we use the street cameras ourselves for facial recognition to track anybody we can, so I suspect they will too."

"Do we really think it's that high class for Hinkleman and his crew?"

"No," Kerrick said. "I doubt *high class* has anything to do with it. But a lot of money and time went into outfitting that prison and keeping you all fed. There were pallets and pallets of food in the loading docks, so chances are quite a few people are involved. And it wouldn't take much to have security cams and traffic cameras searched. I've already done it myself to find the vehicle you were kidnapped in. That's ultimately how I found you at the sanitorium."

She looked at him in surprise. "We never did go over those details, did we?"

He gave her a half smile, paired with warm eyes. "You were a little tired."

"And weak, true," she said. "But that's hardly an excuse."

He cocked his head curiously. "You don't let yourself off the hook much, do you?"

"I feel like I'm always playing catch-up," she said, then smiled and nodded. "Well, I would much prefer to come along for the walk to get the food. But if you think it's that dangerous …"

"We can't take the chance right now," Griffin said, his tone a little brisker. "Kerrick, if you want to go now, we'll try to rouse Brandon. In the meantime …"

Kerrick laughed and took the hint. He was out the door within seconds.

Amanda glanced at Griffin. "Is it safe for him to go alone?"

"It's not safe to leave you guys alone," Griffin answered quietly. "So, we stay together as much as possible, but one of us will always have to leave to run various errands."

She nodded and sipped her coffee again. "I don't even know anything about the two of you or how you came together or who sent you after us."

"Unfortunately I have yet to find anybody who's reported Brandon missing, not even his dad, Mr. Coleman," he whispered, changing the topic. "I'm not sure how long Brandon was there either."

Her gaze dropped to the sleeping boy, and she shook her head, whispering, "I only met him yesterday. He tapped Morse code on the floor of his cell, which was the ceiling of my cell, and I answered."

"And how many people in the world," Griffin said with a headshake, "could communicate via Morse code?"

"Well, thankfully he tried," she said. "Otherwise, I wouldn't have known he was there."

"How many doors did you try on his floor?"

"All of them," she said immediately. "Also I tried every door I came to on my floor, but they were all locked except for one, a broom closet. Then I went up one floor, did the same, and found another closet where several coveralls were stored plus some keys, including *the* master key."

He leaned forward and asked, "You serious?"

She got up and felt her pockets. Down at the bottom, she pulled out the key and held it up. "That's how I got into

Brandon's cell."

He looked at it and whistled.

"We need to go back and see if anybody's left in that place," Amanda said, sitting down hard and staring at him. "And we've wasted the rest of the night and this morning sleeping instead of helping them."

"No need. Another group, like me and Kerrick, was there, keeping watch."

"Well, they shouldn't have let the kidnappers leave with those victims. The other team should have gone in and found as many of the victims as they could."

"They're also tracking where the kidnappers are taking their victims now. And I know that's hard to hear, but this is more than just finding those kidnapped people. We have to go to the evil beginning of all this."

She sagged into place, staring at him, and then shook her head. "Not if still more people are there."

"If they haven't already done that third check of the facility, I can get this key to somebody who will send in a team, and they'll check every room."

"I feel so terrible," she whispered. "I should have remembered this last night."

"Hey, this key is not the end of the world. Most of the guys in my world can get into those doors without a key. I know that a search was done, so let's hold off until I can get more information."

She nodded, but inside she felt sick to her stomach. "For those people to stay even one more night, it's too much."

"And the kidnappers are being followed and tracked too, but we also can't afford to get involved in heavy gunfire where some of these patients might get hurt as collateral damage. You also have to consider that maybe they'll kill some of these people in order to stop them from talking."

"According to Brandon, they were all unconscious."

"Which begs the question, why weren't you and him?"

She frowned at him, but her mind was agile. "I was knocked out originally."

"So maybe they didn't need to drug you because you already couldn't fight back."

"Or because Hinkleman needed me lucid, at least at certain times."

Just then Griffin's phone went off with a weird buzzing sound. He lifted it, looked down, and smiled. "Kerrick's ordering."

"Can he carry it all back?"

Griffin nodded. "But it'll be a lot just because of Brandon's appetite."

"Fine," she said, "but I'd rather have news about that prison."

He typed away on his laptop, and she stared at him suspiciously, wondering if he had access to information that he wasn't sharing. But, of course, he did. She didn't even know what group he was affiliated with. "What country do you work for?"

He lifted his head, stared at her, and smiled. "And why would you assume that I'm from another country?"

"Because of your accent," she said.

"And what accent do I have?"

"American," she said decisively. "Is this a US-government operation?"

"Well, if it is, it sure had better be with the agreement of England's MI6 and MI5 divisions."

She sank back on her chair. "Good luck with that. Everybody does the secret spy stuff. I wonder how much any country knows what goes on in another country, much less in their own backyard."

"Just as a courtesy," he said, "we always operate by letting people know where and what we're up to."

"Sure you do," she said with a knowing smile. "But that doesn't mean that they've acknowledged it or allowed it, have they?"

"We are here with the full agreement of your French government, the UK government, even Norway's government."

She wondered about that. "So my father's behind this? Didn't somebody say that he contacted you?" Griffin was silent on that, but she nodded. "Kerrick said something about that. He told me that my father put out the call."

"Are you close to him?"

Her smile flashed. "Yes, we're very close."

"How close?"

She sipped her coffee several more times and studied him over in the rim of the cup. "I'm not sure what you're asking."

"Would he have had a hand in keeping you as a prisoner?"

She shook her head in an instant. "No, of course not."

Griffin didn't say anything. He just continued to watch her steadily.

She could feel the flush walking up her cheeks, but she remained adamant. "No, he would *not* have been behind this. I'm surprised he still doesn't have one of his security details following me around all the time, like he did during my college days. Because of his wealth and his life in politics, he's become very defensive." She stopped, inhaled a gasp, and stared. "He still has a security detail on me, doesn't he?"

Her gaze widened. "That's how he knew I was missing, isn't it?"

Griffin's eyebrows shot up. "That's something we can check."

"We need to and then find out how they lost me. I believe Hinkleman said," she recalled, as the memory flooded back in, "that somebody was trying to punish my father, I think. Or maybe it was blackmail." She rubbed at her temples. "Sorry, the details are really fuzzy. I don't know what damn drugs they gave me, but I'd wake up in the morning to realize that people had been in my cell while I was out cold. It's a very disconcerting feeling."

"How did you know?"

"The chamber pot had been emptied," she said with a grimace. "I was really surprised at that, but they were full, so what can you do?"

"Well, if they wanted to keep you healthy, then they had to keep you disease-free. And that means emptying chamber pots," he said with a nod. "The drug was probably just something to help you sleep deeper, so that they could come in and do what they needed to do without you waking up."

"Maybe," she said, "but it's an awful feeling to wake up and to know that somebody has been there, looking at you while you sleep."

"That stage of your life is over now. I'm surprised you slept as well as you did."

She flushed but didn't say anything. A voice from one of the beds saved her from that moment as Brandon called out, "Hello?"

What a painful and lonely cry, as if Brandon were still at the prison. Amanda immediately stood, headed to the bed, and said, "Hey, glad you're awake."

He rubbed his eyes and sat up. "We really are safe, right?"

She nodded. "We really are, yes."

He opened his arms, and she reached down, sitting on the edge of the bed, and hugged him.

"Thank you for helping me sleep in the night," he said. "I kept waking up, thinking somebody bad was there, but it was always you."

"Hey," she said, "not an issue. I'm just happy that you're doing okay. It was a pretty long night."

"Yeah," he said. He yawned and then rubbed his face back and forth against her shoulder. "And I'm still tired."

"That's because it's been a rough couple days. Do you know how long you've been in that prison?"

"Nine nights."

Amanda glanced at Griffin. He stared at Brandon in surprise. "So," Griffin said, "you didn't come in at the same time as Amanda?"

Amanda shook her head. "I was only there a few nights, I think. I honestly can't tell you that because I don't know how long I might have been drugged. For all I know, I was brought in the same time as these other people, and what I thought was my first day when I finally woke up could have been my second or third day there." She frowned at that, not liking the idea at all. "What day is it?"

Griffin smiled. "Tuesday. The Tuesday after your kidnapping on the previous Sunday. So you were with the kidnappers about thirty-six hours."

"Seemed longer," Amanda said, turning to Brandon. "I'm so sorry you were there for so long." She hugged him again. "The darkness distorted all my senses. Not to mention the drugs. So my stay felt interminable."

Griffin said, "Let's get you a little more awake, Brandon. Kerrick is coming back with food any moment now."

At that, Brandon hopped out of bed and ran to the bathroom. While he was gone, Amanda quickly made up his bed, picked up the clothes he had dumped on the side, walked over to the bathroom, and knocked. He opened the door, and she handed him his shorts, T-shirt, and socks. "Get fully dressed so that we can be ready to move if needed."

His face was serious as he nodded, and she loved the fact that he understood. As she returned to join Griffin, he smiled. "You'll enjoy being a mother."

"Well, that's an interesting issue because who knows if I'll ever be a mom? It's not like I've had much practice at it."

"No other siblings?" he asked.

She shook her head. "No, none. Although I was married for six months, I never got pregnant during that time. Which turned out to be a good thing."

When Brandon came out fully dressed, his face was washed, and the hair around the edges of his face was damp from his ablutions. She chuckled and motioned at the table. Kerrick was just coming up the stairs outside, and Griffin was already clearing off his work from the table.

"Go sit down," Griffin told Brandon. "Food's coming."

Brandon raced to the edge of the table and sat, looking at the front door.

As soon as the door opened, and Kerrick stepped in, Brandon gave him a huge cheerful wave and said, "Good timing. I'm starved."

KERRICK CHUCKLED AS he unloaded the multiple bags he

carried. "Needed two people to haul this load," he complained good-naturedly.

"Well, I offered to go with you," Amanda said as she opened the first bag and took out a selection of items. "What did you get?"

"Four stacks of pancakes," he said. "Hash browns, patties, scrambled eggs, sausages, breakfast sandwiches." Then he shrugged. "I bought as much as I could reasonably carry in one load."

She looked at him in astonishment. "Were you expecting us to eat it all?"

"I highly suspect that, what we as a group can't eat, Brandon will finish off later," he said. "Particularly if he's anything like I was at his age."

"Did you order the same for everybody?"

He nodded. "Check the other bags for more food. I ordered four of everything."

Beside her, Brandon cried out a yes as he was handed a stack of pancakes. And then Amanda upended a massive baggie of small individual servings of syrup and butter. Brandon dug in without waiting for anybody else. Kerrick sat down, looked at Griffin, and asked, "Any changes or any updates?"

"No, nothing yet from our assistants. But Brandon says he was there for nine days, and Amanda found a master key to the prison rooms," he said, holding it up from where he had it on the table. Kerrick looked from the key to Amanda and raised an eyebrow. She quickly explained.

He nodded and said, "Good thinking and lucky that you found it."

"At that time, I have to admit I didn't question it. But now I'm wondering if it wasn't a setup."

"Possibly," he said. "But nobody came after us, so, if it was, and they expected to catch you, it doesn't really matter now because you're free."

"But I want to make sure that nobody else was left behind and that some operation is overseeing the kidnappers taking off with their victims."

"There was an operation in motion, yes. We'll be told when we're told."

He could see she didn't like that answer though. He seemed to be on a need-to-know basis as it was. If he asked the right question, he would get answers, but it was hard to imagine all the questions that he needed to ask. He wished his new boss was more forthcoming.

He bit into a big breakfast sandwich with sausage patties and eggs, as Brandon beside him dove into the pancakes. Kerrick loved to see the kid eat, especially since he had apparently gone without meals for a long time. Even one meal a day for nine days wasn't enough for any growing child. The food on their table disappeared at a rate that Kerrick expected, but the look on Amanda's face was surprise at Brandon's appetite. Finally Kerrick reached out a hand and said to Brandon in a low voice, "It's okay. There'll be more food."

He could see Brandon almost stopping, as if really understanding what Kerrick said, then the boy nodded slowly. "Meaning, I don't have to eat it all right now, correct?"

"Exactly."

Brandon nodded, put down his fork, and settled back. "Then I think I'm full."

"Good," Amanda said. "There will be some leftovers. Not too many though."

"And we can get more food if we need to," Griffin added

with a wink to Brandon.

Brandon was all smiles.

"I'll drop this in the garbage bin outside." Kerrick rose and cleaned up the empty dishes and packaging. Not very much was left at all. One breakfast sandwich, a couple sausage patties, and a few hash browns. He put everything together in one of the containers and set it atop the table and then left the room and tossed their garbage into a big trash bin in the back of the motel. After that, he took a quick pass around the perimeter of the motel to make sure everything was clear.

Ever since he'd left this morning to go to the restaurant, he'd had that feeling of being followed. A sense of something not quite right. As he came around to the parking lot again, he saw a large suburban against the fence on the far side of the front parking area. It had smoked-out windows and looked government-issued. And that was disturbing because, as far as Kerrick understood, *he* was government, and his UK counterpart was to keep him in the loop.

Slipping around back, taking the external staircase to the second floor, he made half a lap around the building on the walkway that led to all the motel room doors. Now at the front of the motel, yet on the far corner from the suspect vehicle, he would be exposed on these exterior stairs and landings. So he crouched below the railing level and crept all the way across to the far side. Around this corner should be the SUV. He stood up and carefully peered around the edge to see if the vehicle was still there. It was. At least he knew where the interlopers were, but, not liking anything about this, Kerrick sent a text to Griffin.

Griffin stood, opened the door, and didn't show his face. Kerrick dashed inside and looked at him. "This can't be good," he said.

Then the chat window pinged, followed by the ring of a weird little bell.

Griffin looked at the laptop screen and said, "*Move now.*"

The two men galvanized into action. While Amanda collected their few belongings, Kerrick raced to the back of the motel room and looked out the window at the fire escape. He opened up the window enough so that they could scramble out, but it would take precious minutes to get everybody outside. He quickly ordered Amanda out the window and got her into the fire escape with his help. Instead of going down, they went up to the rooftop, Kerrick explaining to her that Griffin had Brandon in his care. Then, from his rooftop perch, Kerrick chose another fire escape for them to take all the way down.

Meanwhile, Griffin brought up the last of the equipment, and he tossed Brandon on his back, and said, "Hang on." He quickly landed in the fire escape, and, with Brandon still holding tight, Griffin raced up the fire escape, onto the rooftop, and then to the far side, taking another fire escape, meeting Kerrick and Amanda at the bottom. Griffin handed off the equipment, transferred Brandon to Kerrick's back, and said, "I'll be back in two." He disappeared around the left of the motel.

With Amanda looking on with terror on her face, Kerrick knew Brandon was in the same fearful state because of the grip he had around his neck. He smiled at her reassuringly. "Griffin's gone to get his wheels."

She nodded slowly. "But won't they know it's him?"

"Maybe," he said. "If they follow us, we will lose them again. It's what we do."

Just then a vehicle came around and headed right for them. Amanda, crying out a muffled surprise, dashed to the side. Kerrick reached out and caught her, then held her close and said, "It's Griffin."

"But it's not our car."

Griffin heard her. He opened the window and gave her a grim smile. "Ours had a tracker on it. Whether that's factory original or a very new addition, not good for our purposes."

With them stashed in the back seat, Kerrick quickly ran to the far side and hopped into the passenger's seat as Griffin took off. Kerrick brought up his laptop, ready to access the chat box and get some safe house info. When they pulled out of the parking lot on the far side, he glanced behind to see if they were being followed. But, so far, he saw no sign of anybody. "Well," he said, "I wish I knew who that vehicle belonged to."

"Check their license plate number," Griffin said, tossing him his phone. "I took a photo of it."

Kerrick quickly grabbed the phone, typed in the license plate info into his laptop, and did a check. "It's not coming up."

"Interesting," Griffin said.

Kerrick typed it into the chat window and asked for clarification.

The answer came back. **British Secret Intelligence Service.**

Legit?

Yes. But driver isn't. Vehicle was stolen in the last forty-eight hours.

He swore softly.

BTW, Jimmy was found dead in his jail cell just an hour ago.

No surprise there. We're on the move.

We have a safe house.

The address was typed into the bottom. He quickly brought it up on the GPS so that Griffin could follow the computer directions to get where they were going. Then he settled back to keep his eyes peeled on the roads around him. He didn't know what had just happened, how they had been found, but any change at this point wasn't good. Into the chat window, he asked for an update. Just then his phone rang. It was ID'd as Unknown Caller, and he answered it to hear the same tumblers clicking in his ear. After giving the preauthorized code word, a computerized voice came on, which sounded suspiciously like his friend Beta from the pub.

"The kidnappers' initial location was searched at five o'clock this morning," the computer said. "It's completely empty. No patients were left behind. It appears that only about ten rooms were in use, based on the garbage left behind. We have tracked three of the ambulances to two different locations. We're getting ready to do a sweep on those locations now."

Kerrick asked, "What about the other patients on Brandon's list?"

"No confirmation yet," he said. "But, from the time when you arrived there, we have had eyes on the place. Potentially they were taken out before."

"I can ask Brandon. He might have more to add."

"Maybe, but don't trust him too much. Also we don't know if either Brandon or Amanda has been inserted with a subcutaneous tracking device. They need to be fully checked out."

"Where will that happen?"

"At the safe house."

And then his phone went dead. The thought of a tracking device didn't thrill him. But it would have been an easy thing to do when they were unconscious, particularly with the child. It would also explain why they'd been allowed to escape because they could easily track Amanda and Brandon and find out who was helping them. He looked at Griffin and said, "Tracking devices, the injected kind."

Griffin shot him a surprised look, contemplated it for a moment, and then nodded. "I presume a physical is in order?"

"Yes. At the safe house." Kerrick settled back for the drive ahead.

CHAPTER 11

"TRACKING? WHAT THE hell does that mean?" Amanda had watched her fair share of spy movies, but this sounded like a script gone bad. She glanced at Brandon, who was calmer and more relaxed this time. He stared out the car window, almost inhaling the information as it flew by. But a tracking device could have been injected into either of them. She understood what a safe house meant in theory, but anything that was different and unique right now didn't make her feel any more confident. Sure, the men had taken them away from the motel when a threat had surfaced, and they'd had some good quality sleep there and had been fed, multiple times and in unending quantities. Now they were on the move but to where?

As she sat back, Brandon slipped his fingers into hers. She squeezed his hand gently and just held his. She, as an adult, had to give at least the outward appearance of being confident. To her, however, just the unknown element and the newness of this experience made for a rather terrifying experience. She lived in her lab, especially since her divorce. She rarely went out. She rarely dated. Everything that had happened in the last few days was well out of her comfort zone.

As were her out-of-the-blue maternal instincts. She'd never put much thought into having a family of her own after her divorce, choosing to bury herself in her work, but, after connecting with Brandon, how could she not want a son? Especially if he turned out anything like Brandon.

But, in order to see that future, she had to deal with her current mess. Hinkleman was one of the bigger and more urgent mysteries to solve here. What purpose did kidnapping her do for him? He still had all her research regardless. Could promote it as his alone.

Okay, yeah, joining forces with two other idiots who wanted her out of the way had lined his pockets with money. Money to do even more research. But wasn't that what Scion Labs was doing for him already? He was the chairman after all. A position that held a lot of prestige and power. How he got that position was a mystery for another day.

She couldn't find the logic in any of this because the bad guys weren't using logic as their metric. Theirs were more about money, power, greed. Again she shook her head.

Brandon squeezed her hand.

Very intuitive kid. She smiled down at him, squeezed his hand back, fighting another wave of anger at Mr. Coleman, Brandon's father. His actions were unthinkable. Kidnapping any child and mistreating him this way was evil, but allowing his own child to suffer through this? That was evil on a massive level. What she wouldn't do to get this sorry excuse for a father in a torture chamber and let her own rage take over.

But a tiny voice reminded her that she didn't have all the information. Yet.

And these thoughts brought her to her own failed marriage, which made no more sense than Hinkleman or Mr. Coleman. She had been so unimpressed with the state of her marriage that she'd promptly dumped her cheating spouse.

And fast. No man since had made her want to change her mind about the hallowed but flawed institution of marriage—until Kerrick.

Even with his ethics and honor and transparent communication evident for all to see, she wasn't sure what she was feeling. Just ... something. Heat. Curiosity. Gratitude ... and damn more heat. Now here she was—on the run, out of a job, her most precious research in the hands of a greedy madman—wishing for some kind of true real-life romance. *Stupid timing.*

Frowning, she remembered Kerrick mentioning that her ex-husband was off-grid. She leaned forward and said, "My ex has a cabin in Wales. If he's missing, he could very well be there. It's part of his original family homestead."

"Do you have an address?"

She frowned and shook her head. "No. I just remember him having grown up there and saying that he went back every year."

Kerrick nodded and said, "Let me pass that along." He pulled out his phone and sent some texts. "Do you know anything about his family?" he asked.

"Nothing that you can trust," she said simply. "As I found out too late, he was a consummate liar. He did tell me that he *supposedly* had an older brother and that his parents were *supposedly* dead and that his brother and he used to meet up at the cabin every once in a while. I guess I believe that last part most of all. Take it all for what it's worth, coming from a very unreliable narrator."

"So, you don't know if he has a brother or if his parents are dead is what you're saying?"

"Exactly. But I do think the cabin was for real because he talked about learning to fish there. And he always spoke with so much emotion tied to those memories."

"That's often a good indicator," Griffin said. He pulled to an intersection, put on his blinker, and turned left. "We are only a couple blocks away from our destination."

"Good," she said, "but is it any safer than our last one?"

"We'll have to see," he said. "I've never been to this one."

And that didn't inspire confidence either. She stiffened as they came around to what looked like a common residential area and pulled into a home with a double garage door that opened automatically as they approached.

"And that's not suspicious," she murmured.

"Just means we're expected," Kerrick said cheerfully.

"Sure, but do we know by whom?" she asked.

"We'll find out," he said, sending a quick text. "Remember. We're here to have your backs."

At that, Brandon piped up and said, "It's a safe house, so it's government-run, by one faction or the other. What we don't know at this point in time is which country. The governments like to keep it that way."

"Maybe so but don't you guys know which government?" Amanda asked Kerrick, then looked to Griffin.

"Good question," Griffin said.

"Wish we knew the answer," Kerrick added. Then his phone beeped, and he read the screen, smiling.

Amanda caught sight of that exchange and felt slightly more at ease. She turned to Brandon, hoping to distract him from the reality of his life right now. "I guess you're a big fan of spy movies too, huh?"

He grinned and said, "Absolutely. Especially the *Bond, James Bond* series."

"I like all those too," she murmured with a chuckle,

amused at Brandon's attempt to sound like Sean Connery, and also very surprised someone his age was familiar with the actor who first played James Bond.

Griffin shut off the engine and, after a quick and silent exchange of hand signals, both men hopped out. She was much slower to get out, and Brandon slid over to her side and exited the vehicle with her. As soon as they were inside, the garage door came down, and they walked into the main part of the house.

She froze. Two men and a nurse stood in front of them. The men nodded, acknowledging the presence of Kerrick and Griffin, but their eyes were on Amanda and Brandon.

One of the men was obviously the brawn, but the guy in the lab coat seemed to be the leader and spoke up. "We'll run some scans to make sure that you haven't been injected with anything. Particularly to confirm you're not carrying a tracking device."

"What kind of scans? Will they be invasive?" she asked, stepping closer to Brandon. Instinctively Brandon reached up and put his hand in hers.

"Just the swipe of a handheld wand for basic metal detection, like used in some American schools, and another one that's pretty high-tech to see if there are any foreign bodies within you, not just those minute metal invaders overlooked by the wand but those made of plastics or whatever."

"And what's the nurse for?" she asked, not moving from her spot. Griffin and Kerrick had aligned themselves on either side of the two of them, still protecting them. That did help a lot, but still she and Brandon were now in somebody else's stronghold and under somebody else's rules, and she didn't think much of that at all.

The nurse stepped forward and swept a handheld wand

over both her and the boy. "Clear," she announced to all in the room. "No large metal foreign objects found."

The lead man smiled at Amanda and said, "Just lie down on the bed. We're not doing any major surgery."

After a glance at both Griffin and Kerrick—who nodded gently to her—she walked slowly toward the man. He motioned for her to enter the next room, and she stepped forward hesitantly. There she saw some kind of a portable X-ray machine. Different but the same. She frowned. "Is this the only way?"

"It's the best way, the least invasive way," he said. Then he reached out a hand and introduced himself. "I'm Dr. Claussen."

Because he seemed to be a medical doctor, as evidenced by his white lab coat, her brows immediately came together in a frown. "If no major surgery will be done here today, are you expecting *some* level of your medical services to be needed?"

"I hope not," he said quietly. "But, if you do have a tracking device, it's likely subcutaneous, and somebody will need to remove it."

"I haven't noticed any recent injury," she said, slowly realizing she had had no way to adequately check any part of her back. She'd had had more pressing health issues to address, both of the physical and mental kinds, like surviving, like escaping, like dealing with poor Brandon's nightmares.

"Good," the doctor said. "Maybe you should go first. That'll make Brandon feel a little better about the process."

"Do I get to watch?" Brandon asked, in serious mode now. Obviously he wanted firsthand information on this.

Amanda spoke up. "I vote yes," her stare locking in on

Kerrick first, then Griffin.

"I don't think that is a good idea," stated Dr. Claussen.

"This boy has a higher IQ than me—and probably you," Amanda responded to Dr. Claussen, slightly amazed at the heat in her words. "If it's such a good idea for me to go first to convince Brandon how safe this procedure is, then Brandon should be an eyewitness of that before he decides whether to do this himself." In the lull that followed, Amanda added, "And he does get to decide himself. Right?" Again she stared at Kerrick and Griffin.

Kerrick grinned, sharing a knowing glance with Griffin, before speaking to the doc. "Mama Bear has spoken."

"Let me just state for the record," Dr. Claussen began with a huff, "that I do not agree to any of this."

Kerrick pulled out his special disposable phone. "No problem. We'll arrange for another doctor." He was already texting when Dr. Claussen cleared his throat.

The nurse with him nodded her head, giving him a pat on his arm.

"That won't be necessary. While highly irregular and not our standard methodology in my field, I realize these are trying times for the two of you and that your emotional health is as important as your physical health." Dr. Claussen faced Brandon. "I'll leave your medical decision up to you, young man."

Brandon was all smiles, and yet, surprised as he looked into the faces of all who surrounded him. "Cool!"

His simple happy reaction was a very welcome respite from the rest of this. And then reality brought Amanda back to the present. ... Hating to go first, but smiling for Brandon's sake, Amanda shot a nervous glance at Kerrick, but he again nodded at her reassuringly. Following the doctor's instructions, she laid down on the temporary hospital bed that they had set up.

She noted the brawny stranger was camped out near the front windows of the safe house and felt a bit reassured.

"I want Brandon behind a lead shield," she said as he held her hand and stood beside the bed. "But... you two aren't wearing lead vests. Is there any chance of radiation exposure for Brandon?"

Dr. Claussen shook his head. "Not with this machine. It uses lasers instead."

Amanda felt somewhat better and smiled down at Brandon, whose entire focus was on the machinery in the room.

With the doctor's click of a handheld toggle switch, a series of X-rays were taken while the others remained standing nearby in the other room, with a direct view of the procedures.

She frowned, not that she had really stopped frowning since leaving the motel, and asked, "Won't it take a while to develop them?"

The nurse smiled. "No, not for this kind of X-ray. We'll have results very quickly."

"And, if I don't have a tracker, we still have to X-ray Brandon?"

The nurse nodded. "It's best if we do, yes."

Dr. Claussen asked Brandon if he could be X-rayed as well.

"Sure." Brandon was already climbing up on the hospital bed as Amanda stood up.

"Why don't you sit in the chair in the other room, Amanda, while we await your results?"

She was already shaking her head when Brandon piped up. "No. Why can't she stay here with me?"

The doctor gave in easily and quickly completed Brandon's scan. When done, the doctor said, "We expect your results, Amanda, in just a couple minutes."

"Literally?" she asked.

Dr. Claussen chuckled. And the nurse was already pulling something from the strange X-ray machine, like copies from a photocopier.

Over the instant objections of Dr. Claussen, both Kerrick and Griffin joined them in the makeshift hospital room, ready to see the official results.

With a resigned sigh, the doctor walked over and held the odd sheet in his hand. He held it up for her and the others to see. He pointed to the picture, at the base of the back of her neck, where something metallic was identified. It appeared on the picture as just a small dot.

Her hand immediately went to her hairline at the nape of her neck, and she felt a little bit of a scab but thought it was just a scratch from her rough treatment in the initial kidnapping event, not to mention Dr. Hinkleman's slap.

Dr. Claussen leaned forward to take a closer look at her neck, while the others gathered around the end of bed to stare at the photo laying there. "There are no stitches," he said. "It's simply been injected. The body is amazing in the sense that it will cover any injuries, no matter how slight, with scar tissue very quickly."

"So how do you get it out?" she asked, while seeing a picture of her head on the hospital bed and surrounded by everyone except their guard.

"I'll have to cut it out," he said quietly.

She stiffened, but Kerrick grabbed her shoulder and squeezed. "It'll be fine."

"So you say," she muttered, turning her head his way.

"It's not your head they're cutting into." And honestly, she didn't even realize they would do it right now until she felt the doctor's hand on her head, telling her to remain still. Then she felt a tiny cut slicing her skin, followed by a probe inserted briefly, before the doctor pulled out something so small she almost missed it. She studied the edge of his tweezers and saw a small metal ball, which could have been the end of the tweezers for all she knew. She looked up at him and said, "That's it?"

"Yes, that's that," he said. He put it carefully into a little test tube for safekeeping, slipping a metal casing over it. "This metal sleeve stops the tracking unit from sending out any signals."

The nurse now came over with Brandon's X-rays.

After a quick look, the doctor pulled out a second tube and turned to Brandon. "May I do a quick check of your neck, young man?"

"Sure." Brandon seemed to be in total research mode, happily taking in this new experience as both fieldwork and lab work. "Do I have the same thing in my head as Amanda?"

"Looks like it," the doctor said amiably. "Same place too."

Amanda gripped Brandon's hands and said, "It'll be over before you know it, and I hardly even felt it."

Brandon nodded, trying to be brave, but it was obvious that doctors and needles and surgical knives were a bit of an issue. She hugged him tightly. "I'll stay right here, holding you. Just focus on my face. Okay?"

Brandon's neck was exposed for the doctor to work with. He bent closer, took a quick look at the back of the child's neck. "It looks the same, like the scabbed-over scratch that I saw on the back on your neck, Amanda."

She and Brandon exchanged a look and then a nod. She squeezed his fingers when the doctor held Brandon's head still and made a tiny slice and popped out the same type of microdot that had been in her. He washed the wound carefully and then told Brandon that he was all done.

She frowned, asking the doctor, "Did you wash my incision?"

He chuckled. "Yes, I did."

"I didn't even realize it."

Brandon sat up and instinctively raised his hand to the wound, but she stopped him and said, "Let it heal for a few minutes, so you don't transfer any dirt or germs from your fingers and put it on the open cut."

He nodded and then immediately turned and asked the doctor, "May I see it?"

And there was that same bright and inquisitive child back again, jumping down from the hospital bed to stand closer to his tracking dot. *The miracle of youth.*

The doctor chuckled and held up the tube that contained his microdot, then placed a metal sleeve over it too.

"So what's on those dots?" Amanda asked.

"We assume tracking information," the doctor said, "but, until we get it analyzed, we don't know."

"So is it likely to have things like our medical records or what they did to us while imprisoned or just something to keep track of where we've been moved to?" She wrapped one arm around Brandon's shoulders and held him close.

"We expect just tracking info, but I don't know for sure yet."

On that note, she jerked, turned to look at Kerrick, and said, "That means they tracked us here. We can't stay now."

He nodded. "We never intended to. This is just a temporary stop to make sure that we don't get followed beyond this point."

"Were we followed?" she asked. "Are these people in danger too?" She pointed to the doc and his nurse, frowning again.

"Not followed that we noticed, no, but that doesn't mean the kidnappers aren't keeping track of us on a computer somewhere and, therefore, could come attack this place to reclaim its victims."

She looked back at the doctor. "So, you'll set up something here? To capture the kidnappers, or the people they'll send here, expecting to attack us?"

"That's a good idea," Dr. Claussen said, with a hand extended toward Kerrick and Griffin. "I don't handle that type of thing, but I'm sure the people in the know will have it all organized."

"It's already being set up," Kerrick said, a smile on his face.

"But we need to be long gone," Brandon piped up. "So where are we going next?"

Now that the ordeal with the surgeon's knife was over, Brandon seemed to be right in the midst of the action. And loving it.

She smiled down at him and said, "You're a brave little guy, aren't you?"

He grinned up at her. "Hey, we're in a spy movie. This is awesome."

She laughed, looked at Kerrick, and said, "Well, you appear to be our intrepid leader. Where to next?"

His phone beeped. He pulled it out and checked the screen. "I have the new address for us, so I suggest we fall back into the vehicle and head off again."

"How long to the next stop?" Brandon asked.

He shrugged. "Maybe fifty-five minutes."

"Good," Brandon said. "We need to stop somewhere on the way to pick up lunch."

Kerrick looked at him and raised an eyebrow. "There's still leftover breakfast."

"No, there isn't," he said. "I ate that already. And, besides, it's almost lunchtime." He rubbed his hands together with glee and raced toward the garage.

KERRICK DROVE CAREFULLY and steadily. He wondered how long before Amanda and Brandon noticed, considering they were both incredible geniuses. He wasn't sure if they were that practically minded when so blessed intellectually. But shortly thereafter Amanda leaned forward from the back seat and whispered, "Where are we going?"

He caught her gaze in the rearview mirror of the car. "You'll find out soon."

She gave him a quick frown but settled again in her seat. Brandon leaned against her as soon as she resettled. The farther away from the safe house they traveled, the clingier Brandon got. But she understood. She didn't know what would happen to him. His father hadn't reported him missing. Did he even know that Brandon was gone? How could he not be aware? What parent could be that clueless?

Unless Brandon was enrolled in some private school, but even school officials take note of student attendances—or absences. Or had Mr. Coleman, Brandon's own father, had a hand in this atrocity? That thought really bothered her.

Already she was game to adopt the boy. Legally.

Or whatever it took.

AS HE DROVE, Griffin talked on his phone incessantly in the passenger front seat, continually distracting Kerrick because the bits and pieces he heard were disturbing, to say the least. Brandon's father still couldn't be located, which, in Kerrick's opinion, could work out for the best for his kid and for people in general. Neither could their associates locate Hinkleman or Amanda's ex but not for lack of trying.

Kerrick was afraid that, every step of the way, people were being taken out of the equation so as to not leave any living witnesses.

Which didn't bode well for Amanda, Brandon, or any of the other kidnapped victims from that original prison location. Kerrick worried about the well-being of those other victims now. While Kerrick's new organization had tracked those victims to their new prison, were they still alive at this very moment? His new employer was taking care of that element with a separate team of men. Kerrick understood the viability of compartmentalization in any op, but ... hell. He had a vested interest and wanted continued updates on all aspects of this mission.

Even worse, how many other kidnap operations were active, just involving these lowlifes? He didn't even want to consider how many other separate criminal elements out there were responsible for other such kidnappings.

Maybe Mr. Coleman, Brandon's father, was dead, either as a witness or maybe as a willing partner in all this. Kerrick still awaited more information regarding his own damn op.

His phone beeped in his pocket, and, while he drove, he pulled it out and speed-read the text.

Brandon piped up, "You shouldn't text and drive."

He glanced into the rearview mirror and said, "You're right. I shouldn't." He dropped the phone beside him, but he'd already seen the message. His assistants had identified two of the faces on the gurneys that Griffin had supplied via his nighttime op immediately after rescuing Amanda and Brandon. One was the daughter of an opera singer and the other was the wife of a billionaire from Saudi Arabia.

To Kerrick, this seemed to be a pure blackmail scheme, just extorting money from the rich families so the kidnappers would return their loved ones relatively unharmed. Like a stream of income to fund the bad guys' main objective: the illegal harvesting of body parts.

Yet Amanda's kidnapping was to force her to divulge her cancer cure. And Brandon? While a brilliant kid, he seemed to be collateral damage for whatever his father had been up to. Kerrick wanted to ask his associates in his chat window if this was a working theory on their end too but knew that they would be heads down, already involved in doing their own research as well. Better to leave them alone to do what they do.

He and Griffin and their two special *packages* were long past the time frame when they were expected at the new safe house. But he and his partner had chosen not to share with anybody their actual whereabouts. Not now. Not yet. And the three people back at the first safe house seemed to know about the next safe house location, and that was too many people "in the know" for Kerrick.

Griffin had scouted out another location. Hence all the phone calls he had been making, including one to Delta, his old buddy, thinking he might give some updates that the others weren't willing to do. No such luck.

Up ahead was a fast-food place. Kerrick glanced into the back seat and asked, "Brandon, are you hungry?"

"Always," Brandon piped up. He looked out his window, saw the burger joint, and cried out, "Yes! Fries."

Kerrick pulled in and parked. Then he said, "We might as well all go in."

Griffin tore his attention from his phone and put it away, looking surprised.

Kerrick shrugged and said, "We could all use a chance to get out and to stretch our legs."

With everyone out, Kerrick glanced into the back seat of the car and pointed. "Is that yours, Brandon?"

It was a small pad of paper and a pen. Brandon nodded and dove into the back seat, then grabbed it up.

In a low tone, Kerrick told Amanda, "Don't leave anything in the car."

After giving him a quizzical glance, she nodded and cast a quick look into the back seat and nodded.

Griffin had pulled their stuff from the trunk. With a backpack each and a duffel bag at their sides, the two men walked in with everything they had into the restaurant. They led the way inside, and Kerrick didn't make any attempt to hide his face from any security cameras either.

He didn't care at this point, as he needed a few minutes to change vehicles. And that meant they had to exit one vehicle in order to get in the next one. They chose a booth at the far back, and he and Griffin stowed their gear at their feet. Once done, Griffin kept on walking. He called back as he headed for the men's room, "Order me a coffee."

Kerrick nodded. Knew Griffin from their previous time

in the navy. And the man was a master at finding new vehicles. As the waitress walked over with a big smile on her face, she asked if they wanted menus.

Brandon piped up. "I want a big burger with fries, no pickles," he announced without any warning.

Kerrick chuckled. "I guess that means two burgers for him for sure. And I'll need another two as well." Then he looked at Amanda. "What would you like, honey?"

As if understanding to keep it in the spirit of a family outing, she smiled at him and said, "I'd love a bowl of soup and a salad." The waitress immediately rattled off the soup of the day, and Amanda nodded. "That would be good."

Then the waitress asked Kerrick, "Anything else?"

He smiled and said, "Got any sandwiches to-go?"

"We have big sub sandwiches," she said. "I could make up a few of those for you."

He thought about it and then said, "Make four, please."

She nodded and disappeared in the back.

Amanda then glanced at Kerrick. "What about Griffin?"

"We'll get something to-go for him," he said.

Brandon looked at them, from one adult to the other, and then shook his head. "He shouldn't be that long in the bathroom."

"No," Kerrick announced. "And we can't be that long either. Hopefully the service here is very fast."

Not only was it fast but the food came piping hot, and it was good.

Kerrick bit into his burger and watched as Brandon very carefully laid his tomato off to the side and placed it just so on his napkin. Kerrick hadn't remembered him doing that the last time, but then the kid had been starving. Once he started to eat though, he didn't slow down, and he plowed through both burgers and all the fries. He kept looking at Kerrick's fries too.

Kerrick shook his head. "My fries, buddy."

At the crestfallen look Brandon gave him, Kerrick lifted his plate and dumped one-third of his fries onto Brandon's plate. Brandon quickly polished those off too. By the time they were gone, he still looked hungry.

When Kerrick got up and walked over to pay for the bill, he found their sub sandwiches waiting and also saw an apple pie sitting under the glass counter. "How much is the pie?"

"If they're cooked and ready to go, I sell them by the piece," she said. "But I do have a cooked spare, if you want one to take with you."

"Absolutely," he said. "And do you have any more of those fries? That kid's empty to his toes."

She chuckled. "Just a minute." Then she walked around into the back, pulled out a cardboard carryout container, and completely stuffed it full of fries. After putting a lid on it and putting it in a bag, she handed it to Brandon. "There you go, big guy. Eat up."

His face lit up the room as he cried out, "Thanks."

Kerrick asked Amanda, "Do we need anything else, honey?"

"Water," she said. Amanda took the bag with the sandwiches and the pie, then walked to the cooler and grabbed several water bottles.

"Good idea. I should have thought of that. Plus a couple coffees to-go for me for the road," he said. "Amanda, do you want one?"

"Yes, please," she said.

He ordered two more coffees to-go and said, "It's a long trip." The woman behind the counter just laughed, filled their order, and totaled their bill. Kerrick paid, and they headed outside with their food and drinks.

Arms now ladened, they walked around the side of the building, as if they'd parked there. Kerrick knew exactly how this worked, but Amanda and Brandon looked at him in confusion. Their vehicle was gone. As Kerrick walked farther down the side of the building, he spotted Griffin on his phone—of course—sitting in the cab of a big jacked-up F-250 pickup. Kerrick opened the passenger side, set down the groceries, putting the coffee on the floorboard so it was safely stowed. Brandon was superexcited about the pickup, but it was so high up he could hardly climb in, needing some help from Kerrick. Even Amanda needed a hand to get into the back. But, once they were all loaded up, Kerrick looked at Griffin and said, "How much food do you need?"

Griffin shrugged. "One of those sandwiches will do. Unless you only ordered enough for the three of you."

But Brandon popped up from the back and said, "I have a lot of fries for you."

Kerrick was amused at his generosity. Brandon ripped off the top of the cardboard box, split up the fries, and handed the bigger half forward for Griffin.

Pleased, Griffin smiled at him and said, "Thanks, Brandon. That was thoughtful of you."

"Only because I'm already full," Brandon said, munching away on his own fries.

Griffin gave a shout of laughter and pulled the pickup out of the restaurant's rear parking lot. Then they circled around to hit the highway going in the opposite direction.

Brandon cried out, "I know this area."

"What do you mean, you know this area?" Kerrick asked, sure the alarm in his tone was evident to all. "Have you ever been to that café before?"

"No," he said, "but coming down the left"—and he pointed out a bunch of buildings that looked like old farmhouses—"I've been there before."

"Why and what for?"

"With my father. He's got some friends down there."

"Do you know how to get home from here?"

Brandon screwed up his face and then nodded. "I think so, yes." Then he fired off directions, which made sense somewhat.

Kerrick could see these details came from the total-recall part of Brandon's brain. On a hunch, Kerrick had Griffin follow the kid's instructions for the next twenty minutes, trying to see if they would find out where Brandon lived. When they came down a residential street, Brandon said, "This is close but not quite."

Kerrick turned to look at him. "So we're in the right area?"

Brandon stared around, mystified. "We are, but I think we're like a block over." He looked ahead and saw a popular ice cream place and cried out, "Yes! I've been to that one." He quickly adjusted his directions, and, before long, they drove down a street no longer filled with middle-class homes. In fact, it was in a commercial district with a lot of warehouses but heading toward the lower end of the business class.

"So is this where your home is or where your father works?"

"Both," he said. "He lives and does his business from home."

"The selling of the body organs?" Amanda asked, worried. Her gaze kept going around the area.

Brandon nodded. "We live up top."

"That can't be very nice," Kerrick mentioned.

"You get used to seeing dead bodies all the time," he said with a shrug. "We're organic organisms, so it's not like it makes a difference."

"I guess."

They drove down the road slower now, giving Brandon time to process his surroundings, when he called out and leaned forward between the two men in the front seat. "Stop."

Griffin pulled off to the side of the road and asked, "What are we looking at?"

"That building in the front of the warehouse on the next block? That blue one? That's home."

Kerrick looked at him and whispered, "Was it always burned up like that?"

Brandon shook his head slowly, fear on his face as he whispered, "No. That's new."

CHAPTER 12

THE PAIN IN Brandon's voice broke Amanda's heart. This kid had lost so much so recently and had been so stalwart for so long. She gently massaged his back. "We don't know if your father was in there," she said reassuringly. "He could be fine."

Brandon stared at the building with a haunted look on his face. "No, but it wouldn't surprise me. That was arson."

"Your dad has some pretty big enemies, correct?"

"Yes," Brandon said in a small voice. "He's in a bad business, and he has a lot of bad friends."

"I'm sorry," Amanda said. She looked at the two men. "Is there any point in going inside and checking it out?"

"I think we need to," Kerrick said. He glanced back at Brandon. "Should I take a closer look at any particular part of the building?"

Brandon shrugged and said, "The offices, especially the back wall on the right side, but Dad had a safe in his bedroom, above the office. He also had a fire escape out the back, so maybe he got out safely." He looked into the faces of the three adults with him, some hope creeping into his expression. "Like we did when we left the motel."

Kerrick studied the extent of the burn. Not a whole lot of the outside shell remained, but the fire looked like it had been stopped midburn. Who was the arsonist? That wasn't his job right now, but he was curious. Still, to cover his tracks, Mr. Coleman might have set it himself.

Kerrick glanced at Griffin and said, "I'll get out. You take them around the block a couple times." And without giving anybody a chance to argue, he exited the pickup and disappeared into the closest building on this block, another warehouse.

Amanda leaned forward and asked Griffin, "What's the point in getting out here and going into a building right beside us?"

Griffin smiled at her. "It's not for you to wonder why."

"Well, you can't quote poetry to me and expect to shut me up here," she said in exasperation. "He's out there alone. This could be dangerous."

"Exactly," Griffin said. "Which is why he told me to drive you around the block, so that you two don't look like you're a party to any of this." And, on that note, he pulled back into the street and headed down the block. As they drove past the scorched building, he slowed slightly so they could stare at it. She could still see the second floor was largely intact, but nobody appeared to be around, and no windows were left. And, if it hadn't been ramshackled beforehand, it would have been well and truly looted by now.

KERRICK MADE IT to the edge of the burned-up building without seeing anybody—or anybody seeing him. He quickly moved down what was left of one side of the building, just to make a quick first-pass inspection, hating the acid-burn smell emanating from it. Had anybody even come to take a look at what was inside this building after the fire had died down? He saw freezers and cold storage units, but none of those would be powered at this point.

What happened to the "perishable goods" that Mr. Coleman kept? Kerrick hated to think that body parts were still in there. Yet it was all too possible. No way would he open one to confirm. He'd leave that to the authorities. Or to Mr. Coleman.

Holding his T-shirt over his nose to keep from inhaling too much of the acidic smell inside, Kerrick stepped into the charred building and walked through carefully. Everything here was black and crispy, like it had been fried at high temperatures. Back toward the smaller rooms, the offices, however, there was much less damage, as if the fire had begun in the front area and had burned backward.

He checked out the biggest office and the charred desk but didn't see very much. Singed papers were atop the filing cabinet, but he found no computers or electronics. But then, why would there be? Somebody else would have been here before him, either taking the electronics before starting the fire or the locals had cleared out anything worth pawning after the fire.

The wooden stairs going up to the second floor were badly damaged, but the metal fire escape outside looked like a viable option. He quickly scooted up the ladder and made his way inside, then stopped. Most of the flooring was gone, leaving only the rafters. The bedroom perimeter was still intact, but its contents were quite badly charred. The bed itself had caught fire. He should have asked Brandon where the safe was. He pulled out his phone and called Griffin to ask Brandon.

Inset into the wall near the fire escape but on the

outside exterior wall.

From where he stood, he looked, then took two careful steps, to where the safe supposedly was. Enough of the wall had burned away that he caught a glimpse of black metal. If the safe was still intact, still locked, then anybody who knew it was here hadn't come back to empty it yet. Probably waiting to make sure the fire was completely out. Or to hire a safecracker. The other option was that the safe was empty to begin with.

He took one step closer, carefully balancing on the rafters, and bent down, peeling off the wallboard. The safe itself was small and would be easy to remove from the studs around it now since they were badly charred. It took a few moments longer to completely uncover the safe. The combination lock was still secured. He couldn't open it safely here as he didn't trust the rafter he stood on, but the safe was small enough that he could carry it.

With it securely under his arm, he made his way back down the fire escape and headed around the back corner to meet up with the rest of them. As soon as the pickup pulled alongside him, he hopped inside, and they drove away.

Brandon leaned over and asked, in a hushed tone, "You took the whole safe?"

"The wall was damaged enough that it was easier to remove the whole thing than to take the time to open it there."

"Can you open it?" Amanda asked.

"I hope so," he said, studying the front of the safe. "It's not really that complicated. Without Brandon's personal knowledge of its location, finding it would have been more complicated. Without that tip, if it hadn't been for the fire, it wouldn't have been easy to find the safe at all." He quickly said something about cracking the combination code. It took him four minutes and thirty seconds to open the safe.

Griffin laughed at him. "You should have had that done in under four minutes," he teased Kerrick.

Kerrick shot him a look. "If we weren't driving around corners like madmen, I would have." He slowly dug inside to find it full of bookkeeping ledgers and cash.

Brandon whistled long and hard. "That's a lot of moolah."

Kerrick nodded slowly. "It is. So why didn't your father come back for it?" He twisted to look at Brandon.

And Brandon looked at him and sniffled once.

Kerrick nodded. "Because you know and I know that, if there was any way he could have, your father would have come back to get this, wouldn't he?"

Brandon slowly nodded.

Kerrick glanced at Griffin and said, "You and I need to analyze what's in these ledgers. We'll probably need your help, Brandon. I'm sorry, but it's not looking good for your father."

"Which also would explain why nobody had put out the word that Brandon was missing," Amanda said. "Because your father would have done that too, if he could, right?" she asked Brandon.

Brandon sniffled again, nodding his head.

"True enough," Griffin added.

While Kerrick pulled out the money, he roughly counted it, noting at least ten but possibly upward of twenty thousand US dollars in bundles here, but there were also bundles of different currencies. With the ledgers open, he checked to see if anything else suspicious could be found at first glance.

Inside one were passports for Brandon and for Mr.

Coleman, as well as other legal documents, like Brandon's birth certificate. Those were all good to have when leaving the country. And it appeared that Brandon's father intended to take Brandon with him. Kerrick showed Brandon his passport to help ease the boy's current pain.

Brandon grabbed it like a lifeline, tracing the small book in his hands, while Amanda wrapped an arm around him and pulled him closer.

With the ledgers on his lap, Kerrick quickly flipped through them, not understanding the codes for everything listed herein, codes using shorthand or acronyms to hide the real transactions. Maybe after Brandon had some time to deal with this, Kerrick might approach him for help with his dad's shorthand. A lot of money was involved. The other ledger held bank account info, security information, and listings of companies that Mr. Coleman had business dealings with. *That* was interesting.

At the top of the list was the company that Amanda worked for, that she held a major shareholder interest in—Scion Labs. He lifted it up for her to see. Had she not been involved in the kidnapping event herself, she would have been one major person of interest. Even now, investigators who didn't know her might still consider her involved in her own kidnapping.

When she sucked in her breath, he nodded and said, "And here is another link between Mr. Coleman and Scion Labs."

She sighed. "Besides Hinkleman kidnapping Mr. Coleman's own son and jailing him." She shook her head.

Brandon read off the name and turned to look at her. "Is that the company you work for?"

She sank into the back seat and nodded slowly. "It is,

indeed," she said faintly. "But I don't think we've ever bought body parts before."

"If you were doing business with my dad," Brandon said, "then you were. Or you could have been using the cadavers for further research. He was selling everything from cellular tissue to brain matter."

"It's possible that somebody doing research at Scion needed some cadaver tissue," she said. "We work on all different levels of the body's systems at different times."

"Yes, but dead bodies? How does that help you?" Kerrick asked.

"Scion is first and foremost a research facility, and examining a dead body that died from cancer or whatever does leave clues," she said, making excuses. "So I can't really say that it isn't possible that we dealt with Brandon's father or purchased body parts from him. It is quite likely possible that somebody was using your father's services. However, I don't imagine too many places would purchase these items."

"You mean, *legally*," Griffin said, his tone dry. They made several quick turns, and he pulled into an underground parking area. Once the gate opened, letting them through, he drove farther inside and then into a parking space marked with the number forty-two on it. He shut off the engine and said, "We're home."

"Whose home?" Brandon asked.

Griffin chuckled. "The driver of the lorry, that's who."

The dead *driver of the lorry*, Kerrick thought, feeling Amanda's stare along the back of his head, but he ignored her. He took the contents of the safe but left the safe behind, and, with the rest of the food and their gear, they hopped out of the pickup, locked it up, and went upstairs. He knew Griffin had made arrangements to get this apartment, one way or another.

Standing before door number forty-two, they didn't find any duplicate keys left behind in the expected hiding places. Not that Kerrick had expected as much, now that they were off-grid themselves. Griffin quickly picked the lock and let them in. He waited at the doorway with the other two while Kerrick made a quick search through the apartment, and then everybody came inside. He locked up after them.

The apartment was furnished in a contemporary style, more of a single-male variety than catering to that of a family. Brandon bounced through it, excited to see something new and different, including the furniture, which was pretty New Age stuff. As he danced around, he called out, "I like it."

Amanda looked like she was wilting. She went over to the nearest large recliner and sagged into the plushy softness.

Kerrick looked at her with worry. "Do you need a nap?"

"I'm okay still," she said. "I got a few hours last night, but don't want to ruin a good night tonight."

"Your body's still recovering," he said. "So, if you need to sleep, let us know."

"And what? Sleep in this *dead* guy's bed?" she whispered.

Kerrick looked at her and said, "It's necessary for the time being."

Her shoulders sagged, and she nodded. "I know. It doesn't mean I have to like it though."

"It's your company noted on that ledger …" he reminded her.

"I know I didn't purchase anything from Brandon's father," she said. "But Hinkleman could have, as CEO of Scion. But did the board of directors know too? Or was Hinkleman just using his position for some off-the-books deals?"

Kerrick's face was grim. "That's what we need to find out."

She was silent as she pulled her knees to her chest and curled up in the big chair.

Immediately Brandon hopped over, snagged a blanket off one of the other chairs, and draped it over her. He gave her a pat on the shoulder. "You just sleep."

She chuckled and said, "What will you do?"

"I'll check out one of those sandwiches they brought."

She stared at him in disbelief, but Kerrick had heard it all and seen it all with young boys. They ate until they dropped in a food coma, like after a big Thanksgiving Day meal of seven courses. He brought the sandwiches into the kitchen, handing one to Brandon, then poked around to make sure there was coffee in this place, real coffee, and put on a pot. Griffin was once again on his phone.

Kerrick himself needed to check to see where they were at for further details, but it looked like there was more of a connection to her company than Amanda had fully realized. That had to be hard in itself. When he glanced back at her, her eyes were closed, and her chest rose and fell in a deep and steady motion. He next checked Brandon, who was watching her between bites of his sandwich.

"We'll let her sleep while she can," he cautioned.

Brandon nodded, swallowed. "I don't think she's having an easy time of this."

"And why is that?"

Brandon looked up at him, chewed a bit more, and smiled. "She's too much of an adult to not find the worry in this, and I'm too much of a child not to find the joy."

Talk about being old beyond his years. Kerrick stared at

the boy in astonishment, but Brandon just shrugged and attacked his sandwich. When the coffee was done dripping, Brandon had finished his sandwich, then skipped off to inspect the apartment further, while Kerrick took his coffee cup over to the kitchen table, set up his laptop and his notepad, and sat down to get to work. He would require more sleep himself, but he needed to sort out with Griffin the roster for their security shifts.

They couldn't stay here for too long, and he wasn't sure if Griffin had made actual arrangements with the apartment management or was just taking advantage. Either way, they were doing what they needed to stay safe. At least, until tomorrow, when they could arrange for another location. Only one night per each. As he checked out his emails, the mysterious but helpful chat box opened. Kerrick decided to call it the Mavericks chat box now, due to their unfettered approach to justice. He read the new message.

Where are you?
New place.
Where?
Outside of town.

He wasn't sure why he was being evasive, but, so far, he hadn't exactly had any reason to trust anybody.

You were supposed to be at a safe house.
Didn't feel right.

Silence came first. **Okay.**

He gave a nod at that. "Damn right. The reason you hired me," he muttered, "is because my instincts are solid. And nothing about this case feels right. In fact, it's all gone to hell."

CHAPTER 13

BY MIDAFTERNOON THEY had settled into Stanley's apartment, their newest safe house. Brandon had crashed on the couch, still sound asleep. Griffin was on the floor on the carpet just in front of him, protecting the boy even while asleep, whereas both Kerrick and Amanda sat at the kitchen table. She cast her mind back to the day when she had been kidnapped. If she had realized it had been Dr. Hinkleman right from the beginning, it would have made a lot more sense. He hadn't shown up to work on that Friday before. He had been very controlling, hovering over everyone's work recently—more so than normal. So missing a normal workday without any explanation was unusual.

"What are you thinking so heavily about?" Kerrick asked, his tone low.

She glanced at the other two, still sleeping soundly, and whispered, "Those two look good together."

"I was thinking the same thing," Kerrick said, "while I watched over you and Brandon early this morning."

She glanced at him. "It's the first time you've mentioned that, holding me close as I fought my own demons."

His smile was gentle but filled with understanding. "We all have demons, and it's no shame in wanting to be held. It's a human comfort we all need from time to time."

"Well, thank you for that and for continuing to look

after us."

He shrugged. "Honestly, I'm not sure what to do with you."

She stared at him in astonishment.

He flashed her a wicked grin. "Other than the usual things a man might want to share with a woman."

She flushed. "I don't think so."

"Are you sure?" he teased. "According to my file, you haven't had a boyfriend since your ex."

She rolled her eyes at him. "So what? And that doesn't mean I haven't hooked up during that time, although that's hardly a replacement for a real relationship."

He shook his head. "Absolutely it's not, but it doesn't mean we can't have both. Besides anyone can see we're attracted to each other. That's not something to ignore."

She stared at him again in shock. "Where's this coming from, all of a sudden?"

"I'm not sure, honestly." He shrugged. "But, ever since I saw your picture, I couldn't get you out of my mind. And then there's the fact that I admire you very much. Well, that's the best basis I know for a relationship."

"Wow." She didn't even know what to say. Her heart knew how to feel though as it warmed to the idea in a big way. She sat back and smirked at him. "Do you always fall in love with women's pictures?"

"Well, I wouldn't go that far," he said, chuckling. "But I do appreciate what you've been doing with your research, and I admire how you've handled yourself since the kidnapping. You got yourself out of a really sticky situation, and you rescued the boy too."

At the mention of Brandon, she glanced over at him, and her smile fell away. "What happens to him if his father's dead?"

"I don't know how that works here," he said quietly. "There will be a system in place, but I can't even begin to guess what that is."

She nodded slowly. "And generally I live in Paris. But I really would like to talk to my father." She smiled. "He has a place in England," she said. "Just a little coastal holiday home, where we used to meet up for holidays. Loved those times."

He stared at her in surprise.

"I was hoping to come over and spend a couple weeks there this year. I just could never find the time."

"A workaholic," he said with a nod.

"I highly doubt you're any different," she said with a chuckle.

"Not so sure about that," he said. "I was at a crossroads myself, trying to figure out where and what I would do next—when I got the call to come rescue you."

"You're not Special Forces?"

"I am, in a way," he said, "but I was a Navy SEAL before. It was time for a switch."

He didn't go into all the details, and she respected his privacy too much to ask. Most likely he couldn't answer either way. But her insides felt pretty warm and fuzzy that he had opened up about how he felt about her. "How is this a switch?" she asked with a note of humor.

"Well, I'm not on a ship, for one."

"Too bad," she said. "I wouldn't mind being on one. The water always soothes my soul."

He stopped and stared at her, one eyebrow raised. "And that's a good idea too." He considered the small apartment around him. "That could be our next step."

She frowned at him. "And what exactly would that next step be?"

"Let me think about it," he said. "It wouldn't work for long, but you'd certainly be safe."

Just then a hard rap came at the apartment door.

All laughter fell from his face. He held up a finger and rose from the kitchen table. Her heart pounding, she dashed to hide beside the fridge. Griffin was already up on his feet, moving smoothly and lightly, picking up Brandon and ducking into one of the bedrooms. She wished she could go with him.

When the pounding came again, a voice called out, "Kerrick!"

Swearing gently, Kerrick opened the door and let somebody in.

"What the hell's going on?" the man asked.

"I didn't like the safe house alternatives," Kerrick snapped. "I do what I do because of my instincts. And my instincts said that other plan sucked."

That brought the stranger up short. He glanced around and said, "Where are they?"

Something about Kerrick's attitude had her stepping back a little bit farther behind the fridge as Kerrick answered, "They're safe."

"Are they here with you?"

"No," he said. "Griffin's got them."

"Shit."

She could just barely see the stranger as he ran his fingers through his hair. "I'll have to fix this."

"Fix what?"

"This." And he turned and stormed from the apartment.

Kerrick slowly closed the door behind him and locked it.

She stepped around the corner and asked, "Who was that?"

"I'm not exactly sure," Kerrick said. "Most of the men I work with in this group are strangers."

Griffin stepped forward from the back and said, "That was Delta."

Kerrick looked at him and said, "Seriously?"

Griffin nodded. "He's a friend of mine."

"Well, he's a rattled friend now," Amanda said curiously. "You guys don't even know who you work with?"

"We each know someone from our past," Kerrick said. "And Griffin and I know each other obviously, but we don't necessarily know who all else is in the team at any given time."

"Yeah, I got that, what with the Greek letters of the alphabet for designations instead of real names. I'd be hard-pressed to trust people without their real names too." She shook her head. "He didn't sound happy that you're here. And how did he know we *were* here?"

Kerrick stared at her and said, "I was just trying to figure that out." He looked again at Griffin. "Did you give them a heads-up?"

Griffin shook his head. "No."

"Are you tracked?"

Griffin shook his head again. "Better not be." He stared at Kerrick and asked, "You?"

"No, not that I know of." Then he frowned, studied the rest of them, and said, "But that's the only way they would know." He stared at Griffin. "It must be our disposable phones." Then he froze. "No. They can track us through the Mavericks chat window." He swore. "I should have thought of that."

"It makes sense though. They are the ones we keep asking for intel."

"*Mavericks* chat window?" Amanda asked, her lips quirking at the corners.

Kerrick gave her a silly grin and shrugged. "I coined the term. But the Mavericks is our code name."

"*Mavericks* works for me," Griffin said. "I like it." His grin was huge, and a mischievous gleam was in his gaze.

"You two may be mavericks, but you're still the good guys."

"Well, maybe we do need to sneak into France and see what we can come up with."

"About what?" Amanda asked.

"More information on Hinkleman and the purchase of body parts by the Scion Labs company, whether Hinkleman acted alone or in concert with the company, whether Hinkleman or Scion were involved in both ends of the body-parts transactions," Kerrick said, watching as Amanda's face contorted more and more at each theory.

"Oh, my God. You don't think … Would my company tell you the truth? Even if they weren't involved, would you believe them?" she asked in exasperation.

"That's why we need to check them out more closely," Griffin added.

"Wait a minute. … At work, that last Friday I was there, I overhead a conversation about Scion's big research vessel being off the coast of Norway. How most of the Scion people would be there soon. Or should be there right now. For some conference."

"On a research vessel?"

She nodded.

The two men looked at each other, their gazes intent, as

if sorting their way through this.

"We'd have to get across the water without leaving a trail, without alerting anybody at Scion," Kerrick noted, to himself mostly.

"I don't understand," she said. "Unless your bags, any of our clothing, or our persons are being tracked by Hinkleman or his goons, how else would they know where we are when we leave here?"

"Satellite," Griffin stated. "Traffic cams."

"We still have to sort out what's going on with the UK kidnapping ring and the fact that everything seems tied to France and now Norway, what with that Norwegian research ship and your father living in Norway and most of Scion Labs' France-based employees, your coworkers, gathering there too. It makes me nervous, but I also wonder if we should be on that ship too."

She snorted. "Good luck with that. It's massive, but, regardless of space and accommodations, it's not like those invitations are just handed out."

"So what kind of conference is going on?" he asked, slowly turning to look at her.

"I don't really know," she said. "I was going to check into it further, but then my life went sideways. I thought, as a board member and a major shareholder and one of their top researchers, that I would have been invited, but I wasn't."

"Maybe Hinkleman had something to do with that?" Griffin said. Then he frowned. "I agree, Kerrick. I think we need to catch a ride."

Kerrick nodded. "I was thinking that too. We could pull the secret card."

Griffin snorted. "How many times had we just boarded

a ship before moving out on a new mission, leaving in silence?"

"Often," Kerrick said with a smirk. "No reason we can't do it again."

Griffin's eyes lit up at that idea. "Let me see who's close by." And he turned and headed to his laptop. Before he typed anything, he added, "I'm using my own computer. It's been swept and not out of my sight."

Kerrick turned toward Amanda. "We'll be on the move soon. You should crash now, while you can."

She slowly shook her head. "I'm not sure I can. All of a sudden, you're talking about how we have to get onto this research vessel. I don't even think that's possible. Or are you thinking that you and Griffin would go, leaving me and Brandon stashed somewhere?" When she saw the truth acknowledged in his eyes, she shook her head. "Hell, no. Brandon, yes. But me, no."

"You're not leaving me behind," Brandon shouted. He came out of the bedroom and raced toward Amanda, throwing his arms around her waist. She wrapped him up tight in her arms.

"Everybody can't go," Kerrick said. "More chances of us being caught. Someone could recognize Amanda. A blond female stands out. And way too dangerous a situation to bring a child into."

"Dangerous on a research ship? For some meeting?" Brandon argued, but he faced Amanda.

Kerrick just stared at her and waited. She filtered through what Kerrick had said, and then she slowly sighed. "Is there another ship we can stay on while you guys head out there?"

He flashed a grin. "Maybe. Depends."

She glared at him, and he shrugged and said, "I can't answer that yet."

She looked down at Brandon. "We'll have to leave soon. Can you go back to sleep?"

He immediately shook his head. "No, I can't. I'm hungry again."

She shook her head, then just raised her hands in surrender and said, "There are still a few leftovers."

A couple sandwiches remained. She put one on a plate and handed it to him as he sat at the table and promptly scoffed it up. She turned when she heard Griffin and Kerrick whispering behind her and glared at them. "Now what?"

But they were setting their watches and talking about buying new phones. "I'll be right back," Griffin said walking to the door.

"We're leaving soon," Kerrick said with a smile to both Amanda and Brandon. "So be ready."

"I've been nothing but ready," she snapped. "I, however, don't even have a change of clothes."

"Well, we have to get you some interim gear," he said, looking at Griffin, who nodded in return. "It won't be fancy though."

Griffin promptly left, only to return in an hour, distributing one new cell phone to each of them, including Brandon, with strict instructions to not use them unless their life depended on it. That 9-1-1 calls were allowed, as long as they were no longer than thirty seconds in duration. "I've keyed in one new cell number into these phones. For Amanda, it's Kerrick's. For Brandon, it's Amanda's. Dial that number if you get lost and keep it close."

Amanda and Brandon nodded.

"I mean it, Brandon. Your life is at stake here, so you

must do as we say. Or you lose this privilege. Do you understand?" Kerrick asked.

"Sure. Got it."

"Your life and Amanda's life too." Kerrick stared at the boy, who nodded and stared at Amanda with a very serious look on his face. Kerrick could only hope he truly understood how serious this was. "No calls to your father for either of you. Understand?"

Amanda and Brandon nodded again.

When everyone agreed to these terms, the guys made their calls. She sat here and waited until they were done, her fingers thrumming on the tabletop. But she smiled at Brandon and said, "If nothing else, we'll have an exciting adventure."

Brandon immediately bobbed his head, his mouth full of sandwich. "I hope we get to go on one of those big naval warships. That would be awesome."

She stared at him, then glanced up at the two men, and wondered just what they had planned. She hoped it wasn't a naval ship. That sounded noisy and crowded. And she didn't think they would blend in very easily, particularly not a child on a naval vessel—not even a woman on a navy ship, not even in 2019—hence the problem with her and Brandon going aboard a military ship. Maybe it *was* better if they stayed on land. Only she didn't want to be separated from any of them.

ONE OF THE last calls Kerrick made had been to the Mavericks organization. They had been more efficient than Kerrick had expected once his request had gone out and plans were made. He told them that they were leaving in four hours but they were on the road in thirty minutes—in a new vehicle compliments of Griffin. They hit the coastline late that afternoon and boarded a small ship heading out toward the deeper waters. This particular ship was known for moving people in the dark of night. A contact he planned to keep for future reference.

For now, they moved in broad daylight; night would fall before they reached their destination.

As for Amanda and Brandon, they were both dressed in black. Amanda's hair had been covered with a soft fishing cap. Brandon sat by her side. He had promised to always stay within arm's reach of Amanda, and that promise was something he took very seriously.

Kerrick turned to face the ocean, closing his eyes and lifting his face into the breeze. The waves were a bit choppy but not enough to slow their schedule.

He stood at the front of the boat, letting the pilot cross the water as hard and as fast as the boat would go. He turned back and motioned at Amanda and Brandon to go down below. She nodded and led the boy underneath. She shot Kerrick a special smile and a little finger wave as the two of them tucked up into one of the big bunks underneath. He smiled, caught Griffin's raised eyebrows, and then shrugged as he turned around.

His sea legs were something he never lost. The water was his element. It didn't matter whether he was in the water or on a boat like now. On any water vessel, he felt at home. He stood here for a long moment, his mind formulating the next step of the plan. Griffin tapped him on the shoulder. He turned, and Griffin motioned toward the back of the boat, where they could sit and talk.

As he sat down, Griffin said, "I have the location of the research ship." He held out his phone to show him.

Kerrick looked at the map Griffin had and pulled out his laptop. Kerrick brought up real-time photos. "And our ship is where?"

Griffin enlarged the map, so they could see the red dot showing their destination. They would transfer to a helicopter sometime after they arrived there, which would take them to the USS *Antietam*, which was even closer to Norway. Kerrick was fine with that. They had avoided any street cams so far. The satellites? Well, … they all had on some kind of a hat, so their faces had been covered somewhat. That would hinder any facial recognition software from getting a valid hit. He hoped …

Now it was just a hop, skip, and a jump from the *Antietam* to the research vessel. It would have been easier and faster to fly straight into Norway and then catch a ride out to the Scion ship. But this way, they didn't leave a paper trail, and nobody at Scion had a clue what they were doing or even who they were.

They traveled for hours before the pilot called to Kerrick. He looked up to see the majestic carrier before them, lighting up the dark evening and the darker ocean. They pulled up slowly to it, next to the affixed ladder on its side, where the four of them would disembark. It was a long way up the side of this navy transport. These ships easily stood one hundred feet tall, just the part sitting atop the water, but a landing was not too far up its side where Brandon and Amanda must get to.

Kerrick quickly woke them up, and, as they shook the sleep out of their gazes, he told them how this would work. He would usher them over the side of this small boat, where they must climb up a ladder on the huge ship, with Kerrick ahead of them and Griffin behind them—to make sure they didn't fall and to navigate them successfully into the cargo levels within.

Brandon's jaw dropped as he stared around. He whispered, "This is huge."

Kerrick placed a finger on his lips and whispered, "From here on in, not a word. Not until you reach your quarters, all right?"

BRANDON'S GAZE WIDENED again, and he quickly nodded. Amanda wrapped an arm around the kid's shoulders and tucked him up closer to her as they got into line. She was cursing her own lack of fitness by the time they climbed the ladder and stepped onto a landing. Brandon made the climb much more easily.

One navy officer met them, led them through a series of steps up and down, and then filed them into one small room. In all that time, not one word had been spoken. As soon as they were inside, Kerrick motioned to the bunk on the bottom and said softly, "That's for you two."

Amanda nodded, laid down, and urged in low voice, "Brandon, come lie down with me."

Immediately he hopped into the bed beside her and curled up tight. Kerrick grabbed a blanket by her feet and threw it over them. "One of us will always be here," he murmured. "But no talking. If you have to, whisper."

Griffin sat down on the small bench space opposite them. As soon as Amanda closed her eyes, Kerrick smacked Griffin lightly on the shoulder and said, "I'll be back soon."

Then he disappeared.

KERRICK HEADED BACK onto the landing where they had come from, having memorized his path easily. There, he met the one person who had helped him off the boat and into the ship's belly. The hired boat they'd arrived on was long gone.

Kerrick was handed an envelope. He nodded, opened it up, quickly took a look. He checked the time; they were leaving in six hours. With a pat on his buddy's shoulder, Kerrick returned to their room. By the time he got there, Amanda and Brandon were sound asleep, and Griffin was working on his computer. Kerrick stepped inside, closed the door carefully so that he didn't wake anybody, and dropped the envelope beside Griffin. "Helicopter out in six hours," he said.

Griffin nodded. "Perfect." Then the man glanced at Brandon. "He'll need food before then."

"He'll get it." Kerrick shrugged. "Meals will be delivered."

Griffin nodded. "Secrecy at all costs. Still, I think we should have left them on shore."

"I wish," he said. "But there's just the two of us, so who were we to leave them with?"

Griffin winced. "I know. That's why they're still with us."

"Any news on the other kidnappers?"

"The Mavericks have a location pinpointed," Griffin said in a low voice. "Already setting up a sting operation to get in."

"Good," Kerrick said. "I don't understand exactly what

the bottom line is here with the company, Scion Labs. What does it seek to gain? To think they were holding Amanda and Brandon under those conditions is beyond belief."

"Our guys might have found Brandon's father," Griffin said, his voice dropping even lower. But his tone told Kerrick so much.

"They found him in the warehouse?"

He nodded. "Crispy critter, no ID on him, and no way to know for sure. But it's highly suspected that's who he is."

"I hate results like that," Kerrick muttered. "We need one hundred percent ID."

"I agree. We can send over some DNA."

"We could, but they should have enough to confirm Mr. Coleman's DNA via Brandon's DNA found on his body tracker."

"Exactly," Griffin said. Then he waited a heartbeat and added, "But that wasn't mentioned."

"That's *not* good news." Kerrick's gaze flew to meet his partner's. "An oversight? Haven't gotten to it yet? My gut's talking to me." He brought out a phone and quickly asked.

He read out the almost immediate response. "DNA was too degraded to match."

"Convenient for the killer." The two men frowned at each other.

Griffin said, sending a wary look to Kerrick. "But, ever since meeting up with that threesome ... that's why we switched out that next safe house, why we left our Mavericks-issued phones behind. Something there wasn't right. At least we have a secure connection to the Maverick team. They can track us. But we don't want Hinkleman's goons doing so."

Kerrick sat here, pondering that further. "But *Brandon*?"

"Might have been kidnapped to keep his father in line. Particularly if Mr. Coleman was supplying the Scion Labs company with his very specialized products, which Coleman's ledger seems to indicate. Then killed when he wouldn't cooperate? Or Brandon's father faked his own death? It's not like he wouldn't have access to a body as a substitute?"

"So, no political ties that we know of, but a potentially worldwide service industry that Amanda's kidnappers, that Scion Labs, needed?" Kerrick nodded slowly. "God, this could be so much bigger than just those three holding facilities we know of in London. I mean, illegal organ harvesting brings to mind kidnapping, human trafficking, just to kill them for their organs. The legal version would hardly be pretty, except for the intended end result—saving a person's life. Otherwise, it would be a damn ugly business if Mr. Coleman were illegally harvesting."

"The question is," Griffin began, "whether he wanted to stop doing it or whether they were looking for something a little more unusual."

"Are you talking about illegally harvesting stem cells?"

The room went quiet.

There was absolutely nothing good about that line of thought. If Brandon's father dealt in legal donations of human organs, that was one thing. Kerrick could only hope that the people donating their body parts were dead from natural causes. But what if Brandon's dad had been requested by the kidnappers—aka Scion Labs—to find a particular body part? Of course with a matching blood type, to use in black-market organ transplant surgeries. Or, in properly matched human volunteers, for those human trials that Amanda needs to prove her cure, which were so hard to get official permission for.

Regardless of which purpose, maybe Scion had placed too many orders for organs or cadavers not currently in stock at Mr. Coleman's?

Or was this ultimately about finding the more universal body part: stem cells that grew into various other body parts? And in numbers that Brandon's dad couldn't foresee supplying in normal legal situations. That would certainly be a valid reason to hold his son hostage and, once Brandon escaped, to then burn down Mr. Coleman's warehouse with him in it. "We have to get onto the research vessel," Kerrick said.

"Well, we're getting there, just another hop, skip and a jump away. At least they're having an exciting adventure," Griffin said, with a nod to their sleeping companions. "Brandon's quite the character."

Kerrick nodded, but he kept quiet.

"And you and Amanda seem to have hit it off," Griffin pushed.

"What's not to like? She's nice. I admire her strength, resourcefulness, and especially the fact that she's a brainiac and doing something worthwhile with it. Obviously it's easy to respect her for that too."

"Well, I saw an awful lot of heat and sparks between you two that had nothing to do with respect and admiration," Griffin said, chuckling. "But that's all right. You're entitled to your privacy."

"I wish," Kerrick said. "As you know we have had no privacy."

"I know. ... I was really surprised to hear you were in."

"Ditto."

The two men looked at each other, taking their measure.

"Are you staying in?" Griffin asked.

"I'm not sure. I wasn't expecting this at all," he said. "This opportunity that arose." Then he studied Griffin and asked, "You?"

Griffin nodded. "Same. Although I'm not sure that I was quite as ready as you to leave the navy. The SEALs team that I worked with was great. But you get to the point where you wake up in the morning and wonder when it's enough."

"Exactly," Kerrick said. "And this seemed like something worthwhile that I could move on to."

"Exactly," Griffin said. "You'll do more?"

Kerrick snorted. "Got to survive this one first."

"I'm surprised, given the sophistication of this kidnapping operation, how they have obviously done this before," Griffin said slowly, "that we haven't been attacked. In my head, there were a couple opportunities where the local goons could have taken us out."

Kerrick stared at his buddy, his mind going back over everything they had encountered so far. "Well, I could confirm one opportunity. Potentially a second one, yes. The fact that they haven't is interesting, isn't it?"

"And dangerous," Griffin said. "I can't help but think it's a trap."

"The research ship itself? Or every step of the way getting there?"

"The vessel," he said slowly. "Where's Hinkleman? And is that body Mr. Coleman's? Were the Scion employees all in on this, even at the board and its leadership and management levels? In which case, *everybody* is collateral damage."

"In which case, they're more than happy for all of us to show up on the vessel," Kerrick said, sitting back and staring at Griffin. "And take us all out."

"Well, that's the problem, isn't it? We would hope not, but how can we not consider that?"

"I don't want to consider any of it. I'd like to take Amanda and Brandon away from here and find some peace and quiet."

"Me too," Griffin said. "But you and I both know the world's a much uglier place than most of the average people know about."

"True enough, and that's not very nice to consider either."

"No, but the problem is, it never seems to get any better."

"Which is why we're doing what we're doing, to bring down this ring of people. But exactly what are they doing and why? Holding political prisoners for political favors or for ransom? Or holding these victims for body parts or for human trafficking? Or first to sell them off and then to harvest them once their buyer is done with them? For whatever reason they're being kidnapped and held in a prison environment. Plus research is involved, the kind of research that involves ordering body parts. … What's the chance those kidnapped people were kept strictly for body parts?" he asked with a frown. "Not about politics. Not about ransom money. Totally about body parts."

"No clue," Griffin said. "But damn I don't like that thought."

"We needed a small team for this job initially, but, at the same time, a part of me says we need some analysts to go through the company."

"The cyberteam is on it. So far they haven't found anything."

Kerrick wandered around the small room, restless. He

should be sleeping, but finally he decided that he needed to disengage his brain. "I'm catching twenty," he said as he kicked off his shoes, climbed onto the top bunk, and stretched out. After years of experience, he knew exactly how hard it was to go to sleep anywhere at any time, but he had perfected a lot of skills to help him get to the top of his game.

Within two minutes, he had his eyes closed and had already drifted into a deep sleep.

CHAPTER 14

SHE WOKE UP when a hand gently shook her shoulder. Amanda stared up at Kerrick and whispered, her throat hoarse and her voice raspy, "Hey. What's up?" Her hands automatically stroked the side of his face.

"We'll be leaving in a couple hours," he whispered gently. "Sorry to wake you but thought you might want to freshen up before we eat. Food will be here soon."

Her brain still foggy, she attempted to focus on what was going on. And then it all came rushing back. She rolled over to her back and groaned lightly. "Seriously?"

He nodded. "Seriously."

She realized Brandon was no longer beside her and sat upright. "Where is he?"

"With Griffin. Brandon wanted to see a little bit before we left."

"Is that wise?"

"It's about 2:30 a.m. Less crew members are needed at this time. Plus, this ship is not in enemy waters. Griffin knows the deal, but he figured this would help take Brandon's mind off his father. Besides, this graveyard shift has a crew meeting happening on one of the upper floors. So … even less seamen about."

"Still …"

Kerrick sat on the bench beside her. He reached up and

stroked her face. "We all have to leave in a couple hours."

She yawned gently and tilted her head into his hand. "Okay. But I wish we could stay here. At least long enough to recover."

"I don't," Kerrick said with a chuckle. "I'd rather be back at a motel or an apartment."

"I thought you loved being out on the ocean."

"I do," he said. "There's nowhere I'd rather be, except for the fact that we've got hundreds of people around us." And, at those words, in a surprising move, he leaned over until their faces were almost touching, nose tip to nose tip. Then he whispered, "And it would be awfully nice if we were alone." He leaned over a little bit more and kissed her gently.

What was supposed to be just a brush of his lips was an instant melding of the two of them. He pressed hard, kissing her deep and long. Still half asleep, she woke up fast, but she also woke up every other body part of Kerrick's as she wrapped her arms around his neck and held him close. When he finally pulled free, he whispered, "Hold that thought."

"WHY?" SHE ASKED. "It doesn't sound like we'll have any privacy or be alone anytime soon."

"Not necessarily," he whispered as he leaned over and kissed her again.

Her heart quickened once more.

"We have an hour at least." Then Kerrick said, backing off slightly, "Or we can make it happen when this nightmare is over."

She took a deep breath, trying to slow her heart rate and

to calm down her racing hormones. She never did one-night stands, so this constant reaction to him had to be from her long-term abstinence added to the adrenaline-filled situation. But she didn't want to let him go. She couldn't see ever wanting to, ... but what if he disappeared from her life when this nightmare was over? Her instincts said, *Grab the moment while you can.* Slowly she let her hand drift down his arm until her fingers clenched his. "An hour?"

He nodded. "Can you be quiet?" He got up, locked the door and returned so he was lying alongside her, his breath warm against her neck.

"No." Yet her head was nodding.

"Can you try?" He chuckled softly.

"Maybe."

He noted the change in her voice and smiled. "I like the thought of an hour alone with you."

"*Mmm*," she murmured, closing her eyes and shifting slightly as his breath washed across her cheek and ear. Shivers whispered down her spine. His fingers slipped under her T-shirt, stroking across her ribs and down her flat belly. She sucked in her breath.

"Problems?"

"No," she gasped, "just sensitive."

He nuzzled her ear and, with that same warm breath driving her crazy, whispered, "Good. Sensitive works for me."

She'd have chuckled, but just then he slipped a finger inside her waistband, and it came out as a moan instead.

He took the lobe of her ear into his mouth and suckled as his fingers delved deeper under her panties. The double onslaught sent her senses soaring. Those damnable fingers. ... She arched her back and twisted slightly, but he held her still, his fingers sliding deeper and deeper. She couldn't stand it, pushed up against him, mewling in need.

"Easy," he whispered.

"Not possible," she gasped, shuddering as he ratcheted up his devilish fingers. "So damn close."

"Good," he murmured. "It's great for stress release."

Her short laugh turned to a groan as her body exploded like minifireworks and ran throughout her body. Her nerves, already sensitive, sent shudders through her body.

He held her close, gently stroking up and down her body. "Perfect," he murmured. "So sweet."

"For me, yes," she whispered as her body slowed down, leaving her replete and toasty warm inside and out. "But not for you."

"We still have time."

She burst out laughing. "Oh, so that's your nefarious plan. I'm hardly likely to argue now."

"You weren't arguing a few moments ago either," he said, his gaze twinkling.

"So true," she readily admitted, snaking her arms around his neck and pulling him on top of her. "Not now either."

"Except for this next part, where we're both wearing too many clothes." He rolled off her and, within minutes, was down to his skin. He eyed her clothing, then, with typical military efficiency, had her stripped down to the buff just as fast. She lay here and let him work, amazed at the speed with which he got things done. With their clothes dumped on the floor, she opened her arms and whispered, "I'm so ready for round two."

His gaze heated up, and he came down beside her. "Good," he whispered, "as I find I can't wait anymore."

With their fingers linked, he raised her arms overhead

and slid down her body, suckling, licking, … kissing …

Her senses, already simmering, flashed with heat once again. She gasped at the sensations surging through her, the fire licking at her nerve endings. "Kerrick," she demanded, "I want you with me this time."

His breath rasped heavily in reaction, but he worked his way back up before claiming her lips once again. She widened her thighs, wrapping her legs around his hips and urging him closer. When he accepted the offer, the emotions that overtook her were too much; … she turned her head away as he simply entered her, her body suddenly liquid, molten fire pouring through her. Simply his touch, his arms tight about her, his breath featherlight on her neck, the warmth of his body, the ultimate physical joining …

Just when she thought she couldn't take any more, he started to move. Deeper and deeper he drove in a slow and steady tempo, until he gasped and broke the rhythm to drive harder and faster, until he ground his pelvis tighter against her. Even his somewhat muted guttural cry, an erotic sound of his own completion, sent her over the edge right after him.

HE CUDDLED HER close, his body satiated and replete. In more ways than one. He couldn't remember sharing this sense of joy, this heartwarming closeness before. She was so damn special, and he had no intention of losing her when this mission was over. That they had a long way to go to get to the end of this nightmare would just give him more time to cement this beginning.

His job itself was problematic but not an insurmountable one. Besides, Amanda would likely be so driven in her work that he'd be the one making adjustments along that way more than she would. He smiled at the thought. He'd be okay with that. He admired the work she was doing. And understood her passion. That was important. When one followed their heart, it would take them where they needed to go.

That's what he'd done, and he couldn't stop anyone else from following their own heart. As long as she was willing to share her heart with him too.

CHAPTER 15

AMANDA WOKE TO warm kisses at her neck. She curled toward Kerrick only to hear his muted laughter. "Sorry, sweetheart, not this time."

"We're leaving?" She opened her eyes and smothered a yawn.

"Soon. We used up all that spare time." He kissed her nose. "And we'll have company soon." He shifted off the bunk and dressed quickly.

"Is it safe to leave the ship, you think?"

"I'm not sure," he said. "But you haven't been totally safe so far, and you're still doing better than when you were in that prison."

She gave a clipped nod. "Good point."

She swung her legs over and sat up on the bunk. "I guess no showers, huh?"

"No time," he said. "You can have a quick wash, and then Griffin'll be back with Brandon. We'll eat some food and leave right away."

She nodded, scooped up her discarded clothing, and made her way to the bathroom. After using the facilities, she indulged in a quick wash, then did the best she could with her hair, but it was well past the point of doing very much. Still, when she stepped back into the main part of the room, she found Brandon, holding up toast topped with something.

"Didn't realize the food was here already," she exclaimed, studying the makeshift table, the food and ... "Coffee," she exclaimed a little too loudly, clapping a hand over her grin.

Kerrick smiled at her as he held out a cup. "I gave you a few more minutes in the bathroom."

She nodded and accepted the coffee from him. "I didn't even think there would be much in the way of food here."

"Special circumstances," he said.

At that, she studied his face, frowned, and said, "Nobody on board knows we're here, do they?"

She caught Griffin's gaze, and he shook his head. "No, they don't. And we'll keep it that way."

She nodded slowly and took several sips of her coffee. She eyed the breakfast options, everything from muffins to breakfast sandwiches. Brandon ate eggs on toast. She picked up a muffin and quickly unwrapped it and ate it, even as Kerrick handed her a breakfast sandwich. Then, with both of those down, and the rest of her coffee too, the tray was polished off. Soon came a subtle knock on the door. Kerrick immediately stood, walked the tray over, handed it out, and said to the others, "It's time to go."

He ushered them out one at a time, Brandon still chewing the last bite of his food, whereas Amanda busily wiped her hands off as she followed them out single file. There was no sign of anybody except for their special host. They were led through another maze and into an enclosed narrow circular ladder, where they climbed and kept climbing and then kept climbing some more. If she had been claustrophobic, their small room would have done her in, but here, for sure, she would have not handled it well.

When they were at the top of the flight of stairs, the hatch was opened, and they were let outside to find themselves on a huge deck. The wind gusted at them, but very early morning gray clouds reigned. They were atop the ship now, nearing a helicopter pad—with a helicopter ready to go, its engine running and its rotors cutting into the air, awaiting them. Crouching down, they quickly raced over to the side of the chopper, where they were lifted into place.

Brandon exclaimed in joy. "Wow, a helicopter and we were just on one of those great big warships!" He kept bouncing from seat to seat, trying all four behind the chopper pilot. Amanda immediately sat down closest to the window and out of the way. Brandon took the opposite seat, and Griffin sat beside him. With Kerrick beside her, they were buckled in, each given a headset, and the helicopter lifted off.

She noticed several large black bags were to one side. *Probably Griffin's and Kerrick's gear.* She wished it were clothes for her, but all she had were the black clothes she had been given to wear for this trip. She was thankful for these. Her old ones were gone. She also dreamed of a good shower followed by a long soak in a hot bath with bubbles and fresh clean clothes of her own, but that wasn't to be. Not yet. She stared out the window.

"You okay?" Kerrick asked through their headset.

She smiled and nodded.

"Ever been on a helicopter before?"

"A couple times."

Brandon heard her and leaned forward to stare at her in awe. She just grinned at him and said, "Enjoy. They're fun."

At that point in time, Brandon peppered Griffin with question after question after question. But Griffin was patient and calm as he answered as many as he could. She wondered if he could keep it up the whole way, but, after about twenty minutes, it seemed like everything overwhelmed Brandon, and he sank back into his seat and watched in silence.

She didn't know how long they would be gone or how far they would travel, but, at this point in time, this was all about trust. And she had placed her trust in Kerrick right from the first time they'd met. It wouldn't change anytime soon.

Kerrick laced his fingers with hers. She squeezed his fingers and smiled.

"All right?" he asked.

"I was just thinking about how much my life has changed since somebody threw a hood over my head," she said, half joking.

"Any idea who it was?"

"No," she said, "not really. But I remember Hinkleman wasn't at work that Friday before the Sunday I was taken. Granted, he didn't work weekends, but I always did. And he knew it. So he must have informed the kidnappers, and they just waited until I left the building, because I didn't keep to any schedule. Meanwhile, Hinkleman was probably already at that old sanitorium, that prison, waiting for me to arrive."

"It's quite possible," he said. "Hopefully we can bring this to an end soon."

"I still don't understand what the research ship is supposed to tell us."

"Hopefully everything," he said cheerfully. "At least if we're lucky."

"Good," she said, "but it's still a little disturbing."

"Of course it is," he said. "But we'll get the answers we

need from the people on that ship."

It took them several more hours, where they traveled by helicopter to another naval ship; then they were switched out to another helicopter aboard that ship and finally landed at a small port off the Norwegian coast, where they were thereafter put into the smaller ship and taken out to open waters. Brandon continued to find the experience amazing, whereas Amanda had gone quiet. She never argued or questioned. She just followed.

Kerrick was amazed at the amount of trust she had put in him. He mentioned it once, and she shrugged and said, "In for a penny, in for a pound apparently."

He squeezed her hand, realizing he kept physical contact with her the whole way, even at one point in time wrapping an arm around her shoulders and tucking her up close. Now they sat on a small bench behind a table in this last ship. "This is the final stop."

She nodded. "We've already slept and ate our way through this set of travels. What is it that you want us to do when we get to the research ship?"

"That'll be a little tricky. Chances are, you'll stay on this vessel."

"Why?" she asked in surprise.

He nodded at Brandon, who had crashed once again. "I don't want him there."

"So why bring us here at all?"

"Because we couldn't leave you behind," Griffin answered from the seat across from her. "We thought about leaving you with various people, but we didn't want to take the chance that it would be the wrong person."

She frowned and then gave a clipped nod. "That makes sense, so thank you for that. But I still think we should all get on the research ship together."

"Have you been on it before?"

"Yes," she said, "I have. For other conferences. As part of one of my degrees, I spent several weeks out on this particular ship."

"Good," Kerrick said. "What can you tell us about the layout?"

There followed a discussion of the different levels of the ship, the way the cabins were laid out, where the labs were, where the computer centers were, and where the pilot's center was. Kerrick was fascinated by the insights she provided. "This should be very helpful," he said.

She nodded. "I hope so."

Just as they finished up, the pilot called down and said, "We're two nautical miles away."

KERRICK HOPPED UP to take a look at the research ship up ahead. "And we're delivering for them, correct?"

The ship captain nodded. "A bunch of supplies they were supposed to take but were missed. So, good timing on your part."

And suddenly they arrived at the side of the ship. Immediately Kerrick went on board and became one of the two men helping to unload the parcels and the packages, the foodstuffs, and the computer gear. He helped carry everything up the ladder and onto the vessel. If these supplies had been loaded while the ship was still docked, heavy equipment would have been used.

But, while the ship was at sea, it all had to be hand lifted, some with the use of a winch. And as soon as he found the opportunity, Kerrick disappeared into the bowels of the research ship. He knew Griffin would take the same opportunity. He tapped his comm twice to let Griffin know he was safely on board. Kerrick knew the pilot would take his place to help unload.

He quickly moved to the far side of the research vessel, keeping to the blueprints he carried in his head, as he raced toward the engine room. He was doing a full sweep, checking to see how much security and what kind of manpower they had on board. After he cleared the bottom level and moved up, he found the sleeping cabins. Some were opened; some were closed, and some were locked. But, so far, he saw nothing suspicious.

It looked like a good fifty people or so were on board. There was a galley and a full kitchen, in which they had five or six kitchen and housekeeping staff. The vessel was not fully loaded as far as hired help. But then it was a research ship, not a cruise ship. Neither was it a private yacht.

He kept out of sight and, when he had an opportunity, snagged one of the uniform shirts from a supply closet and put it on over his regular clothes. It was a rough fit, but it would work. It would allow him to move a little more publicly. He kept going through floor after floor. Meanwhile, Griffin, after he cleared each floor, gave back a clear signal. Finally Kerrick stepped up on one of the upper levels where the big conference rooms were, with all the glass windows overlooking the water.

He heard voices in the background and a speaker. Part of the conference was ongoing. So far, he hadn't seen anything suspicious as to what the hell was going on and how this was connected. He went back down a level, which was just above water level and had open decks. He walked through, looking like he had a purpose. A few people worked behind the fully stocked bar. He headed for the more internal lab room.

Just then Griffin tapped his comm—but only once. Kerrick tapped back once and got the same answer—that meant to warn him something was off. He disappeared quickly down the hallway and headed for the labs. It was a big area that he had yet to check out. As he neared it, inside the lab, he could hear two men arguing.

"What the hell are you doing here?" one asked.

There was silence and then a hard smack.

In his heart, Kerrick wondered if Griffin had been caught.

Instead, a whiny voice answered, "You know I have a reason for being here."

"Nobody comes on board without our approval first," came the first voice and then an audible sneer. "And that doesn't include you."

"Hey, you know I'm valuable. I'm the one who gets you all the stuff you need," the whiny voice said.

Mr. Coleman, Kerrick guessed.

"Sure, and still you asked for more money and tried to blackmail us," the first voice snapped. "Research is important. We're trying to save the world. Remember?"

"Dr. Hinkleman, I'm trying to help you" came the whiny voice.

"And what about your son?"

Bingo. Mr. Coleman.

"What about him? I told you that he didn't matter."

"And yet, we had to hold him, to control him, when you couldn't."

"I know," his father said. "So let me be useful again. Let me help you fulfill some of these orders. You know you have these special requests. If you need to keep my son a bit longer, then keep him. Otherwise, send him home, so he is not your responsibility."

"Your son blackmailed us," the man snapped.

"He's a kid. He didn't know what he was doing."

Kerrick froze and wondered at that. Was it really possible that Brandon had blackmailed Hinkleman? *Absolutely.* Brandon was smart enough. And maybe he hadn't realized what the consequences could be, and maybe he was trying to help his dad or trying to get his dad to stop doing what he was doing. Is that really why Brandon had been kidnapped? It would be interesting to get Brandon's take on that. It's not like he'd proffered any of this information earlier. But Kerrick felt the boy got an unexpected education from the evil side of the real world this week. Poor kid.

"The kid's not important," his father said. "You need to let me help you guys. You know I have the ability to do more."

There was silence. The other man appeared to consider it. "I'll talk to a couple people," he said. "But the fact that your son was privy to such sensitive data and then blackmailed us makes us very leery about the security of your operation and your accounting system."

"He's just one of those genius kids," the father said. "Look. I'll take care of it."

"Meaning, you'll take care of Brandon?"

"If ... I ... have to," the whiny voice said. Now there was a sullenness to it.

"His brain would be interesting to study," the other man said.

Mr. Coleman sucked in a loud breath.

And then the other man laughed and said, "See? You

don't really intend on silencing your son."

"There's got to be another way without killing him," the father said. "I'll send him away so he never comes back again. He won't know anything now."

"Which is why we're keeping him," the same voice said with a snarl.

"Still doesn't change the fact I can get you what you need," he said.

"I said," the man screamed, "I'd think about it!"

Then shuffling sounds were heard, and suddenly the door to the lab room opened, and a man was shoved out into the hall. The door was slammed hard in his face. The man, a small one, a weasel with haunted eyes, caught sight of Kerrick and sneered. "What do you want?"

Kerrick crossed his arms over his chest and said, "I guess it depends if you wish to see Brandon alive or not anymore." He caught the flash of fear in Mr. Coleman's eyes and realized Brandon's father really did care.

"And with one call, you are done," the father snapped.

"Says the guy who sells body parts," Kerrick said slowly.

He nodded. "Yes, I do. But they're necessary for research, and, all over the world, medical research is important."

"But maybe you supply them a little too fresh, don't you?"

The weasel stiffened in front of him. "You don't know anything about it." And he stormed off down the hallway.

Kerrick wasn't sure if he should let Mr. Coleman go or not, but it had been an interesting conversation. It confirmed Brandon's father was alive, so that crispy critter in the morgue had the wrong name on his toe tag. It also confirmed that the father still cared about his son. What would he do if he knew that his son was close by?

Kerrick hoped the boat-for-hire had pulled off far enough away that Brandon and Amanda weren't being questioned. On that note, he turned the knob on the door beside him and pushed. It opened easily under his hand. He stepped inside to see somebody in a white lab coat sitting between a computer and several unknown specimens near a microscope. None were identifiable. Not to him anyway.

The man turned, looked at him, and glared. "Not just anybody is allowed in here. Get out."

"I have something you need."

"And what's that?" he sneered.

Your punishment. "And, of course, you have the one thing I want."

Confused, the man straightened and walked closer. The name on his white lab coat read Hinkleman.

Kerrick gave a feral grin. Exactly who he'd hoped to find.

"What is it that you want? Not that I give a shit."

"What is it? I have questions, and you should have answers. That's all that there is to know," Kerrick said as he reached behind him and locked the door.

The man studied him, saw the movement, and frowned. "I'll call security."

"Go ahead. But, before they get in here, you'll answer a few questions, like why you had your cohort Amanda Berg kidnapped and imprisoned."

"Oh, you overheard that conversation, didn't you?" He sneered. "Well, I don't expect you to be smart enough to understand, but she was a problem. We take care of our problems."

"And how many problems are you taking care of?"

"Who cares? People always want somebody to take care of problems. I just happened to be in a position where I had a problem of my own that I could take care of at the same time."

"So, do you kidnap all your victims for your research purposes?"

"God, no," he said. "Although a tempting proposition. But, if it ever got found out that we were using humans for live trials without approval and then killing them when our research fails and selling their body parts ..." He shuddered. "Just the paperwork alone is a disgusting thought."

Kerrick knew all this confessing by Hinkleman would be safeguarded by Kerrick's ultimate death on board this ship. *Not today, Doc.* Kerrick decided to take advantage of the doc's willingness to share by asking more questions. "So, what were you doing with Amanda? Would you kill her eventually or just keep her imprisoned for life?"

"Well, if her damn research had worked, I would have killed her," he said. "But the fact is, it doesn't work, so I need her."

"Too bad she escaped then, isn't it?"

At that, Hinkleman froze. "You shouldn't be here." He stared at him and asked, "Who are you?"

Kerrick smiled and said, "One of the men who helped rescue her." The words were barely out his mouth when he lunged for the doctor, his fingers going around his throat and the back of his neck. He hit a pressure point, and the doctor opened his mouth to scream, but only a half gasp came out, and he sank to his knees.

Kerrick kept up the pressure until the doctor fell face-forward to the hard floor, knocked out. Kerrick quickly took the lab coat off Hinkleman, tied him up with zip ties—he never left home without them—and dragged his captive around to the back of the labs. He found a closet that would barely hold him.

Then, with Hinkleman's lab jacket replacing the uniform shirt that he wore, Kerrick quickly went through the information sitting on the computers. He sent a message to Griffin and to his Mavericks cyberteam. He got a response back from the chat people that made him smile. But he had no time to deal with that.

He studied the monitors full of information. *Interesting.* Hinkleman had ledgers and correspondences opened. There were letters with Norway addresses. So Hinkleman was doing business there as well. Kerrick quickly downloaded the material and sent it off to the US government, the UK government, the French government, and the Norwegian government. Somebody needed to know what the hell had been going on. With all the computers up and running, and with information flowing as fast as the internet signal could carry it, he heard a sound outside in the hallway. He tapped his comm to see if it was Griffin, but Kerrick got no answer. He tapped again and got no answer. *Shit.*

Suddenly the door opened, and Griffin stumbled in, falling to his knees, where he was then kicked to the ground. The two men behind Griffin pointed their handguns at Kerrick. "You, get away from the computers."

Kerrick stood and slowly stepped to the side, acting like he belonged here. "Of course. What's the problem?"

And somebody else came from behind the two gunmen and shoved Brandon to the floor beside Griffin. Amanda was then pushed inside as well by a few more people—none of those armed as far as Kerrick could see.

More people filed in the room, pushing everyone else

forward. Looked like the conference-goers had gone vigilante.

She looked up at Kerrick, each walking slowly to the other, and smiled sadly. "It was the pilot from the ship."

He swore softly.

She nodded. "Everybody's into betrayal these days." The look on Amanda's face was pitiful. She whispered, "I'm sorry."

He gave a tiny shake of his head and reached out a hand. She placed her hand in his, and he yanked her beside him, just narrowly avoiding Amanda being knocked to the ground by one of the gunmen. "Wow, what a big man you are. Beating up a woman and a child."

The group of men standing in front of him just jeered. "We knew you were coming. You know that, right? We were ready for you."

"Hardly," he said calmly. "Is this the geek brigade? A bunch of desk jockeys with guns in their hands for the first time? Where is the real security team?" He glanced at the computers, all the screens showing signs that his transmissions were in progress but hadn't yet been completed. As he looked, so did they.

"What did you do?" The closest gunman, the one with the curly hair and glasses, raced to the computers and quickly tapped on its keys.

Kerrick just shrugged and said, "Figured your information needed to be shared with the world."

The gunman turned and belted Kerrick across the face.

His head snapped to the side, and he let his body turn in the same direction. As he flipped around, using the force of the blow to drive him along, he heaved a healthy right cross, making contact with the gunman's jaw. He must have had one of those weak jaws because he went down with a slump.

In an instant, more guns were raised in Kerrick's direction. He looked at the gunmen insolently and said, "Who'll sign your paychecks now?"

Frowning, a man in the back stepped forward. "You can't stop our paychecks."

"Good," he said, "more proof of what you've done. Because all the data found here on this ship, documenting all your illegal acts, is right now going out into the ether and spreading far and wide to various countries' governments, so they all know what you've been up to."

"*We're* not up to anything," the man in front sneered. "What do you know? You're a pirate trying to take over our ship."

Kerrick laughed. "Is that what you think we are? Is that what the *good* Dr. Hinkleman told you? Do you want to know what Hinkleman's really been up to? He's been kidnapping people and holding them prisoner, taking money from other people to make certain individuals disappear, who then become body parts, special-ordered organs." His gaze was hard and glassy.

The man in front frowned. "I don't know what you're talking about. We're here for a conference. If we had realized we would come up against pirates in this area, trying to steal our research, we would have brought in more security. But as it is ..."

"As it is, you have a lot of security—where is the real security detail, by the way?—considering this is deemed a medical or scientific conference," Kerrick said. "You can't be so naive as to think this company and the scientists here are do-gooders, can you?"

One of the men standing off to the side, another white-lab-coat wearer, protested, "We are do-gooders. We're trying to cure some of the deadliest diseases."

"Only with very unorthodox methods and purchased by blackmail money, right?"

He had the grace to look shamefaced. "I don't know what you're talking about with the body parts that are special ordered, but we had to raise additional money somehow. Hence the new facility."

"Where you kidnap people and keep them as prisoners?" Amanda cried out in shock, pointing to Brandon. "He was taken, and he's a ten-year-old boy."

At that, even more confusion crossed that speaker's face. He looked down at the boy and back up at her, then frowned. "Well, he wasn't a prisoner. And what do you mean by *prisoners*? These were people who needed special care. We had to develop a special sanitarium with very high-end solutions, and these people were very grateful."

"Absolutely. I know *I* was *very* grateful," Amanda said, almost screaming in frustration. "Don't you realize what's being done to those people? They're held in a comatose state. I know because I was held in that prison. I got a tray of shitty food full of drugs once a day, if I was lucky, with one flimsy blanket and nothing but a chamber pot and a floor. That's all we had for facilities and cleanliness! And this child endured the same treatment."

The man just stared at her in shock. "No, no, no. We created and built a very high-end sanitarium for people who have extraspecial problems and require extraspecial medical attention, where the families don't want anybody to know."

"Have you ever visited the facility? I suggest you do. And the families too would be interested in seeing that."

"You mean, the families pay you to keep these people

drugged out of their minds and away from their fortunes?" Kerrick asked.

The scientists all looked at him in shock.

"No."

"Not possible."

"Certainly not."

"Yes," Amanda snapped. "Just like you're stealing these people's lives, Hinkleman wanted my research to call his own."

"Your research?" Several of the scientists turned to look at her.

She nodded. "I'm Dr. Amanda Berg. I work at and am a major shareholder of Scion Labs, but, gee, I wasn't invited to this meeting, was I?"

"We heard you were dead."

"From Hinkleman, I suppose?" she growled. "I was kidnapped on the way from work. Thrown into the back of a lorry and drugged for a day so they could transport me from Paris to that London sanitarium and then inject me with a tracking device without my knowledge. When I woke up, I was a prisoner in a cold concrete cell with no windows and only a thin blanket on a rickety cot and a tray of drugged food once a day.

"Hinkleman visited me twice. He walked in and told me that my data was corrupt. He was so furious that he couldn't read my research notes that he smashed my face with his fist and walked off. I suspected that, after another day or two, he would have been chaining me to my computer chair to fix my data," she snapped. "Instead, I escaped and found this little boy in another prison cell and got him out of there too."

"Dr. Hinkleman said he had a breakthrough," one of the

men in the back shouted.

"Of course he did," Amanda said wearily. "He's that kind of guy, isn't he? Makes everybody else do all the work, and, when they find a breakthrough, he steals their work, takes the credit." She shook her head. "The animal trials were complete. I needed to move on to the human phase, but my results have been excellent."

"So, how do you explain that your data is corrupt?"

She gave him a half smile. "I often work in a partial shorthand style for my own use. It's faster, and I've been doing so much research that I know exactly what I'm talking about. But Hinkleman hadn't even looked at my research at that point. Until one of my coworkers told Hinkleman that my cure was working. So he had me kidnapped so he could steal my work, so he could be known as curing cancer. Yet he's too stupid to decipher my notes."

A hard rumble of conversations began before them.

"How many of you are a part of Hinkleman's research team? Here at this conference?" Kerrick asked the maybe one dozen men who crowded around the doorway or had stepped inside the room.

"Twenty-five of us are from Scion," one of the men said. "We came because we expected to hear an excellent announcement from the company."

She nodded. "Likely about the success of my cancer cure research."

"And some of us purchase items via Scion," said the other man who'd been horrified to hear about the prison firsthand. "I need a certain amount of pancreatic tissue for the type of work I'm doing, and I get that through the company."

"Of course you do," she said, "but you can also get it

from other companies. The boy's father is the one who supplies Scion with organs and tissue, and it can be a very dodgy business. We're hoping to determine if the body parts he's been dealing in are hand selected by someone *other* than the donor."

The men's faces expressed shock and dismay and absolute horror.

"And why can't you go through established biomedical companies?" Kerrick asked. "Many people donate their bodies to science. You could certainly get a tremendous amount of pancreatic tissue that way."

"But I needed it fresh," the man explained. "Within hours of curating it. And preferably not preserved with the chemicals that are usually administered."

"So, when Hinkleman gets one, is it airlifted to you?"

He nodded. "Absolutely."

"And how many do you order?"

He shrugged. "A couple a week maybe?"

She nodded again. "It'd be interesting to see where they came from. Don't you agree?"

His face paled. "I sure hope you're not implying that he killed people to bring me pancreatic tissue," he said, his voice faint. "That goes against everything I believe in."

Kerrick spoke up. "All we need is a tissue sample from all your Scion purchases, and a DNA match can be run. I'm guessing all your donors have been murdered."

A collective round of gasps could be heard about the room.

"And you each paid Scion Labs to attend this conference?" Kerrick continued.

"Yes, we all do. Even the employees at Scion, I understand, pay a conference fee as usual," the pancreatic customer stated. "Scion Labs puts it on every year, but this year they said they had some great announcements for customers and employees alike, so we should all attend. Plus, they had new supply lines of various products that are needed by us and others. And we can only get through the company."

"Such as the pancreatic tissue?" Kerrick asked.

He and several other men nodded.

"I need adrenal glands," one said. "And that's just part of it. We need fresh tissue samples in order to accurately determine the effects of our testing."

"You don't know what it's like trying to get the permissions to do human trials," one of the men said. "The red tape is notorious. And we're all applying, but, in the meantime, we're working on a limited amount of testing material."

"So you've expanded into working on human volunteers? People who are past the point of being cured, so that you have some test data?" Kerrick asked.

He shrugged.

"Willing volunteers who have nothing to lose and have lost all hope otherwise? But the sample size is still too small, right?" Kerrick asked.

"What most of you need to understand, both employees and customers, is that the Scion Labs itself has become diseased," Amanda said. "Yes, I'm a majority shareholder, but Hinkleman, who is the chairman of the board, has been leading Scion Labs down an ugly path."

"It still doesn't explain why all these people have been kidnapped and imprisoned, and yet, haven't been killed and harvested for body parts already," Griffin said, straightening up in front of her.

"I think it's for blackmail money, another source of steady income to add to the funds collected through the fake sanitorium project," she said. "I think it's pure and simple all about money, power, and greed. Because someone has to fund all this research. You who are customers of Scion all have received grant monies from the company, didn't you? That's why, when they called, you jumped?"

At once, many of the men looked around to the group and then said, "Yes. That's exactly right."

Amanda nodded. "I presume an audit of the company will find that an accurate accounting will not cover all the grants given out to customers, like those gathered here today. Hinkleman was working many angles here, even both sides against the middle—like kidnapping people for blackmail money, to hand out as grants to customers, who then buy body parts from Hinkleman, which he freshly provides from people he's murdered, all while charging you to attend conferences such as this one. I believe Hinkleman may even be surgically removing the organs at the sanitarium where I was jailed. We will set out to prove that as well."

The sounds coming from their audience grew louder.

Amanda turned to Kerrick. "Where is Hinkleman?"

"He's got a bit of a headache," Kerrick said with a grin.

"Can he answer questions?"

"Maybe," he said to Amanda, "but we need to make sure we have everybody rounded up, so nobody is left to cause trouble when we aren't looking." Turning to the crowd, he asked, "Where is the real security team?"

"And sharing all we know with all gathered here today," Amanda said.

Kerrick grinned. *Inciting a riot ... directed at Hinkleman.* He liked how this woman thought.

Several gunshots were fired into the air behind the collection of men gathered in the lab. Several cries of alarm followed as everyone turned to face a new threat. Brandon clutched Griffin's waist and stood behind him, while Amanda was tight against Kerrick, his arm wrapped around her shoulders.

She whispered, "You were right. I should have figured Hinkleman had more security around here somewhere."

Kerrick glanced around, moving her farther behind him. A large refrigerator-freezer cooler was off to the side, to hold working samples, Kerrick imagined. He glanced at it, wondering if she could be safe from gunfire inside it.

She firmly shook her head and said, "Not a chance." However, a letter opener was off to the side of a nearby table. She quickly grabbed it and slipped it up her sleeve.

He grinned. He admired her quick wit. Although he had two weapons on him, it wasn't the right time to show his hand. He needed a distraction first. Seems Amanda was preparing for that.

As the scientists were urged to crowd in closer, four more gunmen stepped forward, their faces grim as they surveyed the group.

"We were hoping to not have to do this," one of the men said.

"Head of security, I presume?" Kerrick asked.

He shrugged. "And a shareholder in the company."

"If I had kept my mouth shut," Amanda said cheerfully, "you wouldn't be in the position of having to kill all these scientists and researchers now, would you?"

He glared at her. But the gasps from the people around them rose in horror.

"There's no need to kill anybody," another security guard said in a soothing tone. "Nobody here will talk. They're all involved."

At that, there was a dead silence. Yes, the scientists, the researchers, the customers, the employees would all soon realize just how much their *involvement* now meant.

CHAPTER 16

AMANDA WATCHED AS the group was quickly separated. Scientists, Kerrick, Griffin, Brandon and herself were off to the other side. She hoped that Hinkleman's security team would at least let a child live. But she wasn't so sure. She heard a pounding on the door behind her. She glanced over when the head security gunman motioned at one of his men to open the door.

Hinkleman struggled to get out, blood flowing from an injury to his temple. He tried to remain steady on his feet, but he was clearly woozy. "Shoot them," he screamed uncontrollably. "Shoot them dead." He spun toward the head of security. "Drayden, you promised me that you'd take care of everyone. Shoot them, damn it."

Drayden? Something was familiar about the large man's bearded face. She frowned. "Were you the one who kidnapped me off the street?"

He sneered at her. "No."

"Are you sure?" she insisted. "You look very familiar."

"It wasn't him," Hinkleman cried out, almost dancing in place. "It was his brother, Haron. He worked on your father's secret security detail." And he laughed as though crazed. "You were so easy."

Shocked, she had the puzzle pieces falling in place now. "No wonder we never could get in touch with Father's security detail to figure out why they lost track of me. Because they were silenced or were part of my kidnapping," she cried out in outrage.

Just then another man stepped forward, who she hadn't seen yet in the background. His features were immediately recognizable. "Haron, I presume?"

He grinned. "Absolutely."

"Why?" She shook her head, dazed. "Why would you be a part of this?"

"For the oldest reason in the world," he said in a smug tone. "Money."

"And my ex? Is he a part of this?"

An odd light lit up Haron's gaze as he glanced over at Hinkleman. "That was Father's idea."

Father? Stunned, she spun to Hinkleman. The shocks just wouldn't quit. "You had your sons kidnap me?" she asked him, but little sanity remained in that gaze. She pivoted back to Haron. "What role did my ex play in my imprisonment?"

He laughed. "Not much but the one meal and one bottle of water a day was his request …"

"That slimy little bastard! It's been five years. What's his beef with me now?"

"Something about how that's all you left him with—enough money for one meal a day."

"But he won't get even that now, will he?" Kerrick asked shrewdly, an arm tucked around Amanda. She curled in closer.

The smile disappeared from Haron's face. "What do you know about it?"

"Well, if you took out the three delivery guys from the Dover side of the ferry, I highly doubt you planned to leave

Amanda's ex-husband alive to talk either. Once you charged him as much money as you could get from him—and it wouldn't have been much, I imagine—then you took him out."

"It's none of your business," Drayden said. "That's enough talking."

"Not quite," Amanda snapped, turning to Hinkleman. "What about those other people you imprisoned? What were you doing with them?"

Hinkleman glared at her at first. Yet, when he finally spoke, his tone was placating, as if talking to a child. "I can hardly let them go, can I? They are a great source of income, month after month after month. Rich people will pay an incredible amount of money to remove a *problem*."

"Like Cynthia and Peter?" Brandon shouted. "They didn't want to be there any more than I did."

"Kids *may* be seen but *not* heard," Drayden snapped.

"It's all right, Brandon," Kerrick said. "A full sweep was carried out, and they've been found. They are in a proper hospital, getting treated even now."

Amanda looked at Kerrick, catching his smile, and felt her heart lighten as he explained, "I only heard a few minutes ago. I just hadn't had a chance to tell you."

"Well, I'm glad to hear that."

"It doesn't matter," Hinkleman snapped. "We'll start again."

"Not from prison, you won't," Amanda stated.

He stopped, stared at her, and said, "You can't stop me. Besides, how did you get here?"

"They were in the boat that came with the supplies," the head of security said. "We told you when we left port that nothing else was to get on board exactly because of shit like this happening." He motioned in disgust at Kerrick and Griffin.

Hinkleman saw Kerrick and pointed a finger at him. "That man attacked me," he roared. "Shoot him right now."

Seeing the confused yet horrified looks on all the scientists' faces as they witnessed this unfolding drama meant more and more of them were now Team Amanda, abandoning Team Hinkleman like a sinking ship. Kerrick grinned at Hinkleman. "What's the matter, Doc? Everybody now knows that you're behind all this nastiness. That you're getting paid by families to keep certain relatives, who they don't want to deal with, in a drugged-out state in a fake sanitarium that is really a jail cell. That you're keeping a little boy prisoner so his father continues to remain silent and will still provide all those lovely special-order body parts that you want at low prices and at speedy time frames.

"But here's some further bad news for you. I only heard about it five minutes after I stepped inside this lab. Did you know that the rest of the board wants to remove you as the chairman? That they want to open a full and complete investigation into your dealings?"

Spittle formed at the doctor's lips. His face turned bloodred, and his hands were fisted and shaking with rage. He turned to the head of security and reached for his rifle, but the gunman lifted it up and out of his way. "No killing, Dad. That's up to us."

"You kill him right now!" Hinkleman screamed, his voice dead hard, his eyes wild. "I don't want to see that man take one more step."

Kerrick smiled, took two steps toward Hinkleman, and watched him back away, his eyes wide and afraid.

"Is what he said true, Hinkleman?" asked one of the scientists. "Did you get us all involved in something so despicable?"

Hinkleman stood up straight, gathering his courage again maybe. "You had no problems getting involved. All you cared about was getting your grant money. Well, we gave you the grant money," he sneered. "So, you owe us, and *we own you*."

Then he turned, stared at his son, the head of security, and pointed at Kerrick, saying, "And I trust that that man does not get off this boat alive."

As Hinkleman took several steps past the head of security, Amanda called out, "If he doesn't get out alive, I'll publish my research under my own name while you rot in jail—that is, if you make it off this ship alive."

Hinkleman turned, stared at her with an ugly twisted expression, and said, "What is he, your lover? I'm sure these gunmen will take care of you, so you won't need him further. That's all you're good for anyway. Goddamn females."

Amanda laughed, making him angrier. "What you really mean is, isn't it too bad that a *woman* found the cancer cure, which you've been looking for after all these decades. You didn't even have the brainpower to figure out my research notes." Her tone bordered on insolence, hoping to push him over the edge. She'd seen it happen once before, and it was a scary sight. But she needed him to lose it right now because it was the diversion they needed.

"You're old. Washed-up," she taunted. "Never did have the brains for this. Just another strutting rooster. *Useless.*" Then she added the coup de grâce. "No wonder the board wants to get rid of you."

He stared at her as a scream of pure rage let loose from

his mouth. "Shut up! Shut up!" Spittle flew from his mouth as he backed up a step, his head shaking, as if incapable of seeing anything but her.

Definitely, he did not see reason.

"No, Dad, stop!"

But he was beyond hearing anyone.

He screamed a second time, but this was a cry of that evil rage from deep inside him as he raced toward her. "Bitch! Stupid cunt! You don't know anything!"

Drayden tried to grab his father to hold him back, but Hinkleman launched himself into the air, his fingers out like claws.

Amanda stepped to the side as he stumbled to the ground. Then she kicked him as hard as she could in the temple. He didn't move. She turned and looked at the curly-haired gunman, still pointing his weapon at her, and asked, "Really? Even now, hearing all we've said, this is the kind of man you choose to work for?"

Curly shrugged. "A paycheck's a paycheck."

"So nobody in your family has died of cancer or lost a breast because of breast cancer?" she asked gently. Curly stiffened. Her gaze zeroed in on him. She nodded. "That's the research I'm doing. I've turned a corner on perfecting my cure, and this guy wanted to steal it from me. He's the true pirate here. And yet, he can't even read my notes. He's not smart enough to do the science. Is that what you want to stand for?"

He stared at her, trying not to reveal his thoughts.

Then Drayden, Hinkelman's son and the head of security, said, "It doesn't matter if anybody in his family has cancer or not. They'll probably be dead before your medicine gets out there."

"Maybe," she said. "I mean, after all, Hinkleman kept me as a prisoner for days, with barely enough food to stay alive and only one bottle of water a day. Hard for me to work on a cure in that condition."

More of the gunmen frowned, and she nodded. "Yeah, didn't you know that was the evil you were working for? That people like me, the brains in this world, are being drugged, yet who were trying to find answers, but who stood in Hinkleman's way of getting his name declared as the one who found the cure for cancer or the next big breakthrough. Then there's the boy, ... and those of us who didn't even know that we were crossing a line, and yet, we got thrown in Hinkleman's fake sanitorium, which is nothing but a prison."

"I don't know anything about kids," Curly said defiantly.

"Well, you're hearing about it right now," she said. "Hinkleman had his goons kidnap Brandon here," she motioned to where he stood watching the scenario intently, "a ten-year-old boy and locked him up all alone in a cell with little food and water and a chamber pot and a cot with one threadbare blanket *for nine days.* Just like they did to me, but I only had to endure a couple days in his jail. You know why? Fear is a great carrot to force people to do something they wouldn't want to do. I can't even imagine how many other people they've done this to before killing them.

"Of course some misguided family members or plain evil people are paying Hinkleman to hide away problem family members, while some people Hinkleman has targeted to be kidnapped simply because their family is rich or because Hinkleman wants fresher body parts."

She sauntered closer to where the good doctor lay unconscious on the floor and gave him a shove with her foot. "If you've got a spare bullet, you should put it in his head. He's the lunatic mastermind behind all this shit. Just what the world needs. Another guy who takes money to lock up innocent people and then to throw away the key. Who has people killed for money. Who has people kidnapped when his supply of illegal body parts runs low."

She reached down, but the gunman said, "Don't touch him."

She straightened and looked at Curly. "Or what?"

He immediately lowered the rifle and pointed it at her chest.

She smiled and walked right up to the rifle until it touched her. "Then pull the trigger, and you can kiss that cancer cure goodbye."

Curly stared at her, his gaze hard. "My mother," he said, "she died of breast cancer."

"And she probably carried the gene too," she said gently. "I'm sorry for that, but, if any other females were born into your family, they're in trouble too."

He swallowed and jerked his head. "My daughter."

"I can't help her in here," she said. "I can't guarantee to cure her, but we're getting incredible results now. That's why Hinkleman put all this together and locked me up, so that he could steal my research and be the king of the cancer cure."

Curly stared at her, undecided.

She shrugged. "Your choice." Then she turned and walked over to Drayden. "So now what? This is your game now that the doctor, your nutty father, is out of commission. It's all about you and your brother now." She couldn't believe all the people who had lost their lives for their mistake in becoming involved with this group. And for what? Just money? That seems to be all Jimmy, Stanley, and Tom got out of it.

Drayden sneered. "He's my father, not my boss, you know? We were willing to work with him when the money was flowing, but he's always been difficult. Now ..." He shrugged.

She smiled and nodded. "Good thing because now you'll have to figure out exactly what you'll do with all of us. I presume about fifty people are on board this ship, counting everybody, whether working or drinking or sleeping?"

He nodded.

"It'll look very suspicious when everybody aboard this one ship shows up dead or missing."

"I'm just here for security purposes, to keep everybody in line and to make sure it's going well. This was our father's show."

"So, are you letting us go or not?"

In response, he lifted the rifle and pointed at her. "Not."

"Okay," she said in that determined voice of hers. She turned her back on him.

BALLSY MOVE, THOUGHT Kerrick. *Might be time for some gunplay.*

When she looked at Kerrick, she held up three fingers against her shirt, then immediately put one down.

He raised his eyebrows.

When she put down another finger, he sent a subtle hand signal to Griffin.

When her final finger was lowered, three people moved in concert: her, Kerrick, and Griffin.

All found their targets.

She stepped to the side of her gunman, pivoted, pulled the letter opener from her sleeve, and stabbed Drayden in the throat. Haran cried out as his brother collapsed.

Meanwhile Griffin took out one of the two civilian gunmen with one chop to the throat, while Kerrick did the same to Curly.

And, just like that, Amanda held a machine gun herself, facing off the rest of the real security team, as did Kerrick and Griffin, but from behind.

She coolly took stock of the other gunmen and asked, "So, what'll it be? A bloodbath or will you lay down your weapons?"

The three remaining security officers, looking down the steady aim of her machine gun, turned just enough to see Kerrick and Griffin behind them. Armed too. They all stared at her in shock, slowly lowering their weapons to the floor.

Kerrick looked at her over the security team caught in the middle and said, "What the hell …?"

"My father taught me to stand up to bullies." She smiled. "You're welcome."

"If you ever pull a stunt like that again …" he snarled, but then he and Griffin knocked out the last of the gunmen. Kerrick stood, hands on hips, shaking his head, his stare locked on Amanda.

She walked up, kissed Kerrick gently on the lips, and said, "Or what?"

A high-pitched giggle came from behind the group of scientists who'd been holding Brandon back during the chaos. Released Brandon raced toward them and launched himself in the air. She held out her weapon to Kerrick, who snagged it from her hand. Then, she grabbed Brandon, picked him up, swinging him around.

He held on tight. Just then another voice cried out, "Not so fast."

She turned to see a scrawny old man in the doorway, tentatively holding a gun. "Not again …"

Brandon looked at him and cried out, "Dad!" He ripped himself free of Amanda's arms and raced over to the man.

The man stared as his son raced toward him, shock on his face. "Brandon?" He threw down his weapon, opened his arms, and crushed Brandon tightly against his chest.

It brought tears to Amanda's eyes to see how well-loved Brandon truly was.

His father had tears dripping down his face as he raised his head from embracing Brandon to look at her. "I don't know what the hell happened," he said, "but thank you for bringing my son here."

"You're welcome," she said with a smile.

Kerrick spoke up, saying, "She rescued him from Hinkleman's prison."

The older man, his throat working hard as he held his boy tightly, nodded and said, "And I'm damn glad to see him. Even after kidnapping my boy, then setting fire to our home, to my place of work, I did everything I could—from groveling to blackmail to get my son back—but they weren't having anything to do with it."

"That's because I'm special," Brandon said, pulling back and looking up at his father. "But she's special too."

His father looked over at her and said, "Special?"

Brandon smiled. "She's just like me."

Brandon's father reached out a hand and said, "My name is Willie, and you have my ever-grateful thanks."

She eagerly shook his hand. "You're welcome. He talked

to me in Morse code," she said with a big smile. "Not sure how many people in the world can do that."

"He's been talking in Morse code since he was a toddler," Willie said. "The fact that you even understood him is a miracle."

She turned and introduced Kerrick and Griffin. "And these are the men who rescued both of us."

"We obviously have a lot of answers and information to share with each other," Willie said to Amanda. "Why don't we all gather in the boardroom?

"Griffin and I'll get these guys secured and stowed away, and we'll join you."

"That works for me," she said, watching Kerrick, who already had four of the six gunmen tied up and secured. She smiled at the others gathered in the lab and asked, "Shall we discuss science, or shall we discuss the future of the company, or shall we discuss both?"

"How many shares do you hold in the company?" asked one of them.

"I'm a thirty percent shareholder," she said gently. "There could be a corporate takeover happening after this fallout settles."

A lot of nods and murmurs of agreement followed as Willie ushered everyone else from the room, staying behind with Kerrick, Griffin, Brandon, and Amanda.

Kerrick laughed. "I can see you doing that too. Are you sure you want to run a boardroom?"

She gave him a horrified look. "Hell no. Absolutely no way. But I'd love to get back to my lab. Somebody else gets to run the company, not me." She looked over at him with a cheesy smile on her lips. "Come on. How about you?"

"The only weapons I like in my hand," he said, "are rifles. Or handguns. But never a pen."

"I'm not so sure about that," she said. "I did some research on my own, and you've got an MBA in business." She didn't mention the loss of his wife and daughter. They had time to discuss that in the years to come.

He shrugged. "Still don't like a boardroom. I'll take a shoot-out any day."

"We'll see," she said with a smile. "As long as you stay close, I don't mind."

"But what if somebody else needs my help way across the world?"

She nodded. "Then you go. But you have to promise me that you'll always come back."

He gave her a special smile and whispered, "I can make that happen."

Brandon followed the exchange like a tennis game, then turned to look at Amanda, then at Kerrick, and back at Amanda. His gaze landed on Griffin, and he said, "See? I told you."

Griffin laughed. "You did, indeed."

Brandon held out his hand. "You owe me."

Griffin pulled his wallet from his pocket, selected a five-dollar bill, and said, "You will make a great con man someday."

"No con about it," he said as he tucked his winnings in his pocket. "You just gotta have the smarts." He tapped his head and smiled, turning back to his dad. "I told you that you should get rid of these guys."

His father nodded. "Well, maybe now that we have a new major shareholder in the company to deal with, we can make some big changes."

And, with that, they all trooped to the boardroom.

But Kerrick grabbed Amanda by the hand and pulled her back. She spun so fast that she found herself in his arms, pressed against his chest. He looked down at her and whispered, "Meaning?"

She looked up at him, her eyes soft and gentle. "You've been in the cold for so long, I think it's time that you found a way home."

"And where's home?" His tone was brisk, but she could see the vulnerability in his eyes.

She grabbed his hand and placed it over her breast. "Home is here. In my heart." She nodded gently and whispered, "I knew as soon as I met you. That's the problem with being smart. Sometimes I know things before others do."

A slow smile stretched across his lips as something dawned in his eyes. He whispered, "No. I knew as soon as I saw your photo." He gently tapped her lips. "I was hooked." He leaned over and kissed her gently, once, twice, and then she wrapped her arms around him and kissed him hungrily.

She whispered, "I'll admit defeat as long as you stay with me."

"Forever?"

"Forever," she affirmed, reaching up and kissing him again, their bodies locked together, heart, mind, and soul. It wasn't just him who had come in from the cold. So had she.

GRIFFIN

The Mavericks, Book 2

Dale Mayer

CHAPTER 1

GRIFFIN TOMAS WOKE to an odd buzzing on his night table. He glanced at the clock—2:03 a.m.—then around at his surroundings. Still in the same hotel room stateside that he had been living out of for the last week. Like Kerrick, Griffin was at a crossroads. He needed a real home but had no idea where it should be. If he continued to work with the Mavericks, he could live any damn place. They'd fly him to his op. He had some ideas but ...

His phone's insistent buzz brought him to full awareness. He grabbed it and frowned. "What?"

"Your services are needed," said the stoic voice on the other end.

"Again? So soon?"

"What can I say? The world's a mess," the voice said.

"Not sure if I want to do any more of these specialized jobs," he said quietly.

"Understood, but you have a unique skill set."

"And what's that?"

The other end went quiet.

Griffin wiped the sleep from his eyes. "Am I going in alone?"

"You can choose one. You'll have all the support you need in the background as usual. And, if you need more backup, you only have to ask."

"What about Kerrick?"

The voice hesitated. "How about Asher or Jax?"

"Jax? Jax Darrum?"

"Yes."

"I didn't realize he was part of the team."

"We're considering it."

Griffin laughed. "Meaning, he hasn't said yes, and you're hoping that, if you can get me to work a job with him, it'll be a yes."

"Potentially." That voice held a dry sense of humor. "Kerrick is around, so he'll run communications on this one."

"You mean, that mysterious chat window?"

A slightly muffled cough could have easily been a chuckle when the voice said, "And maybe a little more."

Griffin frowned. "What's the job?"

"You're heading out in the USS *Anzio*."

"Wait," Griffin said. "I'm not going anywhere until I hear what the job is."

A loud sigh traveled between the phones. "The daughter of a US newspaper mogul with a home base in London has been kidnapped in Thailand and is being held there. The father has got pull in high places and is dealing with us and MI6."

"And what's stopping the military from going in and grabbing her?"

"We only have one garbled message, saying that she's married now and that she belongs with them."

"And what does she say?" he asked, frowning. "Since when did a marriage keep somebody prisoner?"

"In many countries, it does keep them a prisoner, which is why she couldn't get the word out to us that she's being held."

"How long has she been detained?"

"Three days."

At that, Griffin straightened up in bed and threw off his blanket. "Three days? And you knew about it all this time?"

"No, we only got intel that this was a possible kidnapping at midnight. We've been waiting to get confirmation."

"Well, I have to get there fast then," he said. "That's not any two-hour trip."

"True," the voice said. "We can fly you partway, but we don't want you entering the country using any of the normal methods. You're too well-known."

He swore. "So my face isn't to be anywhere?"

"No, hence the ship entering and leaving any country."

"Sure, but going from California to Southeast Asia? That's hardly a twenty-four-hour event."

"True enough. But, as you'll see, we have multiple methods. Be by the docks at 0600 sharp."

And, just like that, the voice rang off. Swearing silently, Griffin had less than four hours. He got up, quickly packed, then showered and dressed. He would need food, depending on what was going on with his transportation. He stared at the Chinese food he'd had last night and shrugged. "Cold Chinese food. Yum. I've had worse." He used food as sustenance and an energy source, hence keeping a selection of protein bars in his ready bag.

But still it wouldn't be enough. Depending on what was happening on board ship—and whether he was there officially or secretly—he might or might not be fed. He quickly finished off the chow mein, tossed the empty containers, and exited his hotel room.

He had called for a cab, but instead a black military-issued vehicle pulled up. He stepped into the passenger side and looked at the driver, surprised to see Jax. "Wow," Griffin said. "They did convince you after all. That was fast."

Jax shot him a hard look. "A one-time deal," he said. "And only because I know you're the one going out on this op."

"Not alone if you're coming with me," Griffin said, returning his friend's hard look with one of his own. He knew Jax from several overseas missions. He was a good man to have in your corner but an even better one if it entailed night work. "Apparently we're supposed to get in and out without anyone knowing we were there."

Jax shrugged his shoulders. "So what else is new?"

They parked as close to the wharf as they could. Each picked up their duffel bags and tossed it over one shoulder. Then the two men walked to the end of the docks. A Zodiac waited for them. The pilot caught sight of them, nodded toward the back, and said, "Let's go. We're late."

Shrugging at that, both men hopped into the Zodiac, and it took off without any fanfare. By the time they reached the docked cruiser, they were led to a separate room, a small sleeping area, by one silent seaman who promptly left them there. With shades of Kerrick's mission in his mind, Griffin walked in the claustrophobic room, dumped his duffel bag, and planted his hands on his hips as he stared around. "Do you know anything more about this than I do?"

"I know Jax shit," Jax said with a grin at the play on his name.

"Well, I don't know anything either," Griffin said, his tone harsh.

Just then a single rap came at the door, and a red envelope was slid underneath. Griffin quickly opened the door, hoping to see who had delivered the letter, but nobody was in the hallway. Like this was some ghost ship. He snatched up the envelope and tore it open. *Travel instructions.*

"Interesting," he said. "We're supposed to be in Thailand by noon tomorrow. *Thailand time.*"

"So we're flying parts of it then," Jax said.

"Yeah, but I already checked. Any commercial flight takes nineteen to twenty-five hours. We better be flying Air Force One to make Thailand by then. Right off the bat, we're short like fourteen hours, just because of the time differences. Could be more like fifteen hours ahead, depending on which part of Thailand we're dealing with."

Jax groaned, then threw himself on the top bunk. "In that case, … I have time to sleep now. I didn't get much shut-eye last night."

"Who did?" Griffin muttered. Trouble was, he was hungry again. The leftover Chinese food hadn't done the job. He quickly pulled out his phone to check if he had any internet. He did, since they were still in port. He sent off a text message. **Envelope received. Travel instructions received. No damn food. No coffee.**

He put away his phone and dropped to the bottom bunk, an arm across his eyes. It was one thing to be part of a well-oiled Navy SEAL team on board a ship. They did constant training when they went out to sea. Everybody had orders; everybody had instructions, and everybody had a part to play. In this scenario though, Griffin didn't know what part he was supposed to play. That had been the same problem for Kerrick. After all those years of the disciplined navy life, Griffin found the sudden freedom in his daily routines something to adjust to. But he'd do just fine, he just needed time. Something he didn't have right now.

Helping out Kerrick had been a hell of a way to drop into this all-new Mavericks system. Griffin wasn't even sure it's what he wanted to do long-term. He'd been on the fence when he'd been tagged to help out Kerrick—who was going in alone—and, well, that wasn't Griffin's kind of a play. Nobody should go into these shitstorms without backup.

And, if some woman had been kidnapped, ... well, two former SEALs would have a better chance of survival and success versus a larger team from another agency. His phone buzzed, and an encrypted file popped up with a note. His eyebrows shot up at that. He quickly followed instructions to decode it and went through the file on Amelia Rose.

"That's the daughter we're supposed to find," he said, raising his phone to flash her picture to Jax. "Except the photo's beyond dated. And chances are someone else put out the cry for help."

"Is she really being held against her will?" Jax asked. "That's one of the biggest issues here. Did she put out the cry for help, or did somebody else?"

Griffin was still going through her file when he froze, looked at the date, and swore. "I'll say it wasn't her choice," Griffin snapped, studying the data in front of him.

"And how do you know that?" Jax asked.

"She's eleven years old."

Jax peered over his top bunk at Griffin on the bottom bunk and said, "What the hell?"

Griffin nodded with a grimace. "She's just a child. It says here she was kidnapped, along with her nurse and her tutor."

"And how old's the nurse? If she's gray-haired and sixty, we're in trouble."

"The nurse is sixty-eight. So, yeah, we're in trouble. The tutor, however, is thirty-two and speaks three languages. Her name is Lorelei. Lorelei James."

"So Lorelei got the word out?" Jax asked curiously.

"Most likely," he said. "But, as usual, our intel is very skimpy."

"It seems like we go into these jobs with less and less intel each time," Jax said. He waited a moment and then said, "I heard a few details about your job with Kerrick, but it went okay, didn't it?"

Griffin groaned. "It did, but it was touch-and-go a couple times. That kid, Brandon, he was something else."

"Didn't Kerrick say something about the woman he rescued being part of the same high-IQ group?"

"Yes, she's back in her lab. The entire corporate organization has been reshuffled as she stepped up in power after all the changes. Her father had also stepped up and bought a whole pile of shares and handed over voting power to her to give her complete control of the company."

"Wow," Jax said. "Not bad for her. And I guess Kerrick is sticking around Paris."

"Yeah, and he's running communications for us this time."

"What the hell does that mean?" Jax asked.

"I think it's the Mavericks command center. Nobody is allowed to know what we do, where we're from, or what our histories are."

"So, are fake IDs in that envelope for us?"

"Maybe," he said, "but I didn't think so." He grabbed the red envelope, opened it again, and then whistled gently. "Well, there are now. They were stuck to the inside of the envelope." He quickly ripped off the tape, releasing the IDs. He handed one to Jax. "This is you, *Malcolm*."

"Whoever invented these names," Jax said, "should be

shot."

"Hey, it's way more normal than your real one," Griffin said with a laugh.

"You're one to talk," Jax said. "Who names their kid after some legendary creature in Greek mythology?"

"I think Griffins are found in many different societies back then," he said. "So, whatever. It's unusual enough, but I've always liked it."

"I like mine too. But can't say much about *Malcolm*. Malcolm Harris."

"Well, that's all right in my opinion," Griffin said, groaning. "I've been renamed as *George*. George Honeycutt."

At that, Jax chuckled. "That sounds lovely."

"It makes me sound beyond old. It's supposedly an unassuming name," he said. "At least this guy has brown hair and gray eyes. Close enough to pass for me." This time he checked the inside of the envelope more thoroughly—to the point where he ripped it open. "Okay, I don't see anything else in here. But this is a journalist's media pass, and, if you look on the back, it's got a British citizen's ID card."

"As if we look like Brits," Jax said with a scoff. "And I certainly don't have an English accent."

"I don't think you need to worry about that," he said. "I think it's a case of nobody gets to look at these close enough to double-check."

Just then another single knock came. Both men hopped up, with Jax standing behind the door. Griffin hurriedly opened the door, hoping to surprise whoever was on the other side. But, once again, he saw no one. There were, however, two large trays of covered food. He looked at it and smiled. "Well, at least my text did something."

"What? Did you text, asking for food?" Jax asked, chuckling.

"Hey, if we've got a lot of traveling to do, I want to make sure I'm fed. I cannot do anything if I don't have energy."

"Oh, I agree with you. I'm just surprised you got service so fast."

"One thing I learned from that last op with Kerrick," he said, "is that anything, *absolutely anything you want*, you just ask for it. They do their best to deliver."

"Good to know." They brought the trays inside, sat down, and stared at the covered dishes. "It's still cafeteria food though, isn't it, just under a fancy domed plate?" Jax asked.

Griffin uncovered his. "But a step above," he said. "I don't know about you, but I got steak and prawns."

Jax looked at Griffin's plate in shock and said, "Seriously?" And then he lifted the lid to his plate and said, "Look at that. I do too."

"But you don't like prawns, do you?"

"No. I'll trade you for your steak."

"Hell no," Griffin said. "I'll just eat your prawns when you're done with your steak. I know you won't eat them, so I don't have to give you anything." He gave Jax a big grin. "Good deal for me."

With that, the two men quickly polished off their meals, and then, even though it was early in the morning, they stretched out, and this time both crashed.

LORELEI JAMES SAT quietly in the corner of the room. Amelia Rose was sound asleep in her arms. Finally the little girl's tears—loaded with homesickness, loss, and grief—had dried, then had sent her crashing into a deep and restorative sleep. Lorelei, still conscious, still awake, still dealt with the terror of what these bastards had done to Nurse. Lorelei had long ago forgotten the older woman's real name as everyone called her *Nurse*. It's how she wanted it.

Why had she been killed outright? And yet, Lorelei and Amelia Rose had been also kidnapped and kept alive. In Lorelei's mind, she figured that their kidnappers had deemed Lorelei an asset whereas Nurse had been a liability. Nurse was definitely older, walked with a heavy limp, and was cantankerous and fussy, whereas Lorelei had done what they'd asked and had tried hard to be obedient. She knew in no way they would ever get out of this nightmare if she caused any more trouble. Nurse's death had been a well-heeded lesson—if that's what the kidnappers had intended.

But poor Nurse—no, Mary. That was her name. She had been with Amelia Rose since birth. And Lorelei believed Mary had been nurse to Amelia Rose's father too.

Gerard, Amelia Rose's father, would be devastated. She couldn't help but think this nightmare was due to his massive global business dealings. His media company had morphed into a worldwide media and information services company, distributing content, including book publishing, digital RE services, cable network programming, and pay-TV. Yet even though he ran his massive conglomerate from his base in England, the transplanted New Englander was, at heart, first and foremost, a family man. Nurse had sat at the dinner table with them every night.

It was very American of the entire family, but Nurse had loved it. So did Lorelei. She loved the continuity of the generations, and she loved the loyalty and affection shared between one another. Only it had suddenly shifted and not in a good way. Amelia Rose was desperately struggling to come to terms with their new reality. Lorelei could only hope the message she had managed to send off had been received. She'd taken that chance, while they were in the last hotel, with one of the cleaning ladies who had been new. Lorelei had quickly passed her the note with her plea for the cleaning lady's help, and now all Lorelei could do was wait.

At present, in their new location, no such opportunity had presented itself. Just then the door opened. She froze, the child still sleeping in her arms. One of the men came in, noted the sleeping Amelia Rose, and his face softened. That was a good-enough sign. He nodded and quickly turned and left. But then anybody who was used to dealing with children knew they were much easier to handle if they had sleep. And Amelia Rose definitely needed sleep. Then again Lorelei did too.

She closed her eyes and laid her head against the wall. A bed sat beside them, but Lorelei couldn't get up while carrying the child in her arms. Lorelei wasn't that strong. And she didn't want to drop Amelia Rose, so this is where they were. They'd both sleep better though, if Lorelei could get them onto the bed.

Except she'd do anything to keep the girl asleep. Amelia Rose was exhausted and heartbroken. This had been too much for the young preteen on the brink of puberty. She was sheltered yet worldly, ever fascinated by her father's massive media enterprise, yet kept out of its day-to-day business. She was deemed too young, although the girl had a brilliant mind. Still, she spent many fun hours in her father's office, soaking up the atmosphere of his big business. She was due to inherit a sizeable portion of the company when the time came. But not until her father's passing. In the meantime, Gerard ran the business with an iron grip on its total control.

Lorelei couldn't help but think that had something to do with this kidnapping. Where there was big money… someone was always trying to steal it.

Footsteps sounded in the hallway. Her heart sank as she watched the doorknob turn.

The door opened again.

CHAPTER 2

THE SAME MAN walked in, and he was accompanied by two different men—not dressed in suits, like some of the others, yet not in combat uniforms either, like some of the rest. They wore jeans and T-shirts, and they gently swept Amelia Rose from Lorelei's arms and laid her down on the bed.

Half expecting them to do something horrible, Lorelei scrambled to her feet and raced over, hoping they wouldn't separate them. Amelia Rose had been through too much. These men, or maybe the other men—she no longer knew who was who—had killed Nurse in front of them after holding Mary captive and beating her. She was harmless, but they hadn't cared. Amelia Rose had screamed and cried out, struggling to get free, only to collapse in Lorelei's arms.

It had all been about lessons, making sure Lorelei and Amelia Rose learned theirs.

They'd already escaped once, hence the punishment to Nurse.

The punishment had been anything but fair.

Still, the girls had learned their lesson.

Now with Lorelei standing protectively over the sleeping Amelia Rose, the men were already backing out of the room, and the door was closed and locked behind them. Grateful for that much, Lorelei laid on the bed beside her charge and closed her eyes. She kept thinking of ways that they could escape, ways that Lorelei could get the word out again. To let Gerard know. He was powerful, had money and friends in all different kinds of places—and obviously enemies too.

It wasn't even thinkable that something like this had happened. Gerard was supposed to meet them at Island Retreat, a favorite resort where they'd planned a family holiday. Well, except not with Wendy, Amelia Rose's mother. But Gerard—or Poppy, as Amelia Rose called him—would join them. The girl had been beside herself with joy. She loved her poppy. Lorelei and Amelia Rose had come a few days early with Nurse, and then they'd been snatched up and moved to a different hotel.

They'd all escaped soon afterward, but Nurse had ordered the two girls to go one way, and Nurse would go another, hoping all would find help and would gather later today. Yet when Lorelei and Amelia Rose had returned to their original hotel, they found Nurse Mary held there as a prisoner. It had gone downhill from there.

Now they were in this new hotel. At least Lorelei assumed it was a hotel since she could see green foliage everywhere out the window. They were in a decent-size room, and it had that hotel feel to its sheets—which made a noise when you laid down. The beds were solid though, almost too solid to be comfortable.

As she lay here on the bed, Amelia Rose sniffled in her sleep and reached out in a panic.

Immediately Lorelei wrapped her arms around her charge and whispered against her ear, "It's okay. You're fine."

Only when Amelia Rose took a deep, tremulous breath and sank back into a sound sleep could Lorelei do the same.

THEY ARRIVED TWENTY minutes to noon, Thai time. Right on schedule. After a mixture of military transportation—flights, speedboats, cruisers, and helicopters—Griffin was here, and Jax was still with him. It's a good thing they'd eaten well at the beginning because food had been scarce afterward as they had been secreted away for most of their travels.

They had no instructions as they were dropped off on a wharf in one of Thailand's poorest areas. With their duffel bags over one shoulder, the two of them strode ahead to find a place to make their headquarters. They hadn't gone ten feet when Griffin's phone buzzed. He pulled it out and found an address texted to him. He checked it out online, lifted it so Jax could see what came up, and then hit the Map icon on his cell. The location was two miles ahead and down about six blocks. Both of them set off in the direction of their next stop. As they walked up to the address, they found a tourist-type hotel.

Griffin frowned. It wasn't their usual place. The two walked inside to see several clerks busy with tourists checking in. A man from a side office stepped forward and motioned for them to join him. They walked in, sat down on the chairs, and gave him hard glances while he shut the door, and no one ever exchanged a word. The fake IDs were handed over. The man quickly typed away on his keyboard, printed off several forms, and gave them keys. "Here you go, Mr. Honeycutt. Mr. Harris."

Then he opened a safe and handed a stack of money in the local currency to each of them. After that, he got up, opened the door, and sent them on their way. "Enjoy your stay."

Stuffing the money in their pockets and holding the keys in their hands, they followed the man's instructions up to their two rooms. They entered both, dropped their bags, and Griffin unlocked the connecting door. Jax pulled out a small device from his duffel bag and quickly scanned both rooms. He nodded. "They're clean."

"Interesting," Griffin said. He looked around, instinctively checking corners for video cameras and anything that might have passed the bug detector. As much as they tried to stay up on technology, it was hard to. Especially when it came to anything available in North America because China was often way ahead. He walked over to the window and took a look at the streets outside. Their beds were turned down, as if the men were ready to sleep, but it was just after noon, so that wouldn't happen.

"Do we have any intel on timing or where our kidnap victims are located?" Jax asked.

Griffin shook his head. He sat down at the table and pulled out his laptop. "We need food too."

Jax nodded. "I'll scrounge up some."

Griffin raised one finger, thinking about it, and then said, "Get enough so we don't have to go back out today for more."

"Are you hoping to make a move on her today?"

"I want to do some reconnaissance tonight," he said. "In the dark, after we have a chance to get a better location of where she is. If an opportunity presents itself, then we'll take it, but that's not likely."

"We can do that," Jax said. "I might do a little bit of looking around myself while I'm out."

"Do that," he said. Just then his phone buzzed. Jax

stopped while Griffin looked at the latest message. "Check your phone. Make sure you got these photos."

The photos were a new set, more up-to-date, of both the girl and the tutor, plus a less clear photo of the nurse.

Jax checked his phone and said, "Got it." Then he quickly disappeared out the door.

Griffin pulled up the Mavericks chat window and typed into the box. **Intel on kidnappers' location? We've landed.**

He searched online for histories on the victims, the people they were looking for, starting with Amelia Rose, who was probably the main target for the kidnappers, given who her father was. The one thing about intel was, you never knew what was important until you found it. Not a whole lot was to be found on any of these three kidnap victims—a strategic move on the part of Gerard, for sure—but then a link popped up in his chat.

He quickly clicked on it to see full background files on Mary, the nanny, Amelia Rose, and Lorelei, the tutor, completely making his last ten minutes spent online useless. In these reports, he had everything from birth date to favorite color and the outfit the little girl wore when kidnapped, as well the private school she once attended and the reason why she had a nanny and a tutor now. Apparently there had been an incident at her private preschool, and she'd been tutored ever since. She appeared well-adjusted and intelligent, though on a short leash by her protective father.

He opened the chat window asking for any updates as he studied the photo.

The chat immediately said that Mary's body had been found at the hotel where the three had gone missing.

He sucked in his breath as he stared at that message. A murder upped the stakes to critical. And why her unless she was going to hamper their progress. She was older and not in the best of health. That alone was going to have a huge impact on Amelia Rose. Emotionally and psychologically as the reports said she was close to both her nanny and tutor.

"Poor girl," he whispered. She was small and fair with a china-doll look and blue eyes and ringlets. He shook his head and sighed. "Yeah, that's not troublesome at all." She was the epitome of what a lot of people considered the perfect face. She had a cherubic innocence. And, for that, he had to hope the kidnappers hadn't had a chance to touch her yet.

Then he read the file on the tutor. She was part of a marine family and had gone her own way to become a teacher.

"At least you're not part of the Mensa group," he said. "That would be a little bit too much to handle a second time around." He'd gone a lifetime without meeting anybody with an IQ like the two people in their last case. It was fascinating, but, at the same time, as he read through Lorelei's folder, he had to wonder if she was just as brilliant, also a genius, but who had simply never been tested. She was fluent in three languages but could read and speak in five.

"Still not all that incredible," he said, downplaying it. He could handle three languages himself, but that was it. Plus, so many people born in European countries were multilingual and never thought anything about it. However, she also was licensed to teach in the arts and sciences. Her file spelled out all her upper-level university work and diplomas received.

"Interesting," he muttered as he kept going through the update. And that's when he found what he was looking for. After all her degrees had been earned, the last one as she had turned twenty-three, a big hole appeared in her background history, until she moved from the States to England seven years ago, when she was twenty-five. Followed by confirmation of her hire by Gerard as a tutor for his daughter, some five years ago, when she was twenty-seven.

Frowning, he returned to look at Lorelei's photo and asked, "What did you do after your college graduation before moving to England? And what did you do during those first two years in the UK before hiring on with Gerard?" But then she'd been young. Maybe after graduating, she had spent a year backpacking in the States or abroad. Who knew? Or two years with the Peace Corps. Or on a church mission. Still, he shook his head. Any of those suppositions would have been unearthed by the clever Mavericks team.

He quickly went back to her file and brought up another photo of her face. It wasn't beautiful or angelic like the child's, but still Lorelei had something strikingly attractive about her. It was the determined look in her face, the stern lines to her jawbone and cheeks. This woman wouldn't be taken lightly. But she was also somebody who had plans and would go wherever her plans took her, regardless of other people's opinions. If he was less than kind, he would have said she had a stubborn tilt to her chin, as if whoever took the photo had had to coax her into sitting still long enough. And her eyes had a glint in them as if to say, "Do your worst."

And he was fascinated. *Why didn't you ever marry?* He checked her photo again. She was definitely pretty enough to catch many guys' attention. And the background check on her proved she was plenty smart. The fact that she was collateral damage in this kidnapping of Amelia Rose was one thing, but, added to that, Griffin had to rescue them both.

He couldn't lose either one of them. Lorelei was needed in order to keep the young girl in a decent mental and emotional state. The tutor could be a huge help moving forward as the child dealt with this adversity. So he couldn't just learn about one victim. He had to learn about both.

By the time Jax returned to their rooms and came over to his side with large containers full of street food, Griffin had a pretty good grasp on the two people they were going after here. So he had asked the chat box for background on the father, since his daughter's kidnapping was more than likely to target her mega-rich father. The Mavericks team had already anticipated this and sent the file immediately after his request.

The father was a little bit more elusive, but he was a newspaper mogul, used to getting his own way. As a big business owner, he was stubborn and likely arrogant as hell. This was his third marriage and his daughter was his third living child. His first marriage had produced a son, who was killed at the age of two when both father and son were kidnapped. Kidnappers never captured. Griffin stalled when he read that. *How do you ever get over that loss?*

His second marriage had produced two offspring, both sons, and they were set to take over the business. But then they were much older, already in their thirties. Gerard Whitaker was in his sixties, and, from the look on his face in the photo that Griffin had been sent, Gerard wasn't an easy man to get along with, not with his hawkish nose, stern countenance, and hard eyes.

So either his relationship with his daughter was one similar to how he'd probably raised his sons, with lots of discipline and a lack of affection, or it had been the complete opposite, and she'd been the apple of his eye. Griffin leaned toward that. He moved his laptop off to the side, smiled up at Jax, and said, "Do you have enough money?"

Jax nodded. "Yes. We're good to go. And, no. Nobody's seen the girl or women."

Griffin nodded. "It was taking a chance asking. I did find out one disturbing bit of news. The nanny's body has shown up at the hotel. She's been shot. No suspects at this time."

"Jesus." Jax stared. "I wasn't expecting that."

"None of us were," Griffin said grimly. "But it's upped the ante now. Asking about the missing woman could set off another killing."

"I doubt it, it was all very casual. That's all right," Jax said. "They showed me pictures of their kids, so I brought out the photos of the girl and her tutor. I said I was here visiting them and how proud I was of their accomplishments."

Griffin laughed. "Yeah, nothing like family pride to set in. It does make me wonder how it affected the father's sons, though, at the thought of him having another family and a daughter."

"Give me the rundown."

Griffin quickly shared the information he had found online and recapped what he had been sent and said, "I just want to make sure we can write off the sons on our list as being behind this."

"So neither of our kidnap victims are married to some political type in Thailand?" Jax asked.

"I highly suspect that any political angle has nothing to do with the kidnapping, but we can't knock anything completely off our radar at this point. The kidnappers had said that she'd been married, but is that even legal?"

"In Thailand, you can probably buy a marriage for five bucks," Jax said grimly. "And child sex workers start as young as newborns."

"So the marriage angle was about rape of a child?" Griffin's stomach twisted at the thought. "That's just sick."

"The pedophiles are. It doesn't stop them from coming over here and abusing the locals for money because they can. And here, sadly some of the parents throw their kids into the industry just to make money so they can have more themselves."

Griffin shook his head. "I know all this to be true, but I don't want to sit here and focus on them. Otherwise I'll go on a rampage and free all these child sex workers out there."

"And you know they'll just kidnap another thousand to replace them. It's a messed-up world."

"It is, isn't it?" Then he dove into the food, not stopping until he was halfway through the first carton. He slowed down and said, "*Hmm*, it's not bad."

"A couple vendors are not too far from here, so we won't starve."

"Good," Griffin said. "Just when I think that I've eaten too much, I remember Brandon, that little kid from the last mission, who never even seemed to slow down."

"Are he and his dad okay now?"

"I think so. Although the father is trying to make his business a little more formally legit."

"I'm sure Brandon and Amanda want to stay connected. They're two of a kind."

"They're more than two of a kind," Griffin said. "They're seriously two halves of the same pea. That was amazing, just seeing how much brainpower was in that room."

"Make you feel bad?" Jax asked.

"No," Griffin said. "But it was definitely daunting to see just how much these people could change the world, what cures they could create, what new IT systems could be invented …" He shook his head. "It was pretty wild being around them."

"And yet, they were normal?"

"So normal," Griffin said. "Like unbelievably normal. Like you would have no clue that they were among the most intelligent people on the planet."

"And what about our Lorelei, the tutor?" Jax asked. "Apparently she's pretty smart too."

"Yes, but big gaps are missing in her history. She has four years unaccounted for, from age twenty-three to twenty-seven. She never married, yet she's thirty-two. And pretty. Don't you find that odd? Although being a live-in tutor of an eleven-year-old kid would probably seriously interfere with dating."

"If nothing showed up in the Mavericks background check, it was probably harmless stuff back then. Lots of us make mistakes when we're young and stupid," Jax said. He lifted his head, looked at Griffin, and said, "And I would think her not being married would be a plus in your view. Didn't you do something stupid when you were young?"

Griffin nodded. "Yep, I married at eighteen because I thought she was pregnant."

"But she wasn't?" Jax stared at him, his eyebrows heading to his hairline.

Griffin smiled. "Her father might have had something to do with that quick service too."

"And how long did you stay married?"

"Well, we were together for six months, but then I got

into the navy, and, on the return from my first leave, I found her in bed with somebody else. Divorce proceedings started immediately after that, and I sent a picture to her father to let him know to get off my back as she'd already found somebody else."

Jax let out a long whistle. "Wow, bet that went over well."

"No clue if it did or not," Griffin said. "She was too young to settle down, and so was I. And the father needed to let her live her life."

"Have you seen her since?"

Griffin shook his head. "Hell no. Don't care to either."

"So you should be able to relate to Lorelei choosing not to marry young."

He nodded. "I can. Something about her set of features …" He shook his head. "I'm not sure why, but she's mesmerizing."

Jax raised his eyebrows again.

Griffin laughed. "No, not like that."

"It's always like that," Jax said with a smirk. "Kerrick was the same after seeing Amanda's picture."

"Well, I won't be hooking up with this one," Griffin said drily.

"But if she's single, and you're single …"

"Single and have been ever since," he said. "Came close once or twice but I just couldn't quite get myself to pull the trigger. Not sure why. I'm going on the assumption each wasn't the right one. But then I did pull the trigger under coercion, and she wasn't the right one either. So it'll be a long, cold day in hell before I do it again."

"Unless it's the right one," Jax said.

"Well, it won't be her," he said, pointing at Lorelei's

picture. "She looks like she wouldn't be very easy to live with."

"Or maybe she would be very easy to live with if it was the right person for her," Jax said, "but hasn't found him yet."

"Whatever," Griffin said. His phone buzzed once more, and the chat box on his laptop popped up again. He quickly reached over and hit the link. It was a picture of Lorelei and Amelia Rose walking around the beachfront in Thailand. "This is from one of the resorts less than one mile away from here," he said slowly. "Taken four days ago."

"They were free then?"

"Yes. How does that work? I thought they were taken before then."

"Either this was for their good health and a ton of guards surrounded them or they escaped."

Griffin quickly zoomed in on the image and caught the look in Lorelei's eyes. "They've escaped. *There*. She's terrified, and the little girl is barely walking on her own. She's hanging on to Lorelei so tight."

"Escaped and then recaptured?"

"Quite possibly." He quickly asked that question in the chat box, and, when the answer returned in the affirmative, he nodded. "So she did her best to get them out of there, but now they've been recaptured and will be locked down even tighter."

"Well, that's not good," Jax said. "But kudos to her for getting free."

Griffin typed into the chat window. **Location?**

We're getting a suspected location.

When it showed up one minute later, the link was a photo of guarded compound. Griffin flashed it Jax's way.

"It's well-armed," Griffin said. "Likely under heavy security."

"And how do our people know that the little girl's still there?"

Griffin typed in that question.

Chip, the chat box replied.

He sat back and looked at Jax. "That makes sense. The father probably had a microchip implanted in Amelia Rose to keep track of her, in case anybody tried something like this."

"That brings up another point," Jax said. He rose, went to his adjoining room, came back with his laptop, and typed. A few moments later, he lifted his head and said, "You mentioned this before. The father and his first-born son were kidnapped some thirty years ago. Gerard obviously survived, but his son didn't."

"Can't imagine living through that," Griffin said.

"And that explains the daughter's microchip. So now we do have a confirmed location, via the chip. That's huge. But why isn't a bigger team going in to take them out?"

"Casualties? Small team is quiet, easier to hide—just the two of us."

Jax stared at him. "I'd still feel better if we had more. Don't we have backup?"

"Let me see what we've got," Griffin said as he typed in the chat box. **Reconnaissance tonight. Any backup for the plan?**

No.

Griffin winced, and Jax's jaw dropped in horror. "None?"

"Not at the moment." Griffin shook his head.

"What about Kerrick?"

"Right. I forgot he was supposed to play a part in this."

He typed in **Kerrick?**
That's me.
Wish you were here, buddy.
Paris.
Damn.
Sorry.
We need somebody else.
Let me check availability and proximity.

"Kerrick's on the other end of this chat," Griffin said with a smile. "That's good news. But then he's in Paris, not here, and that's the bad news."

"First things first," Jax said. "We need to set up a reconnaissance and take a look at exactly what we have for issues. I want satellite feed."

Griffin quickly requested the feed. When the link popped up a few minutes later, he shared it with Jax.

"Let's see what we're looking for," Griffin said. The compound itself appeared to be about ten acres total, had a high stone wall about eight, maybe ten, even twelve feet high all the way around the perimeter, with a walkway on the top. "Damn." Immediately he typed into the chat window **Can we narrow down the girl's location via her chip?**

No. Either her location is somehow blocking her chip's abilities or her chip can't narrow down her location.

Griffin grumbled as he showed Jax the recent chat window conversation. Then Griffin pointed at the satellite feed. "Interesting design," he muttered, while Jax sat again before his own laptop.

"Hey, the rules and regulations here are much less than at home," Jax said. "And permits are a joke."

"What permits?" Griffin studied the compound and said, "I'm seeing watch guards on each of the four corners and two dogs with handlers."

"I'm seeing a third pair, a dog and his handler, in the back north corner at forty-five degrees."

"Got him. So, three dogs, three handlers, and four guards." He sat back, looked at Jax, and grinned. "That's not a bad ratio. Seven men to two?"

"Make that eight, if the three dogs count as one man, if not more," Jax said, "but definitely doable."

"The trick is, we can't be seen. Not per the Mavericks contact guy and not for our general health and not for the success of this rescue op. Yet no trees are around that wall. Scaling it won't be a problem, but somehow we have to get up without any of the guards seeing us and none of the dogs smelling us."

"And getting up won't help if we're not planning on going in."

"Right. We don't want them to detect us when we're just in recon mode and then double up security before we get our rescue plan organized and put into effect. The house itself looks like it's ten thousand square feet roughly."

"Bringing up blueprints right now," Jax said, tapping his laptop keys busily on the other side of the table. "Hard to say where the prisoners are located in this mausoleum though."

A beep had Griffin checking the chat box.

Nobody local available. You guys are on your own tonight.

Griffin groaned, pointed at his drop-down chat box message for Jax's benefit.

"It is what it is," Jax said.

Griffin continued to study the external layout. "There's one driveway in with double doors. Full-size, more like seen on a medieval castle. It's pretty ironic considering they have a wall, not a moat. But the wall is too short to provide an adequate defense against a determined intruder and also too thin that it won't withstand much."

"C-4 then?"

"Potentially. We could set charges on all four corners, take down the perimeter wall, but we have to make sure that somebody's already inside and uses that as a distraction to extract the girl and the tutor."

"I think we both have to go in. Two victims, one a child, we need one man assigned per victim."

"Then we have nobody on watch outside," Griffin muttered. He grabbed a pen and paper and jotted down the details.

"We don't have any time to waste either. These kidnappers have had the girl for way too long as it is."

"Potentially we do have some leeway here, as long as the girl's safely inside, and they haven't done anything more to get themselves in even deeper shit. We need to make sure the girls don't get moved again. We're losing time with each change in location made. Or, now that we have a confirmed location for them, if the kidnappers do make a move, we catch them in transit."

"Exactly."

CHAPTER 3

LORELEI WOKE TO the door opening. She lifted her head, groggy and disoriented, Amelia Rose still sleeping against her chest. A trolley was pushed into the room, and the same man who'd been here earlier motioned at it and said, "Eat." Then he turned and walked out.

She stretched, kissed Amelia Rose gently on the temple, and said, "Wake up, little one."

Amelia Rose nodded, reached up with a fist, and tried to rub the sleep out of her eyes. She opened them to look up at Lorelei and around the room, only to have tears immediately flood her cheeks. Lorelei quickly pulled the child into her arms and said, "Yes, we're still here. Yes, we're still prisoners. But we had a chance to get some sleep. Today's a different day."

Amelia Rose looked up at her, and her bottom lip trembled. Then she saw the tray. And with the precociousness of a child, she asked, "Food?"

"Yes," Lorelei said as she got up and walked over to lift the lids on the pans. It looked to be meat, vegetables, and rice of some kind. She pulled up a chair to the little trolley so Amelia Rose could sit down. Then Lorelei poured water for them both, grabbed a roll for herself, and stood on the far side. Amelia Rose immediately wanted Lorelei to sit down, but she shook her head and said, "I need to stretch my legs."

She grinned at her charge. Even with her tear-streaked cheeks, she was busy plowing into the food. "It's good that you have an appetite."

"We need the energy," Amelia Rose said.

"We do," Lorelei agreed. She walked over to the window with the fresh bun in her hand and studied the greenery outside.

"Do you know where we are now?"

Lorelei turned, keeping a bright smile on her face, and said, "No, but lots of nice trees are outside. And it's a decent-enough room. We have our own bathroom. That's something."

"Is this a new hotel?"

"I thought so at first," Lorelei said, "but now I'm wondering if maybe it's a private home."

One thing about Amelia Rose was, she didn't think like a child. She stopped, looked at Lorelei, nodded, and said, "They can't take the chance of us escaping again."

"I know," Lorelei said. "We had our chance."

"It's my fault we got caught." Immediately the tears flowed again.

"Oh, sweetheart. No, it isn't." Lorelei rushed to Amelia Rose's side. "They were looking for us. It was only a matter of time."

"I was so scared," Amelia Rose said, looking up at Lorelei and biting her bottom lip. "If I could have run, it would have made a huge difference."

It would have, but no way would she let Amelia Rose take on this guilt. "We'll be fine."

Amelia Rose nodded and kept eating. "I don't think anybody here will get a message out for us."

"Probably not, no. Particularly since I've seen armed

men who look like staff around here. If this is a private home, which I think it is, that's most likely the answer. So I'm pretty sure the people here are paid to look after us, and they won't betray the people who pay them."

"Of course," Amelia Rose said. As soon as she was done eating, she pushed the chair back and got up and walked to the window. "It's so pretty here," she said, "but I didn't know it held such darkness."

Immediately Lorelei placed a hand on the child's shoulder and gently rubbed her arm. "You know your father's looking for us," she said. "Stay strong."

"Do you think my brothers are too?" she asked in an almost muted tone.

Lorelei winced. Her brothers had been incredibly cold and standoffish all of Amelia Rose's life, as if they hadn't wanted or needed any more siblings. And Lorelei could understand their point. But it would've been good if they could have let a little girl into their world. This little girl could bring in the sunshine. "I think they're probably rethinking their whole world right now," Lorelei said. "And you know your mother must be missing you terribly."

Amelia Rose's bottom lip trembled again. "Then why didn't she come with us?"

Lorelei didn't know what to say. Although the girl's mother did love her daughter, she wasn't the maternal type. And traveling to Thailand at this time of year had not been on Wendy's list of things to do. "I'm sorry. I'm sure she was just busy."

"She's always busy," Amelia Rose muttered. "That doesn't make it right."

"No," Lorelei said, "it doesn't, but it doesn't make it wrong either. She knew that you would be with me."

Amelia Rose nodded, squeezed Lorelei's fingers, and said, "So is this where we stay now? I really could use a computer."

"Well, you might *want* a computer," Lorelei said gently, "but I doubt they'll let us have access to the outside world. Obviously we'd try to send emails to escape again."

"I know, but I do love my games, and they're a great way to pass the time." She returned to the food trolley and said, "Do you think anything else in here is edible?"

Lorelei laughed. "Normally you like trying foods in other places of the world."

"Only if I know what they are."

Lorelei lifted the rest of the lids from the dishes so that Amelia Rose could see. "There's cake, cheese, and fruit," she said. "What would you like?"

"I'd like a pot of tea, and I'd like some cake and fruit."

There was a shelf below, and Lorelei bent to take a closer look and cried out in delight. "It looks like a pot of tea. It might be a bit strong though because we didn't see it right away." She pulled out the tea tray and set it on the floor. There were no dressers or night tables in this room. Nothing but the bed and now the trolley. She quickly cleaned off the dishes atop the trolley, then lifted the tea tray there. "And you know what? If we had thought of this earlier, it looks like this comes up." She quickly pulled a swinging shelf, topped by a sheet of wood, and locked it underneath with the proper brace.

"That would help," Amelia Rose said with a laugh. Sitting down again, they had tea and dessert.

They were almost done when the door suddenly opened again. Three men came in, and immediately Amelia Rose jumped off her chair and threw herself into Lorelei's arms.

Lorelei smiled at the men and said, "Thank you for dinner."

One of the men nodded, and the cart was taken away. Then, without hesitation, the door was slammed in their faces.

Amelia Rose looked up at her and asked, "Are they gone?"

She hugged her gently and whispered, "Yes, they're gone."

"I don't like them." Amelia Rose stepped away, looked around, and said, "At least they didn't starve us. But I really wish I had a computer."

"Or at least some books to read or a puzzle to do?" Lorelei teased. She wasn't sure what to do with her charge. It was one thing to sleep eight hours in the day and to spend another hour eating, but that left an awful lot of hours left to do nothing. The room was bare except for the single bed.

Amelia Rose looked over at Lorelei and then walked up to the door and turned the knob.

When the door opened easily, Lorelei raced to her side. A guard stood there. He frowned and slammed the door shut.

"So," Amelia Rose said with a pouting face, "I guess we don't get to leave."

"No, of course not," Lorelei said gently. "But you knew that."

"I know, but I had to check."

And, of course, Lorelei should have done that earlier too. She'd already assumed that they were under guard. Just then she stepped around Amelia Rose, opened the door, and smiled at the guard. "Is there any chance we could have some books or a computer or some games to play to fill our time?"

He frowned at her and shrugged.

"If you could ask, that would be lovely." And then she closed the door herself so that he wasn't forced to do so to keep them inside. After that, she walked to the bed, sat down, and opened her arms. As Amelia Rose piled onto her lap, Lorelei said, "Now we sit and wait."

"I'm really glad you're with me."

Lorelei's heart broke, and she held her charge closer. "I am too."

"Do you think Nurse is in heaven?"

"Absolutely she is," Lorelei said. "That's where all the good people go, and Nurse was a very good person."

"She loved me," Amelia Rose said, tears once again forming in the corner of her eyes.

"I know she did," Lorelei said. "And you loved her. And it's always hard to lose anybody so loved."

"She shouldn't have had to die that way," Amelia Rose said. "She didn't want to come on this trip in the first place."

Unfortunately that was all too true. But Amelia Rose's mother had insisted. As long as Wendy wasn't here, Amelia Rose was to have all the people who she cared about with her. Especially when she couldn't have the ones who she really loved with her, like her mother and her father.

IT WAS ONE thing to look at the compound on satellite, and it was another thing to stand in the shadows and assess the height of the wall. Twelve feet was what they'd measured off, but it was a sheer twelve feet. It looked like a smooth coat of cement on the outside. They could probably do a run and jump up and over it, but doing it quietly and silently in the night might not be quite so easy. Ropes would work though. But grappling hooks were hard to keep silent. They'd need a cover sound to be effective in close quarters like this.

The walls were smooth, but he saw gates every two yards, with small windows cut into each. *Could work with that.*

Jax tapped Griffin's shoulder and pointed off to the side.

One guard walked across the top of the wall. No railings were up there, so the wall had to be at least two feet wide for him to make that journey as casually as he did. The fact that he walked with a rifle over his shoulder said a lot about how the community would view the owners of the compound. As nobody to mess with.

Griffin watched as the guard walked around the perimeter wall, timing him. Twelve minutes for a three-quarter turn, where he met up with somebody else climbing the opposite side of the wall. Griffin and Jax had satellite images on their phones to sync with the reality on the ground while they searched the area. Two people were on the wall, two on the ground walking one dog each. Griffin hadn't seen all three dogs and their handlers patrolling yet.

The two of them moved silently in the night, taking a good assessment of what challenges and weaknesses they faced here. When they slipped back around to the far side, a large clump of trees was close enough to the wall that they could scale the trees and potentially get up on to the wall to take a look inside the compound.

As Griffin assessed the distance to the wall, he noted that the kidnappers had completely missed this weakness. In fact, it was something that, if it were up to him, he'd have fired his man over.

The tree had grown up tall and straight but had also

branched out at the top. While maybe the kidnappers had assumed that nobody would cross the wall because no branches were close enough, Griffin was high enough that, from his perch, he could drop down onto the wall. He shook his head at that.

Hearing an owl call in the night, he twisted to look at Jax in another tree, pointing to the north.

Griffin checked it out to see one of the dogs sniffing along the inside edge of the wall.

No handler was with him.

Using his night vision binoculars, Griffin checked to confirm a holding pen for the dogs was here. So this dog wasn't on duty tonight. He was just checking out the area, minding his own business. That worked for Griffin. But it was also darn close to where he would most likely land on the wall.

Not good.

Using his binoculars again, he carefully assessed the windows on the building closest to him. Several smaller buildings were inside the compound as well, but he had no way of knowing where the girls were being held. Intel said they were here somewhere, but, so far, he and Jax had no proof to back that up.

This closest building in front of Griffin had six windows accessible, where he could see how the people lived and worked inside. In one window a man sat at an office desk, talking on a phone. In another was a guard. At least he looked like a guard since a weapon was over his shoulder. He was having a cup of coffee as he stood and stared out into the night.

Not wanting him to get an instinctive feeling of being watched, Griffin quickly changed his view to check out the other windows. Two of the windows showed nothing, while one revealed a hallway all the way down as far as he could see. The question was, were the girls in this part of the building or in another area of this same huge building, or were they in one of the smaller buildings?

When the owl hoot came again, Griffin glanced once more at Jax to see him holding up his phone with a satellite image on the screen. Griffin quickly pulled out his cell and checked his satellite feed to see several men walking from one of the smaller buildings to the largest one.

He nodded. That would be the guardroom they were leaving. And that likely meant that Amelia Rose and Lorelei were housed in the bigger building.

Griffin sighed. They had at least ten thousand square feet of building to search. That would take time. They needed a way to narrow the search area. Infrared would be lovely. He frowned and sent a text. **Need infrared or better to find out where the prisoners are being kept inside the building.**

Not the usual request. Not available in that area. Will let you know.

He pocketed his phone and slipped back down, then headed to the north corner. A few trees were over here, not as big or as easy to hide in but strong enough so he could certainly scale them. On his way, he heard a dog bark. He froze, dropped to the ground, and waited. He could hear voices but saw no flashlights or heard any sounds of movement coming toward him.

When it was silent again, he moved quietly in the night and made his way to the other trees. He chose the tree with the most coverage and scaled it to the top. From his new vantage point he checked out the activity on this side of the building. Once again, he found windows that let him into little corners of the compound's world.

At one, he saw a woman staring out, but it didn't mean it was the woman he was looking for. Her features were too indistinct due to the many small panes in the window. If it had been daylight, he might have had a better look. But through the binoculars? He was just getting a female shadow.

He studied her features to see long hair and watched as she rubbed her temple. Then, hearing something, she spun quickly and disappeared from his sight. Those were good signs that maybe she was Lorelei. He mapped the location in his head and turned to study the rest of the people on this side of the building. The guards were doing their pass yet again atop the perimeter wall. Griffin stopped, checked on his timing, and nodded. Then he muttered, "At least they're consistent."

He waited another ten minutes for them to complete their pass and to see if the woman would return to the window, but she didn't. If Griffin could make it from this tree to the wall, he could quickly jump off the wall and get into the compound from that spot, then use this as a way out again. But that only worked for him doing further recon. He couldn't expect the woman and the child to make this climb. Plus the trees weren't close enough on this side to help him get onto the wall, but it would be a good area for somebody to stand guard. With that in mind, he quickly dropped to the ground and headed deeper into the trees and away from the compound.

Jax joined him very quickly. "Thoughts?"

"The best option would be to get in and to get out without waking up or having the guards notice," Griffin said.

Jax had his hands curled as fists as he glared back at the

compound. "Except they've got the dogs running free right on the side of the wall that we're likely to climb."

"Yes, and chances are those dogs will be trained to not take any gifts from strangers. We can't drop steaks in there."

"And a dog'll hear our every move."

"True, but will the dogs know us from the guards? Maybe instead of avoiding the guards, we should take out the two on top of the wall, put on their uniforms, and go in that way."

Jax thought about that and nodded slowly. "We don't know how they're getting up and down either."

"I think I saw a ladder on the inside of one of the walls," Griffin said. "It would make sense. Fast up and fast down."

"No railings to help us get up and over otherwise."

"The trees will give us access from this side, so, if we can use a ladder once inside to climb the wall out again, we'll be fine. To take out the guards, we'll need some equipment with us. And if we run into trouble inside …"

"I have a backpack with C-4 and some weapons," Jax said. "Do we know if the girls are ambulatory?"

"No clue," Griffin said. "I did see a woman in one of the windows. When somebody made a noise, like it was behind her, she quickly spun and disappeared."

"That's promising. What floor?"

"Third."

"Of course. The building won't be easy to scale from the outside."

"No, and I've seen no decks on the third floor either. There are some on the second but not above."

"So where do you want to go in?"

"I was thinking the one side door between the two tree points."

After that, they spent an hour looking for exits. Not just one but four different ways. By the time they made it back to their hotel rooms, they crashed.

Griffin woke four hours later to hear his phone buzz. He reached over, groggy.

No luck with infrared. Not a problem now that they're being moved.

"Shit," he said, sitting up. **Where and when?**

Now. To an unidentified location.

Time to overtake them?

No. Already leaving compound.

Are we tracking? He wiped the sleep from his eyes, quickly threw on some clothes, and grabbed his laptop.

Yes, satellite.

I'm on it if you've got a link.

He was given a link in an instant. He brought it up to see the satellite feed, showing the moving vehicle.

Do we have a destination?

No.

How many?

Woman, child, two men.

Including driver?

Yes.

We need a place to take them out, he said as he studied the feed.

Trying to set it up now. A blockade?

Didn't a second vehicle go with the gunmen? He hated to think about it but had to consider it.

No. We didn't see a second vehicle. You must have been seen.

No. He refused to believe that he'd triggered any alarms and that the kidnappers were leaving with their victims because of anything Griffin and Jax did. **Must be moving**

them daily. But, of course, it was possible, so he couldn't discount it. **We need wheels.**

Already on the way.

Just then an envelope was shoved under the door. He got up, walked over, and picked it up to find a set of keys. He smiled and muttered, "Kerrick's good."

Then back at the chat window, he typed **Got the keys.**

Good.

You're damn fast.

And you've been sleeping. Otherwise you'd have been on this.

He frowned. **Still had to grab some shut-eye. Can't run all the time.**

I know. That's why we've got your back.

At that, Griffin settled back and smiled.

Jax woke up, sat upright, and asked, "What's up?"

Griffin looked his way. "Looks like we wasted our time earlier doing recon. They're moving the girls."

Jax immediately bolted from bed and dressed. "Let's go."

"Go where? We're tracking them but have no clue where they're heading."

"Doesn't matter. As long as they're on the road, they're weaker than when they're in a stronghold."

Griffin laughed, throwing his duffel over his shoulder. Everything was already packed up and ready to go. Jax groaned and grabbed his bag, then the two men headed outside. Griffin hit the button on the fob with the vehicle keys and turned toward the sound of the beep. A small truck-SUV hybrid. *That would work.* They tossed their bags in the back and were on the road within minutes. He brought up the satellite on Amelia Rose's implanted tracker and held his breath until it showed him where the kidnappers were traveling.

"We need to plot an intersection," Griffin said. "They can't drive forever. They'll need gas too, but we want to make sure they're not heading to an airport. If that's the case, we want to take them out first."

With Jax running navigation, Griffin quickly drove as instructed so he could catch up with the kidnappers, who were a good forty minutes ahead, if not an hour. But they weren't traveling fast. He, on the other hand, was really moving it. He whipped through the streets, grateful that it was still the wee hours of Tuesday morning and that the traffic wasn't heavy.

"You're gaining on them," Jax said. "Looks like they've taken a turn up ahead."

"What kind of a turn?"

"Might be a pit stop."

"Good. That'll help us to make up for some lost time."

"The kidnappers shouldn't give the girls too long out of the car," Jax said. "Probably just a bathroom break."

"They have a child with them."

"We have to pick up at least twenty miles though," Jax warned him. "So go faster."

He snorted. "This bucket won't go any faster."

"I'll find you a faster route."

"Off-road works for me." On that note, the two of them focused on moving as fast as possible and catching up with their prey.

CHAPTER 4

LORELEI STOOD ASIDE, waiting while Amelia Rose washed her hands. She'd begged for a bathroom break from their two kidnappers, who had only given in after the two females had badgered them. Now their guard stood outside the washroom. When she was done, Amelia Rose reached for a hand towel and looked up at Lorelei. "I don't want to go out there again," she muttered.

Lorelei smiled gently. "Neither do I. But I've checked here, and there's no way to get out of this room, so we have to be brave a little longer."

Amelia Rose nodded. "I know. Do you think anybody in the restaurant would help us?"

"I doubt it," Lorelei said. "It's possible, but nobody wants to get involved. Obviously these are very powerful people, and they'll make things very difficult for anybody who tries to help us."

Amelia Rose wiped her eyes and said, "All I do is cry."

"And crying is just fine. There's no shame in being afraid."

"Maybe not but you're not crying."

"Inside, I am," Lorelei whispered.

Amelia Rose reached out and clung to her, clasping her hand.

"Let's go before they come in here."

As they stepped out, one of the men stood in the hallway, waiting for them. He glanced at them, did a cursory look inside the ladies' room, and then motioned for them to go ahead.

"May I get a glass of water, please?" Amelia Rose asked.

He frowned and glanced at Lorelei, who nodded and said, "A couple bottles of water would be helpful."

He shrugged and motioned them back toward the vehicle. But he did say, "I'll see."

She smiled and nodded. "Thank you. It'd be appreciated. Oh, and she might need food soon too."

He nodded but said, "Not yet. We're arriving at another place soon."

"Okay," she said. She led the way to the vehicle, her gaze searching around without making it seem she was looking too much. Dawn's light came over the horizon. The café was empty except for a couple rough-looking guys. She figured they wouldn't help her out. As a matter of fact, they were more likely to help out the driver and their guard instead of her. She motioned for Amelia Rose to head to the car. They walked over slowly. The driver waited for them outside, standing by the vehicle, pumping gas it seemed. He opened the car door, and they got inside.

Lorelei smiled at him and thanked him. She figured being polite and friendly couldn't hurt. It might make the difference between having their faces smashed in or not. Yet this violence could happen whether they liked it or not, whether they were nice or not.

Amelia Rose snuggled up closer. "Why are they doing this?" she whispered.

"Likely because of your father and his businesses," Lorelei said in a low tone. "He's very powerful. That means he's made a lot of enemies."

"But I haven't," Amelia Rose said in a voice that almost broke Lorelei's heart. "I haven't done anything mean to anybody."

"And that's good," Lorelei said. "We'll keep it that way, okay?" Lorelei smiled at her charge and whispered, "It's all right. We'll just stay friendly and do what we're told, and we hopefully will get out of this without anyone else getting hurt."

The trouble was that, as she stared down at her charge, curled up against her body, she knew avoiding further violence wouldn't be so easily done as said. This was bad news all around, and she had no clue who or if anybody gave a damn. As she stared out into the rising morning sun, she thought it was Tuesday, but time was hard to track in her mind. She'd never felt lonelier or more terrified.

And then she caught sight of another vehicle parked off to the side, in front of the restaurant area, the two men inside that car seemingly studying her. She frowned, trying to figure out who they were. One of the men got out and walked casually toward the restaurant. He stepped inside, and she wished she was still inside. At least he might have helped them. He looked like some badass warrior. There was a can-do attitude about him that she really appreciated. At least, if nothing else, he'd be the kind of person who would stop the others in the restaurant from hurting her and her charge. She leaned forward to speak to the driver, who still stood out front, manning the pump while filling the car with gas.

"May I go into the restaurant and get some food for Amelia Rose?"

He frowned at her and shook his head.

"Please. She needs food for the trip."

"We won't be that long," the driver said, his tone brooking no argument.

Her shoulders sagged. "Coffee? May I buy you some coffee?" He looked at her, and his gaze slid toward her hand. She held up a little bit of money that she still had from her pocket. "I don't know how much this will buy," she confessed, "but maybe a snack and some coffee for us all?"

He hesitated, but she hopped out of the car and said, "I'll leave Amelia Rose with you. Obviously I'm not escaping, leaving the child behind."

He relented and said, "My partner's inside, so don't try anything funny. Otherwise you won't see her again."

Amelia Rose hopped out. "She can't take me with her?"

The driver grabbed her arm, shuffling Amelia Rose back inside the car.

Lorelei smiled at her. "I'll return in a moment. Getting coffee and water."

Then she ran inside. At the cashier station, she quickly ordered coffee and a couple bottled waters and picked up what looked like some fresh bread from this morning plus a bag of treats for Amelia Rose. As they made up her order, she glanced around, her gaze catching the man who had just walked in ahead of her. He stared at her with a raised eyebrow. A question was in that gaze, like he was asking her if she was all right. She just didn't know how to give him an answer. She subtly held out one hand in a thumbs-down signal, as in *No, I am not all right.*

He walked toward her, and, while her coffees were being served, he ordered coffee for himself as well. "Is the coffee any good here?"

She looked up at him and shook her head, trying not to

attract her guard's attention.

"Interesting," he murmured.

"Help me, please," she whispered.

He nodded. "It's on the way."

She wasn't sure what he meant by that. Just then the driver called for her from outside. She looked over, smiled, and quickly scooped up the coffee that the cashier had just placed into the holder for her and showed it to the driver outside and to the nearby guard. She waited for her change and raced out with her guard, all the while the driver still busily yelled at her about her recent activities, but she could barely understand.

When he was done, she smiled and said, "Thank you for this." Then she handed him a coffee.

He still growled.

She handed the guard one too and then got into the back of the vehicle with her charge. She got water for Amelia Rose while Lorelei had a coffee for herself. She still had some change left in her hand, which she stuffed into her pocket. She quickly gave Amelia Rose her treats and one of the fresh rolls, grabbed another roll for herself, and then handed the bag of food to the occupants in the front seat. It was snatched from her hands. She knew they weren't happy with her, but this was a small gesture to make things a little easier.

Then she sank into her seat, wondering who the hell that man had been and if he had meant what he said. As if understanding how disturbed she was, Amelia Rose grabbed her fingers and squeezed hard. She looked down at her and saw the worry in the girl's eyes. Lorelei smiled at her and said, "It's all right, sweetie. Remember. We'll be okay."

Amelia Rose sat back and munched away as the car pulled away from the combination café and gas station and drove onto the main road. She didn't know how long they kept driving afterward. And, for the first time in a long time, she felt a whole lot better. She didn't know who that man was and what his role in all of this could be, but he'd understood that she was in trouble. That was more than she could have hoped for. Now she just had to wait and hope for an opportunity. She wasn't sure why the newcomers hadn't done anything about this at the restaurant. Then maybe it wasn't the best location? For instance, the fact that he didn't know for sure that she was even in trouble. But he knew now, so hopefully he could find a way to contact somebody to help.

She settled back and whispered, "Have a nap and rest."

Amelia Rose handed over the last of her treat and said, "I don't want this." She had a sip of water and then stretched out on the seat behind her and closed her eyes.

Not wanting the food to go to waste, Lorelei quickly polished off the last few bites and drank her coffee. She watched the two men in the front seat. They were talking, but their voices were low. She couldn't see anything. She shifted slightly so that she leaned against the far corner of the back seat but couldn't really see behind her. Shifting a little bit, she could look around the countryside as they drove. She had no clue where they were or where they were going. Only as they went around a corner did she catch sight of another vehicle far behind them.

It was the man from the restaurant.

He had believed her. Her heart lit with joy, but immediately she got worried. What if the Good Samaritans were found out? What if her driver saw they were being followed? Would they blame her? Punish her? Like they had Mary? She hoped not because Amelia Rose would have to witness that too.

She hoped it wouldn't be as bad as what they'd done to Nurse Mary, but she couldn't stop her fingers from clenching. These weren't the same men who had tortured and then killed Nurse, but the memory of what they'd done to that innocent old woman would fill Lorelei's nightmares for years. She tried to relax, slowly taking deep breaths, trying to unwind, but just knowing somebody was behind them, that somebody was looking out for them was a ray of sunshine to her heart. In her mind, she whispered to the unknown man, *Please find a way to help us. Please.*

When a shout came from the driver, she leaned forward to see him avoiding a traffic accident up ahead. He hit the brakes hard, and Amelia Rose woke up, crying. She rolled half off the seat, and Lorelei immediately grabbed her to stop her from banging into the driver's seat. The men in the front seat were cussing and swearing, but four vehicles were at odd angles across the road, two of them badly smashed.

Lorelei cried out in shock when she saw how extensive the damage was. She couldn't understand their language, but the men were talking constantly over and around her. The driver seemed to want to keep driving, but the road was completely blocked, giving him no place to go. The guard in the passenger seat got out, walked up to the accident scene, and argued with somebody on the road. Two of the vehicles were being moved off the road so the traffic could keep moving, at least in one lane.

She looked back to see the vehicle from far behind had now pulled right up to their vehicle's bumper. Her driver yelled and shouted from the window at the people hindering their path. Swiveling, she checked the vehicle behind her again. It was now empty. Both its driver and passenger were nowhere to be seen. Then she caught sight of brown hair before it sank down behind her car window. She glanced at Amelia Rose, who sat up with tears in her eyes as she stared at the accident in horror. Lorelei pulled her close. With her tight against her side, she whispered, "Be ready. This might be our chance."

Amelia Rose's jaw dropped, and she whispered back, "Now?"

"I don't know," she said, "but I want you ready, and I don't want you to cry out. And I don't want you to argue. When I tell you to run, you stay close to me. Do you hear me?"

Amelia Rose nodded.

Just then the driver opened his door, got out, and yelled at someone ahead of him.

The brown-haired man now popped up again, motioning for Lorelei to come to him.

Sitting on the far side, she silently opened her door, slid out and kept low, urging Amelia Rose to join her, then bolted backward toward the other vehicle. She came face-to-face with the man from the restaurant, and, before she could say a word, she was picked up and moved into the back of the second vehicle, Amelia Rose with her, both of them trying to stay out of sight when a blanket was thrown over them. Then the man hopped back in, and his buddy turned on the engine.

She kept Amelia Rose huddled low with her. She was darn grateful to be driving away from her captors, but what if these men were worse? She twisted upward, poked her head out, and whispered, "Do you think we're safe now?"

"No. Not at all," said the man she'd spoken to earlier. "But hopefully we will be soon."

GRIFFIN KEPT A warning hand on the girls' heads, whispering, "Stay low. Stay low."

Jax was at the wheel. He'd slowly backed up, turned around their car, and drove away, trying not to make it look like he was escaping, but, in truth, they were not only escaping but doing it as fast as possible but inconspicuously. As Griffin turned to look behind them, the two men returned to their car, only to stop and scream and yell at each other as they realized the girls had vanished.

"Now they know they're missing," Griffin said. "Pick up the speed a bit but not to draw any real attention."

Jax already had goosed his gas pedal, waiting for Griffin to give him the all clear to get this vehicle in high gear.

As Griffin watched, the other vehicles now joining in this traffic jam had pulled up behind the kidnapper's vehicle, effectively boxing them in, filling in the void their leaving had opened. Another one pulled out of the row and turned around, doing what Jax and Griffin were doing, rather than waiting for the vehicles in the accident to clear off. It effectively jammed in the kidnappers' car.

"They're on their phones, calling for help," Griffin said, "since they can't get out of the traffic jam."

"Good," Lorelei snapped from behind the front seat. "They deserved that."

When they rounded a bend in the road that cut them off from the kidnappers' sights, Griffin told Jax to floor it.

Jax put the pedal to the metal, but then he coaxed it up another gear. "Let's hope we have enough of a head start."

Griffin leaned over his seat and looked down at the two girls. Lorelei's eyes were brown and wide, filled with a bit of temper and a little bit of uncertainty. But Amelia Rose's eyes broke his heart. She was clearly terrified. He smiled at her and whispered, "It's okay. We're the good guys." But it didn't look like his words had any effect. He looked at Lorelei. "Do you know what they wanted from you?"

She pointed toward Amelia Rose. "They want her."

"We heard from your dad," Griffin said gruffly. "So, Amelia Rose, you'll be okay. We just have to get you to safety."

At the mention of her father, her eyebrows rose, and her eyes widened. "Did Poppy send you?"

"In a roundabout way, he did," Griffin said, not having a clue who was behind his orders. "The bottom line is, we were sent to rescue you and to get you out of here safely."

"I'm not going without Lorelei," Amelia Rose said, her tone stubborn.

Griffin chuckled. "We're taking both of you." He kept an eye on the road behind him. "Looks like we've lost them for the moment, but I'm sure they've radioed ahead. We have to switch vehicles."

Just then his phone buzzed. He glanced down to read an address, punched in for the map, and held it up for Jax.

Jax looked at it and nodded.

Griffin typed in the address into the car's GPS. As soon as Jax understood where the address was, Griffin wiped the GPS from their car and from his phone. Griffin then forwarded the image he'd taken of the kidnappers' license plate to his Mavericks contact. They should be able to track the car and, with any luck, the drivers.

"Can they really track your car, your phone, see your recent activity?" Lorelei asked in confusion, having seen what Griffin had done.

"We don't want to take the chance that they can," he said. "Worse than that is if they're tracking us via satellite."

She stared at him in horror and then cried out, "We have to ditch this vehicle."

"Like I said," he said, "we have to switch vehicles."

Just then they went through a series of turns as Jax took the vehicle on a roundabout trip and pulled into a parking lot. There wasn't much in the way of decent vehicles here, but Jax obviously had a plan. He headed to the far side where two vehicles had pulled up beside each other. The men stood off to one side, arguing something fierce, and they didn't notice Jax slide into the driver's side and take off with one their vehicles toward Griffin and the girls.

"Move," Griffin said, "now." He was out and opening the door to assist Amelia Rose. Lorelei was already out on Jax's side. She had yet to notice that there was no sign of Jax. She came racing around to Griffin's side of the vehicle and held out her arms. Amelia Rose ran into them.

Their new transport pulled up; they dashed inside and hit the road. Griffin watched behind them again, but neither man, still intent on their argument, had yet to notice that one of their cars had been stolen. A few blocks later he smiled and said, "Clear." He turned to face the girls in the back seat. "Now"—Griffin pulled the armband he'd been carrying in his pocket for just this moment—"Amelia Rose, lift your right arm please."

Shocked, she slowly lifted it to rest on his seat in front of her. "Why?"

He smiled, reached around, and placed the band in the middle of her upper arm. "You have a tracking chip in your arm. This will block the signal."

She twisted her new accessory. "It should come in better

colors."

He laughed. "No such luck. Black is all I've got. Don't take it off, *unless* you become separated from us. And then we'll use that signal to track you two down again. But blocking it now should stop the kidnappers from tracking you again."

"That's how they knew where we were after we escaped." Lorelei cried out, studying the new arm band. "We never had a chance."

Jax took another rough corner, sending the girls sliding along the back seat.

"Wow," Amelia Rose said. "He doesn't drive very well, does he?"

Jax snorted from the front seat. "I drive better than you think," he said. "I just have to make sure that we're not being followed."

At that, Amelia Rose stayed quiet.

Griffin looked at her and said, "My name is Griffin, and that's Jax."

She looked up at Griffin and said, "You're a winged horse?"

"Winged lion," he corrected with a big smile. "And you're Amelia Rose, and you're Lorelei, right?" When both nodded, he could feel their relief settling inside. "Now that we got that straight, I need to know if either of you are hurt." His gaze was searching as he studied the child and then the woman. He didn't want to ask if they'd been assaulted in any way, but it happened so often that he knew he had to be sure.

Immediately Lorelei shook her head and whispered, "We're both okay. I don't know for how long that would've lasted though."

"Any idea why you were being moved?" Jax interrupted.

"No, not really."

"They had to move us. To get us away from what they'd done to Nurse. She's in heaven," Amelia Rose said tearfully. "They killed her so we'd behave."

CHAPTER 5

LORELEI STUDIED THE two men who now held their lives in their hands. She hadn't seen anything that showed her something was off with them, but, at the same time, it was hard for her to be too complacent. She didn't know them. They'd helped her and Amelia Rose escape, but who were they exactly? "Are you sure her father sent you?" she asked cautiously.

"We're special ops," Griffin said. "Her father initiated the request, but the government sent us. I doubt he knows who the two of us are personally."

"I guess I wonder which government it is," she said smoothly.

The corner of his eyes crinkled, and he nodded. "Good question. We're both American."

Lorelei's heart froze, and her eyes widened. "But her father's British."

"One of those joint task forces," Griffin said, which made Jax snort. "Except he's an American citizen."

"I'd like to see the *joint* part of this," Jax said.

Griffin turned that light gray stare in her direction. There was no deceit, but there was also no give in them. "We were given a mission, given orders to extract both of you from the difficult situation you were in. So that's what we did."

She frowned. "Orders?"

"Yes," he said, "that's how this works. We're offered a mission, and, if we accept, we're all in."

She hated to say it, but something was almost depressing about that. She hated to be just another mission; yet, if they hadn't been designated as a mission, the two of them would still be prisoners. But she nodded and said, in a more formal tone, "Then thank you."

"Don't thank us yet," Jax said cheerfully from the driver's side. "We could have gone from the soup into the stew."

She hated that analogy. She twisted to look behind them, but nothing was there. Thankfully it looked like they'd lost their kidnappers. "Well, at the moment, the kidnappers aren't behind us, so I'll take that as a blessing."

"Yes," Griffin said, "but we need to know who's behind the kidnapping. I'm not prepared to turn you over until we're sure this is resolved and the two of you are safe."

Something about his wording sent unease sliding through her. Surely they'd not hold them hostage too, would they? "Presumably you'll turn us over to our British government," she said smoothly, "so we can go home."

"Is that where you are from?" Griffin asked, testing her honesty.

She nodded. "I'm American, but I've been living in England for the last seven years, and I've been with Amelia Rose for five of those seven."

"So her father sent you to Thailand for a holiday?"

"Her mother did," she said quietly, glancing at Amelia Rose, who was still lying on the back seat and staring at the men. Lorelei nodded and added, "Just the three of us but her father was to join us there."

"They killed Nurse Mary," Amelia Rose said in a faint

voice.

Griffin stared at her and nodded. "I'm sorry, little one. It's hard to lose someone at any time, but, under these circumstances, it's much worse. We did hear that one of your party was dead. I'm sorry about that."

"They shot her," Lorelei said. "And I think it was a lesson and a warning to us to behave, or we'd follow the same suit."

"It makes sense," Griffin said. "But apparently there wasn't any ransom note. Instead they said that Amelia Rose had been married. I thought it was you, Lorelei, originally, because I didn't understand child marriages here. Still don't for that matter," he muttered under his breath.

"They're big in many parts of the world," Lorelei said. "But the fact remains, she would not ever partake of or agree to any arranged marriage at any age, and, since she is not of age, they don't have her father's permission. None of that was mentioned to us, so I doubt any intended marriage had anything to do with this. And, although they had no hesitation killing Nurse, they didn't hurt us."

"Either way, you were both being held against your will."

Lorelei gave a strong nod. "We three were originally kidnapped on the street and were taken to some hotel. When our guard was called away from the front door to our hotel room, we escaped out the patio door. We all three left but separated soon afterward. I was to stay with Amelia Rose, and Nurse was to return to our hotel room to gather our things and wait for us to meet up with her there as soon as we could.

"As we went back to our original hotel room, they were inside the room waiting for us. They already had Nurse—

Mary, but she preferred to be called Nurse. She'd gone down for a nap, and they woke her up and had her tied in a chair when we returned. They'd hit her a couple of times. Poor Nurse. I should have known better than for any of us to return to our registered hotel rooms. We were told we were to cooperate or else. Then, as a warning, they shot her—in front of us."

Griffin winced. "They probably planned on killing her anyway," he said gently. "They couldn't leave any witnesses behind."

She hated to think of that, but it had crossed her mind. She nodded slowly and said, "I'm just so sorry that her last minutes on earth were full of terror. I'm also sorry poor Amelia Rose was subjected to seeing that. She loved Nurse very much. It's traumatizing for her."

"And I'm glad that you two are not facing your last few minutes on earth right now," he reminded her. "And, with any luck, we can get you out of this mess. Her father can get a specialist to help her deal with the trauma when you are home."

That reminder Lorelei needed to keep close to her heart. They'd been through a lot already. And she wanted to trust these two men. But something devastatingly attractive about both of them made her instinctively not want to trust them either. She'd had more than her fair share of smooth slick males. Not that these guys were like that, but she didn't want to take the chance.

Amelia Rose needed to feel secure right now, and Lorelei couldn't take the chance of these men betraying them too. "We figured her father was being blackmailed," she said in a low tone. "That maybe something related to his businesses was involved in this."

"Well, Gerard has two sons and then Amelia Rose, correct?" He kept his gaze on her.

She turned to look at Amelia Rose to find her eyes were closed. Lorelei gently shifted the little girl so that her head lay on Lorelei's lap and brushed the hair off her head. "Yes," she said. "Two adult sons who run part of the business and a dad who's old enough that he's thinking about easing back, so he can spend more time with his new family."

"And sometimes that doesn't always go over well in the family," Griffin said. His tone was bleak.

She wondered what he was getting at. She understood some of his suspicions about the sons, and she had to wonder herself. "The brothers have no deep love for Amelia Rose," she said quietly. "As sad as that is, there are an awful lot of years between them. Decades, in fact, and probably not a wish to share the very hefty inheritance pot either. However, I'm not sure risking all that would be worth it to get rid of her."

"I think, at this point in time, there's probably more than enough inheritance for three."

"Probably," she said, "but some people will never have enough."

"True enough," Jax said. "We're five minutes out."

She looked around the area with interest. "And where are we going?"

Griffin shrugged and said, "To our next destination." He flashed her a wicked grin and turned to study their surroundings.

Even though he had been speaking with her, he never really lost that sense of alertness. And it was back in full force now too. She wondered if this was because of an already pretty intense scenario or if that was just the kind of guy he was. Did he work all the time? Did one take a break from this kind of a living? Was there even a break, or is that what they did until they died? Did these men die with their boots on? She had no clue, but it was an interesting thing to contemplate. He hardly looked like a 9-to-5 office-type guy.

He was obviously the one in charge here, but Jax was an equal partner from appearances. She listened as the two discussed entryways. She didn't quite understand the wording or what they meant, but her thoughts were now consumed with Amelia Rose's brothers. She had met both of them a few times. They'd been arrogant but friendly. Both of them had been born into big money, and both of them had gone to business school, rising rapidly up through the ranks of their father's company, like their father had for his father. Yet Gerard retained full control.

The sons felt they had earned their positions, whereas she was sure the sons had viewed Amelia Rose as just an observer, a pretty little tagalong who would spend money and not make it. As long as she kept to her little pile of money off to the side and just had fun on her own, the sons probably wouldn't bother with her.

Yet her father had constantly mentioned bringing her into the business when she was old enough. Maybe that was enough to set this off. Lorelei didn't know. She hoped not because how wrong would that be to be worried about your kid sister taking part of your inheritance pot when the pot was so damn big? Taking an active role in the mega-business that surely needed more bosses? But it was so hard to know what people were thinking, and sometimes they weren't thinking at all. They were just reacting.

Griffin turned suddenly and asked, "Was her mother supposed to come on this trip?"

Lorelei shrugged. "Maybe ... originally. I don't know. I'm not privy to those kinds of plans."

"What kind of relationship does Amelia Rose have with her mother?"

Not really liking where this conversation was going, Lorelei pinched her lips together and tried to be detached about it. Obviously somebody was behind this nightmare, so they needed to consider everyone and everything. "They were friendly," she said, "but not necessarily very loving. Her mother is not very motherly, shall I say. Amelia Rose is closer to her father."

"So, if somebody wanted to hurt her mother, would doing something like kidnapping Amelia Rose be the worst way to do it?"

She shook her head. "No, it would be her horses."

Griffin went still, then gave a clipped nod. "And the best way to hurt her father?"

"Either his sons or Amelia Rose," she affirmed. "She and her father have a very caring relationship." She smiled. "We should all be so lucky."

"THAT CONFIRMS WHAT I was thinking, that maybe she was the apple of his eye," Griffin said, keeping his voice neutral and not letting Lorelei know exactly what he was thinking. Because, at the moment, he wasn't even sure what he was thinking himself. His thoughts were firing off in random directions, still putting the pieces together. But, one thing was for sure, the mother was a suspect, and so were both sons. Yet he highly suspected that was just the tip of the iceberg in this case. Hell, there were too many suspects at this point. Best if they could knock some off the list. He hated to think that either parent was involved.

He looked over at Jax, who pointed ahead. Immediately Griffin leaned forward to study the neighborhood. The address was the fifth floor of a high-rise. Underneath in the parking garage, he helped Lorelei out, then leaned in and quickly scooped up the sleeping child.

With the duffel bags now carried by Jax, a procession headed up to apartment 504. The door was unlocked. They stepped inside, and Griffin walked right through to one of the bedrooms and laid the little girl down. He pulled a blanket off the second bed and quickly covered her up. Then he stood for a long moment in the doorway, wondering what kind of a bastard would hurt a young girl. He didn't understand the child-marriage part of it at all.

However, in many countries, women were nothing but chattel, and marrying them off meant they had become somebody else's possession. In many cases, it was legally binding too. He wasn't sure about an eleven-year-old being of marriage age, but, having heard nightmare stories about child brides in many parts of the world, he wouldn't be at all surprised in theory. But, in this case, there was no parental permission. She'd been kidnapped. And that was the key.

She was also a British citizen, but women disappeared into the sex trade all too often. From everywhere. Hell, many were young girls too. It's possible marriage would be the end result for some but not for the majority. Boys had value but in a different sense; girls were valuable for blending marriages and powerful families. It was a scary world out there.

Griffin couldn't see that as being anything other than a punishment for the father though. Particularly if they thought that they could get him to believe she had been raped. Griffin presumed any parent would do anything to rescue their child from that scenario.

He stared down at his clenched fists, hating that, even now, the thought of child rape could disturb him so much. He'd seen such atrocities in the war and had tried to avoid coming in contact with much of it because he tended to lose his temper and take it out on anybody and everybody involved.

Griffin had gotten in trouble in the navy as a young seaman after finding out one of his colleagues had taken advantage of a Thai girl. She'd only been nine. The man in question had taken a hard beating from Griffin and then had been thrown in the brig until his trial, which all had helped Griffin deal with this issue, but it hadn't been enough. That little girl had to carry the childhood trauma of that rape for the rest of her life, and that wasn't fair.

Hating the thoughts in his mind, he walked to where Lorelei had collapsed into a recliner and crouched beside her and said, "Please tell me for sure that she wasn't raped."

Immediately Lorelei shook her head. "No, she wasn't. Neither of us were."

"Did a marriage of any kind take place?"

She shook her head. "No. They did treat us better this last twenty-four hours though. Amelia Rose was given food and water and a bed to sleep in."

"Probably realizing that a child being treated a little bit better would be easier to deal with."

"Or make her prettier," Lorelei said caustically. "It's all about the value of the child."

"But there could be all kinds of value involved in something like this," Griffin said. "Even if it's to make her father's business holdings look shaky because he can't look after his family. Stock prices on his US newspaper holdings have already started to drop."

"Why would people do things like that?"

"To make money," he said. "To make lots and lots of money."

"If someone did that," Jax said from behind her, "they would have sold their stock immediately. And now that the shares are dropping, it's pretty easy to buy up shares cheap when it hits its low point. Then you wait until they bounce back up again and sell them off for a tidy profit."

She shook her head, stood from the chair, and walked to check on Amelia Rose. Lorelei wrung her hands as she paced back and forth, obviously distressed. "The only ones I can think of who would have anything to do with this," she said, "would be either Gerard's sons—because they're part of the bigger business picture—or one of Gerard's enemies. And I'm sure he has more than a few of those."

"What's he like to work for?"

"As long as you're on his good side," she said with a wry smile, "it's fine. But the minute you cross him, like anybody, it's not much fun."

"Is he fair?"

She tilted her head to the side, thought about it, then nodded slowly. "Anytime I've had any dealings with him, it seems like he was fair. But then my job is looking after Amelia Rose, to teach her, to guide her, and to help her grow up. As long as I do that, and she appears to be in good health emotionally and physically, then he's happy with me. But, when he does test her on her knowledge, if she slips up, I'm the one who gets blamed."

"That's because the father never wants to believe the child is not doing what she's supposed to," Jax said with a smirk. "Did he ever show any signs of violence toward her or his wife?"

Immediately Lorelei shook her head. "Not that I ever saw. I'm with Amelia Rose most of the time."

"What about Nurse?"

"No," she said, her face softening. "Gerard had a soft spot for Nurse."

"And his wife?"

She winced and exclaimed, "I hate saying bad things about anybody."

"You don't have to," Jax said, his tone quiet but giving no quarter. "But, if you want to get out of this nightmare scenario and get back to England and be completely free of this threat, we need the truth."

"I would say it's a loveless marriage then," she said promptly. "I don't think they even have meals together."

"Any sign of a divorce in the offing?"

"I think Gerard's tired of divorces," she said. "He lost out pretty badly on the last one. Likely the one before that too."

"There would have been a prenup on this one though," Griffin said. "I can't believe he wouldn't have that in place."

"True," she said, "but it's also important to understand that he doesn't want to disrupt Amelia Rose's life."

"Sure. But one has to find happiness somehow," Griffin said. "I don't believe in staying together for the children. Those kids feel the tension, see the fights, the lack of real communication. It leaves a mark on them, in my opinion. And a child witnessing a bad marriage is not setting a good example for her either. Every child should be so lucky as to have two loving parents, who love and respect each other, and who love their children unconditionally."

Lorelei sighed. "There are more divorced families now than not in some places," she said with a nod. "All I can tell you is that there doesn't seem to be any affection or love between Amelia's parents."

"Do you ever see the three of them together?"

"Yes, but not often," she said, slowly crossing her arms over her chest as she stood, her legs slightly wide. She stared at the two men. "Is this really necessary?"

"Yes," Griffin said. "We have to figure out exactly what's going on, and, to know that, we have to figure out who the major players are and what their role in this is."

"I don't believe that either Gerard or Amelia Rose's mother has anything to do with this," she said. "Gerard adores Amelia Rose. As for Wendy, I don't think she wants anything to change the status quo." Lorelei held up her hand. "Let me qualify that. Wendy doesn't want to be poor. Wendy loves money and what it can buy. That's her status quo. Her status quo has nothing to do with being married to Gerard but that she married a rich man. Any rich man would do, in my opinion. She obviously has no respect for marriage as an institution—or even motherhood for that matter."

"Meaning, if she were to instigate matters, she'd have, more than likely, targeted Gerard instead of her daughter?"

"Exactly," Lorelei said. "When you think about it, she doesn't want a divorce, but that doesn't mean being a wealthy widow would be a bad thing."

Griffin nodded, walked to the window, and stared outward from one of the corners. He knew enough to not stand fully in front of the window and to let anybody even see him. He didn't know what the deal was on this apartment—who it belonged to; where the owners were; how their Mavericks boss came to know about—and it didn't matter.

It was a place to stay. He glanced at her and asked, "When did you eat last?"

"I picked up coffee and a few treats at that coffee shop where I met you," she said. "I shared them with the driver to make the relationship a little less strained, but that was our last meal."

"So you need food then?"

She nodded. "As does Amelia Rose. But we need good food, like real food."

Jax was in the kitchen, opening cupboards. When he opened the fridge, he said, "Aha."

Griffin looked at him and asked, "What did you find?"

"All the food's here, just like I asked," Jax said with a big smirk. "We got a roasted chicken, a cooked beef roast, lots of sliced deli meats, cheeses, and salad makings." He opened another cupboard and brought out bread and buns, then quickly took the food from the fridge, and they stared at the assortment.

"You guys came better prepared than I expected," she said in surprise. "This is definitely food, and it's people food. But Amelia Rose'll want kid food."

Jax nodded as he studied Lorelei. "If we stay another night together, we'll get whatever Amelia Rose wants. Just tell us what she likes."

"In the meantime, this is what's here," Griffin said. "If she's hungry, I'm sure she'll find something to eat."

CHAPTER 6

"I DON'T KNOW. I don't think it's quite that easy," Lorelei said with a smile as she walked over to see the possible choices for Amelia Rose. *Eggs, cream, and cheese.* Lorelei nodded. "She'll have a cheese omelet with this."

"Good," Jax said. "I, on the other hand, will have a huge salad with lots of protein." He looked over at Griffin. "You?"

"Absolutely."

The men prepped a large salad while she watched. She frowned because she hadn't been asked herself. When they had a load of salad mixed up with veggies in a large bowl, Griffin looked at her and said, "Are you having an omelet with her or a salad?"

"Just salad?"

"A whole roasted chicken is here," he said. "I'll chop up some on the side, like a Cobb salad or a chef salad."

She smiled. "I'll have some of that then, please."

He nodded and got back to work.

She wandered the small living room, hating the sense of not knowing what to do next. "Does her father know?"

"By now, probably yes," Jax said. "But we can't get confirmation."

"Why is that? You guys are just the leg men?"

"We're the ones who go in and get the job down," Griffin said, his voice harsh. "We leave the glory and kudos to everybody else."

She stilled, studied his face, and smiled gently. "And that's what your life's been like? Rescuing people from situations in foreign countries, and nobody even knows who you are?"

"Yes. And I'm okay with that," Griffin said. "If you do a job, you do it right. And, if you do it right, it doesn't matter who else knows."

"That's a quote I haven't heard before," she said curiously. "Where'd you get that one from?"

"From myself," he said. "It's a motto I live by."

"It's a good way to live," she said. "As somebody who's involved in raising a young girl in this world and explaining to her how all this works, it's not a bad one for her to understand."

"If it works for you," he said, "use it. But just keep in mind that a lot of people don't understand the hardships in life. We're never really challenged until life throws us some of the shittiest things. Then we have to pull up and out of it."

"So, besides the fact that you're very busy saving the world," she said, "what personal challenges have you had to suffer through?"

He looked up at her, surprised. "Do I have to have had some?"

She nodded. "Yes, I think so. Personal challenges ensure changes on a whole different level. It sounds like you've been through both."

"Maybe," he said noncommittally. He reached for the roasted chicken, cut it through the breastbone and through the back, and then deboned the breast, dissecting off the pieces. He placed everything on a plate as he worked.

She watched, realizing he was avoiding her question. "Have you ever been married?" He almost cut his finger. He swore softly, and she took that for a yes. "What happened?"

"What often happens when men are away at war," he said.

"She hooked up with somebody else?"

He nodded, glanced at Jax, but he was happy being by himself as he continued to build up the salad. He was listening to the conversation but not getting involved.

She walked closer, not sure exactly why she felt like she needed to prod, but there was just something about this man, so capable and so strong, so determined to follow his own rules. It's as if he was not looking at other parts of his life, the other areas where the rules might need to be bent slightly in order for him to have some peace inside. "So, did you just walk away then, not have any more relationships with women?"

He raised an eyebrow. "Hell no."

She chuckled. "Well, it's good to know. But you can't let one bad experience taint the rest of us. But I suspect something else in your past drives you to avoid marriage."

"Of course," he said. "But not my cheating wife. She's not worth the effort, but I've seen the hardships war has wrought on the women and children left behind and the dangers from other military men. It's not a pretty sight, and one I've seen way too often." He cleaned his hands and the knife. "But you'd be wrong to think it's made me avoid relationships. It's helped me stay focused on my career, but I've dated lots."

"True, but you didn't let yourself get too involved, huh?"

"Yes, but don't go thinking that I loved her dearly and

was totally betrayed by it," he said with a shake of his head. "It wasn't like that at all."

She frowned at him and said, "Then what was your marriage like?"

So he told her. She took a step back, shook her head. "Surely that doesn't still happen in this day and age?"

"Her father felt very strongly about it all and made it clear what I would do to fix the problem," Griffin said with a hard smile. "I have no idea how he feels about her now though."

"That was kind of a bitchy move to send him the photo but understandable," she said. "He forced you to live what—eight months of your life according to his will, so I guess it makes sense that you had a little retribution."

"Exactly," he said, "but I left that alone a long time ago."

"No, you haven't," she said. "Otherwise you could laugh at it. Instead your mouth still tenses and your shoulders stiffen when you think about it."

He stared at her with that same hard look again. "Doesn't mean that I'm not over it."

She shrugged. "But neither are you relaxed enough to go back into a relationship to that level again."

"I don't want to go into a relationship to that level," he said. "That relationship was at the surface level. It wasn't based on truth, faith, honesty, or loyalty. Why would I ever want to go back to that?"

"So, you should do something different," she said. "Something better."

"Maybe," he said, "but that's not quite so easy. One doesn't just conjure up a good relationship that can withstand the test of time."

She snagged a piece of cucumber from the salad bowl.

"True enough. And you never will if you don't put yourself out there."

At this point, Jax laughed. "What are you doing? Matchmaking on the run?"

She shrugged. "No, not really, but it's my attempt at a more lighthearted conversation that's not related to what we've just been through. So I'm more than happy to keep going with this train of thought and leave off discussing all this ugliness around us."

"Good answer," Jax said. He picked up the large bowl of salad, carried it over to the small table, and quickly handed her plates and cutlery. As she set the table, he asked, "What about you? Have you been married?"

"No," she said. "I wasn't going to jump into anything too early after watching several friends married and divorced within a couple years. Most now with young children to look after on their own as single parents. I decided that wasn't for me. However, when the time came, I fell in love hard and fast. I came close to marrying him, but I didn't get to the altar."

"Why? Did he fall in love with somebody else?" Griffin asked, his tone rough.

"He died in a rowing accident," she said suddenly, a catch in her voice. "We were in England for a holiday. It would be an extended holiday, while he considered going to school there. He was offered to join a rowing team. Anyway, he went out early one morning and didn't come home."

"Do they know what happened?"

"He was diabetic," she said, "and he got too cold, and they figured that he ended up without enough energy to make it back again, then fell into a coma and drowned."

"And are you satisfied with that explanation?"

She shot him the briefest of smiles. "It's an unhappy one but, yes, because I've seen him do it before. We used to hike a lot, and he was really crappy about looking after himself. If he didn't have something sugary to get him through, I could see him definitely falling into a coma."

"So then what did you do?"

"I stayed in England," she said. "Very soon afterward, I ended up with this tutoring position, looking after Amelia Rose."

"You could do something very different from that with your qualifications."

He watched as she hesitated and looked at him, and then she said, "And, of course, you guys have investigated me, right?"

They shrugged and then nodded.

"Right, so you already know about my fiancé, and the gaping hole in my life that he left behind brought me here," she said. "And, well, I could have done something different but was lost and needed something—someone—to love. By then, I'd already fallen in love with Amelia Rose. Back then I couldn't see leaving her too. Besides the pay is way beyond what I'd make in the public or private education system. Sure I could go into the political arena as a translator or work for the UN possibly, but, as I said, Amelia Rose gives me more love and job satisfaction than any other option I've looked at. So, whether others agree or not, I'm happy."

"What do you mean—leaving her *too*?"

"Her father had a relationship with the child's maid," she said, sitting down hard on one of the kitchen table chairs. "When the relationship was over, of course, the maid was gone. Plus that wasn't the first time. But each and every time it's another blow to Amelia Rose. She needed some stability in her life, somebody who could care for her and be there for her and not be her father's latest paramour."

"And you're not in line for that position?"

She chuckled. "No. Let's just say I prefer Amelia Rose over her father any day."

Griffin smiled at her approvingly. "See? Being single isn't so bad. And being faithful isn't bad either."

"No," she said. "I'm both of those. But it was also hard to lose my partner before, so I haven't exactly jumped back into the relationship setting too easily. I'm entitled to have a relationship, but it's not something I really want to pursue, especially not while I have Amelia Rose to look after."

"True," Jax said, "but you can't be single forever because of a child. She's eleven, and she's getting old enough to understand."

"She's getting old enough that she's pushing me into dating," Lorelei said with a groan. "She kept telling me which waiters and people at the hotel would be ideal partners for me." Both men laughed. She stood and said, "Speaking of which, I should check on her."

"I'll do it. You're tired. Just rest," Griffin said. He walked down the hallway.

Soon enough, Lorelei heard voices and realized her charge was awake.

She was about to jump up when Jax placed a hand on hers and said, "Let him."

She raised her brows at that but subsided. When she looked up again, Griffin carried Amelia Rose, the two of them smiling and laughing together. Wow. That was great to see Amelia Rose so comfortable with Griffin after the nightmare she had been through. "He's good with her," she murmured to Jax. When Amelia Rose was set gently on her feet, she raced over to Lorelei, and the two hugged.

Lorelei motioned to the chair beside her and said, "This one's for you."

She hopped up, looked at the food on the table, and frowned. "I don't like veggies."

"Don't you like to run far and fast?" Griffin asked. "You need veggies for that."

Lorelei looked up at him in surprise, wondering if he knew about how they had been recaptured.

"You need energy. You need food. You have to feed the body in order to keep the energy supplies running so that, when you need to run, you can run."

Without another word, Amelia Rose reached for the salad and put some on her plate. Lorelei helped her pick out the rest of what she wanted, some sliced chicken breast and her choice of dressing, and then, before long, she was tucking into the salad like she was an old veggie champ.

Lorelei shook her head in a slight way and told Griffin, "That's not the tact I would have used, but it was effective."

"It's also the truth," he said, "and I am a believer in being truthful whenever we can. Surely it's better for kids too."

She wasn't sure if that was a criticism or not, and, of course, he didn't know enough about Lorelei to understand the problems they had getting Amelia Rose to eat healthily. But, if Amelia Rose was finally understanding that she needed to eat better, then that was all good.

Lorelei thoroughly enjoyed her meal, but she caught herself yawning now that all the adrenaline had worn off and that they were more or less safe at the moment. She needed a good night's sleep tonight, but she didn't know how long they were staying. So far the men hadn't said anything to her about their plans. Whether that was on purpose or not, she didn't know.

Amelia Rose piped up and said, "I want to talk to my daddy."

"When we're in a safe place," Griffin said, "then you can."

"Are we not safe?" the little girl stared up at him, her bottom lip trembling.

He gripped her hand gently and said, "This is step one. We can't take a chance that somebody may have followed us here or that they're tracking our transmissions. So, when we do get to a place where we can be sure that we have a safe line, then you can talk to your father."

She nodded slowly and went back to eating.

Griffin turned to Lorelei and asked, "Is there anybody we should contact about your disappearance?"

She shook her head. "My parents would just worry, and they don't know even what I do on a day-to-day basis, so it's not an issue."

"Did they disapprove of your job?"

"Not so much disapprove as just thought it was below me," she said with a half smile. "Like you, they thought I was destined for bigger and better things."

Immediately Amelia Rose gripped Lorelei's fingers. "You're not leaving me, are you?"

"No," Lorelei said. "I've told you that before."

Amelia Rose sank back and smiled. "Good. Then I don't have to worry about waking up one day to find out you're gone too."

That too broke her heart. "I know," Lorelei whispered. "I've told you before that I won't leave without giving you lots of notice, and probably, at that point in time, you'll be ready for me to go, to give you some freedom."

Amelia Rose shook her head. "No, I can't imagine that."

"Well, you might want to go to another school and have friends your own age," Lorelei murmured. "But you never really know what opportunities may arise, what surprises your dad may have for you. Who knows? Your family might move to France or Greece. Or maybe you want to be a travel writer for your dad's newspaper someday, living in other cultures, or maybe a political writer, understanding what's going on in the world as things happen."

"Like what happened to Nurse?" Amelia Rose whispered.

"Kind of," Lorelei said, wishing she hadn't brought it up. "But there are good things in life too."

"Like what?" Amelia Rose demanded.

"Griffin and Jax, for one," Lorelei reminded her. "They saved us. We're not in the back of a car being carted off to some odd location to be watched by guards."

"That's true," Amelia Rose said as she turned her solemn and direct gaze to both men. "Thank you for that."

Both men nodded. Jax smiled and said, "No problem. Now let's make sure that they can't come after you again."

"That wouldn't be good," Amelia Rose said. "I don't know how many times anybody can escape before the odds are against you."

Lorelei watched as Griffin studied the young girl. Every once in a while, she said things that were almost too adult. She was caught up between a child and a young teen. Sometimes she could figure things out well beyond the ability of most adults, and, at other times, it was as if she were a two-year-old. They continued to eat until Griffin's phone went off. Everybody stilled in that instant.

Griffin placed his fork down, picked up his phone, and

checked it. "We're here for the night," he said and placed his phone on the table, then went back to eating.

Lorelei resumed eating too. "But we don't know beyond that?"

"No," he said with a smile, "we don't know beyond that."

"We should know beyond that," Amelia Rose said. "How come you don't know what happens later? Aren't you in charge?"

"Plans are happening, and people are being contacted," Griffin said. "For all you know, they're contacting your dad."

She frowned but still nodded. "My dad's not easy to get a hold of."

"Except for the red phone," Lorelei mentioned.

Griffin immediately turned toward her. "What red phone?"

"It's the phone that my dad only takes those calls directly," Amelia Rose said. "It's the one that he knows I can contact him on and not have to go through all his secretaries."

"That's a good phone number to have," he said as he stared at her. "Do you know what that number is?"

She rattled off the number before anybody had a chance to consider whether she should or not. "Don't worry. Poppy told me to only give that number to people I trust. So it's okay that I gave it to you."

Griffin immediately asked, "Did your kidnappers ask for that number or any number for your father or mother?"

"No." Amelia Rose shook her head, then smiled.

Griffin turned to Lorelei, a really worried look on his face.

She frowned. "No. They never asked me or Amelia Rose. ... Does that seem odd to you? Or is this normal? Normal for a kidnapping, I mean?"

"Not sure," Griffin said. "But I'm really glad to hear that Amelia Rose knew not to give out this number to the bad men."

Amelia Rose perked up and smiled again.

Jax dialed the number and then handed the phone to Griffin. "It's a safe phone," Jax explained to Lorelei.

When a man answered, Griffin asked, "Gerard?"

"Yes, who is this?" he snapped. "And how did you get this number?"

Griffin immediately put the phone on speaker and looked at Lorelei and Amelia Rose. "Say hi."

Amelia Rose piped up. "Poppy?"

There was silence, then the man on the other phone exploded. "Amelia Rose, is that you, honey?"

"Yes," she said. "We're safe. Griffin and Jax saved us." She gave Poppy a rambling and an almost incoherent explanation of everything they've been through. Finally the father interrupted her gently to make sure that she was not hurt and that she was okay, and then he asked, "Is Lorelei with you?"

"Yes, I'm here too, Gerard." Lorelei's tone was friendly enough but more businesslike. She quickly confirmed what Amelia Rose had been trying to say. "Jax and Griffin are special ops," she said. "We're in a safe house, eating right now."

"Well, thank heavens for that," Gerard snapped. "Let me talk to the men again."

She returned the phone to Griffin. Then she gazed at Amelia Rose, who was now plowing through food but still talking with a bright smile on her face. "See? We're safe now," Amelia Rose said. "And Daddy knows it too."

"Exactly," Lorelei said. "But remember. We're not out of danger. We're still not back in England, and we still have men chasing after us." She tried to keep an ear to the conversation that Griffin was having with Gerard, but it was hard because Amelia Rose kept talking in her other ear. Now that the child had spoken to her father, she was doing much better.

"I understand you were supposed to come to the hotel, sir. Is that plan still happening?"

"No, not now," Gerard said briskly. "I want the two of them back in England immediately."

"Well, we're still in Thailand, but I don't know for how long," Griffin said. "I just need to know if we have more people we need to look after."

"No," Gerard said. "Your orders are to bring her straight home."

"I'll relay that upward," Griffin said formally. And then he hung up and looked at Amelia Rose. "Good thing you could remember that number."

"It's the one thing my poppy made me memorize," she said. "And I didn't forget, did I?" She turned to look at Lorelei. "He can't be mad at you this time."

"I don't think he'll be mad at me for a while," Lorelei said, "although I could be wrong."

"Will he blame you for the kidnapping?" Griffin asked in confusion.

"It's possible," she said. "I was following instructions, but I wasn't expecting to be kidnapped at a hotel."

"And both of you escaped once too, didn't you?"

Lorelei slid a glance toward her charge, but she nodded.

"Yes, but that didn't work out so well in the end, so it's not something that we're worrying about right now."

"It's my fault," Amelia Rose said. "I couldn't run anymore. And they caught us." She grabbed the salad and put more veggies on her plate. "Nobody told me veggies would make me run more."

"Well, now you know," Jax said in a serious tone. "You always need to keep fit, and you always need to eat the proper food. You never know when you'll get into a tough spot and need that energy."

Amelia Rose nodded soberly. "Now that I know, I'll look after myself better."

Lorelei was surprised to hear that. She faced Griffin. "Can you get us out of the country?"

"Do you have any documents with you?"

"No," she said, "everything was stolen when we were kidnapped."

"What about at your hotel? Is any of that material still there?"

"Possibly," she said, "but I don't really want anybody from that location to know that we're still alive."

"Meaning, that they're involved?"

"Or meaning, that they don't need to lose their jobs over us," she said. "And, if they are in trouble, we don't want them to get into more trouble. Not with those men. Not with what they are capable of."

"One of us will return to your hotel," Jax said. "See if any of your stuff is there that we can retrieve."

"I doubt they held the rooms for us," she said.

"How long were you booked for?"

She stopped, stared, and nodded. "That's right. We were booked for seven days."

"So, even if you weren't physically there, they have no reason to take away your room or to store your belongings elsewhere." Griffin glanced at Jax. "I'll go there later tonight."

"Good," Jax said. "I'll stay here on watch."

And that's what they did. As soon as the dishes were done. and the table was cleared off, Griffin stood, snagged his laptop and phone, and he turned to Jax. "I'm taking the bug detector, but I'm leaving the car in case you need to move quickly. I'll pick up a ride for me. Track me via my phone."

"I'm on it," Jax said it.

Then Lorelei watched Griffin walk out the door.

GRIFFIN ARRIVED IN his stolen vehicle and parked it five zigzagged blocks away, near a commercial district, so, even if the kidnappers tracked him to this car, they would have no idea which business he went into. Yet, if the kidnappers had any brains, they'd know he was too close to this hotel not to be coming here. So Griffin would make this a fast trip in and out.

He approached the hotel with a nonchalance that he was far from feeling. He'd already done a quick check around the perimeter, careful to avoid any cameras. And found neither security nor armed guards. Nobody had shown any signs of extra force. He walked inside with another group, choosing one with a couple tall guys that he could effectively hide behind while facing away from any cameras in the lobby, casually watching the elevators and jumping on with another group of tall visitors, and headed up to the rooms that

Lorelei had told him they had for themselves. Amelia Rose's father was supposed to get the room across from them. It was an interesting choice. They could have had a family suite that would have been a little grander. But maybe the father planned to switch it when he got here. Or he wanted privacy for a female guest traveling with him.

Griffin still wanted confirmation that the father was supposed to come, not just because the father said so. He sent a quick text to Jax to ask the chat window people.

On it.

Because, if the father was involved in something like this, Griffin needed a little more proof of what was going on. And it didn't make any sense that the father would be involved, but Griffin didn't want to exclude anybody at this point. That way just led to problems.

Once upstairs, other people stepped off the elevator with him, and the only camera on the floor seemed to be here, so it captured his back at best. Standing at the hotel room door, he stopped, double-checked the room number, and then quickly unlocked it with his tools. He stepped inside; the bedroom appeared to be just as the women had left it. Their clothes were here; their suitcases were here; everything they needed was here. And more—Nurse's belongings too.

He quickly searched for cameras. Found none. He gave the bug detector a good sweep over the rooms. Again nothing. At least that was good. He surveyed the rooms again, reminding himself to get in and to get out fast.

He frowned, thought about it, and decided he might as well take what he could with him. He quickly packed everything up in the first bedroom, then went through to the second bedroom and found the same thing. Only here, Amelia Rose and all her clothes had been unpacked neatly and placed in the dresser. He quickly packed it all back up and then did a sort through to make sure that all the beddings and clothes were clean of listening devices or cameras, just to make sure the bug detector didn't miss anything.

He found no messages left here by the girls or the kidnappers as far as Griffin could tell. He found no cell phones. The kidnapper had at least taken them. Yet Griffin found a couple laptops as he packed up their belongings.

He knew that the girls were a little suspicious of everyone else still, and rightfully so, but as long as he could get their gear to them, that would help them feel like they were a little bit safer.

His phone beeped. A text from Jax.

Earlier airline reservations for father confirmed, then canceled after we were alerted of kidnapping event.

Well, it didn't exonerate Gerard. Maybe he was just good at covering his bases. But it seemed to substantiate his statement.

With four suitcases now making his exit a little bit more awkward, Griffin stepped out of the hotel room and wheeled the two big ones, with the other two thrown over each shoulder, while heading toward the service elevator, where thankfully there were no cameras. He stepped inside and let it take him down to the very bottom, which was the service garage, where he'd have more choices as to which vehicle to steal this time.

Once inside the dim, gloomy area, he found a dark corner, moved the luggage off to the side, and quickly chose his ride. He had just unlocked the passenger side when a vehicle entered the underground parking area on the far side. He quietly loaded up his new vehicle with the girls' stuff, and, as he hopped into the driver's side, he watched as four men got out of a van, carrying weapons.

They had his undivided attention now.

They walked over to the door that led directly into the hotel and stood on either side, as if standing guard. He frowned, but then another vehicle showed up with two more men inside. One man hopped out and walked toward the other four, shouting in a rapid-fire way.

Using his camera, Griffin took photos of the man approaching the hotel and of the four gunmen. When somebody glanced in his direction, Griffin turned his head, as he started up the engine and slowly drove past. When he came near the two vehicles that they had driven, he took several photos, including the license plates, but couldn't get decent shots of the driver, still in the second vehicle. He got several but doubted they'd lead to any facial match. He drove past them, up and out onto the street. He parked around the corner, locked up the vehicle, and rushed back into the garage. There he could see the four armed men standing around the vehicles and discussing something. So the head guy and the driver with him must have entered the hotel, as there was no sign of those two.

Frowning, Griffin sent the photos to Jax, asking him to look up these men. And then Griffin headed to the side of the van so he could hear their conversation. Some words were in English, and some were not. It was a guttural mix of both. But from what he understood, the boss man got immediate word from a hotel staff member that the suite of rooms had been cleaned out.

His heart sank that his visit had been discovered so quickly. Obviously this was a trap to get another chance at kidnapping the girls. Well, at least that part of the kidnappers' plan didn't happen. But the last thing Griffin wanted to do was throw any extra eyes in their direction. He needed to get the girls away from this whole area, not bring up more questions. Knowing that these armed men were still looking for the girls, and now him, he headed out of the garage but had every intention of entering Lorelei's hotel via the front door.

When his phone buzzed in his pocket, he quickly ducked between two other vehicles and pulled out his cell. And the message came back from Jax saying that the person photographed going into the hotel was the same one who had originally kidnapped the girls. He was the organizer behind it all, as far as Lorelei could tell. License plates were stolen from different vehicles. So no leads there.

Griffin walked up the front steps and through the lobby. It was evening, and a few people wandered around, but mostly the lobby sported muted lighting and a more relaxed and romantic atmosphere as only a hotel could offer. Griffin saw no sign of the man he was looking for.

As Griffin sat in the shadows of the lobby and watched, the elevator opened up, and the same man that he had photographed earlier came walking forward, sending rapid-fire questions at the staff at the front desk. From the bewildered look on their faces, they didn't have a clue what he was talking about. Still, the man kept pointing to the elevator, and then he switched to English and said, "All their stuff is gone. Where did you put it?"

They looked from one to the other and said, "We didn't touch it. Nobody's touched the room as per your orders. All of it was left exactly the same, as you told us to. Nobody's been allowed in."

The kidnapper was obviously well-respected and came with a lot of power.

"Well, somebody not only got in," he said, "but everything's been cleaned out too." He turned, firing off orders to anybody who would listen. "You go and find out now," he roared. "Check the cameras, check everywhere. I want to know who took their luggage."

With everybody focused on the man clearly in charge, Griffin slowly rose to his feet and casually walked out and around the side of the hotel to his new vehicle. There, he hopped into the driver's seat and turned on the engine, and drove slowly back to the apartment. Interesting. They were after all of the girls' possessions now. Why hadn't they taken them in the first place? And why did they want them now?

Unless they planned to recapture the girls—and soon.

CHAPTER 7

LORELEI, ALTHOUGH GRATEFUL to have her belongings back, was more than a little worried with Griffin and Jax in the corner, busy, heads bent together, whispering hard and fast. Griffin showed Jax some photos, and both men then separated, sat down at their laptops, and pounded the keys furiously. She crossed her arms, waited for the right time, and then asked, "So what's happening?"

Griffin didn't even look up. He kept pounding away.

She walked over to him, reached out a hand, and touched him on the shoulder. When he didn't respond, she dug her nails into the cords alongside his neck and said, "Don't ignore me."

He dropped his hands from the keyboard and glared up at her. "Just because I choose not to answer doesn't mean I'm ignoring you."

She raised an eyebrow. "You're not answering me."

"You don't have a question that I can answer."

She brought a chair up and around so she could sit beside him. "Meaning, you don't know what's going on, or you don't want to tell me?"

Jax laughed. "Both."

"And that's not good enough. I've been to hell and back, and I'm very concerned about Amelia Rose. So somebody should start talking."

Griffin, instead, picked up his phone, swiped through, and brought up several photos. "Do you know this man?"

She nodded slowly. "We saw him at the very beginning, but I don't know who he is."

"I do," Jax said. "He's security for a big arms dealer in Thailand. His boss owns the compound you were held at. He's got business deals with governments on a global scale."

"What's that got to do with Gerard's businesses? He's in media."

"I'd say," Griffin added, "that your kidnapper was more into military privatization than anything."

"So that sounds like a rebel, a vigilante, a guerrilla, not an enemy of Gerard's."

"Probably an enemy. Most likely a competitor. Or possibly hired for this job. But then who in Gerard's company would know this guy?"

"Gerard and his sons all deal with international business deals. But you're wasting your time there," she snapped. "Gerard's not into military stuff."

Griffin gave her a flat stare. "How would you know?"

She blinked in confusion, then shook her head. In a low voice, she said, "He's not that kind of guy."

"Yes, he is," Griffin said in a low tone. "The media is a major part of his business, but he's involved in a lot of military contracts for communications as well."

At that, Lorelei sat back and stared at him, stunned. Then she muttered, "I never even considered something like that. But I should have. Communications is a big business, and who needs it the most? Well, *the military*."

"Exactly. And, quite often, communications companies supply their tech—whether software or hardware—for other countries as well."

"So, this guy didn't like the price of Gerard's services?"

"Or Gerard wouldn't do business with him is another possibility. So who would know who he does business with and who he doesn't?" Griffin asked. She winced. "Does any of that sound familiar?"

"I have no clue," she said. "I have nothing to do with his business, and, no, I haven't overheard any conversations about military communications for sure. My job is Amelia Rose."

"Sure," Jax said, "but you're an intelligent woman. You must have gotten some impression as to what's going on."

"But not about this," she protested. "Gerard has had lots of business meetings in his home, but we're always off in a different wing."

"Have you seen many different nationalities come through the house?"

She nodded slowly. "Sure, but I couldn't tell you which ones they were."

"Makes sense," Jax said. "I hate to say it, but Gerard could be dealing with both sides of a war at the same time."

"I couldn't tell you who these people were, not their names," she said, "and all the black limos look the same. I never really saw anybody get out of them. The limos drive in, and they drive out. I don't know who was inside those limos." She motioned at his phone. "Why aren't you sending that photo to Gerard and asking him?"

"I am," he said, "but I've gotten a little more devious, and I'm checking the cameras at the house." He pointed to the monitor in front of her, and she gasped to realize it was the front door of Gerard's biggest family estate that she and Amelia Rose normally lived at.

"Oh, my gosh, how can you do that?"

"I'm doing it for your sake and for her sake," he said bluntly. "And, no, Gerard would not be happy if he knew." Just then a black limo pulled up in the video.

"See? They all look like that," she said. "I think Gerard owns three or four himself."

The driver hopped out, opened up the door behind him, then walked around, and opened up the other door. Several men in business suits exited the vehicle and walked toward the front steps.

"When was this?" she asked, peering closer.

"Three days ago," he said. "I wasn't sure how far back to go in a video feed, but three days earlier brings up some interesting possibilities."

"But this could be legitimate business," she said. "It doesn't mean it has anything to do with our kidnapping."

"Maybe not, but it doesn't mean it doesn't either. In order to understand the enemy, we have to understand the people involved."

She stared at him and said, "I really don't like the way your mind thinks."

He turned, flashed her bright white teeth, and said, "Why don't you lie down and rest?"

She glared at him and leaned closer. "Why don't *you* lie down and rest?"

In a surprise move, he stole a kiss and cheerfully said, "Can't. I'm on duty."

Stunned at the shock of his lips against hers and the spark that had flashed between them, she sat back awkwardly. She crossed her arms over her chest as she tried to figure out what to do next. A gentle exit would have been nice, but she'd passed that point. She looked at Jax and caught him grinning. She glared at him, then announced, "It's not funny."

Immediately he wiped the smile off his face, and, in the gravest of voices, he said, "Absolutely not."

She raised both hands in frustration and said, "You two are impossible."

"Hardly," Griffin said. "You should be grateful to us."

"Yeah? What do you want as thanks?" she asked suspiciously.

He looked at her, and she could see the anger in his eyes. "Not that."

"I didn't think so," she said.

"You'd better not think so," he said in a warning note.

She shrugged and whispered, "Everything's topsy-turvy these days." Then she rubbed her temple. "And I'm getting a hell of a headache sorting my way through it."

"Well, you need to remember," he said gently, "that you're not alone anymore."

She thought about that and brightened. "You're right. I'm not. So you should be able to handle it all." She got up to check on Amelia Rose.

He called out as she walked away, "That's what we've been trying to say."

"Oh, and here I thought you're telling the little woman to go lie down and to not worry her pretty little head about it."

When she heard an odd spluttering sound, she turned to see Jax barely containing his mirth as he stared between the two of them. "You know, if we weren't on the job," he'd said, "I'd suggest you guys grab a hotel for a couple nights and work this through your system."

She spun around yet again, her hands on her hips, and glared at him.

Jax shrugged and said, "I'm just saying. There's enough electricity in this room to crack and cook an egg. If you guys ever let loose that firepower, you two would burn up the sheets."

"I'm not interested in burning up the sheets," she said stiffly.

"I am," Griffin said immediately. "So, if you ever change your mind, let me know."

She gasped out loud and then realized he was teasing, looking at her with the most innocent of looks on his face, but his eyes twinkled. She stormed over and pointed her finger in his face.

"Careful," he whispered in a low tone.

"No, you be careful. Amelia Rose could hear you."

Griffin's gaze hardened. "You should know better than that. I wouldn't tease you like this in front of the child. And you really don't want to get me mad on this subject."

But instead of backing down, she shoved her face against his and said, "Why?"

He grabbed her on either side of her face, tucked her just a little bit closer, and kissed her hard. And, damn, if the passion didn't arise once again, and sparks flashed all around them. She groaned softly, and he forcibly pushed her away and said, "Jax is right. We'd better watch what we're doing."

She shook her head. "What the hell is this?"

"Adrenaline," he said. "Fear, gratitude, danger. It mixes hormones and passion all together. Now leave. Keep temptation away from me, woman."

She snorted. "No problem." And she stormed off to visit Amelia Rose.

IT WAS ALL Griffin could do to stop the laughter from bubbling up and outward. She'd look shocked, frustrated, and frustrated in another way too. He could relate. He shifted back to his laptop and tried to refocus. He knew that Jax was grinning like a crazy man. Griffin just shook his head at him. "Don't say anything."

"I don't have to say anything, aside from maybe I'm the one who'll have to go for a walk and leave you two alone."

"Not with the kid," he muttered.

"Good point," Jax said. "Maybe the kid and I will go for a walk then. For just the briefest of moments."

Griffin considered what that opportunity could mean, and then he shook his head. "Not going to happen. Not while we're on the job. And definitely need longer than *the briefest of moments.*"

"You may have to make do," Jax said, "because, when the job's over, there's a good chance you two will be on opposite ends of the earth."

"True." He sighed, his shoulders sagging as he thought about it. But he wasn't a randy teenager anymore, and keeping his own sexual passion in check was something he was used to. He'd sent the photos to his team and had asked them to forward those to Amelia Rose's father. Within minutes, his phone rang. He looked at it. *Gerard.* He quickly answered, putting it on speaker. Jax moved closer.

"So you do recognize that first picture we sent you?" Griffin asked.

"Yes," he said in a harsh tone. "He's one of the men who threatened me if I didn't do business with them. I was supplying China and South Korea with special communications, and they wanted the same deal."

"And you didn't give it to them, I presume?"

"No," Gerard snapped. "I didn't like anything about the deal. And I didn't like anything about the people behind the deal."

"With good reason, it's one of the reasons I went back to the hotel and retrieved their personal belongings," Griffin said. "But now we've got a problem because I think they were behind the kidnapping."

"You went back to the hotel and got their stuff?" Gerard asked curiously. "I don't understand why."

"Because I didn't want to leave anything behind," he said honestly. "It's much better to remove it and not leave bits and pieces the kidnappers can come back for, using them as signs of proof of kidnapping, by sending you a jacket or a skirt or something worse."

"I never thought of that," Amelia Rose's father said. "That's a little disturbing."

"I also wanted to see if somebody at the hotel had been ordered to clean out their rooms. Instead, the staff had been ordered by that man to leave everything left behind as it was."

"They were held in their rooms originally and then moved," Gerard said.

"And how do you know that?" Griffin asked curiously.

"Because the staff said that they couldn't raise anybody in the room, but the doors were all locked, and they were told to stay away. But then, when they went back again for housekeeping, the rooms were empty."

"Likely when they tried to escape out on the beach," Griffin said, his tone low. "Your daughter's feeling very guilty for not keeping up with Lorelei as they ran away."

"She's never been very physically active," her father said with a sigh.

"Well, the good news is, she's at least eating vegetables now," Griffin said drily.

Gerard gave a short bark of laughter. "Well, that's something. She's pure and innocent," he said, soft and gentle. "And I want to make sure she stays that way."

"Until when?" Griffin asked. "You know that she'll grow up at one point in time. This alone has helped her to grow up a lot more. You do realize that she saw Nurse killed in front of her, right?"

There was silence on the other end of the phone, and then Gerard swore deep and heavy. "My poor baby," he whispered finally.

"Nurse's death was to set an example that the two of them behave and follow orders. Nurse was also grabbed and held in the hotel room, the same room that they were in."

"Yes, they had a suite," he said. "I always do that."

"Same suite as for you?"

"No, I reserved my suite across the hall. But it's not like we've traveled to Thailand annually or even every few years, and we don't stay at the same hotel regardless," he said, his voice distant. "The girls must have been seen at the reception desk or on their way back and forth to the hotel."

"Time to get them fake IDs then when they travel, to register them at hotels under those fake names too."

"Maybe … if she ever travels again. I understand the microchip helped you to identify where they were?"

"Yes. They were being held in a compound owned by that well-known arms dealer the kidnapper works for," Griffin confirmed. "But the girls were then moved that night, and we caught up with them when the kidnapper's vehicle was sidelined by an accident."

"Did you cause the accident?"

Griffin gave a short laugh. "No, not this time. Otherwise the chase would have gone on much longer. As it was, there was a big pileup, and it was a pretty ugly crash site. The kidnappers were at the head of the line. I came up behind, managed to get the girls, and we turned around and got out of there, while more cars drove up and boxed in the kidnappers."

"Well, I'm grateful for that," he said. "Have you any idea who else might be involved?"

"No. We're still running background checks on everybody in your company and your family, especially anyone who would know the arms dealer," Griffin said smoothly. Then he waited. And Gerard didn't disappoint.

"My company and my family?" he roared.

"Yes," Griffin said. "It could be that this is a complete blackmail scheme from the outside, perhaps orchestrated by your denied military man. But somebody had to know your schedule pretty well. Somebody had to understand that the three females would be completely alone on this trip. This wasn't just by chance that they got kidnapped. No 'Oh, look. There are three people we can kidnap and run a ransom deal through.'"

"The way you put it," Gerard said, "I guess that makes sense. But I run heavy security checks on everybody in my company. Nobody would dare cross me."

"And that just means that somebody already has," Griffin said with a heavy sigh. "Look. I know that you run communications and consider yourself high-tech. Often though, shit like this is very close to home."

"How close?" Gerard asked, but his voice held a warning, as if Griffin wasn't to cross the line.

"Well, if you don't think that I'll check in on your sons

and your wife, you're wrong," Griffin said coolly. "Because this kidnapping event won't happen again. That little girl's been through enough shit. And Nurse did not deserve to be murdered on a holiday a long way away from home."

"No, she didn't even want to go," Gerard groaned. "My wife insisted."

"And I understand that your wife and your daughter don't have a close relationship."

There was silence on the other end. "That's quite true, but that doesn't mean Wendy would do anything to harm Amelia Rose," he said briskly, almost dismissing the concept out of hand.

"And, for that, I need to understand how the inheritance works, upon your death." Griffin knew he was crossing some major personal lines here. "A lot of people would benefit if your daughter doesn't survive either."

"There's enough money to go around," he snapped. "And I don't want you making accusations against my family."

"Outside of your sons and your wife, who else stands to inherit?"

"My brother and his family," he said. "My brother's been my vice president for a good twenty years."

"And do they all get a big-enough piece of the pie that they're all happy?"

"They should be," he said. "They get a decent voting block now, but that doesn't change much with my death."

"And how do your sons feel about that?"

"They are fine with it," he said, his tone turning bewildered. "You don't really think somebody is angling for more, do you?"

"The problem with being greedy," Griffin said, "is that

generally you're too greedy to see where enough is enough." On that note, he changed tact and said, "I need the name of your brother and the names of the family members that work for you."

Gerard gave him the list and then said, "You better be wrong about this."

"I hope I am," Griffin said. "But, so far, somebody has already kidnapped your daughter, twice, and killed your nurse. I'm sure you feel that something needs to be done after Amelia Rose has been put through so much."

"Well, as soon as I get my daughter and Lorelei home, Lorelei will get a raise. And Amelia Rose may never leave the country again."

"And that would make sense," Griffin said, "but it's not necessarily the right answer."

"So, what are you thinking?"

"I'm wondering why you didn't send any security with the women, traveling to a foreign country." Griffin stared down at the phone, waiting to hear what response Gerard would give.

In a slow tone, he said, "That was my wife's idea. She felt that traveling with security was stifling. She never did see that there was any danger."

But even Griffin could hear the broken tone in the man's voice. "I know about your first son," Griffin said. "And I'm sorry about that. I guess that's partly why it surprised me that the women were traveling alone."

"Because I got complacent," he said, his voice returning, vibrating with anger. "Something I won't forget again."

"And whose idea was it that the three women travel here on their own?"

"My wife's," he said, "but I agreed."

"And how often does something like this happen?"

Silence. "Not very often. Usually my wife or I travel with them."

"So, when was the one last time that the two women traveled alone with Amelia Rose?"

"I'm not sure they ever have," he said, his voice rising.

"And you still haven't received a blackmail notice?"

"No, I was expecting it anytime now. I was taken with my firstborn son a long time ago, but he was only two years old, and they separated him from me. The kidnappers blackmailed my father, who started this company and was doing quite well at the time. Nothing like it is now, mind you, but enough that the kidnappers figured to cash in on his success. They made him and me sit and sweat and panic for three or four days, and *then* they sent a note with a ransom demand. Immediately he jumped on it and tried to pay"—his tone turned harsh, unforgiving—"but ..."

"And then you were betrayed?"

"Yes, I was betrayed," he agreed. "The money was picked up. I was released at the gate of the estate, still tied up and a hood over my head, and my son's dead body was dumped close by. The cops never found the killers," he said, the old grief still catching his tone.

"So, you assumed that it would be a similar scenario this time?"

"Yes. Only I don't understand this game. Yes, I was expecting a ransom note. Thank God, you have them safe. I need to know what the play is here. I don't understand, but I can't lose another child this way."

"No," Griffin said. "I don't understand either. At least not yet."

CHAPTER 8

LORELEI HAD SPENT some time calming Amelia Rose, especially after hearing her poppy's raised voice on the phone. The child was soon placated, but she clung to Lorelei. Both girls had moved to the couch in the living room of the apartment, where Amelia Rose soon fell asleep and where Lorelei fidgeted, near enough to hear the conversation on speaker still ongoing in the kitchen.

When the call ended, Griffin leaned back in his chair, his face thoughtful and pensive, she hopped to her feet and ran toward him. She didn't even question when he opened his arms, and she threw herself into them to give him a hug. "You don't look so good."

"I'm fine," he said. He frowned and noted that Amelia Rose was once again lying down. "Is she sleeping? Through all that yelling?"

Lorelei nodded. "She's been sleeping a lot lately. I think she sleeps to avoid thinking about the emotional scenarios, like her poppy on the phone just now."

"Stress will do that to you as well," he said. He glanced at Jax, hunkered over his laptop at the kitchen table. Griffin swept his arm in that direction. Lorelei sank into a chair next to Jax, Griffin joining them, and all three of their heads bent together as they spoke in low tones.

"Do you have a suspect?" she whispered. "A business

enemy or family?"

"I'm not sure," Griffin said, "but let's look at this. The brothers gain Amelia Rose's interest in the estate if their sister doesn't get home. Her uncle gains as well if she doesn't get home. And the wife, what would she gain?"

"Depends if she's setting up the blackmail," Jax stated. "Imagine if she gets, say, a ten-million-dollar ransom. She ends up with her daughter and gains the money and is free of Gerard, free to live elsewhere, to remain separated informally if not legally. Plus, like any blackmail, she's free to blackmail Gerard again if Wendy maintains possession of Amelia Rose. It's the ultimate ATM."

"Meaning that, there's a prenup, where she doesn't get very much and can't stand staying with him and wants a new way to start a new life but with tons of money?" she interpreted Jax's comment.

Both men looked at her in surprise but then nodded. "Exactly."

"That's a bit rough," she said. "But honestly, I could see her having her own daughter kidnapped. She's not family oriented but is all about Gerard's money and the house and living the high life."

"Can you give us an example of what you mean?"

Her voice lowered as she leaned closer. "Gerard is no saint but tries to keep his affairs quiet, but she's makes no attempt to be discreet—jumps all men between fifteen and fifty, anywhere and anytime, even if Amelia Rose is around. Drinks like a fish and shows no loyalty to her husband at home or out in public. I know he's sick of her, but I don't know if he's done anything about a divorce yet. Honestly, I can't believe he's put up with her antics this long, even if she is Amelia Rose's mother."

"And that sucks," Griffin said. "It's bad enough to think that you've been kidnapped because of your father's business dealings, but do you really want to hear that all this terror you were put through was because of your mother's machinations?"

"What about Nurse?" Jax asked. "What was the relationship between Amelia Rose's mother and Nurse?"

Lorelei winced. "The worst," she said slowly. "Wendy wanted Mary fired. Said Nurse was old and useless."

The two men exchanged hard glances.

She shrugged, then frowned. "But to go from wanting Nurse fired to then arranging for the woman to be killed, … that's pretty cold, even for Wendy."

"Depends on what ransom money might have come through."

"But they didn't have to kill Nurse for that," she protested. "She could have been rescued, and the mother still gets her money. Then she leaves behind Gerard and Nurse. Maybe even Amelia Rose. Oh my …"

"Surely Wendy or whoever won't even try for a ransom now that Gerard knows his daughter has been rescued, or is another party in play?" Jax asked.

Just then a text message came from Gerard. **Ransom note just came through. Twenty-five million. Unmarked bills tomorrow night at a specified location. Please confirm you still have my daughter.**

Instead of responding by text, Griffin hit Dial and handed the phone to Lorelei, as she turned to watch Amelia Rose still resting on the couch.

As soon as she heard Gerard's voice, she said, "Gerard, this is Lorelei. We have her. She's sound asleep."

"Oh, thank God," he said, and she could hear the fear

and anxiety threatening his voice. "So, what the hell's going on here?"

"I'm putting you on speaker," she said, and she hit the button and laid the phone on the table.

"I highly suspect," Griffin said, "we have kidnappers who lost their bait but will try to get the ransom money anyway. While they still look to recapture your little girl, they'll see if they can get a money drop and run."

"So they're assuming then that you guys have gone to ground and haven't contacted me. Is that it?"

"Well, if it wasn't for your daughter remembering the number of your red phone," Griffin said, "the normal route would be to take the little girl to the police, right?"

"Or at least a consulate, yes," he said.

"In which case, the media would have already found out."

"Particularly given our names," he affirmed. "So, ... because the media hasn't told the story, you're thinking that the kidnappers don't know who has my daughter and Lorelai or if their two victims escaped on their own or if somebody even worse has them. And, while they track down the location of their victims, they'll still stick to the plan."

"Wouldn't you?" Jax challenged.

Gerard sighed. "Of course. Anybody would. So I still have to show up at that meet."

"Get MI6 assistance and set it up so you snag whoever is picking up the money. That event is set to happen on English soil, so MI6 would want to take part in this."

"They are already involved," Gerard said.

"Good. And hopefully, with any luck, we'll snag whoever is behind it on your end. We're still on the lookout here for the kidnappers to make another move on the girls, but just know that, at the moment, we're all safe."

"Good," Gerard said, his voice stronger. "Lorelei, you still there?"

"Yes, Gerard, I'm here."

"I just wanted to say," he said, his voice choked up, "I wanted to say, *thank you*. Thanks for keeping Amelia Rose safe."

She smiled. "I said I would. It's been a pretty rough trip so far. So, the next time you plan a holiday, may I suggest we pick the South of France?"

He gave a burst of shallow laughter and said, "That sounds like a good idea to me. And I will ask that you keep looking after her the same way as you have been. I don't think I could stand to lose another child."

"We have no intention of letting that happen," Griffin said.

"Good," Gerard said. "Losing one was horrific. The thought of losing another one? ... No, I'd rather shoot myself first."

After that conversation ended, Lorelei decided it was time to call it a night. This had been one long ugly Tuesday. She went to bed early after Jax moved Amelia Rose from the couch to a proper bed, hoping that maybe she and Lorelei could finally get a decent night's sleep. They were obviously still in danger, hiding from whoever was after them locally, but there had been an amazing amount of progress. She knew the men were staying up for a while, sorting through the information.

It was all a bit confusing for her because she was more about teaching her charge instead of studying new people close up. She knew Gerard considered himself a great judge of human character, but he'd married Wendy, so how good a judge could he be? Not to mention the fact that they were still married and that confused Lorelei. Unless it was only for Amelia Rose's sake, in which case the marriage would be done relatively soon or at least in seven years when Amelia Rose became an adult. To think though, that the mother might have had a hand in her daughter's abduction was beyond Lorelei's comprehension.

No, she refused to believe it until there was proof.

Amelia Rose was a gorgeous little girl inside and out, and she was just on the brink of entering young womanhood. Lorelei knew Amelia Rose would take the world by storm in whatever direction she chose. But more than that, Lorelei had been privileged to be a part of Amelia Rose's journey so far. At one point in time, Lorelei wanted children of her own, so tutoring Amelia Rose had been an interesting trial. Lorelei laughed at that word because there hadn't been very much in the way of trials with the child. So maybe it wasn't a good test after all for having a child of her own.

And, of course, she'd started on the job when Amelia Rose was already six, so Lorelei had missed her early years. Amelia Rose adored spending time with her poppy but not so much for time spent with her mother. In that way, Amelia Rose instinctively understood the difference between quality time versus just putting in time. Lorelei could easily see the reason why.

Still, it was late. Better she stop this endless mental loop and get some sleep.

Lorelei had her suitcase now, giving her clean PJs for tonight and fresh clothes for tomorrow. She quickly had a shower, taking extra long to do her hair, which was dark blonde and looking almost black with dust and dirt. She rinsed and washed it several times and then, when she stepped out, not wanting to go to bed with it all wet, braided it in a thick plait down the center of her back. Finally clean and realizing she could afford to sleep, at least right now, she dressed in her summer pajamas of a camisole and matching boy shorts and crawled into bed.

She was hoping that the monsters would stay away tonight. But she was afraid, as tired as she was, that was almost an invitation to let them in again. And she'd have no control because she'd be asleep, and her subconscious would be running the show. She slowly closed her eyes and drifted off. But it wasn't long before someone chased her and the child, her lungs burning as she tried to carry Amelia Rose along and to help her move faster and faster. Lorelei could feel the panic threatening to choke her. And, when she finally woke up with a cry choking in her throat and her heart pounding desperately to get free of her chest, she sat up in bed and gulped air.

Griffin stood in her bedroom doorway, staring at her.

He took three short steps to her bedside, sat down, and pulled her into his arms.

She burrowed in deep. "Will the nightmares ever stop?"

"Yes," he said, "they will. But maybe not as fast as you'd like them to."

She didn't even want to contemplate his words. But it was understandable. Time helped heal and added distance to a lot of things. She sighed and tried to pull back, but he had nothing to do with it. He just held her close and whispered against her hair, "Relax and remember that you're not alone. We're here to help, and we're here to protect. Your cry was terrifying enough that it almost gave me a heart attack. So I need these few moments."

That gurgled a laugh out of her. She looked up to see his

grin flash. "You said that on purpose," she murmured.

He grinned, nodded, kissed her on the temple, and said, "I did, but you're obviously feeling a little bit better. Now lay back down, and I'll pull the covers over you. If you want, I'll stay in the chair in the room."

"No," she said, "I should be fine." At least she should be inside. She didn't know if she would be or not. But it was ridiculous to think she would need him to stay in the room with her. She curled up under the covers, and he tucked her in and dropped yet a second kiss on her temple, making her wonder at the ease and naturalness of it on both their parts. And then she listened as he walked away. She counted his steps to the doorway and then couldn't do it. "Stop."

He froze, returned to her side, and whispered, "What?"

She groaned. "I don't want you to stay, mentally, because I know I need to handle this," she whispered in frustration. "But just the thought of you leaving right now is making my heart pound, and I can hardly breathe."

Instead of grabbing the chair on the far side, he nudged her over and laid atop the covers beside her. He wrapped an arm around her and pulled her against him. "Sleep," he said. "It's much easier to deal with everything in life if you have rest. When you don't, the problems seem bigger and much harder to find a way around. So, let's sleep tonight and worry about it later."

She hated being weak. She hated knowing the sense of security that just being in his arms gave her. But she wouldn't look a gift horse in the mouth. As long as he insisted, she could acquiesce. She snuggled deeper into the blankets, yawned once, and then whispered, "Thank you."

He gently hugged her closer and whispered, "You're welcome. Now go to sleep."

When she woke yet again a few hours later, arms were wrapped around her and held her close. She twisted and turned until she saw it was once again or maybe still Griffin. She opened her eyes to reassure herself and, seeing his gentle concerned face, closed her eyes and drifted off to sleep again. When she woke yet again, she struggled less, recognizing his touch, and finally fully woke this time. It was early morning, and he snored gently beside her. She smiled and whispered, "I wonder if you got enough sleep."

She checked the time to see it was past seven in the morning. She slipped out of bed, grabbed her clothes, dressed in the bathroom, and then walked away, leaving him to snooze gently on her bed. She stepped out into the main apartment to find Jax up and making coffee.

He looked at her, smiled, and said, "Is he still sleeping?"

Embarrassed, she nodded and whispered, "I don't think he got much sleep though. I kept waking up, screaming."

"To be expected," he said seriously. "And I would have done the same, but he got there before me." He waggled his eyebrows at her.

She chuckled. "Not likely."

"Absolutely," he said. "Not to make this all about the danger right now, but we need you as focused and as capable of running if need be as we can."

She immediately winced, hearing the reason behind his wish to help her. "In theory," she said, "I know that. But, in reality, it sucks to think that's the reason he was in there."

"No," Jax said, "don't misunderstand." He pressed the button for the coffee and turned to face her. "That's the reason either one of us would have gone to settle you, but he didn't have to stay. He did that because he cares."

She could feel the warmth blossoming inside. "Dangerous time to be caring about somebody," she said lightly. "It's likely the danger that's heightening his emotions."

"Maybe for you," he said bluntly. "But this is the work Griffin has done for years. I don't remember a single case where he spent the night holding a woman close just so she didn't have to battle nightmares on her own."

She sagged into the kitchen chair, thinking about that. "He really lives up to his name, doesn't he?" She tried to add a note of humor to it but there was a softness in her voice, and she knew that Jax caught it.

He nodded. "He's always been a protector. And he's been hurt a couple times."

"Haven't we all?" she asked, staring off in the distance. She gave herself a mental shake and said, "While I was battling demons, what kind of night did Amelia Rose have?"

"She slept like a rock," he said. "Unbelievably so."

"She always has had that ability," Lorelei nodded. "I was very jealous of it, even before this trip."

"You don't sleep most of the time?"

"I do," she said, "when I'm in my own bed, but I'm not as comfortable being out and about in the world, so traveling generally impacts my sleeping."

"That's the same for a lot of people," he said. "But at least you're doing fine now."

"I'm definitely doing a lot better, after some sleep," she said. "Not to mention a shower and a clean change of clothes." She motioned at the clothes she had on. "I wonder why they never cleaned out our rooms before?"

"I bet they're regretting it now," he said, "because they obviously lost that advantage. Not to mention the fact that we knew where you weren't."

"Can they track Griffin?"

"I doubt it," Jax said. "He's a shadow in the night."

"But even shadows …" she whispered, trying hard to still panic in her heart, "shadows create shapes."

He nodded seriously, brought cups over to the table, and sat down as they waited for the pot to drip. "But he's very good at what he does. And we won't be here for long anyway."

She looked at him in surprise. "That's too bad," she said. "I was hoping you'd stay."

"No," he said, "we all have passage back to England."

"Interesting," she said with a frown. "How are we traveling?"

He smiled. "Underwater."

She stared at him in shock. "What?"

"We need to get you out of sight of cameras and away from everybody, so our choices were public transport, private transport, or we had to get creative."

She stared at him. "Underwater? Not scuba diving, right?"

"Don't worry about it," he said. "We got this."

She hated to say it because she knew they did have it, but it was still disconcerting. "Does Gerard know?"

Jax shook his head. "Better that nobody knows. We want to make sure there are no leaks and no betrayals anywhere along this process."

"Fine," she said. "I'm all for that. What's the first step of this unique journey we're taking?"

"Some interesting flights," he said with a grin. "You don't get seasickness or motion sickness, do you?"

She shook her head. "No, both Amelia Rose and I are good travelers that way."

"That's good," he said as the coffeemaker beeped. "Because this could be a fun ride."

He got up, poured the coffee, and wouldn't say another word.

GRIFFIN HAD WOKEN up as she left and took a few moments to go to the bathroom, scrub his face, and begin the day. He walked out hearing Jax telling Lorelei about the next step of the journey. Griffin headed for the coffeepot and poured himself a cup. "Have we confirmed all the details yet?"

"Almost," Jax said. "Just the first leg is in question."

"Right," he said, "and that's the most important one."

"I think it's more or less resolved. We're just waiting for a final confirmation."

"Do we have time for food?" Lorelei asked.

"We do," Jax said.

On that note, Griffin walked to the fridge and pulled out eggs and bacon. A little bit of chicken was left, but they had pretty well scoffed up everything else. He brought out those leftovers from the fridge too and said, "This is what we have to work with." He started the eggs and bacon and watched as Lorelei got up and snagged a piece of chicken and stood there by the table, eating it.

"How did you finally sleep?" he asked, his voice low and soft, but that gaze of hers, well, it would melt his heart if she lit it.

She smiled up at him. "Well, at least I slept, thanks to you. You didn't have to spend the whole night, you know?"

"In order for you to get to sleep, yes," he said, "I did."

"Did you get any sleep?" she asked worriedly. "There's

no point in your rescued kidnap victims being safe and able to run if the guy who is protecting them isn't."

Jax laughed beside her. "She's got a point there, Griffin."

"I slept pretty decently," he said, surprised that he felt strong and capable. As soon as the bacon was perfectly cooked, he laid it on a paper towel and mixed up the rest of the eggs into a scramble. With the last of the bread, he made toast and said, "Food's a bit of a mix-up, but it's what we've got."

Just then a sound came from the other bedroom. Lorelei bolted to her feet and raced in. Both men froze as they listened to the girls' conversation. Then realizing that the child's cry was followed by laughter, they both calmed down.

Jax looked over at Griffin. "You're getting in too deep."

Griffin stopped stirring the scrambled eggs in the pan. He looked over at his friend and said, "Maybe."

"Did you think about that?"

"No," he said, "I didn't. Not sure I can either."

"Meaning?"

"I think it's already too late. I've met a lot of women in my time, but I can't say too many have affected me like this."

"Just stay objective," Jax said.

"I will be," he said. "I have to admit that I'm operating under a new set of parameters. I've never had anybody I cared about to this extent."

"I know," Jax said. "I guess that's why I'm bringing it up. We want to make sure that decisions are still made for the right reasons."

"I'm always a pro. You know that," he said. He turned off the burner and quickly dished up the scrambled eggs into a serving bowl, then he called out, "Lorelei and Amelia Rose, breakfast."

He finished setting the table, holding off looking in the girls' direction as they came toward him because he knew, like Jax had seen, Griffin's gaze would go first to Lorelei, if only for the chance to see her again. And how sad was that? He lifted his gaze to see her warm brown eyes staring at him and a grin at the corner of her lips.

"She slept well," Lorelei announced. "She says two heroes are looking after us, so there's no reason for her to have any nightmares."

Amelia Rose bounced forward and threw her arms around Griffin and gave him a big hug. Then she walked over to the table where Jax sat and hugged him from behind. Jax chuckled, turned around, picked her up, and stood with her in his arms, then tossed her once. She let out a shriek.

Lorelei looked at him in amazement. "How can you even lift her?" she asked enviously. "I don't have that kind of strength."

"You don't need it either," Griffin said as he motioned at the table. "Sit down. Let's get eating."

Obediently she sat on the chair beside him, just like how he would have sat beside her. They were almost like homing pigeons, instinctively seeking each other out in the darkness. And he knew just how bad he really did have it. Amelia Rose, on the other hand, was more than happy to sit beside Jax, even pulling her chair closer toward him.

"Did you get any sleep, Jax?" She chattered away as she dug in, scooping up eggs with a serving spoon but then snagging up bacon with her fingers. Lorelei immediately chided her for her fingers, but she just grinned up at her. "Jax uses his fingers," she said.

And Jax deliberately reached across, used his fingers, and

snagged more bacon.

Lorelei groaned. "You two are incorrigible."

But Griffin, not to be outdone, using his fingers, chose two pieces for himself but also two for her and dropped those in her plate. He raised an eyebrow and said, "One does what one must …"

She gave him a special smile that hit him hard. He dropped his gaze to his plate, confused, irritated, and frustrated at the timing. When he raised his gaze again, Jax looked at him with a warning in his gaze. Griffin gave a brief nod and tucked into his food. Objectivity was everything in this game.

And, in games like this, making a mistake was fatal.

CHAPTER 9

SOMETHING HAD DEFINITELY changed between her and Griffin. Lorelei wanted to spend time in a corner with a cup of tea and really delve into what was going on, but there was no time. As soon as they finished eating, the men had bounced up, cleaned up the kitchen, and packed up the rest of food into a large Ziploc bag, which she didn't quite understand, until she realized that it was all leaving with them. She raced back to her room, quickly made the bed, and checked that there were no obvious signs of anybody having been here. Then she went to Amelia Rose's room and did the same.

With the bags packed and sitting at the front door, Griffin made a final tour through the apartment and opened the front door that led to the hallway. Jax was out first, checking that the coast was clear. And then he nodded toward Griffin. Jax grabbed half their luggage and had his duffel on his back and motioned for Lorelei and Amelia Rose to follow Griffin, who carried the rest of their luggage. He headed forward and hit the button on the elevator, Jax behind them all. As soon as they all stepped in, instead of going down, they went up.

Lorelei's eyebrows went up too. She frowned at him, but Griffin gave a small shake of his head, and she understood it wasn't the time to ask questions. This was the time to go with the flow if she wanted to get her and Amelia Rose out of here safely. With her heart hammering against her ribs, she hung on to Amelia Rose, not giving the girl a chance to back away from her.

Amelia Rose looked at her and whispered, "It'll be okay, Lorelei."

She was probably hurting the child's hand with her panicked grip, so she gentled her hold. Lorelei gave a small chuckle and said, "I hope so."

"It's all good," Amelia Rose said. "These guys will look after us just fine." And her tone was so confident that Lorelei was amazed. Was that the innocence of a child who hadn't seen quite enough of the world to understand just how ugly the underbelly could be? Yet she'd seen Nurse killed. So maybe it was about trusting in *these* heroes.

When they got to the floor they wanted, after they had bypassed all the others, Jax quickly moved to another elevator and motioned them inside. Without question, the four piled in with all their luggage, and he hit another button. When the elevator doors opened this time, they found a small entranceway with glass doors in front.

They were on the roof.

Lorelei gasped as Griffin opened the glass door and stepped outside, getting them to move quickly. Apparently they were on a schedule. They followed her out, and she would have asked a question but couldn't be heard as a helicopter flew overhead and suddenly landed in front of them. She looked at Griffin, and he nodded, grabbed her arm, and said in a low voice against her ear, "Hang on to Amelia Rose."

Jax was already ahead of them. He spoke with the pilot and opened the back door, tossing up luggage. He called over to them, "Come on."

They quickly raced forward, with Griffin showing them how to duck below the rotors. Then he picked up Lorelei and lifted her into the chopper and did the same with Amelia Rose. Jax stowed their luggage safely, belting it in. Once inside, both men climbed up, and they went to town, locking down harnesses on both girls. They took seats across from them, even while the pilot lifted the helicopter. The doors were off, and she got a bird's-eye view of the city as they soared high above.

The pilot flew for about forty minutes and then landed at what looked like a yacht club. He set the helicopter down, and, without another word, the men got off, helping the girls and taking the luggage with them. There, they strode toward the end of a single long dock. They moved quickly and efficiently, not running, but Lorelei and Amelia Rose had to run to keep up. Lorelei was afraid that that in itself would cause attention. But, when she got to the end, a speedboat, and a big one at that, sat nearby.

Surprised—yet nothing really surprised her anymore—she hopped in, accepted the life jackets that they were both given, put hers on, and then helped buckling up Amelia Rose. The girl was well on her way to getting it buckled herself when they were off again.

Lorelei had no clue where they were going, but apparently it was important that they get there fast. The speedboat was noisy, too noisy to talk and be heard. The wind was brutal too. Even behind the windshield, it wasn't enough to stop the cold wind from biting each of them. Even though the temperature and the sun were hot, that wind-shear factor was something else. But they came up against another large yacht and were quickly disembarked onto the new vessel. Finally, when the speedboat left, she turned and looked up at

Griffin. "I get the need for speed but that thing is dangerous to anybody's hearing."

He nodded but didn't say a word about the remark but instead said, "Now we'll stay here on deck for another short trip."

She smiled at him while he pulled out a laptop. She saw he had a satellite feed link that appeared to be directly overhead. "Is that us?"

"Now we wait," he said with a nod.

She smiled and nodded, but the yacht was quite a ways offshore. She didn't have a clue where they would go. That speedboat had taken a tremendous amount of energy from her. They'd been on it for just long enough for her to completely lose her orientation. She sat down with Amelia Rose beside her.

"How long are we waiting?" Amelia Rose asked.

"A while."

Amelia Rose piped up and asked more questions. She wanted to know how big the yacht was, how fast it could go, whose it was, and could they go to one of the rooms on it. Jax answered each and every one of her questions patiently and calmly, with as much information as he could.

And, for the last part, he said, "No, you can't."

She looked up at him and pouted. "My dad has a yacht," she announced.

"I'm sure he does," Jax said with a smile. "But this is one of those mega-yachts. I doubt his is this big, although it could be."

She shrugged. "I never get to go on it. Maybe it's bigger?"

"Maybe that's what we should do next time," Lorelei said. "Maybe you can get your dad to go on the yacht with us."

"Maybe," she said doubtfully. "I think he leases it."

Lorelei didn't know how long they would wait. It seemed like they were expecting another ride immediately, but that didn't happen, and the yacht stormed ahead at a decent rate. She frowned, but, when wondering if they would get a cup of coffee or at least some water, a trolley was pushed down to the far corner.

Jax retrieved it and brought it forward. "Oh, nice, anything anybody could want," he announced. And, sure enough, there was a pot of tea and a pot of coffee, sandwiches, and little extras, like cheese and fruit. She grabbed two plates, took a selection, passing one plate to Amelia Rose and sat back down where she had been, so she could stare out at the ocean. And to sit close to Griffin.

"I have no idea how you made all this happen," she said, "but thank you."

"It's what we do," Griffin said.

"Well, maybe," she said, "but I wonder just how much you do versus how much your team does."

"True enough," he said with a chuckle. "You don't do any of this without a team behind you."

She nodded. "Not to mention money."

"Most people aren't paid for their part in this," he said.

In light of their kidnapping for a multimillion-dollar ransom, Lorelei was happy to hear that. "I can't even imagine where we're going from here," she said. "At least for the moment, it's peaceful. It's quiet, and I don't really feel like we're in any danger."

"And you could be wrong about that," Griffin said. "Not only do we have the normal problems but this particular area is well-known for pirates too."

She stiffened and stared at him in shock. "What?"

He nodded. "The good news is, armed security is on board just for that event."

"But that's ridiculous," Lorelei said, glancing around nervously. "It's like we're at the end of the ocean."

"It is what it is," he said with a nonchalance that surprised her.

"Surely we aren't getting blasé about pirates now, are we?"

"I'm more concerned about the men who kidnapped you two. Let's make sure that we get you home safe and sound with nobody even knowing that you made it there."

"You know we could have gone by private jet, right?"

"We could have," he said cheerfully. "But, as long as you're undercover and out of the way, you have no idea where we are and what we're doing. And neither do the kidnappers."

And just when she thought it was time for a nap, by the position of the afternoon sun, Griffin stood, gathered all the dishes, put it on the tray, motioned to Jax, and said, "It's time."

In a small voice, Lorelei asked, "Time for what?" She hated to admit it, but she was damn afraid that he would pull out scuba gear or something equally dangerous. She'd never been much of a water person, and this was getting scarier and a whole lot more dangerous than she'd first thought it would be.

He looked at her with a grin on his face and said, "You'll see."

And, beside her, something—small—came up out of the water. A round object, until the rest of it broke through. They were coming alongside a submarine. She bolted to her feet and stared in shock. "Oh, my God," she croaked.

"Just like Jax told you. *Underwater.*"

THE TRANSFER WAS made as quietly and as efficiently as possible. And the two girls were now safely in one bunk in a spare cabin on the supply deck. They had been led here by one seaman who made no conversation and neither did he expect any. Griffin noted the four bunks for the four of them. He settled into his lower bunk, placed his laptop underneath his bunk, with Jax already settled up above in the top bunk, and said, "We'll take a nap."

"A nap?" Amelia Rose asked. "Didn't you sleep last night?"

His lips quirked. "I did, indeed," he said, "but I have to be ready for whatever comes. So right now, it's an opportunity to grab some shut-eye." And he closed his eyes but couldn't sleep. It was also time for him to let his mind wander and to get all the information he had in his head organized and reorganized.

Besides the initial checks into Gerard, his previous wives, Lorelei, Nurse, and even Amelia Rose, they had further backgrounds on both sons, on the current wife, and on the brother and his family, but absolutely nothing pointed a finger at any one person. They were still working on the family connections.

Griffin had a suspicion it was all connected to the brother, but he had no proof. Just a question about a man who worked at his brother's company knowing it would never be fully his. Also the brother could be involved with yet another family member, but that led to the big question of, why partner up? Or was it to have the connections to pull this off? One had an idea but couldn't do it alone. Hence the need for the second party.

If so, then they must share the ransom money. That often didn't go well. Unless one partner wanted something much different than the other.

They'd done a deep search on Gerard's business holdings but had found nothing criminal or underhanded. And nothing involving Thailand, other than two of Gerard's companies were buying satellite time and looking at overhauling their global communication systems.

No, this felt like it was much closer than a business-related retaliation, even though that played into this, what with the security guard for the big arms dealer in Thailand being the original kidnapper. Yet they had not found a link between the original kidnapper and someone in Gerard's family. And yet, this was all about family. Griffin knew it in his gut. He had seen takeovers within a family happen before. A lot of times, the younger generation didn't want to wait for the older generation to retire. It usually had fatal consequences for the elder generation.

Gerard though, in this case, was hardly senile or even elderly. But, if his sons were looking for more power, more money, and more status, this would definitely be one way to get it. Both sons were married and, according to the details, have been for several years. No children yet in either marriage. And then there was Gerard's wife.

Griffin felt they were missing something. They were missing *somebody*.

On that note, he rolled over and looked at Lorelei. "Can you make me a list of everybody in the household?"

"Don't you have that already?" she asked without looking at him.

"I have an official one," he said, "but I want an unofficial one from an insider."

She looked over, puzzled.

He nodded. "So include boyfriends, girlfriends, delivery people, and anybody who you see on a regular basis at the house."

Understanding lit her chocolate-colored gaze. She nodded, reached into her bag on the floor for the personal notebook that she always kept with her, and started writing. As he watched, she had already written down more names than he expected. "Also write down in what capacity you know them as," he said. He dropped back onto his pillow, linked his fingers, and placed them under his head, while he continued to think about all the information swirling around in his thoughts.

He knew that Gerard didn't want to think it was anybody in the family, but Griffin was pretty sure Gerard was wrong. He rolled over, looked at Lorelei again, and said, "Add anything you know about his brother's family."

"He's married, has two sons of his own, and was there with Gerard right from the beginning. I'm sure you have intel on all these people," she said in exasperation, "so what difference does it make what I write down?"

He smiled. "Because you see things. You see things differently." And he rolled back over again.

He could hear her snort, but then Amelia Rose said, "He's right, you know? You do see things differently. Any time I get upset or get into an argument with Mom, you always point out another perspective to help me adjust."

"Well then, you help me with this list," Lorelei said. "Who do we see in the house all the time? Because you know that you and I are both invisible."

"That's true," Amelia Rose said. "But we also work on that."

Griffin sat up and looked at her. "What do you mean by that?"

She shrugged. "We work hard to not be seen a lot of the time."

"And why is that?"

"Because, if I go out, I get in trouble," she said with a conspiratorial grin to Lorelei. "My dad likes to think that I'm super smart because I spend hours and hours working on my books. But the thing is, I'm super smart because Lorelei teaches it to me, and I get it fast and easily. So then we have lots of free time, but I'm not allowed lots of free time." She rolled her eyes. "They want me to always work on something else. But I want to have fun too."

"And that all makes sense," he said. "So what do you do to appear invisible?"

She shrugged. "We're very good at listening for footsteps and hearing conversations using back staircases. Even a couple secret entrances and exits to the hallways are in the back."

"Interesting," he said. "I gather then the house that you live in is old."

"Built in the 1500s," she said with a big smile.

"Right. So then you should add people to the list too, Amelia Rose. Maybe you'll remember some who Lorelei forgot." He laid back down, thinking about what a life it was for the two of them. Part of the big machine, full of expectations, and then condemnation if the expectations weren't met. And what kind of a life was it for a child to go from study to study to study? She needed playtime and free time and time to think and time to just be. But then again, that was what life was often like in some of these wealthier families.

He half listened to the girls and half let his mind churn again. To him, it all boiled down to power. Somebody wanted something. Gerard wasn't willing to give it. They took his daughter instead. She was leverage, clear and simple. So, who wanted something from Gerard, and what was it that he wasn't willing to give?

He looked at the two girls. "What is one thing your father really wants in life?"

The two looked at him, nonplussed.

"Let me rephrase that," he said, capturing the angles in his head. "What is the one thing your father isn't willing to give up?"

"His company," Lorelei said instantly. "Power."

He looked over at Amelia Rose. "And do you agree with that?"

"Yes," she said. "But also me. Although, if I'm honest, I'm probably a close second."

He nodded. "Which is why you were kidnapped," he said. "Because you're a close second, so they're forcing him to make a choice. Give up his first choice and keep his second choice, or keep his first choice and lose his second choice. But, if he gives up power, he gets to keep you."

"But then the contest was already lost," Amelia Rose said sadly. "Remember that part about me being second choice?"

"That's how *you* feel," he said with emphasis. "But not necessarily how your father feels. He may not have the ability to show you that you're in first place, and he may not have had the time or the necessity to decide which was in first or second place until now."

"But surely, if it's something like power, once he's got his daughter back, he'll turn around and come after whoever did this," Lorelei said in confusion. "So, whoever is doing this has to make sure they have a loophole to get what they want and to stay safe themselves."

"Or not so much to stay safe," he said softly, "but to ensure …" And then he left it hanging.

Lorelei looked at him for a long moment, puzzled, and then her eyes widened in knowledge. She moved closer to Griffin and whispered, "To make sure he can't come back after them. In other words, although we're in danger, so too is her father."

Amelia Rose watched them but didn't seem able to hear them.

Griffin nodded slowly. "And again I don't think it's a case of *we're in more danger than he is* or *he's in more danger than we are*. But it would look extremely suspicious if something happened after this kidnapping event that suddenly had Gerard out of the picture. If the masterminds behind all this were smart, they'd make it seem like an accident. Because really, if somebody can take both of them out of the equation, what happens to the company?"

"It goes to the sons, I would think," she whispered, curious. "But I don't know how the will is written."

"And let's not forget the brother is the vice president, so he would potentially move up or possibly get fired depending on how many shares he has …"

She nodded slowly. "Can you send a warning to Gerard?"

At that, Jax swung down off his bunk and said, "I'm on it." And he walked out of the room.

As he left, Amelia Rose hopped to her feet and said,

"Can we leave the room? Can we go explore?"

"Unfortunately not," Griffin said. "That's not allowed." When she frowned at him, he shook his head. "By rights, Jax shouldn't have left either."

"We don't want him to get in trouble," Lorelei said.

Amelia Rose didn't bother with words. She raced to the door and tried to open it. When she found it locked, she turned to Griffin in shock. "Will they let him back in?"

Griffin nodded. "They will. He's not far. He'll be out in the hallway, talking to somebody."

"Oh," she said in a small voice.

He realized just how much stress was on her shoulders. He shouldn't have had this conversation when she was sitting here and listening, but, if she was as smart as everybody said, she needed to know that their danger was not something so easily avoided.

"Have you got that list for me?" he asked, looking over at Lorelei. "I've already sorted through information we have on the sons. They both started in the company as young men and worked their way up. Both are respected and well-liked. No hint of being upset that Dad hasn't stepped down yet. So not sure if they are hiding dissent really well or if there isn't any—or rather not much. All young men want to move up, and all men want to be Top Dog, but, while Gerard is there, there's no moving him down and out of the company. It would take something major for that to happen."

"What do you think? Is this everybody?" she asked Amelia Rose, who took a couple minutes to study the sheet and then nodded. Lorelei ripped it off the notepad and handed it to Griffin. He laid back down as Amelia Rose sat beside Lorelei.

"A lot of names are on here," he said. "Some I have never even heard of."

"That's because a lot of people are quiet in that house," Amelia Rose said defiantly. "They like to play games too."

"Games?"

She shrugged. "They're not allowed to be on the premises overnight in some cases, but Lorelei saw one of the maids who lives on the premises and has a boyfriend, and he comes and goes by the back entrance. The maid's boss doesn't like him, so he's not allowed to stay overnight, but he does anyway."

"I wonder if security knows about that?" Griffin muttered.

"That's only one of many instances," Lorelei said quietly. "A lot of the staff do leave and return at odd hours."

"Anything suspicious about it?" he asked.

She shrugged. "I don't think so, but again I don't know."

"Right," he said. It was interesting though. Griffin sat up and grabbed his laptop, checked to see if he had an internet signal, and then sent a text message asking for a moment of internet to send out intel. All communications and emissions were severely restricted on submarines so it might have to wait until they surfaced. He waited, and, sure enough, the chat window opened up, and he was given a black box to type in to. He quickly typed in all the names, one at a time, with the bits and pieces of information the girls had given him. As soon as he was done, the chat box closed, and the link severed.

He frowned, sat back, and said, "Well, we'll see if they can find any more information."

"If you have internet," Lorelei said, "can we use our laptops?"

He looked at her and said, "You can have your laptops but, once again, no outside access."

She stared at him. "Is that for our security or yours?"

He fixed a steady gaze on her. "Just by being here, we're putting hundreds of other men's and women's lives on the line. So my answer is that it is security for *everyone* aboard this sub."

CHAPTER 10

IF LORELEI HAD known how they were traveling, she would have been super excited about this opportunity. But it had happened so fast, and then she was escorted to stay in a room without any chance to even look around, and now she was stuck here. They were on their second day. And she had no clue how long it would be. The men were completely relaxed, taking the time as it passed easily, but, for her and Amelia Rose, time was not going quickly.

She looked at Griffin and asked, "How much longer?"

"Not long," he said.

She snorted. "Pretty sure you've told us that several times already."

"We'll be surfacing soonish."

She raised an eyebrow. "Hours, days, weeks, months, years?" she asked, ending on a caustic tone.

He grinned. "Hours."

Immediately Amelia Rose sat up and stared at him in shock. "Really?"

He nodded. "We're just waiting for the go-ahead."

Just then an odd sound ran through the submarine; Lorelei sat up and looked around. "What was that?" The angle of the people shifted.

He looked at her and said, "We're rising."

She stared at him, then looked around, feeling the sub

rise up to the surface. "Are you sure we couldn't have a tour, even a little one?"

He shook his head. "Not in any way, shape, or form."

Her shoulders sagged. "Are you blindfolding us to get us up and out?"

"No, but nobody else will see us." His phone buzzed. He looked down, nodded, and said, "Let's go."

"What if we weren't packed?" she asked in a curt tone.

"We didn't give you a choice," Jax said, stepping in. "We never know from one day to the next. Now we know, and it's a good thing that you followed our instructions and stay packed."

And, sure enough, they had everything. They were told to repack to be ready to go at a moment's notice, which is why the last couple days had seemed almost anticlimactic. But, with Jax in front, Griffin behind, and Amelia Rose between them, they were led out and back up to the surface. As Lorelei stood here, staring at the ocean around them with just the bare minimum of the sub showing, she was astonished. But right in front of them was a different ship. She looked at it and asked, "And how are we getting on that?"

Griffin tapped her shoulder, and she turned around. A small pontoon boat waited for them. They were quickly transferred to the small boat and then moved out to the larger one. As they made the transfer yet again, Amelia Rose laughed and said, "This has been fun. How long will we be on this ship?"

"Not long," he said. "We're taking a helicopter again."

It was like a replay, only in reverse of their trip out.

"At least you seem to know what you're doing," she said. She was grateful to be off the sub. And, more than that, she was just grateful to have been released from the prison of that small enclosed room. It hadn't been that bad, but they'd been tired and waiting on edge, knowing that they could be moving at any time. They were led up to the top of the current ship, which she had no clue what it even was. It looked like a small tanker, but a helicopter landing pad was on the top deck, with a helicopter waiting for them. She looked at Griffin. "Takes a lot to set up something like this."

He nodded. They rushed onto the helicopter, and it took off almost immediately. And as it went high in the sky, she could look out and see land in the distance. She shook her head. "I have no clue where we are."

"Not a problem," Griffin said. "You will soon."

She snorted. But, when the helicopter settled down on the landing pad of Gerard's home, she cried out in surprise. "I had no clue we were so close," she said. As soon as the rotors slowed enough, several men raced from the estate toward them. The helicopter doors were open, and all four of them were escorted off and quickly led into the house.

There, Amelia Rose turned, looking around. "We're home again," she cried out. As soon as she was inside, she ran through the front hallway, calling out, "Poppy! Poppy!"

Double doors opened, and a man strode toward them. As soon as his gaze fell on his daughter, Lorelei could see the love pouring from his face. He opened his arms, and Amelia Rose ran into them. He picked her up and hugged her close, then twirled her around, holding back the tears. She knew Gerard was an emotional man. Usually they only saw his negative emotions though—not this side.

Lorelei glanced at Griffin and Jax and whispered, "See? He really does care."

"Absolutely he does," Jax said.

"The question is, who's using that to get what they

want?" Griffin asked.

She didn't even want to hazard a guess. After a few minutes of hugging his daughter, Gerard walked over, still with Amelia Rose in his arms, her legs wrapped around his waist as she beamed at Griffin and Jax.

"This is my poppy," Amelia Rose said.

Gerard held out his hand and shook both of the men's hands vigorously. "Thank you so much," he said.

Jax nodded but didn't say anything.

Griffin shook his hand and said, "You're welcome."

Gerard's gaze dropped to Lorelei. He smiled and wrapped an arm around her shoulders and hugged her up close. "I can't believe what you two have been through," he said.

Lorelei stepped back, smiled up at him, and said, "Don't mind if the next time you want to send me to Thailand, I refuse."

He rolled his eyes at that, his face hardening. "Nobody's going anywhere until we know what's going on."

"Good," Griffin said, "because we need to talk."

Gerard looked at him solemnly, then focused on the girls and said, "Let's get you guys to your rooms."

Lorelei desperately wanted to stay with the men so she could hear the details but had the feeling they would be put into their place as to where *the women belong.*

But Griffin surprised her. "I think Lorelei needs to hear this too."

Gerard frowned at him. "What does she have to do with any of this?"

"Outside of being a victim and potentially could still be a victim," Griffin said, his tone brooking no argument, "she needs to know how much danger you're all still in."

"Not her surely," Gerard asked, his arms crossing as he geared up for his more belligerent and domineering wouldn't-budge manner.

Lorelei shook her head. "It's okay, Griffin," she said. "You can fill me in later."

He frowned, not liking her answer, but nodded.

As she turned to walk away, she stopped and said, "Please don't leave without speaking with me," and waited until both men nodded. And then she grabbed Amelia Rose's hand and said, "Let's go unpack our bags."

"But I want to stay with them," Amelia Rose said.

"Amelia Rose, don't you argue," her father ordered.

She turned and glared at him. "You're not the one who was tossed into vehicles and locked up in hotels and treated like you were nothing," she shouted at him. "We have a right to know what's happening now."

Surprised and maybe even astonished at the suddenly disruptive manner of his daughter, Gerard frowned at her. But Lorelei stepped in and said, "She is overwrought. We have been kept abreast of everything up until now. It would help her mind to calm down if she understood that we were safe now."

"Of course we're safe," Gerard said, bewildered. "She's home."

"But you don't know a lot of things yet, like whether or not the reason that we were kidnapped started here," Amelia Rose said, and then she turned and ran away.

Offering an apologetic smile, Lorelei followed her charge. She knew that the men would have a heck of a conversation coming up. She had a good idea what Griffin wanted to say, but way too many uncertain elements were involved. Gerard needed a man-to-man talk. She almost laughed at that. Because if ever there was a position that kept the women in *the women's place*, it was this one.

It's not that she would ever succumb to that mentality, and it bothered her that Amelia Rose was being raised with that mentality, so Lorelei had done what she could to let Amelia Rose know that her opinion matters and what she had to say mattered. Nothing was quite so easy as letting the world dominate you so that you became a silent victim by just not even speaking up.

It wouldn't be an easy conversation in the office. Gerard was very particular about dealing with matters concerning his family. He was also a bit of a control freak, and no way would he entertain any implication that somebody else close to him was involved in this nightmare.

She wished she could be a fly on the wall.

"WHAT IS IT you want to speak to me about?" Gerard asked in a more genial tone than he had expressed at the onset. He motioned at the two visitor chairs in his office and took his spot behind his imposing oak desk. It was a power play to make them feel uncomfortable, but Griffin hadn't lived in this world for as long as he had to allow something like that to throw him.

"We think the kidnapping is connected to your family," he said bluntly.

Gerard's gaze widened, and he shook his head. "No way in hell."

"What happens if you die?"

His eyebrows rose. "The estate's fairly convoluted," he said. "There's no simple answer. It's not as if my wife gains everything up on my death."

"Of course not. What about the company? How does that get divided up?"

Gerard's fingers pounded on the desk as he thrummed them. "My sons get an equal share. My brother stays on as the vice president, and he has a small voting block. He doesn't gain much more."

"Interesting," Griffin said. "So what happens if you willingly sign over more shares to a third party or a fourth party?"

"*Willingly* would mean that I'm handing off some of my control. Not happening."

"How much do your sons each have now?"

"Twenty percent," he said, "and I have fifty. Actually fifty-one and then my brother has nine."

"So your fifty-one gets split evenly?"

"No, not quite," he said, "twenty-five goes to my daughter, the remainder is split by my sons with my brother getting a little more—six, I think."

"Oh, now that's interesting. So your brother goes from nine to fifteen, and then each of the sons end up with thirty."

"Something like that, yes. Why is that interesting? They have to work together to make the company still work."

"And, for that reason, I'm wondering if somebody in there hasn't thrown in his shares with somebody else."

Gerard stared at him in shock. "The only way any of that'll happen is if I'm not here to keep control, so the question is moot."

"Well, not if somebody decides to take you *and* your daughter out, either together, separately, as an accident or a brazen attempt at ownership of the company."

Gerard sank back into his big chair and studied him. "I face death almost weekly," he said. "There was no reason to take my daughter this time instead."

"For the ransom. Except, now that they didn't succeed, their plan A is a wash. Did you, by the way, take the money to the drop as planned?"

He shrugged and nodded. "But nobody picked it up."

"I'm not surprised," he said. "Did you actually take the twenty-five million?"

He shook his head. "I took some, like one hundred thousand, but the rest was fake."

"And so the kidnapper could have known it was fake and didn't show up for that reason?"

"I don't like what you're thinking," he said, "but you can bet only a select few knew anything about this. I don't know how many agents of the MI6 department would have known, but I highly doubt too many people did."

"Did your sons know?"

He nodded.

"Your brother?"

He nodded.

"Your wife?"

"Of course my wife, for God's sake. It's her daughter."

"So, all of the same intimate family members knew that you were lying to and cheating the kidnapper even at this point."

"I don't lie and cheat at any point," he said. "We knew it was a bluff, but I didn't want to take the chance."

"So there was no sign of anybody at any point in time coming to pick up the money?"

"Not that we could tell, no. MI6 ran the cameras all around the area. Nobody came before, and nobody came twenty-four hours afterward."

"Good to know," Griffin said. He turned to look at Jax. "That proves our theory, doesn't it?"

Jax nodded slowly. "It does. It's clearly an inside job."

CHAPTER 11

THE GIRLS COULD hear Gerard's roar from the bottom of the stairwell where they were still lugging their luggage up to the first landing—something Lorelei encouraged so that Amelia Rose learned to be self-sufficient, not relying on staff to help her at all times. Lorelei stopped, looked at Amelia Rose, and whispered, "Oh, that didn't go well."

Amelia Rose shook her head. "He doesn't like whatever they're telling him."

"Isn't that the truth," she said. She quickly grabbed Amelia Rose's bags. "Come on. Let's go upstairs. We don't want to be caught out here if they leave the office."

Amelia Rose raced ahead of Lorelei while she struggled with all the luggage. Now she knew how Jax and Griffin felt. She'd let them carry everything, but now it was up to her. Finally upstairs, she took the two pieces of luggage that were her bags to her room and then carried Amelia Rose's luggage to hers. They quickly unpacked, tossing into the laundry cart what needed to be washed and putting away their luggage.

"Let's go put on laundry too." It was something that Lorelei often did, which was especially convenient with a laundry room on the same floor, even though the housekeepers came in and changed the bedding. Amelia Rose's mother used to come in and criticize the quality of their clothing and whether it was time for them to be tossed rather than be washed. But, not giving anybody a chance to tell her otherwise, Lorelei quickly put Amelia Rose's clothes into the washer and started it. She'd like to do the same for hers but that would have to be the mixed load.

She still heard loud voices downstairs. She wondered if she should find out what the heck was going on. Amelia Rose looked nervous, chewing on her bottom lip, as she stared down the hall toward the stairway.

"I wonder where your mother is?" Lorelei asked suddenly. "I'm sure she's waiting to hear news of your arrival."

Amelia Rose turned, looked up at her. "I'll call her." Lorelei held out her phone, and Amelia Rose called her mother. But it simply rang and rang and rang.

Seeing the despondent sag to the little girl's shoulders, Lorelei reached out and hugged her. "You know what? She's probably out riding."

At that, Amelia Rose nodded. "That's where she'll be. Or maybe in the barn." She brightened. "We should go to the barn and surprise her."

Knowing how that was definitely not a good idea— Wendy was carrying on an affair with one of the trainers— Lorelei shook her head and said, "You wouldn't like to surprise her if she's napping, would you?"

"She wouldn't be napping in the barn," Amelia Rose said. "I'm not a child anymore. Unfortunately I've seen way too much of the world already. What you're saying is, she's probably having sex with one of the stable hands, aren't you?" There was such disdain in her voice that Lorelei had to laugh. It was also typical of Amelia Rose to be so blunt when she wanted to be.

"Well, she certainly might be," she said. "Either way, we

won't disturb her."

Amelia Rose nodded and then said, "But I still want to know what they're yelling about downstairs."

"I do too," Lorelei said. "It has to do with our kidnapping."

"Then we have every right to find out," Amelia Rose protested. And, precocious as always, she raced ahead of Lorelei and slipped into one of the hallways that led to a second staircase. It would take them around behind Gerard's office. Lorelei, not wanting her charge to go off on her own, followed her. She tried calling her, but her voice carried too loudly. Instead, she picked up her feet and ran behind her.

When she finally caught up to her charge, she crept down the stairs on the far side of the office, looking for the bolt-holes they both knew were here. As soon as Amelia Rose found one, she gasped, her face plastered against the wall, spying through the small hole. Immediately Lorelei stepped up to one of the higher ones and looked in. Amelia Rose's father still ranted and raved, stomping about the office like a madman, yelling at the two men both sitting relaxed in the chairs, half looking at each other and half ignoring the tirade enacted out all around them.

Finally Gerard came to a stop, wiped his mouth, then ran his fingers through his hair. "You're wrong," he stated firmly. "I know you are wrong." His voice kept rising on every word. "I refuse to listen to any more of this wild talk against my family," he roared.

Lorelei wasn't sure Jax and Griffin were ever wrong in their world. She was pretty darn sure that they knew exactly what they were doing at all times. It was a little disconcerting actually. Not to mention the fact that they seemed to know so much about everyone. Of course, she hadn't helped when she had deliberately given out more names of staff and visitors in the household too.

But, if it came to keeping Amelia Rose safe, Lorelei would do anything she could. Not that the people on her list would appreciate it. It seemed like nobody ever did. Still, that wasn't her problem. She was bound and determined to keep Amelia Rose as safe as she could. She watched Gerard walk around, sit down at his desk, and bury his face in his hands.

He finally lifted his face and said, "You're wrong. You need to go over your so-called evidence again."

Griffin shook his head, launched to his feet, and said, "No, we're not wrong, but you don't want anything to do with our intel? That's fine. But it's up to you then to keep your daughter and her tutor safe. And to watch your own back."

"Of course I'll keep them safe," he said in exasperation.

"And how do you expect to do that?" Jax asked, standing at a slower rate. "When it's quite likely the threats are coming from within your own family."

"Says you," Gerard said, glaring at both of them. "I thank you for bringing my daughter and Lorelei back home again. But I want you to leave now."

Griffin nodded. "No problem." And he turned and marched from the office.

Amelia Rose gasped and said, "We have to stop them."

Lorelei admitted she didn't want them to leave either, but it was beyond her control. She did, however, want to say goodbye to them.

Amelia Rose raced away and slipped through one of the bookshelves on the library side and ran toward the front door. As she got there, the men walked through the front entrance. One of the manservants closed it behind them. Amelia Rose raced to the front door, but the manservant stepped in front. She screamed, "Get out of the way. I have to say goodbye."

He lifted his head and looked down the hallway, watching Lorelei coming up behind her. Lorelei saw Gerard also coming down the hallway, giving a clipped nod. The manservant stepped aside and opened the front door.

Amelia Rose launched herself outside, Lorelei following her very quickly. Jax picked up Amelia Rose and hugged her carefully. Then Amelia Rose threw herself at Griffin. She shook her head and said, "Poppy shouldn't be so mean to you."

Both men chuckled, and Jax said, "Don't you worry about it, pumpkin. We're fine."

"But we might not be," Amelia Rose cried out. "I don't trust anyone here."

Griffin crouched in front of her. Even though she was eleven, he understood full well that she needed some reassurance. He grabbed both her hands and said, "You can always call us if you run into trouble."

"And how will we do that? You didn't give us your numbers."

Lorelei joined them, coming up behind her charge. She reached out a hand and shook Jax's and said formally, "Thank you so much." And then she reached out to Griffin, but he glared at her and said, "Don't you dare." And the look in his eyes glinted with determination. She let her hand drop, gave him a smile, and said, "It's awkward now."

"Not awkward at all," he said, and he snagged her chin, tilted it up, and kissed her hard. Shaken more by the emotions rolling inside her and the sense of loss already forming, she just stared at him when he pulled away.

"We don't have your numbers," Amelia Rose called out again.

Griffin reached inside his wallet, pulled out a piece of paper, and handed it to Lorelei. "Put that number into your phone, and have Amelia Rose memorize my number as well," he said. "Call that number and ask for me anytime you need to. Or rather, just say you're in trouble, and I'll come."

"But what if they move us somewhere else?" Amelia Rose asked, determined to not be reassured that he wouldn't break contact.

"I'll find you," he said, gently stroking her arm where her chip was. The arm band had already been removed. "Just like I did last time." Then he raised his gaze to look at Lorelei and whispered, "I promise."

She clutched the paper in her hand and turned to look up at Jax. She wanted to say something but didn't know what, and her shoulders fell helplessly as she struggled to control her emotions while her tears threatened. He gently stroked her cheek. "Look after her."

She nodded. "Look after yourselves." And she watched, already groaning, as they both walked away.

Amelia Rose had no intention of staying calm or quiet about it. She turned and raced back inside, yelling at her father, "You can't let them leave."

"Hush now, Amelia Rose," he said, his voice stern, but his arms going around her in a hug. "You don't know what's going on."

She pulled out of his arms and glared up at him. "I know more than you think. Yes, I'm still a child, but I'm not that much of a child any longer," she said bitterly. "They rescued us, and they kept us safe all this time. They know what's going on."

"But you don't," he reiterated. "Now, isn't it time for you to have a nap?"

Lorelei sighed quietly. It was such a typical thing for Gerard to say. He had absolutely no idea how to deal with his daughter.

"I doubt I'll ever sleep again, particularly in this house," Amelia Rose yelled as she stormed up the stairs. However, she stopped at the first landing and yelled again. "Poppy, it's you who doesn't understand. I think people might be mad about me getting thirty-five percent of the company."

Lorelei gasped and stopped abruptly. *Oh, my God. This changes everything.* Once again Lorelei followed her charge, as was her job. *I need to tell Griffin...* Yet she would be abruptly ending her assignment as Amelia Rose's tutor if she did that. She couldn't abandon Amelia Rose now. Her emotions were all stirred up from being kidnapped. And she hadn't even reached puberty yet, when an avalanche of emotions would truly hit her. Lorelei couldn't imagine how things would be when Amelia Rose hit that age. She was already a bundle of nerves now and would need lots of support to get her through this event.

Even if I tell Gerard first, ... he will send me away, just like he did Griffin and Jax.

As Lorelei reached the first landing, Gerard called to her, "Lorelei, I'd like a few moments in the office with you, please."

She hesitated. She had to do what she must to save Amelia Rose. Even if it meant giving up her own relationship with the precious girl. Lorelei swallowed her tears, turned, and then nodded. "Right now?"

He nodded, but it was a crisp and clean nod. A determined nod.

And her heart sank. But her spine became steel as she stood up taller. She slowly walked back down the stairs, feeling a sudden sense of doom as she followed him into his office. Instinctively she took Griffin's spot in his chair and asked, "What can I help you with?"

"Was my daughter touched in any way?" he asked bleakly.

She shook her head. "No, she wasn't." She could see the relief wash over his features.

He nodded again. "I'm really glad to hear that. Is there any chance she might have been, and you didn't know?"

She shook her head. "I've been with her all the time. We were never separated. She was always in my sight. However, she has changed and is very emotional after having Nurse killed in front of her. That event alone will be a trauma she'll struggle with," she said bluntly. "You cannot mitigate all the damage done to her psyche from that event alone."

"Poor Mary. She was the most loving woman." Gerard sank back into his chair. "I wish Amelia Rose hadn't seen that. Who would traumatize a child like that?"

"I wish she had never seen that too," she said. "Hell, I wish I hadn't seen it."

"Nurse suffered at the end, didn't she?"

"Yes," Lorelei said, wincing and shoving her own memories back down again, "she did. There's no easy way to say it. She was terrified. She'd been held until we were returned to the room, and, at that point in time, she was used as a lesson to make us comply with their wishes." She didn't explain how Nurse had urged them to leave, going separate ways, when the chance had presented itself. Even though Lorelei had argued, Nurse had been adamant. She wouldn't be able to keep up, and the two girls could return and rescue her. Instead, none of the women had gotten away, and Nurse had paid the ultimate price.

"Did they beat her up?"

She didn't know why he wanted to torment himself with the details, but a lot of people needed to know everything before they had enough closure to walk away. "They certainly hit her a couple times, but I don't think they did much more than tie her up and maybe threaten her beforehand. However, when we walked in, they proceeded to hit her several times," she said bleakly. "I tried to stop them, and they hit me too. And then I tried to stop Amelia Rose from going to Nurse. That I did manage, but not before they threatened to hurt your daughter as well. And then they said, as a punishment for us escaping, and to make sure we didn't do it again, they had to kill Nurse."

Gerard sat there, his jaw working for a long moment; then he said, "Thank you."

"I wish I could have saved her," she said. "They knew exactly who she was and her relationship to Amelia Rose. She was targeted. We all were but Nurse particularly."

At that, he looked at her in surprise. "Do you really think so?"

She nodded. "I do."

"Do you think this whole thing was about Nurse and not about Amelia Rose?"

"I hadn't considered it from that viewpoint." She tilted her head to one side. "I think that the end result was always supposed to be that Nurse died," she said, slowly formulating her thoughts. "I think that Amelia Rose was also supposed to remain as a captive. For blackmail first, then as leverage for you to do something that the kidnappers wanted."

"And yet, the ransom note was for just money."

"But they didn't pick it up, did they?"

He sat back and studied her. "Did you talk to the two men about this?"

"There wasn't anything else to talk about," she said wearily. "They asked question upon question. And yet, almost everything they said made sense to me too."

"You surely can't think that Amelia Rose's brothers or uncle or mother are involved in this, do you?"

"Nurse's death was personal," she said. "I can't imagine that anybody would have just killed her to teach us a lesson. Obviously I don't understand people like this at all, so maybe that's normal behavior among evil men, but they did not at any time hurt Amelia Rose."

"Was this marriage stuff just all bullshit then?" he asked, worried.

She could see that still the sexual abuse aspect bothered him.

"Likely," she said, "just more emotional torture to overpower you. To traumatize you more."

"Maybe," he said, "but nobody's tried to shift anything within the company. The stocks are down slightly but not crashing. There hasn't been an aggressive buyout or any takeover maneuver. Nothing on a business level."

"I don't think it's business-related in the sense of a takeover by another business or corporation," she said, tiptoeing around the issue. "I think it's all personal."

"But what can anybody possibly gain from this?" he asked, crying out. "I already suffered through this with my son. I shouldn't have to suffer through it with my daughter."

"Which is why she made the perfect weapon," Lorelei said gently. "You're already primed to do anything to keep your daughter safe and to not relive what happened all those years ago."

He stared at her and then pinched the bridge of his nose. "You're right," he said. "You're very right. The trouble is, a lot of people would know what had happened to me already. So it wouldn't take much digging to figure out how to get to me."

"But would they understand how much it devastated you?" *Like Nurse would know. ... And like Wendy would know ...*

He shook his head, waved one hand, but never responded to that question. "Even if I was asked to step down from the companies," he said, "once I got my daughter back, obviously I'd turn around and retaliate."

"Unless they permanently stopped you from retaliating."

He raised his head and looked at her, and she nodded. "And that's why you shouldn't have sent Griffin and Jax away. They firmly believe that your life is in as much danger as Amelia Rose's."

He stared at her, and his face turned gray. "I don't even care about my life, but I do care about hers."

"Imagine if both of you were dead," she said. "A house fire, a car accident, a drowning ..."

"You mean, together?"

She nodded. "You already told the men how the company divides down and that your sons' holdings and your brother's increases, but what about Amelia Rose? If she's living, does she get a portion of the business?"

"She gets a share, as do her brothers," he said softly. "My brother's share is not that much."

"But that was the previous distribution upon your death. ... Did you change your will recently?" she asked.

"Did you make any announcement recently? Did you ever have a new conversation about how the estate would break down upon your death?"

"Yes," he said bleakly. "We had a family meeting about it."

She stayed quiet and waited. "And now, looking back on that family meeting, did you think that maybe some people didn't like what you had to say?"

"Possibly," he said. "But I don't want to believe it's any of them."

"And what if just you died? Each one of them, instead of gaining in power actually loses power, don't they?"

He shook his head. "How is that possible?"

"Because that fifty-one percent that you call *yours* must really be twenty-five percent Amelia Rose's and twenty-six percent yours, right?"

"How do you know that?"

"It's the only way she can end up with thirty-five percent of the business at your death."

Gerard was speechless, which was a rare event.

"She listens to everything you say while she spends the day in your office with you. She's quite a remarkable child and has a great business sense for an eleven-year-old. But you already know that, don't you? You've been grooming her, haven't you? Otherwise you wouldn't have given her a controlling interest in the company upon your death."

Gerard ran his fingers through his hair.

"While you're alive, she can't take part in the company, correct?"

"Of course not. She's a child."

At this point, Lorelei leaned forward and asked, "So, while you are alive, you vote her portion until she becomes of age. And, at your death, she gains ten percent, giving her thirty-five percent—*the* controlling interest in the company. Your sons bump up to twenty-five percent each, your brother to fifteen percent. So, if you should die, who would vote Amelia Rose's controlling portion?"

His jaw dropped as he stared at her, and he said, "Her mother." Then he shook his head. "Hell, no. There's no way she would do anything to hurt Amelia Rose."

"I have nothing to say about that, except to remind you that no one hurt Amelia Rose *physically*," Lorelei said. "And I think you're taking an ugly chance sending those two men away. You don't know who all is involved. Since you ruined the kidnappers' chance at twenty-five million, they may feel pressured to create your accidental death, so they have access to not only *all* your money but also *all* your businesses."

He groaned, grabbed his phone, and called somebody. "Bring them back," he said harshly. Then he tossed his phone down and said, "Those men could be part of the problem."

"They could be," she said drily. "But I highly doubt they want to torture themselves looking after a terrorized young woman and an emotionally fragile child any longer than they have to."

"I gather you weren't the most cooperative."

"We were once we realized they were on our side," she said, "but you have to understand how we both have a lot of trauma that we're facing from the two different kidnappings. Crying, emotional females, having nightmares, not sleeping well, are difficult for these men to handle too."

He nodded. "I'm sorry. I never even thought to ask, but did they hurt you physically?"

"I was hit across the face a couple times," she said, "but

the nightmares..." She stood, smiled at him, and said, "If you don't mind, I need to keep an eye on Amelia Rose. She's very emotional right now."

"Well, tell her that I've got the men coming back," he said. "Maybe that will make her feel better."

"You mean, you've asked somebody to *request* that the men return," she said. "They don't take orders very well from other people. And I'm sure they make decisions on their own—not because you say so."

"Men like that never take orders."

"I agree with you there," she said. And, with a smile, she turned and walked out, but her heart was lighter to realize that maybe, just maybe, she'd keep her job. *And* she might see Griffin again. She would sleep much better knowing that they were here, and she knew Amelia Rose would too. Lorelei didn't know if the wife had planned this kidnapping event or if Gerard's brother or sons were involved in this mess. But now she was suspicious of them all.

Either way, it didn't matter what Lorelei felt because it was all a massive betrayal for Gerard. He'd spent his life building this business and doing his best for his family. It had to suck to think that the betrayal was from within. But that's how life was sometimes. If it was worth doing, it was usually worth doing in a big way. And these people had obviously gone all in. The worst-case scenario would be if it were more than one of them.

As soon as she found Amelia Rose in her bed, Lorelei wrapped her arms around the girl and said, "Your dad asked Jax and Griffin to come back."

Immediately Amelia Rose hopped to her feet, turned, and looked at her. "Really?"

Lorelei nodded. "Yes. I haven't heard if they've agreed to

return or not though. But if we're lucky, they will."

"Call them," Amelia Rose demanded. "Tell them just in case they don't want to listen to Poppy. They'll come if you ask them."

Lorelei laughed. "No, they probably won't."

"Try, please," Amelia Rose said.

Hating to say no, Lorelei pulled out her phone and the piece of paper with Griffin's number on it and quickly dialed. When she heard Griffin's voice on the other side, she said, "Gerard asked some of his men to bring you back."

Griffin snorted. "That's nice. We're already miles down the road."

"Come back," Amelia Rose yelled into the phone. "Please, please, come back."

"Why?" Griffin asked. "Is there a problem?"

"Probably," Lorelei said. "I just spent the time since you left in the office with Gerard, helping him to see that maybe this is personal. If it isn't us in danger, I think he is."

"Then he has his own security staff," Griffin said in exasperation. But she could hear the two men talking. "We're on our way back," he said, "but if we get kicked out again …"

"I'll take the blame," she said. "I was there when he called his men and said to go get you."

She could hear the laughter in his voice when he said, "May not make a difference."

"No, but you're made of sterner stuff. I doubt he'll scare you away."

"Maybe not," he said. "And maybe I'm just coming so I can see you again."

"Well then, you should come when I have days off," she said.

"Do you get those?" he asked.

"Well, I used to. I have no idea what I'm supposed to do now."

"You can't leave me," Amelia Rose called out nervously. She knew that Griffin could hear the child's voice too; she was certainly loud enough.

"As you can tell," Lorelei said drily, "things are still in an upheaval here." She grabbed Amelia Rose's hand and walked over to the far side of the room where they could sit on the window bench. She motioned outside and said, "It's beautiful outside. After we're done talking to Griffin, we'll go for a walk, okay?"

"Over to the barn? To see if Mom's done her thing with the stable hand?"

Catching Griffin's snort on the phone, Lorelei winced and said, "We don't talk about her like that. Remember?"

"Fine," she said, "but that's only if Griffin comes back. And he has to bring Jax with him too."

"He doesn't *have* to do anything," Lorelei scolded. "Where are your manners?"

But Amelia Rose just sat in the corner and said, "Please get them to come home."

Into the phone, Lorelei said, "Did you hear that?"

"Yes," he said, "but you know we can't stay on as babysitters, right?"

"I know," she said, "but it would be nice if you had a day or two off that would line up with mine."

"That is an entirely different story." His voice deepened as he spoke, then became more businesslike as he added, "When we near the master gate again is where we find out if we're allowed back in or not."

"If it doesn't open, I'm sorry. It would mean that he had

called one of his men as a ploy to keep me appeased."

"And I'm sure a lot of men in this world would do a lot to make you happy."

"No, that's not the relationship I have with Gerard. But he would take my advice, especially if I said it was necessary for his daughter's peace of mind."

"And it is," Amelia Rose snapped from beside her. "If they won't let them into the gate, I'll override it and let them in myself." And, with that, Amelia Rose darted off.

"And I'm on the run behind her again." She ran behind her charge all the way down the staircase. "She has more energy than a filly, and I'm feeling very much like an old gray mare," she said sadly. "But, Griffin, she *just* told me that, under Gerard's new will, she would get thirty-five percent, *the* controlling interest."

"That changes everything."

"I know."

The wait was excruciating but finally through the windows of the front door, she would be able to see the gate opening, letting Griffin back in. "What vehicle are you driving?"

"One of our own," he said. "Why?"

"So your team already knew that you were here?"

"Of course," he said. "Why wouldn't they?"

"I don't know," she said. "It just seemed odd that you would already have new wheels."

He laughed. "We get what we need at any time. Remember?"

She smiled and said, "I remember." Then, on impulse, she said, "Too bad you don't need me."

And she hung up.

GRIFFIN FILLED IN Jax with the piece of the puzzle that Amelia Rose had supplied and studied his partner. "What do you think?" Just then his phone buzzed. He looked down, groaned, and said, "It's Gerard." He answered the call with a "Yes" in a noncommittal tone of voice.

"I need you boys to come back here."

Silence. Griffin glanced at Jax, who raised his eyebrows, stared back at him, and shrugged.

"I'm pretty sure our job's done," Griffin said.

"Maybe," Gerard said. "But it appears that Lorelei thinks you're a very necessary part of solving this, keeping the girls safe."

"Maybe, but she's not the boss in this situation, is she?" He couldn't help the cool tone in his voice. It's not as if Gerard had been terribly friendly at the end.

"No," Gerard said a heavy sigh. "But she seems to believe as you do."

That shot his eyebrows up. "Interesting," he said. "I can't say we've discussed it very much."

"No, but she's very intelligent. That's one of the reasons I hired her to tutor Amelia Rose. I do respect her brainpower."

Griffin found that interesting too. "And what is it you're asking us to do?"

"I'm asking you to come back and to help me get to the bottom of this."

"I'll have to talk to my boss about that," Griffin said.

"Don't bother," Gerard said. "It's already cleared. All you have to do is turn your vehicle around and get your asses back here." And, with that, he hung up.

Griffin looked at Jax and said, "Well, apparently Lorelei does have some influence."

"Probably Lorelei and more so Amelia Rose."

He nodded. "I guess we're going back."

"Odd how Gerard knew who to call up the ranks of the Mavericks, and yet, I don't think we have a *boss* to even ask, do we?"

Griffin shrugged. "Just a stalling tactic on my part," he said. "I didn't want him to think that we were jumping at the idea."

"Except that we *are* jumping at the idea," Jax said.

"Well, I am. You don't have to," he said.

"No, no. I'm in this to the end, whatever end that may be."

"Meaning, the little girl got to you?"

Instantly Jax turned it around and said, "Meaning, Lorelei got to you?"

"Well, that's true," he said. "She certainly did."

Jax laughed. "At least you admit it. That's a whole lot easier than ignoring it."

"She's not somebody you can ignore," he said.

"No, she isn't. Particularly when you're on hyperalert when she's around."

"And, like you said, it's not necessarily a good thing."

"No, but, with Gerard's *request*, and Amelia Rose's big announcement, I think it's well past the point of having a choice now, isn't it?"

"It so is." Griffin groaned and said, "Still feels like, you know, somebody calling an untamed puppy to come."

"That's just Gerard. We don't *have* to go," Jax said, "but it would be nice to get that chance to tell him, *I told you so*."

Griffin laughed. "There is that."

"Plus you and I both know those girls are in danger. *And* the jerk Gerard."

"Oh, no," Griffin said. "There's no way we're *not* going. And I'm glad that he was forced to call us back. Let's hope we're not too late even now."

"And that's the thing, isn't it?" Jax said. "We don't even know where *all* the threats are coming from, but we do know that there *are* threats. Multiple threats to deal with."

"Yes," he said, "that sucks. However, we do know where *one* of those threats is coming from now."

It took them another twenty minutes to return to the mansion. And as soon as they arrived, Amelia Rose raced toward them and threw herself into their arms. Jax chuckled, picked her up, and said, "You know we can't keep doing this, right?"

She nodded. "Just until we keep Poppy safe."

Jax squeezed her tight and passed her off to Griffin.

Griffin loved the fact that she was half woman, yet half child. Still wanted to be hugged and picked up and tossed around, and yet, also wanted to be treated like an adult. She was a mature eleven-year-old in many ways, and yet, just a young child in so many others. No sooner had Griffin put Amelia Rose down than Gerard stepped out the front door too.

He walked to meet them, shook the men's hands, and said, "I apologize." His voice was stiff, but at least he was doing what he should do. "And, yes, please, let's go in and have another talk."

"No problem," Griffin said. "Maybe Lorelei should take part in it this time."

Gerard winced. "I've already heard her point of view. Everybody appears to think that it's a family matter and that

I'm in danger as well."

"Where is your wife?" Griffin asked.

"She's taken a short holiday to Venice."

Griffin and Jax exchanged a knowing glance.

"And I presume you've buffed up your security?" Jax said.

"I have," he said. "But, if what you say is true, how do I know who is loyal to me?"

"While we're in place," Griffin said, "we'll sort that out so you have a trustworthy team going forward."

"That's a good idea," he said with relief. "Let's start with my head of security. If he's clear, we can assign a lot of the other clearances to him."

"Good idea."

Back in the office, he ordered coffee for everyone, and they sat down, taking a good look at who they had on his security staff. Sixteen men were assigned across all the family members.

"Any idea if anybody's in financial distress or has a weakness that can be exploited?" Jax asked immediately.

"I wouldn't have thought so," Gerard said, "and that is my head of security's job."

"Which is why we'll check him out first," Griffin said. "He's in a position to put people in place as he wants and not necessarily people who are good for you."

"And that's a disturbing thought," Gerard said. "In my business, I hire the best that I can for the rest of this stuff. Nobody can look after everything."

"No," Jax said. "And the more widespread and diverse you become, the more you have to rely on others. As soon as you do, that's when you can end up in trouble."

Gerard nodded. He brought out files from the nearby

filing cabinet and said, "These are personnel files on everybody I currently employ in my security force, and the head of security's folder is on the top."

Jax looked at the name, chuckled, and said, "I know this guy."

"Do you?" Gerard looked at him and raised an eyebrow. "By reputation?"

"Yes," Jax said. "Up until this moment in time, I've never had any question about him." Jax reviewed the file quickly and then handed it to Griffin.

Griffin looked at it briefly, nodded, and said, "Except for one thing."

"What's that?" Gerard asked.

"His son got into a lot of trouble," Jax said.

"Now you're right there," Griffin agreed, looking further at the folder, nodding. "It's quite possible that Bram here has been compromised. I'd hate to think it though."

"What about his son?" Gerard asked.

"He was caught with a dead woman. Somebody's daughter from Saudi Arabia," Griffin said. "They were doing drugs at the time."

Gerard nodded. "Bram told me about that, as soon as it was discovered. So, not only were drugs not allowed in that area," Gerard said, "but the fact that she died would also have caused quite a kerfuffle. Still, I thought that was settled."

"Regardless, it gives Bram a weakness someone could exploit," Griffin added.

"And, of course, we must remember that just because it could have happened doesn't mean it did happen," Gerard noted.

"Exactly," Jax said.

"Is he around? Can we talk to him?" Griffin asked.

Gerard picked up the phone and made a call. Within ten minutes, they could hear footsteps walking down the hallway. Bram stepped in a side door, nodded at Gerard, and said, "What can I do for you?"

Gerard motioned to the two men standing just behind Bram.

"Well, well, well. Jax and Griffin. Who knew? You guys are like bad pennies," Bram said, smiling.

"Meaning, we show up where we're not wanted?" Griffin asked drily. His comment was certainly appropriate given the fact that Bram was the one being investigated first.

"Absolutely," Glenn Bram said. "And, if you're here, it means something's going on that I currently don't know about."

Griffin nodded and said, "Well, we have some good news but also some bad news."

"The girls," Bram froze. "Did you hear from the kidnapper?"

"No," said a voice from the doorway. Amelia Rose and Lorelei stepped in.

Bram's face broke out into a huge smile. Griffin had been watching, and that man in front of them was overjoyed at their safe rescue. That was huge for Griffin. He looked at Jax, and his partner nodded, whereas Bram held his arms open and Amelia Rose raced into them.

"You got them back," Bram said, when he finally could, his voice breaking slightly. As soon as Amelia Rose had stepped out of his arms, he turned to face Griffin and Jax. "Well, now I know why you guys are here. That's definitely your kind of a job." He turned toward Gerard. "I don't know how you found these guys, but these men are the best."

Gerard's face worked with emotion as he nodded and said, "And they did get Amelia Rose back. Lorelei as well."

"Nurse?"

At that, grief crossed Gerard's features, and he took a moment before he could answer. "They killed her," he said, "as a way to get Lorelei's and Amelia Rose's cooperation. My girls escaped and went looking for help, then were recaptured and Nurse killed, as a threat of what would happen to them if they tried to escape again."

"And yet," Griffin stepped in to say immediately, "that wasn't their fault."

Bram nodded. "Exactly. It doesn't mean the killing wouldn't have happened anyway. There's no real way to know with guys like that." He looked at the two men. "Did you take out the kidnappers?"

Both men shook their heads. "That's partly why we're here now," Griffin said.

Bram's features sharpened. "You think he's from home soil?"

Griffin hesitated, glanced at Gerard, and then said, "Unfortunately I think it's closer than home soil. I think it's a home job. Meaning …"

Bram's back stiffened. There was no doubt that he understood the implication.

"We think it's somebody in the family," Jax filled in immediately. "At least one," he murmured.

But instead of showing any surprise, Bram nodded. "Sorry, Gerard, but I've been wondering about that ever since the kidnapping. But I don't have any reason to look at anyone in particular." Bram held up his hand to quiet Gerard.

Oddly enough Gerard did as asked.

"Hear me out this time," Bram began. "It's just too convenient how everyone's alibis are all nicely locked down as everyone was here. Yet someone is pulling the strings from a distance. Still, that means there are too many possible suspects, and they are all connected to you, Gerard, and the massive corporate network you've built. Requires someone in the know. Someone who could contract men in Thailand. Which brings it back to your sons, your wife, and your brother. Wendy much less so because she is never involved in the businesses, but, with her proclivity for men in her bed, … it's possible."

"And yet, you didn't tell me?" Gerard asked in shock.

Bram faced him with a grimace. "The one thing about you is, I have to come with hard evidence for you to listen. Otherwise nobody gets to say anything about family."

Gerard had the grace to look ashamed, and Griffin understood. After all, he and Jax had pretty well been kicked out of the house themselves for having said or implied something along that same line.

"And I hate to say it," Jax said, "but one of the first people we have to start with—and, of course, we want to completely clear—is the head of security."

Bram nodded. "And that's to be expected. So what do you want to know?"

"Has somebody been blackmailing you or asking you for information that they shouldn't be or contacting you in any way, shape, or form that they shouldn't have?" Griffin asked Bram. "You know the drill."

"I do," he said. "And you're thinking about my son and his troubles, aren't you?"

"Yes," Griffin said instantly. "I am. Obviously that situation is one that we wished hadn't happened in the first place, but it does leave you open as those doors weren't permanently closed."

"And, if they had been permanently closed," Bram said, "then I would be in even more trouble."

"To a certain extent, yes. That's definitely a possibility."

"First let me say …" He nodded at Gerard. "I told Gerard as soon as I found out and have been upfront and honest with him thereafter, keeping him updated." Then Bram addressed all of them. "Well, my son was cleared of all wrongdoing," Bram said. "He's currently in drug rehab and has been for the past three months. It's too early to tell if it'll work this go-round or not. It's not the first time we've had him there. I keep hoping each and every time that it will be the last, but I'm not a fool. I know that, chances are, it won't be his final stint in rehab." There was such sadness in his expression that Griffin didn't get any sense of betrayal from him.

"So nobody's tried to blackmail you or compromise your position here?" Griffin asked for clarity. He wanted Bram to look him in the eye and tell him no. And that's what Bram did.

He looked him in the eye and said, "No, none."

Griffin nodded. "And you have responsibility for hiring all the security for the company and the family?"

At that, Bram looked surprised. He shook his head. "Absolutely not. I'm not sure where you got that idea from."

Griffin looked at Gerard. "Gerard?"

He stared at Bram. "Of course you do."

Bram shook his head. "No, I used to, until that was taken away, and other people hired their own people."

"Who took that away?" Gerard asked in shock. "Who's

usurping my authority?"

Unfortunately Bram just looked at Gerard quietly and said, "I think it's everybody."

Gerard stared at him, completely flabbergasted, and Bram explained. "Remember how your son wanted one of his childhood friends on staff? And the only place that he was in any way qualified was as security. That started it. Then your wife wanted somebody also hired, and again the only place for that person was in security. Even your brother has had his hand in making sure he had somebody on security. And all of that because they wanted to know that somebody was looking after *them* and their interests."

Jax asked slowly, "Is that what's going on here, Bram?"

"I'm not sure if it's that or the fact that, as soon as one manages to wrestle a little bit of control away from Gerard, everybody else tries to as well."

Griffin looked at Jax, and then the two of them faced Gerard. "Did you realize that this has been happening?"

His face worked into a grimace, and he stared at Bram. "I remember them fighting over it, and me telling you it didn't matter."

At that, Bram gave a decisive nod and said, "Exactly. And, once that happened, other people got hired on. There are friends who work in the household staff, and there are *acquaintances*..." He said that part and the next with emphasis. "... who *work* on the grounds..." And he let his voice trail off.

Griffin pulled out the list he'd gotten from Lorelei and Amelia Rose and said, "Do you have any of those names?"

"John Halffinger works in the stables," he said instantly. Then he stopped and looked at Gerard. "A friend of your wife's."

Gerard winced. "I'm paying this guy to shag my wife?"

That got a laugh out of Bram. It was totally inappropriate with Amelia Rose here, but at least Gerard had a sense of humor. Griffin looked to see Lorelei standing beside Jax with Amelia Rose. But then the girls had given them the name of Amelia Rose's mother's lover, so obviously not too many secrets were here.

"And who else?" Jax asked, leaning over so he could look at the list that the girls had given them.

Bram proceeded to name four others on that list.

Gerard shook his head. "I don't even know those names."

"One is on the cooking staff in the kitchen," he said. "It's one of your sons' school friends."

Gerard frowned, remembering that, and then dismissing it. "I'm sure that was somebody he went to school with. What's the problem with that?" A heavy pause ensued as Gerard looked from one to the others around him. "He's in the kitchen, for God's sake."

Lorelei stepped forward and said, "What a perfect place to poison somebody or to kill somebody through allergies."

Gerard just stared at her, his face settling into hard lines. "I'll say it once more. I really hate this, but it's a shitty world we live in."

They went through each and every name that Bram came up with, and then they started in with the actual security people he was responsible for, and the six he hadn't approved who were assigned to other members of the family even though Gerard signed their paychecks. By the time they were done, Gerard was almost gray-faced. "So is there anybody I hired and am paying for who is loyal to me?"

Bram immediately nodded and said, "The men I've

hired who are on staff here specifically to look after you," he said. "As long as I can keep them around, then we can do the job that needs to be done."

"*If you can keep them around*? What does that mean?" Griffin asked.

Bram looked at Gerard and said, "I hate to bring this up again, but your sons often take security away from you when the boys take trips, and often you just don't seem to care."

"Well, because keeping my sons safe is paramount," he said. "That's not the same thing."

"Well, it is," Jax said, "if they're behind any of this."

"And if they want you less guarded while they set up an attack on you personally," Griffin added.

And once again Gerard's face stilled. His big shoulders sagged as he slumped into his chair. "So now what?"

"We compile everybody's movements at least two weeks prior to the girls' first kidnapping event," Griffin said immediately. "We need to know exactly where everybody was and who was on what duty." He looked at Bram. "How many of these questionable men might have had anything to do with this ransom drop where nobody showed up?"

Bram looked at him in surprise and then nodded. "Good point," he said. "Only mine were hired to run the ransom drop and to protect Gerard here, but that then left a lot of the other men to be present for the other side."

"But nobody showed up on the other side," Gerard said in exasperation.

"I know," Griffin said. "And how much of that was because they already had insider information that the money was fake and that the drop was a MI6 trap?" There was silence in the room, and then finally Griffin said, "Look. We can talk until we're blue in the face, but we need to clear

Bram here, and Bram needs to help us go through every staff member on this estate, not just security, and see who might be aiding and abetting that kidnapping."

"If it's anybody on my staff," Gerard said, "I want them fired, and I want them legally charged."

"All fine and dandy," Bram said. "We still have to find out who they are first."

"We'll do a close review of all staff, but we're starting with the security personnel," Griffin stated.

And, at that, they were given a room with computers and areas to interview staff. They compiled a complete rundown on who had been available, who was off doing other work, and what the relationships were between the various staff. When Griffin began the face-to-face interviews, meeting Bram's security guards, they stood out. It wasn't just the look of them, but they were well-trained, used to obeying orders, and understood security from the inside out.

The friends who had been brought in to specifically serve the other family members were a completely different group of security personnel. Not that they were involved in criminal activity in any outward way, but they definitely weren't of the same ilk. They were completely uncomfortable with being questioned. They didn't stand in any neutral position. They looked guilty right from the get-go, most likely because they already knew that they weren't right for those jobs. They hadn't trained for them. They weren't experienced. They had nothing real to offer for a position such as this one.

And yet, they were all taking Gerard's money. Maybe they were learning something, and maybe they were grateful for the opportunity and were doing their best. Griffin would like to think some were. Two of them though, he highly doubted. As soon as both of those men left, Griffin looked at Gerard, snorted, and said, "Seriously?"

He winced and said, "My wife's suggestions."

Griffin jotted that down. His wife obviously had a predilection to young, brawny, and potentially nothing-between-the-ears stud material. Even Lorelei, who'd come and gone several times, smirked as she walked in, crossing paths as one of those men walked out.

"Do you know those last two men?" he asked her.

"Sure, insofar as they showed up one day with jobs," she said cheerfully.

"Did you ever see them working?"

Her tone was completely bland as she said with twinkling eyes, "Tell me what their job was, and I might be able to answer you."

Gerard snapped at her. "I get that this is funny to you, but it's not funny to me."

Immediately her face sobered. She nodded and said, "So, therefore, to be direct, I highly doubt I've seen them doing anything that you would be paying them for."

He glared at her, then groaned and said, "Really? That pair too?"

She nodded. "Yes. That pair too."

"Please tell me that my daughter didn't see them ... together."

"Not that last one," Amelia Rose said. "Just the two in the barn and the gardener."

Her father stared at her in horror.

She shrugged and said, "Living here is an education too. Into human relationships. How to treat people, whether family, friends, or coworkers." She giggled. "Besides, Poppy, your business is to write all about the news. Well, at least some of your businesses do that. So Lorelei said I should research my poppy's company of companies to figure out what I want to do with my life. To figure out where I would best fit in, where I would enjoy my work. Right, Lorelei?" On that, she smirked and walked out.

Gerard sat there, clearly overwhelmed. "When did eleven-year-olds become so worldly?"

Griffin wisely stayed quiet. So did Jax.

Bram, on the other hand, said, "She's still probably better off being more worldly and wise than vulnerable through blind innocence."

Gerard nodded, yet said, "Still way too young."

"Maybe," Griffin said, "but I don't think *young* means *naive* anymore."

Gerard studied him for a long moment, sighed, and said, "Back to work. And then I'll take steps to stop being the laughingstock of my own household," he growled.

Lorelei shook her head. "You're not the laughingstock," she said. "Your wife is."

He looked at her and said, "But I'm being conned."

"Sure, but you're allowing your wife's dalliances, and you don't care. That's the difference. She thinks she's deceiving everybody, yet nobody is unaware of her affairs. That changes others' perceptions entirely."

"Thank you. I'll take that as a small salve to my conscience," he said.

She chuckled. "You know something has to be done about it, other than firing her lovers. When you're ready, you'll do it."

"What am I to do about Wendy? She's Amelia Rose's mother," he growled.

"While you certainly have grounds for a divorce," Lorelei

said, proving that once again she had a unique position in the household, "it's all up to you to do whatever you feel is right."

"If anything," he said, "I was hoping my daughter would get a little older first."

"She clearly is old enough to understand too much now," Lorelei said gently. "You can hear it in her words alone. Keeping this marriage going for her sake is more about teaching her that marital vows have no meaning. Of course that's a very British way to look at things. It's supposed to be the heir and the spare, but you already had those to begin with, so there really are no rules to wealthy British marriages now, are there?"

He snorted and said, "That's one way to look at it. Not the easiest and not the nicest but the old way. Yet the fact that Wendy's a tramp doesn't mean that she's done anything criminal. I still refuse to believe that she would do anything to hurt her daughter."

"Quite possibly," Griffin said, "but is there anything she's done that would put her in a position of being compromised?"

Jax snorted. "Sounds like the much harder question would be finding things she's done where she wasn't compromised."

They all sat here for a moment in silence, thinking about the woman with the blatant disregard for her husband's reputation and who had complete disregard for her daughter's well-being.

"The thing is, it would have to be something *so* major," Lorelei said, "for Wendy to even care about any repercussions from her actions."

"She's not likely done anything like that," Gerard said

heavily. "She cares about studs, two- and four-legged ones. When we found out she was pregnant, I was ecstatic—she was not. She wanted an abortion or an open marriage. It was no contest to me. She's no different now than when I first met her. I just can't keep living like this. And I can't keep putting Amelia Rose in these unhealthy situations."

CHAPTER 12

LISTENING TO THE men discuss the issues was fascinating. Lorelei wasn't sure how she'd been allowed to stay as a party to this except for the list that she had created with Amelia Rose's assistance. Amelia Rose had taken off to play, as they certainly didn't have any school lessons scheduled for right now while they both recuperated from their ordeal. When lunch had been served, Lorelei sat beside Griffin. And, when the day was finally done, she looked at the two men and said, "Does that give you any answers?"

Bram answered, "More to the point, it narrowed the field. We have everybody in a security position cleared except for two."

"Which two?" she asked. "And were they not cleared just because they aren't here?" The men shrugged but didn't offer more information. "And what about the family?"

"Family is the next layer," Bram said. "We have to know who we can trust before we start combating the war that's being waged from within."

"Do you think it was insidious intent or is this all by accident, this salting of unqualified men within the actual family members?" Lorelei asked. "Are they just circumstantial and random hires? Because you know now that hand-picked people are inside the house. More hand-picked people are inside the kitchen, even in the other security team, for

God's sake. Therefore, all facets of Gerard's working life here from home are handled by people who were hired by somebody other than himself."

Griffin looked at her and smiled. "Figured that out, did you?"

She nodded, a sad expression on her face.

"I'm not sure how this plays out though," Bram said. "That's what we're still figuring out."

Gerard growled and looked at Lorelei. "Where's Amelia Rose?"

"She's in her room, playing computer games."

"Could you please check?"

"I can." She didn't worry about Amelia Rose in her own home before, but, as they looked at the problems Gerard had with the household staffing, it would certainly be something Lorelei considered moving forward. With them doing this investigation, it would just bring up even more issues of trust for Amelia Rose among the staff. Lorelei pulled out her phone and called her charge.

Amelia Rose immediately answered the landline in her bedroom. "Yes, I'm here. Yes, I'm fine and exactly the same since the last ten minutes when you contacted me."

Lorelei chuckled. "It was an hour ago, and your father asked me to check this time."

Lorelei raised her voice and said, "Poppy, I'm fine."

"Good," he grumbled. "But you didn't come for food."

"I ate earlier," she said. "And I'm going to bed early too. I'm really tired." And her voice did sound pretty rough.

Lorelei took that as a hint and said to the girl, "I'm on my way up."

"Thank you," Amelia Rose said, her words filled with obvious relief as she spoke.

When Amelia Rose hung up, Lorelei looked at Gerard and said, "It'll take her a while to settle down and to know that she isn't in danger anymore."

"And, for that," her father said, "we'll keep working on getting to the bottom of this from our end. But please, Bram, make sure my daughter is safe, particularly while she sleeps in her own bed."

"I'll post a man at her door right now," Bram said.

Lorelei winced. "That's not guaranteed to make any of us sleep well tonight."

"I know," Gerard said. "But this first gambit's been tossed, and the kidnappers lost. I mean, it would make sense for them to try it again, from home now."

"Well, I hope you're wrong," she said. "It's not what I want to consider at all."

He nodded. "I'll be up to say good night to my daughter in a little bit. Tell her that, will you?"

She nodded. "You know that she does understand that you do love her and that you will do anything to keep her safe."

Gerard smiled. "Thank you for that. She's very important to me."

"All your children are," Lorelei said. "I hope they all know it."

"I do too," he said as he stared down at the list. "God, I hope so."

NOT LONG AFTER Lorelei left, the men wrapped it up. Gerard's sons were both coming for a meeting the next morning, both of them perturbed at the call from Gerard's home to theirs. And Gerard's wife, who apparently was still out of town, would return as well. Gerard was determined to get to the bottom of this and have face-to-face meetings with everyone. Griffin didn't have a problem with that. He just knew that those kinds of meetings rarely turned out the way people expected them to. But, hey, good luck to Gerard.

Griffin was shown to a first-floor guest room not long afterward, with Jax in the guest room next door. As Griffin got ready for bed, he checked his watch. *Already one in the morning.* Somehow their entire Thursday had disappeared. Then that tended to happen on these jobs. That's what he was used to, but he couldn't get Lorelei off his mind.

He'd slept beside her for the last several nights, if only for her own comfort, but he found that he was used to it himself, and he wanted to continue sleeping beside her. Walking away from that tonight was hard, and it would likely be every night from now on too. He walked into his en suite bathroom, closed the door, and had a quick shower. When he came out, he felt a deep sense of unease. And instinctively he knew Lorelei was suffering. He sat down, pulled out his phone, and texted her. **You okay?**

There was a delayed response, which, for a moment, he thought meant that she was sound asleep, and then she texted back. **How did you know?**

Instinct. I just got out of a shower, and it felt wrong. If we were anywhere close, I would have automatically come to see if you were okay. As it is, a text is about all I can do.

I have to get used to sleeping alone. I can't depend on you to chase away the boogeymen.

No, he typed in. **But I'm sorry if you're not getting any sleep. How was Amelia Rose?**

She seems to be sleeping fine came the response.

Wish I could.

He understood. **Well, I can't walk through the halls of this place easily. I don't even know where your room is. But you can always come visit me.**

And he left it hanging of course. For all he knew, she'd lose her job if she did come to him. And he didn't want to put that on her either. Knowing that there was probably no way for them to be together under Gerard's roof, Griffin got into bed and closed his eyes. When his door opened ten minutes later, he was already alert and watching.

She poked her head around the corner and stepped in. He didn't say a word. He just pulled back the blankets, and she crawled in. With a heavy sigh, she rolled over, backed up against him, and fell asleep.

He whispered against her hair, "This is really a bad habit."

He thought she was out cold, but she responded. "I know, but I figured there'll be lots of times to learn to adjust, and I shouldn't have to do it tonight." And, with that, she shuffled closer, and this time she did fall asleep.

He laid here with her in his arms for a long time. He needed sleep too, but this bundle of crazy comfort that he himself gained from holding her made him realize just how important she was to him. That in itself wouldn't be easy to handle. It was pretty damn hard to have a relationship, given their professions. And, even if they did get that far, it's not like he would be changing his. Although this was supposed to be a one-time deal, and he was already on a second Mavericks op, so he didn't know how that would work out long-term.

He laid here for a long moment and then thought he heard something. He froze, not wanting to disturb Lorelei, and, when a text beep came through, he reached for his phone.

Are you there? Jax asked.

Yeah, he replied. **Heard something out in the hall. Don't know if Lorelei was followed.** That was something he hadn't considered, and maybe he should have with everything going on. This wasn't likely the best idea they'd had.

Jax sent back a smiley face, then added, **I'll check it out.**

Griffin heard just the hint of a sound from his partner's bedroom, but, even then, he knew something was off about this whole thing. Never, at any point in time, had he considered that Lorelei might have been an inciting party to this kidnapping, working with whoever else had planned this fiasco. And he sure as hell would hate to think of it now because it would mean his instincts were completely off, but he had to wonder.

And then he realized, no, it just wasn't part of who she was, no matter how people might look at this. No one understood how hard it was to get over a kidnapping. Besides, she'd had lots of opportunities to take him or Jax out. And she had done nothing but protect Amelia Rose.

When he heard something again outside, he gently stepped out of bed, made sure that she didn't rouse from his movements, and texted Jax. When Griffin got no reply, he went to the door and listened. He heard something. *A scuffle.*

He opened the door silently and stuck his head out. Somebody came out of nowhere and smacked him hard on his jaw. He went down but was already rolling to come back up again. He lashed out with his foot, catching his assailant, dropping him hard on the floor beside him. He continued to fight hard and fast, and he caught sight of Jax's fight going on beside him.

But the thought uppermost in Griffin's mind was that Lorelei was here. Hopefully she was sound asleep. But what if she wasn't? He hated the dangling suspicion that said, what if she was behind this attack? He knew it couldn't be true, but, until he got to the bottom of this, he had willingly forgone taking a closer look at her.

And just when he took another blow and a hard boot to a rib, he heard a loud crash. He turned to see his assailant dropping. Lorelei stood trembling in the doorway with a lamp in her hand. The glass had been shattered over his assailant's head. Well, that answered that question. He bounced to his feet, kissed her hard, and whispered, "Thank you. Now go inside and lock the door." And he shut the door in her face.

He then went after Jax's attacker. Within minutes, he had him subdued and tied up beside the other one. "Those two men we haven't interviewed," he said.

"I know," Jax said, gasping, bent over, regaining his breath. "So, are they the missing two, or are they part of some completely different group that is involved?"

"This is getting ridiculous," Griffin said. He pulled out his phone and phoned Gerard.

A sleepy voice answered.

"This is Griffin. Two assailants attacked Jax and me. We have them both tied up in the hallway. What do you want to do?"

Gerard became fully awake. Immediately he roared, "What? In my own house?"

"We need to check on Amelia Rose."

Gerard was already up and running. "I'm racing toward her bedroom right now. I don't know who else they would be after."

"Well, they came after us," Griffin said, "but I'm not sure why."

"It has to be the investigations into my staff," Gerard said over the phone.

"Maybe," Griffin said, still thinking it through.

Griffin could hear Gerard speaking to the guard before opening the door and then the relief in his voice when he said, "Amelia Rose is in bed, sound asleep."

"Thank heavens for that." He gave Jax a thumbs-up.

"I'll wake Lorelei and bring her here."

"Don't worry about it," Griffin said. "I'll send her up."

An edgy silence followed on the other end as Gerard assimilated that information. But his voice was hard when he said, "You do that, and then we'll talk."

Just then Lorelei stepped through the doorway, listening from the other side. She reached out for Griffin's phone. "There's nothing to talk about," she said in a cool tone to Gerard. "I can't sleep since the kidnapping. I'm the one who came down to Griffin. And these two intruders may have followed me. I don't know. But both have been secured, and I don't recognize either of them."

"You come up here to Amelia Rose," Gerard said, his tone back to normal. "I'm coming there. Maybe I'll know them."

As Lorelei raced past them, Jax punched Griffin lightly in the shoulder. "Nice woman," he said, "especially when she stands up and defends you."

"That *is* why she came down here," Griffin said with a wry smile. "She hasn't slept since."

"And we both understand that," Jax said. "Still doesn't change the fact that there's something between you guys."

"Sure, but what?"

"Well, it's not like either of you are involved with anyone else. So there's nothing really stopping you from having a relationship."

"Just our jobs," Griffin said with a note of laughter.

"Yeah, well, there is that. Not sure that we are even full-time with the Mavericks much less that we know what we're doing with our futures now, do we?"

"I thought the Mavericks gig was temporary," Griffin said. "But I thought that when I helped out Kerrick. That's when I was called into play. Now I'm not sure what the deal is. Except this seems almost like an initiation."

"The Mavericks team is not for everyone," Jax said. "Yet I think a lot of navy guys, those with families, end up leaving the navy before they really want to. And this Mavericks life might work better for them. Or maybe those family guys just wanted the navy to change some of its rules."

"Hell, I'm single, and I was ready to leave before they tagged me for this job," Griffin said. "I just hadn't figured out what I would do in the meantime."

"Well, figure it out, and, if they need to tag you for jobs like this, that's an option too," he said. "Nobody said it had to be permanent and forever with the Mavericks."

"I know. Just feels odd."

"That's because this op got to you. Because it's been a while since you had a real relationship," Jax said. "It hurts you when someone you care about gets hurt."

"Absolutely it does." Gerard barged into the hallway, having obviously heard part of their conversation. "And if there's anything there worth keeping, then you fight for it. But I really won't take kindly to you playing fast and loose with Lorelei, and she'd have my head if I were to say that in her hearing."

"She would, indeed," Griffin said. "And I don't know what's going on between us. So far, it's been a case of comfort." He let them know quite clearly that they hadn't crossed that line. But it showed how he wanted to.

"Well, it won't be for long," Gerard said. "She's a hell of a good woman, and I really don't want to think of her getting hurt."

"Well, you're a little late for that," Griffin said, glaring at him. "She got hurt on this trip."

"That's why I'm trying to stop it from happening again," Gerard roared.

Griffin motioned to the two men on the ground. "Who the hell are these guys?"

One was conscious, a T-shirt of Griffin's stuck in his mouth; the other was still out cold. Griffin rolled the one out cold over so that Gerard could see his face too. He stared at them in shock. "They both work for me. These are the two security men who we never got around to interviewing because we couldn't find them."

"Who hired them?"

"My brother," he said, frowning. "But that doesn't mean he knew these guys would turn against me."

"No, not at all," Griffin said. "As we know, men are turned all the time. These bad guys prey on that chance."

The two men were lifted and hauled to Gerard's office, and Bram was woken up and brought down to deal with the pair. When he recognized them, his face thinned, and his jaw firmed. He frowned at Gerard, pointed to one, and said, "This is the one I fought against being hired."

"And I overruled you, I suppose," Gerard said, sagging into his oversize leather chair.

Bram nodded. "That you did. Your brother wanted this one brought in and trained, and why was that?"

"I don't know," he said. "Son of a friend of his or some such bullshit."

"Well, we need to know exactly what that was all about," Griffin stated firmly, "because now, apparently, it's a bigger issue than it was before."

"It is, indeed," Bram said. "It is, indeed."

Very quickly Gerard's brother, Joe, was ordered to attend the meeting that morning with Gerard's sons. Groggy from being woken up, Joe said, "I'll be there in a few hours."

Gerard interrupted. "Don't bother. I'm sending the chopper now."

"This must be important," Joe said.

"It is," he said. "I'm calling a family meeting." And he proceeded to wake up the rest of his family, ordering them all to attend earlier than planned.

Griffin had asked that Gerard make the calls with speaker engaged, so Griffin heard a lot of groaning and bitching on the other end of the calls, but nobody flat-out said no. Gerard was the money and the power behind the company and the ultimate head of the family hierarchy. When he said jump, they all jumped. But it was easy for Griffin to see that some of them were very tired of jumping.

When he hung up the phone, Gerard stared at it for a long time. "A lot of dissent is all around, isn't it?"

"It could very well be too tight a glove on some of them for too long," Griffin said boldly. "Everybody starts to chafe after a while."

"So what's the answer? I'm not ready to retire."

"Bring them in more," Jax said. "Give them more responsibility, and give them a bigger role in running the company."

"They already are though."

Bram made an odd sound.

Gerard looked at him and asked, "Aren't they?"

Bram shrugged. "Not as much as they'd like to be. You do keep them fairly tightly held."

"Well, that's because I'm not ready to hand over control of the company," he snapped.

"Of course not," Bram said. "But then you have to expect that people want more, want to move up the ladder. And when they want more for a long time, they eventually do something about getting more. So you should listen more closely to what they say. Pick up on these disgruntled moments. Allow people to be honest with you, to share a different opinion. Your sons are capable businessmen in their own right. Your brother has been with you since the beginning. Hell, your father started this company, and you two inherited; but you made it massive, and Joe's been left in a supporting role all this time. That, however, doesn't mean that any of them are behind the kidnapping or this latest assault."

"Have your security feeds been checked?" Jax asked. "Do we know if any other men came onto the grounds overnight?"

"Not that I've seen," Bram said. "I've got two men looking right now." Just then his phone rang. He answered it, frowned, and said, "Make sure you've got a full coalition of men. I want all four of them brought into Gerard's office." He put away his phone and said, "They found two others outside and have a line on two more at the stables."

"Six men?" Gerard asked. "What the hell?"

Bram nodded. "Six. What we're trying to do is make

sure we catch them all right now. So we can finally get to the bottom of this."

"Do you have enough men?" Jax asked. "We can help."

"We're good," Bram said, "and my security team has been fully warned after all the interviews yesterday that something was up."

"Right, so make sure only men who were cleared yesterday are on this," Gerard snapped.

Griffin, already feeling like something else was going on, said, "I don't like it. It still feels like distractions."

"From what?"

"I don't know," he said, "but I don't like it." He pulled out his phone and quickly phoned Lorelei. There was no answer. He bolted to his feet and said, "Where's Amelia Rose's room? I don't like this."

Gerard looked at him, already standing, and asked, "Did you contact Lorelei?"

"Yes, and there's no answer."

"Let's go," Gerard said.

Jax stood guard on the prisoners with Bram while Griffin and Gerard raced up to Lorelei's room. Before they got there, Griffin already knew they would be too late. Gerard bolted into his daughter's room and froze. Her bed was empty, the guard out cold down the hall, and there was no sign of either of the girls. He turned in horror to look at Griffin. "What the hell?"

Griffin didn't bother answering—he was already heading downstairs and outside.

CHAPTER 13

LORELEI WOKE TO a pounding headache. It didn't take long to realize that she'd been knocked out and taken prisoner by somebody. That she had been walking into Amelia Rose's room at the time terrified her even more. Where was Amelia Rose? She desperately tried to stay quiet as she rolled over, searching for her, but the pain almost blacked her out. When she could control her breathing enough to control her pain, she opened her eyes, found Amelia Rose lying beside her.

Her eyes were wide open, and she had a finger to her lips.

Grateful that she was unhurt, Lorelei sank back down and tried hard to get her brain to function again. She could hear voices outside, but the smell told her where she was. At least where she hoped she was.

They were in the stables.

Hay, sweat, and manure filled her nostrils. Surely somebody in the house would notice. Gerard was already well aware of the attack on Griffin and Jax, meaning that she and Amelia Rose should be found soon enough.

Amelia Rose's gaze was terrified as she gently rubbed Lorelei's face, but she didn't say anything.

Lorelei didn't know if the child wasn't speaking because they weren't alone, which was possible, or because she was too shocked to say anything. Lorelei captured her finger and held on. Either way, it was not good.

As she waited for her headache to ease back, Lorelei took stock. She wasn't tied up or restrained in any way, which meant either they were under guard or they were in a locked room. As she looked around, she recognized the horse tack room, confirming that they were, indeed, still on the property. That made her feel much better. She knew where she was, and she wasn't too far away from Griffin.

And, at least for now, Amelia Rose was okay—but not for long. The voices were loud, irate, and close to her. She didn't really recognize any of them though. She rolled over ever-so-softly. The tack room had half doors, and the people arguing were just outside, so it's not like she and Amelia Rose had any way to leave without being seen. That explained why Amelia Rose wasn't talking. Lorelei quickly checked her pocket, found her phone, and sent Griffin a text. **Tack room, stable one.**

Then she slipped her cell back into her pocket, held her finger up to Amelia Rose's lips, and whispered, "Griffin."

Immediately Amelia Rose's eyes grew wide, and she nodded. Hope entered her gaze as she realized that maybe, just maybe, a rescue was coming.

Lorelei lay here, quiet, trying to discern the voices and how far away they were, as she took stock of their options. She needed a weapon, any weapon. The bedroom lamp had done a hell of a job, so what could she use in here? There were bridles and bits, both which, when swung with a hefty motion, would give a hell of a blow. But, if she moved, somebody was likely to know that she was awake. She studied one of the bits hanging on the wall and motioned at it with her head. Amelia Rose followed her gaze, saw the bit, and frowned. Lorelei whispered, "Weapon."

Almost immediately Amelia Rose understood; she snagged the bit off the wall and came back beside Lorelei. The bit was attached to a metal lead. She separated the two so that they each had a weapon, one a little less effective than the other, and, when she heard footsteps, quickly laid on top of both of them, back into the same position, and closed her eyes.

"The oldest one's still out," one of the men said. "How hard did you hit her?"

"Not hard," somebody said.

At that, the man walked away again.

"What about the kid? Is she still asleep?"

"They both look it," he said without much care. "As far as I'm concerned, it's easier if we just kill them now."

"No killing," a sharp voice came from the far side. "We agreed, no killing."

There was something about that tone. The voice had been partially disguised, but it was almost identifiable. Lorelei frowned, thinking about it, but it was hard to focus, not to mention her brain still felt scrambled. She didn't know how long it would take for Griffin to set up a plan. What she didn't want was for them to get caught too. No point in trying to rescue the two of them if they all ended up captured. She pulled out her phone and sent yet another text. **Hurry.**

This time she got a response. **Almost there.**

She held it up for Amelia Rose to see. She smiled and hunkered down closer to Lorelei. The two of them just lay here, waiting and knowing that the attack would come when they least expected it, and they wanted to be ready to take advantage of any opportunity they could. When it happened, it was even more of a surprise because it came from the other end of the stable.

They heard voices, then grunting and sounds of a fight, and then, just like that, Griffin opened the stall door and raced into the room beside them. Gerard was right behind him. He reached for Amelia Rose and hugged her close, whereas Griffin grabbed Lorelei and just held her tight. She cuddled in closer and said, "See? I told you that we shouldn't be apart."

He laughed. "You didn't say anything about that."

"Maybe not," she said, "but I'm saying that now. This is ridiculous every damn time, and who was it this time?"

"Unfortunately it was the same as the last time," Gerard said, his tone thick with emotion.

Only Lorelei didn't have a clue. "Why are we in the barn?" she asked. "Wouldn't it have been smarter to take us immediately off the property?"

"Well, that was in progress," Gerard said. "But who do you know who spends so much time in the barn?"

She looked at him in horror. "Surely not Wendy?"

Gerard nodded ever-so-slowly. "Yes, Amelia Rose's mother. But we have no proof yet."

"Or it was made to look like she'd be the guilty party?" Lorelei suggested, hoping for the best.

Griffin didn't say anything. Lorelei looked to him for confirmation, but a thoughtful look passed his face. She nudged him. "Is that your take too?"

"Partly," he said. "I'm not sure if that's all of it though."

Gerard looked at him in shock. "What are you saying?"

"Not sure yet," he said. "But how about we get the girls back to the house and take our prisoners in for a little interrogation?"

Gerard snorted. "How about we just deep-six them all?"

"Can't get answers off a dead man," he said, "or a dead woman, for that matter."

Trying to stand wasn't easy. Lorelei's legs were still a little bit goofy. She looked up at Griffin, his arms around her, and she said, "You know that it'll be almost impossible to sleep now, right?"

He just smiled and didn't say anything.

She sighed. "I guess I'll have to get used to it though."

"You would anyway," he said. "I still have a job."

"True," she said. "I couldn't possibly be with somebody who was unemployed."

He chuckled. "Is that what we are, somebody with somebody?"

"Hell no," she said. "I'd never sleep alone again if I had a choice."

"Well, I'm hardly just a replacement for a teddy bear," he said smoothly.

"Well, you're very teddy-bear-like, but you make a hell of a better protector."

"What kind of a protector was I? You were kidnapped yet again."

"I wondered for a moment there if that was Gerard's doing."

Gerard looked at her and said, "What?"

"Well, you're the one who sent me to Amelia Rose's room."

"Sure, to keep her safe," he said in outrage. "I wasn't expecting my own wife to be finagling her daughter's kidnapping."

"Well, did you start divorce proceedings?"

He flushed. "I'm thinking about it, but I haven't done

anything officially."

"Well," Griffin added, "somewhere along the line, she got wind of her future, and, before she would let you have Amelia Rose, Wendy decided she would take her daughter and enough money to make sure *Wendy* would be okay. ... I'm not sure if that money was for Amelia Rose too, but most likely it was because the child makes a good bargaining chip later on too."

As the solemn group made their way back to the house, vehicles arrived.

Lorelei glanced at Griffin and asked, "What's this all about?"

"Gerard called a family meeting to get to the bottom of this," he said. "And this is him sending out the word and ordering everybody to show up."

"Right, and Wendy was supposed to as well, wasn't she? I thought someone said she was out of town."

"I'm pretty sure she was already here," Griffon said. They walked into Gerard's adjoining offices, which had been opened to make it more of a boardroom. Griffin approved of everybody being in one spot.

With Bram running security, the prisoners were all led in; Lorelei and Amelia Rose stayed in the hallway, and Gerard's sons gasped, "What on earth, Father?"

"Amelia Rose, Lorelei, and Nurse," Gerard said with great difficulty, "were just in Thailand for a holiday."

"Right. And were kidnapped. We know all that. Are these the men responsible?" asked one of his sons.

"Yes," he said.

"Is Amelia Rose okay?" asked his other son.

Gerard nodded. "I can't tell you what kind of a nightmare I've been through dealing with this."

Amelia Rose and Lorelei stepped inside.

His sons stared at Gerard, then turned to look at Lorelei and Amelia Rose.

Lorelei nodded and said, "Yes, we are safe. We only got home a few hours ago."

"You didn't tell us she was safe," his eldest son protested, staring at Gerard, anger deepening the lines on his face. "Why didn't you tell us? Amelia Rose is our sister too."

"I did tell you that we did a ransom drop, and nobody came to pick it up. It was all very hush-hush. Instead, these men"—he motioned at Jax and Griffin—"rescued both of them in Thailand and returned them here to me."

"And Nurse?" one of the sons asked, looking around. "Is she in bed?"

"She was murdered in Thailand," Gerard said in a heavy voice. "Her death was to make the girls stop trying to escape. It's been a very difficult few days because I was reliving the whole nightmare I had already been through with your older brother. Anyway, the long and short of it is, the girls were rescued, and Mary's body is being returned tomorrow, where we will bury her ourselves."

The brothers looked stricken at the news of what happened to Nurse.

That made Lorelei feel better. Although Nurse was set in her ways and potentially a pain in the butt to a lot of people, Lorelei hadn't had any problem with her. But Mary had raised all of Gerard's children over many years—and even Gerard too as a child—so the family ties were strong. Gerard's sons were still in a daze as they listened.

Joe, Gerard's brother, then spoke. "I don't understand why you didn't tell us about their safe return. You know we would have been there to help and to support you after what you've already been through."

"They've barely been home for one day. Plus I've been sorting out who is behind all this. And fast, before the company was impacted."

"Of course. Always the company. Jesus, even when it was your own daughter," Joe said, shaking his head.

One of Gerard's sons nodded. "But it would have been devastating to the company shares and would have been a sign of weakness," he said. "Lots of our business competitors would have taken the chance to completely annihilate us, if they could have."

"Exactly," Gerard said, sounding surprised at his son's insights.

Lorelei glanced at Griffin and whispered, "Feels weird to be here for a family meeting right now."

"Maybe," he said, "but that's where we need to be with all the players in one room."

Just then Gerard's wife walked in, yawning, tying her robe around her. "Good Lord, I only got in during the wee hours of the morning and look at what's going on here."

"*What's going on?*" Gerard asked, his voice full of contempt.

As soon as she had entered, several security men stepped up, blocking her escape.

"What's going on is that the jig is up for you."

She looked at him in surprise. "What are you talking about?"

Although they suspected Wendy was responsible, they hadn't caught her in the act of doing anything involved with this mess.

Amelia Rose brought it all to a head. She walked over, stood in front of her mother, and said, "Did you really get me kidnapped in Thailand and have Nurse killed?"

Her mother stared at her in horror. "What are you talking about? Of course not. I would never do that!"

"Actually you would," Gerard said. "Particularly after I said no way were you getting custody of Amelia Rose."

At that, his wife turned her fury against him. "She's my daughter."

"She's also my daughter," Gerard said, fatigue in his voice. "I was more than happy to share custody. Until you pulled this stunt."

"I didn't do anything," she snapped. "How can you even begin to think I'd hurt Amelia Rose?"

But then Lorelei understood something else. "I just heard your voice in the stables," she said. "You did something to disguise it, but I figured it out."

Wendy turned to her and, in a mocking and disdainful way, said, "You're already traumatized from being kidnapped, and now you're pointing blame at me and expect anybody in their right minds to believe you? Obviously you need some time off." She turned to her husband. "I suggest we lay her off and give her a paid holiday. I'm sure we can find somebody better suited to teach Amelia Rose whatever it is you think she needs from a private tutor," she continued with a roll of her eyes. "But we certainly don't want somebody who is as mentally unbalanced as Lorelei is now."

"Well, if I am mentally unbalanced," Lorelei said in a calm voice, "I know who to blame."

"And who's that?" Wendy asked, calling her bluff.

"You," Lorelei said, turning to Amelia Rose. "It'll be okay, sweetie." Lorelei took that moment to have Amelia Rose taken from the room by her two security guards.

Lorelei continued, "You wouldn't necessarily hurt Amelia Rose, not physically at least, but you would consider these three kidnappings as, to you, a *small* emotional pain for her to endure if you end up with the twenty-five-million-dollar ransom. Wasn't that the amount Gerard was to pay? It's an interesting figure, but I'm sure, if we worked out what you thought these twelve years with Gerard were worth, you'd probably come up with something like that. And, of course, you had to pay for the men who you hired to do this, both here locally and in Thailand. But the clincher was hearing you in the stables, now that I think about it. I should have recognized your voice right off the bat because even the men who rescued us asked some questions that I didn't put together. Until now."

"What are you talking about?" Wendy asked as she huffed and walked to one of the chairs and threw herself elegantly across the upholstery.

Lorelei had never really understood how women could make simple movements just like that so smooth. Lorelei would look like a galloping horse if she tried to pull off something like that, but, then again, Wendy had good looks and Gerard's money and coaches for every conceivable thing that she could possibly want. So maybe Wendy had a coach for learning how to show disdain with a physical movement.

"You're the only one who would want Nurse killed," Lorelei said. "Nurse hated you, and you hated Nurse."

"Well, I certainly didn't hate her enough to have her murdered," she said in disbelief. "Oh, my Lord, you certainly need a holiday, if that's where your mind is at," she said.

Good God, trouble was, Wendy made everything sound so sensible, that this was all Lorelei's ludicrous beliefs. Lorelei wasn't even sure how to get through to Wendy. Lorelei looked to Griffin with a question in her eyes.

"The thing is, you are the only one who *would* want to kill Mary," Gerard said slowly. "You have always wanted me to get rid of her. You wanted me to buy her a little cottage somewhere and kick her away, even though the only family she had was us."

"She doesn't *have* you," Wendy said. "Good God, she's the hired help. It's not like they are blood. They are servants. They don't mean anything." She looked at Lorelei with a wave of her hand, and she laughed. "You didn't really think you would be wife number two, did you?"

"Oh, you mean, wife number four? Because you're number three, of course. No, I certainly have no intention of becoming wife number four. Gerard and I are definitely not suited. But then neither are you two. Nurse wanted Gerard to get rid of you, though didn't she? Especially lately?" She watched Wendy's face pinch tighter.

Gerard groaned. "Can we stick to the issue at hand?"

"The issue at hand are these preposterous accusations," Wendy said. She got to her feet, another purely elegant movement that had Lorelei wondering how she managed to pull it off. "I need sleep, so I'm going back to bed. Whenever you guys sort this out, you can let me know."

"Not quite," Lorelei said calmly.

When the guards assigned to Wendy boxed her in, she frowned and stepped back.

Lorelei turned toward Griffin and asked him, "Griffin, you have anything to add?"

Griffin smiled and said, "I'd like to know where you were, Wendy, when everybody was in Thailand."

"Well, I certainly don't have to answer your questions," Wendy said. "Good God, Gerard, are you really suggesting that I had something to do with my own daughter's kidnapping? That I would put her through something like that?" She shook her head. "That's low, even for you."

GRIFFIN WATCHED WENDY'S body language, something to reveal who her partner was in this. He already knew she was guilty, but it was a matter of finding who else was guilty with her. She continued to con the crowd, to spread her disdain around the room, her gaze mocking as she glanced at every person, landing on Lorelei at her side, the corner of her mouth turning down with an extra shot of venom for her. But when she looked at Gerard's brother, her gaze slid right by.

And Griffin knew.

"Of course she didn't do it alone," Griffin said. "She couldn't have planned this herself. Not enough smarts. So it's really all about who would partner with you to make sure that you were both looked after in the future. Knowing that, at some point in time, Gerard would retire and would hand over control of his company to his sons, you needed someone who would gain power from this kidnapping plan in addition to you. Or at least to make your partner in crime think he was getting an equal deal. But you didn't have the connections to set up a long-distance kidnapping in Thailand."

"Of course I didn't," she said. "And who are you?"

He waved his hand, as if telling her that her question wasn't important or that she wasn't important. He had no intention of answering her. "So I guess the real question is, what agreement did you make? And the first one to volunteer information and to help out, of course, will get a better deal."

She stared at him in mockery. "Does that work for you often?"

"Oh, it works a whole lot more often than you would think. We can already prove your involvement. You're the one who set up the trip to Thailand, the planning—like for hotel rooms and no security, and made sure that Nurse went, even though Nurse didn't want to go," he said smoothly. "The question is, who found and paid for the local men in Thailand? What about the extra men here?" He remembered the man barking orders at the hotel, where the three females had originally stayed. "I mean, we found several of your cohorts in the barn, of course, but where else would you find men for hire if you wanted a good ride?" He deliberately left the innuendo hanging.

She glared at him and said, "I do believe you're insulting me."

He shook his head immediately. "Good God, no. I couldn't be bothered. There's a time and a place for everything, and I've already figured out who your partner is. So the question is, will you give us the information first or will he?"

"Who is it?" Gerard demanded.

"Oh, no," Griffin said. "She gets one last chance right now. Otherwise MI6 gets her."

"That'll never happen," she said, but her demeanor stiffened as if suddenly worried.

"Well, the problem is, the other person involved has no intention of going down alone and taking the fall for you as the mastermind behind it all. The sentence will be quite a bit stiffer for you, Wendy."

"How does that work?" she asked on a disbelieving

laugh. "It should be easier. It's not like I did anything."

"Right," he said, seeing the first cracks in her facade.

Gerard, staring at his wife in horror, said, "Dear God, you *did* do this." He looked at Griffin. "And who else? I'll fucking kill him."

"Sadly"—Griffin looked at Gerard—"your brother."

On those words, his brother bolted from the office, past the two guards, racing for the front door. He came head-to-head with Jax. And it was all over, just like that.

When Jax pushed Joe back into the office, Wendy stared at him with hatred in her eyes. "All you had to do was sit there and completely deny everything, but, no, that was well beyond you, wasn't it?"

He glared at her. "What kind of a fucking mother would do that to her daughter? And to hate the child's nurse so much that you arranged for her to be killed as a lesson? God, poor Mary. She was my nurse growing up too. But, no, you were adamant on that score." He shook his head. "You're just scum."

"And what are you?" Lorelei asked in shock. "Except the scum's lover?"

Joe stared at her in horror. "You've got to be kidding. I wouldn't touch that well-used body for the life of me."

At that, Wendy screamed in outrage.

But Gerard's roar silenced everyone. He stood and stared at his brother. "After all I've been through, you would do this to me?"

Joe sneered at him. "Even back then, you were father's favorite. You were the poor son who'd been kidnapped, your own son murdered. It's the only reason he gave you the lion's share of the company. He felt sorry for you. He wanted to stop his own guilt for not keeping you safe."

"No," Gerard roared. "He felt guilty, sure, but nothing like I felt. He didn't *give* me the company. I earned it. As I've grown the family business one thousand times over since then, his trust in me has been proven. You were nothing but a wastrel, playing your days away, so damn sure you would get half, and yet, do nothing for it."

"Like hell." Joe shook his head, his face twisted with anger and jealousy. "He never loved me like he loved you. And you were so set on giving your daughter control of the company, over me, who's been working there as long as you have, Gerard? Really? I wanted Amelia Rose to die for many reasons, but especially so you had to deal with that same loss all over again.

"It's only one-quarter of the pain I went through every damn day listening to Father spout off how you were just like him. A businessman through and through, and why couldn't I be more like him and *you*." He spat that last word, making it obvious that was the last thing Joe wanted to be. "And you so generously let me keep my shares and work in the company, keeping a paycheck rolling through so I could support my family, while you rake in millions a year all for yourself."

"Millions I *earn*." Gerard stared at his brother in disgust, but there was no surprise in his expression. "You should be thankful I'm such a family man. I should have cut you loose when I first took over the company for Father. You've always been lazy. A self-centered entitled bastard." He looked at his wife in disgust. "It makes sense now. Joe has been dealing with a lot of Asian companies recently. That's how he found the people to do your dirty work in Thailand. And was he to get half the ransom money?"

The look on her face made him laugh. "Of course not,"

Gerard said, shaking his head, still chuckling. "You weren't giving any of the ransom money to him, were you? So the company went to Joe? But you still didn't have the majority ownership, even pooling Amelia Rose's shares with Joe's. At my death, my sons own fifty percent of the company, with Joe and Amelia Rose owning the other fifty percent. It's still half for the boys and half for Joe and my daughter. No one completely owns the company. Forcing them to work together, which was my plan. But which wouldn't happen until I died. Hell, even with me dead, this wouldn't make Joe happy. Joe doesn't have the ability to be happy." He snorted. "Neither do you, Wendy."

She shrugged. "Causing you pain was a lot of it on my part. Joe wanted you and Amelia Rose dead, but I didn't want my daughter involved any more than she was. So the plan was for me to disappear with her, and then you'd have an accident, Gerard. Maybe your sons too." She glanced at Gerard and Joe, staring at her like she was a nasty virus that might spread. "Not like Joe cares about them either."

Gerard sank back into his big leather chair, the huge man diminished by the family of blackhearts plotting against him.

The room was suddenly filled with MI6 men, as all their prisoners were led away.

CHAPTER 14

LORELEI STARED AT the suddenly silent and almost empty room and gave a broken laugh. "There's nothing, really, to laugh at. But it's either that or cry. This is just too unbelievable."

Griffin wrapped an arm around her, pulled her close, and said, "But now it's over. We have a team picking up the hired men in Thailand."

She buried her head against his chest and whispered, "Thank God for that." As she turned to look around, Amelia Rose was in her father's arms, her arms tight around him too. And Lorelei knew that, although this was one of those life lessons that was almost impossible to forget, Amelia Rose would be fine—eventually. Lorelei wasn't sure how fine she would be though. Amelia Rose would have everything money could buy to help her over this. But she also had the one thing that money couldn't buy which would get her over this the best and which would help her the most.

Her father's love.

It was a good ninety minutes later when Lorelei headed to bed. She was exhausted. Her mind still buzzed with everything that had happened. She'd been separated somewhere along the line from Griffin, so that their statements could be taken by MI6. Now things were getting back to normal. All the MI6 agents had been given rooms to accommodate their stay as they continued their investigation later today, after getting some sleep first. Lorelei suddenly found herself outside Griffin's bedroom. She snorted at that but had no problem walking inside and crashing on his bed. As far as she was concerned, that was the best idea she'd had in a long time. She was just drifting off when the door opened. She smiled and muttered, "Where'd you think I'd be?"

He quickly shucked his clothes and crawled in beside her. He pulled her up close, and she said, "Finally."

"Sleep," he said. "We'll talk in the morning."

"It is morning," she muttered, yet sleep reached up to claim her. The last thing she heard was, "Okay, later this morning." And she drifted off.

When she awoke, she felt a furnace beside her. She rolled into it, welcoming its heat as it chased away the chill in her soul. It was beyond comprehension that Amelia Rose's mother had been behind all of that terror and had used the opportunity to get rid of Nurse at the same time. What was wrong with people who thought murder was considered a reasonable action to take? And, of course, Joe and Wendy hadn't picked up the money because they were well aware it had been a trick and a trap. Lorelei wondered what would have happened if they'd gotten away with kidnapping them the second or third time.

Would there have been yet another ransom, or would that be a case of just *kill them off and who cared?*

She was still so damn tired. She didn't want to move, and she had no idea what would happen in terms of her and Griffin. Obviously he would leave, and she had to rethink what she wanted to do with her life, not to mention about Amelia Rose. Was it time for her to go to school and to meet other friends and not have a private tutor? Probably. She'd grown up a lot over this. Lorelei was good at what she did, and what Amelia Rose really needed to heal now was time with her father.

Lorelei hoped that these horrid circumstances had brought some good to Amelia Rose and her father too—a closeness, a new beginning, a more transparent sense of communication—not to mention to Gerard's sons too. She was glad that they weren't involved. It would be good if Gerard could ease up some of the control that he held over them and over the company, could give them bigger roles, could make them feel like they had a bigger part in the company. Even though both sons worked for the company, they were not high enough in the company to have any actual power.

"What are you thinking?" Griffin murmured.

"I'm wondering about the future," she said honestly. "My job, your job, and Gerard. I'll have to deal with the family dynamics."

"Do you think they'll be okay?" he asked.

"Yes," she said. "And obviously way better off than with a woman who was prepared to do something like that to the family for money."

"Do you think it was for money or to keep custody?"

"With her, maybe I should have said for *power*," she explained, "because I don't think love was the determining factor in this case. As long as she had control over her daughter, she still had access to a lot of money. And how sad is that?"

"Very," he said, nuzzling her neck. "You should be sleeping and not worrying about other people's family problems."

"I know, but while I've been here, I felt like I was part of the family. And now? Now I think it's time for a change, but it might be too soon for Amelia Rose."

"I'm sure it is. She's already lost Nurse and now her mom, at least in any way that counts."

"Right," Lorelei said. "How do you deal with that kind of betrayal?"

"Slowly and one bite at a time," he said. "And with Gerard always around to help her."

"Yes," she said. "I think that's the most important recovery piece that he needs to understand, how his presence is so necessary to her healing."

"She might need you too."

"I think for a little while, yes," she said. "For a transition period but not forever. She's certainly grown up a lot. I mean she's eleven going on twenty-one."

He chuckled at that. "She's a very precocious child. I alternate from calling her woman to child to something in between."

"Because she is, and she's still in that young version of whatever we should call it."

"That preteen. *Precocious* preteen."

She chuckled. "Yeah, exactly."

"And what do you want to do?" he asked. "You've been looking after other people's kid for a long time."

"Well, not in the capacity you mean. I'm a tutor, but I don't know if I want to do that anymore. You learn a lot when your future is suddenly taken away from you. Now that I have one again, I need to rethink things."

"It does happen that way, indeed. You have to put a priority on some things, prioritize your life," he said. "And that can be hard."

"It can be deadly," she said. "I really don't know."

"Well, don't rush into anything," he said. "You have time."

She smiled. "I do now, thanks to you. Do you think they would have killed us?"

"I don't know," he said. "Depending on the brother's level of involvement, it was to his benefit to ensure that Amelia Rose not survive. But I don't know how the mother who would have handled that. Possibly an unfortunate accident down the road. As for you, they couldn't let you live to talk."

"Nice. *Not*. I guess it depended on the money, didn't it?" she said caustically. "Something I'll have a hard time with."

"Sure, just understand that Amelia Rose is young and strong, and she will recover, and this is a terrible family scenario, but it's not *your* family scenario."

"I know," she said. She smiled up into his eyes and said, "What about you?"

"What about me?" he asked, and then he yawned.

She gently rubbed his unshaven cheek and asked, "When are you leaving?"

He winced. "Probably soon. I don't really know."

"Sounds like we both have things to think about," she said.

He nodded. "We do, but just think. We're in control. We can choose what we want to do right now."

"I know what I want to do right now," she said. "The question is, what do we want to do after *right now*?" And she reached up and kissed him gently.

"Well, I like to work on one thing at a time," he said smoothly. "So how about we focus on that *right now* thing, and then we'll worry about the rest?"

She chuckled. "So, in other words, make no plans right now?"

"I know one thing," he said. "I don't want to lose contact with you."

She smiled, nodded, and said, "Agreed. In that case, as long as we do our best to find a way to make something work, then nothing else really matters, does it?"

He smiled and said, "Well, some things matter." And he nudged his hips against her.

She felt the heat and the hard ridge against her smooth skin.

"You're wearing too many clothes," he whispered.

She chuckled. "I'm sure a handy guy like you can take care of that." And, within seconds, she was flipped onto her back, and her nightdress was up and over her head. Laughter, bright and joyous, peeled out as she wrapped her arms around him. "You're such a can-do type of guy. Why don't you show me what you can do?"

"You mean, show you more?" he asked. "I already rescued you twice, by the way."

She placed a finger against his lips, stopping the flow of words, and said, "How about, instead of talking, you just show me?"

He lowered his head, and he kissed her gently several times, and then finally he deepened the kiss until she moaned with joy.

She wrapped her arms snugly around his neck and said, "Not too bad a start. I can't wait to see how you finish."

He chuckled and proceeded to show her with his hands, lips, and tongue, stroking, learning as she moaned and twisted beneath him. Every movement that brought her pleasure, every movement that caused her to still in surprise, only to arch up in need.

She cried out time and time again until finally she demanded, "Enough teasing. I want you now." She hooked her legs around him as he settled between them. She looped her arms around his neck, tugging him close, and whispered, "Kiss me like you mean it."

He stopped, looked at her. "Every kiss I've given you is because I mean it. This isn't a dalliance," he whispered gently, caressing her cheek with his lips, his tongue sliding along the edge of her lower lip and then inside to war with hers. He pulled back ever-so-slightly. "This is for us. Not just for today, not just for tomorrow, but for as long as we want it."

She smiled, wrapping her legs tighter around his hips and whispered, "Then how about forever?"

And he plunged deep, taking her all the way home.

EPILOGUE

JAX HAD SEEN it coming, but he wondered how they would make it work. As far as he understood, Kerrick and Amanda were doing just fine in Paris. But Lorelei and Griffin? ... Well, they had hit it off right from the beginning. But Jax couldn't be happier for his friend. It was a lonely lifestyle these SEALs had chosen to lead, and each and every one of them had come to this point as a jumping off spot to something different, to making a choice to do something else.

He hadn't told Griffin but Jax's agreement to come on this mission was so that he could take the lead on one op and one op only. He was leaving the military, and he was leaving everything to do with this type of life. The Mavericks team had asked Jax specifically to help Griffin as a warm-up to doing his one mission sometime later. He figured that it was the same for Kerrick and for Griffin. Jax wasn't sure about joining the Mavericks unit for what would be his one big job, but the unit trained everybody before they took the lead on their one mission and then were done. But, as Jax thought about it, nobody in the Mavericks unit needed training.

This was like the peak of their careers for them. Jax didn't know if they would all be brought back to do something else. It was possible though, and Jax would consider it.

He also knew that most of them were getting paid enough money that they wouldn't have to work again. He'd never discussed that part either with Griffin or Kerrick. Jax didn't even know if Griffin knew what Kerrick had gone through. What Jax did know was that the next job was his to head up. He hoped that he had a couple weeks or a month or two before then. Hell, he'd be happy to have a year or two in between these particular jobs.

They were hard and intense, but, once done, then the op was done, and so was he. He didn't have friends or family to worry about, so he was in a much easier situation than Griffin and Kerrick. Although, now that they had met and been partnered up for these Mavericks operations, things had changed for those guys too. That didn't mean that they, in any way, shape, or form, were ready to go out the same as Jax was. They'd all come to the point where, if this was the last mission for them, then that was the last mission, and they didn't really care to go on any more missions.

Neither did he. He was moving on to something different. He just didn't know what. He had a hankering for travel, to see the world as a tourist for a change, instead of skulking through the night in the shadows of darkness, watching other shadows move as they tried to take over worlds and governments and individuals.

Sitting on a beach and watching the sunrise would be a pretty decent way to spend his time, and sitting on the same damn beach and watching each new sunset would be a unique opportunity for him to just relax, maybe with a cold beer and with a friend or two. Now that would make his life pretty damn perfect.

He was headed back home again. He had been on his phone, setting up arrangements for his apartment and making sure his landlady knew he would arrive soon. The silly things in life that you had to organize. As he landed back in California and grabbed his single bag and headed outside the airport, his cell buzzed.

He glanced down at the screen, groaned, and said, "Hell no. What?"

"How tired out are you?"

"Fucking tired," he said. "It's not like I got much sleep on the last job."

"That was two days ago," the man said in exasperation.

Jax heard something in that voice, and he said, "Hell, Griffin, is that you?"

Griffin chuckled. "Hell yeah, it's me. Is that okay?"

"I don't know," Jax said. "What do you want?"

Immediately all the humor fled as Griffin said, "We need you."

"Are you coming with me?"

"No. Somebody will though."

"Why is it always like that?" he asked. "Some of these jobs are getting pretty thin for just one or two of us."

"If it can be more, it'll be more. I promise I won't send you out without backup."

He snorted at that. "But it won't be you though, right? You'll be holed up somewhere nice and cozy with Lorelei."

"If I could join you, I would," Griffin said regretfully. "Lorelei and I will see each other on a regular basis now, spending time with Amelia Rose too. We're giving the child time to adapt before Lorelei leaves."

"I'm almost jealous," Jax said. "*Almost* but not quite."

Griffin snorted. "Your time will come. You won't even see it happening, and, before you know it, it'll be right there in your face."

"I doubt it," he said, "but whatever. So, what's the job?"

Griffin took a long, slow breath and said, "You won't like it."

"I never liked any of 'em," he said. "So what's the deal?"

"We've got a cruise ship that's been taken over."

"Pirates? I'm one man. Remember that?"

"It's a one-man job. We need somebody who can go in and take them out, one by one."

"I still am not going alone. Someone has to watch my back."

"Do you remember Beau?"

"Hell yeah, I remember Beau. That man could eat crawfish like nobody else I've ever seen," Jax said. "Then again he's huge. He can't hide anywhere. He's too damn big."

"Well, he won't be eating crawfish this time. And he won't need to hide. As a matter of fact, he'll be shooting bullets at pirates. He always was a dang good sharpshooter. So he'll meet you there."

"Meet me where?"

Griffin snorted. "Off the Florida coast. You should be there right on time."

"No," Jax said. "I just got off the goddamn plane in California."

"So you're already packed, right? You hear your name on the PA system? Yeah, that's to go pick up your tickets. You're flying out now."

And, with that, Griffin hung up.

Jax swore.

This concludes Book 2 of The Mavericks: Griffin.
Read about Jax: The Mavericks, Book 3

The Mavericks: Jax (Book #3)

What happens when the very men—trained to make the hard decisions—come up against the rules and regulations that hold them back from doing what needs to be done? They either stay and work within the constraints given to them or they walk away. Only now, for a select few, they have another option:

The Mavericks. A covert black ops team that steps up and break all the rules ... but gets the job done.

Welcome to a new military romance series by *USA Today* best-selling author Dale Mayer. A series where you meet new friends in this raw and compelling look at the men who keep us safe every day from the darkness where they operate—and live—in the shadows ... until someone special helps them step into the light.

No time to rest. The world is a mess ...

He'd barely made it home from helping Griffin only to find himself called to rescue a doctor on a cruise ship overtaken by pirates in their search for Abigail Dalton. The pirates had no trouble killing passengers until they found the right woman. With one man at his side, Jax sneaks onto the ship to rescue her.

When she heard the gunfire, Abby hid in the venting on the ship. When a man susses out her hiding place, she's sure her world is about to end. Only Jax is on her side; yet he came with just one man to help. Stunned, she stays close as

Jax frees the ship and keeps her safe—until they find out the real reason for this nightmare, when she's forced to England to face the two-legged monster of her nightmares …

The safest place is at Jax's side, but Abby knows all too well how slippery this monster really is and how easily he steps from the shadows to grab his victims …

Find book 3 here!
To find out more visit Dale Mayer's website.
https://geni.us/DMJaxUniversal

Author's Note

Thank you for reading The Mavericks, Books 1–2! If you enjoyed the book, please take a moment and leave a short review.

Dear reader,

I love to hear from readers, and you can contact me at my website: www.dalemayer.com or at my Facebook author page. To be informed of new releases and special offers, sign up for my newsletter or follow me on BookBub. And if you are interested in joining Dale Mayer's Reader Group, here is the Facebook sign up page.
http://geni.us/DaleMayerFBGroup

Cheers,
Dale Mayer

About the Author

Dale Mayer is a *USA Today* best-selling author, best known for her SEALs military romances, her Psychic Visions series, and her Lovely Lethal Garden cozy series. Her contemporary romances are raw and full of passion and emotion (Broken But … Mending, Hathaway House series). Her thrillers will keep you guessing (Kate Morgan, By Death series), and her romantic comedies will keep you giggling (*It's a Dog's Life*, a stand-alone novella; and the Broken Protocols series, starring Charming Marvin, the cat).

Dale honors the stories that come to her—and some of them are crazy, break all the rules and cross multiple genres!

To go with her fiction, she also writes nonfiction in many different fields, with books available on résumé writing, companion gardening, and the US mortgage system. All her books are available in print and ebook format.

Connect with Dale Mayer Online

Dale's Website – www.dalemayer.com
Twitter – @DaleMayer
Facebook Page – geni.us/DaleMayerFBFanPage
Facebook Group – geni.us/DaleMayerFBGroup
BookBub – geni.us/DaleMayerBookbub
Instagram – geni.us/DaleMayerInstagram
Goodreads – geni.us/DaleMayerGoodreads
Newsletter – geni.us/DaleNews

Also by Dale Mayer

Published Adult Books:

Hathaway House
Aaron, Book 1
Brock, Book 2
Cole, Book 3
Denton, Book 4
Elliot, Book 5
Finn, Book 6
Gregory, Book 7
Heath, Book 8
Iain, Book 9
Jaden, Book 10
Keith, Book 11
Lance, Book 12
Melissa, Book 13
Nash, Book 14
Owen, Book 15
Hathaway House, Books 1–3
Hathaway House, Books 4–6
Hathaway House, Books 7–9

The K9 Files
Ethan, Book 1
Pierce, Book 2
Zane, Book 3

Blaze, Book 4
Lucas, Book 5
Parker, Book 6
Carter, Book 7
Weston, Book 8
Greyson, Book 9
Rowan, Book 10
Caleb, Book 11
Kurt, Book 12
Tucker, Book 13
Harley, Book 14
The K9 Files, Books 1–2
The K9 Files, Books 3–4
The K9 Files, Books 5–6
The K9 Files, Books 7–8
The K9 Files, Books 9–10
The K9 Files, Books 11–12

Lovely Lethal Gardens
Arsenic in the Azaleas, Book 1
Bones in the Begonias, Book 2
Corpse in the Carnations, Book 3
Daggers in the Dahlias, Book 4
Evidence in the Echinacea, Book 5
Footprints in the Ferns, Book 6
Gun in the Gardenias, Book 7
Handcuffs in the Heather, Book 8
Ice Pick in the Ivy, Book 9
Jewels in the Juniper, Book 10
Killer in the Kiwis, Book 11
Lifeless in the Lilies, Book 12
Lovely Lethal Gardens, Books 1–2

Lovely Lethal Gardens, Books 3–4
Lovely Lethal Gardens, Books 5–6
Lovely Lethal Gardens, Books 7–8
Lovely Lethal Gardens, Books 9–10

Psychic Vision Series
Tuesday's Child
Hide 'n Go Seek
Maddy's Floor
Garden of Sorrow
Knock Knock…
Rare Find
Eyes to the Soul
Now You See Her
Shattered
Into the Abyss
Seeds of Malice
Eye of the Falcon
Itsy-Bitsy Spider
Unmasked
Deep Beneath
From the Ashes
Stroke of Death
Ice Maiden
Psychic Visions Books 1–3
Psychic Visions Books 4–6
Psychic Visions Books 7–9

By Death Series
Touched by Death
Haunted by Death
Chilled by Death
By Death Books 1–3

Broken Protocols – Romantic Comedy Series
Cat's Meow
Cat's Pajamas
Cat's Cradle
Cat's Claus
Broken Protocols 1-4

Broken and… Mending
Skin
Scars
Scales (of Justice)
Broken but… Mending 1-3

Glory
Genesis
Tori
Celeste
Glory Trilogy

Biker Blues
Morgan: Biker Blues, Volume 1
Cash: Biker Blues, Volume 2

SEALs of Honor
Mason: SEALs of Honor, Book 1
Hawk: SEALs of Honor, Book 2
Dane: SEALs of Honor, Book 3
Swede: SEALs of Honor, Book 4
Shadow: SEALs of Honor, Book 5
Cooper: SEALs of Honor, Book 6
Markus: SEALs of Honor, Book 7
Evan: SEALs of Honor, Book 8
Mason's Wish: SEALs of Honor, Book 9

Chase: SEALs of Honor, Book 10
Brett: SEALs of Honor, Book 11
Devlin: SEALs of Honor, Book 12
Easton: SEALs of Honor, Book 13
Ryder: SEALs of Honor, Book 14
Macklin: SEALs of Honor, Book 15
Corey: SEALs of Honor, Book 16
Warrick: SEALs of Honor, Book 17
Tanner: SEALs of Honor, Book 18
Jackson: SEALs of Honor, Book 19
Kanen: SEALs of Honor, Book 20
Nelson: SEALs of Honor, Book 21
Taylor: SEALs of Honor, Book 22
Colton: SEALs of Honor, Book 23
Troy: SEALs of Honor, Book 24
Axel: SEALs of Honor, Book 25
Baylor: SEALs of Honor, Book 26
SEALs of Honor, Books 1–3
SEALs of Honor, Books 4–6
SEALs of Honor, Books 7–10
SEALs of Honor, Books 11–13
SEALs of Honor, Books 14–16
SEALs of Honor, Books 17–19
SEALs of Honor, Books 20–22
SEALs of Honor, Books 23–25

Heroes for Hire
Levi's Legend: Heroes for Hire, Book 1
Stone's Surrender: Heroes for Hire, Book 2
Merk's Mistake: Heroes for Hire, Book 3
Rhodes's Reward: Heroes for Hire, Book 4
Flynn's Firecracker: Heroes for Hire, Book 5

Logan's Light: Heroes for Hire, Book 6
Harrison's Heart: Heroes for Hire, Book 7
Saul's Sweetheart: Heroes for Hire, Book 8
Dakota's Delight: Heroes for Hire, Book 9
Michael's Mercy (Part of Sleeper SEAL Series)
Tyson's Treasure: Heroes for Hire, Book 10
Jace's Jewel: Heroes for Hire, Book 11
Rory's Rose: Heroes for Hire, Book 12
Brandon's Bliss: Heroes for Hire, Book 13
Liam's Lily: Heroes for Hire, Book 14
North's Nikki: Heroes for Hire, Book 15
Anders's Angel: Heroes for Hire, Book 16
Reyes's Raina: Heroes for Hire, Book 17
Dezi's Diamond: Heroes for Hire, Book 18
Vince's Vixen: Heroes for Hire, Book 19
Ice's Icing: Heroes for Hire, Book 20
Johan's Joy: Heroes for Hire, Book 21
Galen's Gemma: Heroes for Hire, Book 22
Zack's Zest: Heroes for Hire, Book 23
Bonaparte's Belle: Heroes for Hire, Book 24
Heroes for Hire, Books 1–3
Heroes for Hire, Books 4–6
Heroes for Hire, Books 7–9
Heroes for Hire, Books 10–12
Heroes for Hire, Books 13–15

SEALs of Steel
Badger: SEALs of Steel, Book 1
Erick: SEALs of Steel, Book 2
Cade: SEALs of Steel, Book 3
Talon: SEALs of Steel, Book 4
Laszlo: SEALs of Steel, Book 5

Geir: SEALs of Steel, Book 6
Jager: SEALs of Steel, Book 7
The Final Reveal: SEALs of Steel, Book 8
SEALs of Steel, Books 1–4
SEALs of Steel, Books 5–8
SEALs of Steel, Books 1–8

The Mavericks
Kerrick, Book 1
Griffin, Book 2
Jax, Book 3
Beau, Book 4
Asher, Book 5
Ryker, Book 6
Miles, Book 7
Nico, Book 8
Keane, Book 9
Lennox, Book 10
Gavin, Book 11
Shane, Book 12
The Mavericks, Books 1–2
The Mavericks, Books 3–4
The Mavericks, Books 5–6
The Mavericks, Books 7–8
The Mavericks, Books 9–10
The Mavericks, Books 11–12

Bullard's Battle Series
Ryland's Reach, Book 1
Cain's Cross, Book 2
Eton's Escape, Book 3
Garret's Gambit, Book 4
Kano's Keep, Book 5

Fallon's Flaw, Book 6
Quinn's Quest, Book 7
Bullard's Beauty, Book 8

Collections
Dare to Be You…
Dare to Love…
Dare to be Strong…
RomanceX3

Standalone Novellas
It's a Dog's Life
Riana's Revenge
Second Chances

Published Young Adult Books:

Family Blood Ties Series
Vampire in Denial
Vampire in Distress
Vampire in Design
Vampire in Deceit
Vampire in Defiance
Vampire in Conflict
Vampire in Chaos
Vampire in Crisis
Vampire in Control
Vampire in Charge
Family Blood Ties Set 1–3
Family Blood Ties Set 1–5
Family Blood Ties Set 4–6
Family Blood Ties Set 7–9
Sian's Solution, A Family Blood Ties Series Prequel

Novelette

Design series
Dangerous Designs
Deadly Designs
Darkest Designs
Design Series Trilogy

Standalone
In Cassie's Corner
Gem Stone (a Gemma Stone Mystery)
Time Thieves

Published Non-Fiction Books:

Career Essentials
Career Essentials: The Résumé
Career Essentials: The Cover Letter
Career Essentials: The Interview
Career Essentials: 3 in 1

www.ingramcontent.com/pod-product-compliance
Lightning Source LLC
LaVergne TN
LVHW021650060526
838200LV00050B/2286